# Trial of Stone
# Heirs of Destiny (Book 1)

By Andy Peloquin

Copyright. First Edition

Andy Peloquin

©2018, Andy Peloquin

ALL RIGHTS RESERVED. This book contains material protected under International and Federal Copyright Laws and Treaties. Any unauthorized reprint or use of this material is prohibited. No part of this book, including the cover and photos, may be reproduced or transmitted in any form or by any means, electronic or mechanical, including photocopying, recording, or by any information storage and retrieval system without express written permission from the author / publisher. All rights reserved.

Any resemblance to persons, places living or dead is purely coincidental. This is a work of fiction.

# Table of Contents

Chapter One ........................................................................... 1
Chapter Two .......................................................................... 15
Chapter Three ....................................................................... 25
Chapter Four ......................................................................... 33
Chapter Five .......................................................................... 41
Chapter Six ............................................................................ 49
Chapter Seven ....................................................................... 57
Chapter Eight ........................................................................ 63
Chapter Nine ........................................................................ 71
Chapter Ten .......................................................................... 81
Chapter Eleven ..................................................................... 89
Chapter Twelve ..................................................................... 95
Chapter Thirteen ................................................................ 103
Chapter Fourteen ................................................................ 109
Chapter Fifteen ................................................................... 117
Chapter Sixteen ................................................................... 129
Chapter Seventeen .............................................................. 141
Chapter Eighteen ................................................................ 147
Chapter Nineteen ................................................................ 155
Chapter Twenty ................................................................... 165
Chapter Twenty-One .......................................................... 175
Chapter Twenty-Two .......................................................... 181
Chapter Twenty-Three ........................................................ 189
Chapter Twenty-Four .......................................................... 197
Chapter Twenty-Five ........................................................... 207
Chapter Twenty-Six ............................................................. 217
Chapter Twenty-Seven ........................................................ 227
Chapter Twenty-Eight ......................................................... 237
Chapter Twenty-Nine .......................................................... 247

Chapter Thirty ................................................................253
Chapter Thirty-One ........................................................261
Chapter Thirty-Three .....................................................271
Chapter Thirty-Three .....................................................279
Chapter Thirty-Four .......................................................287
Chapter Thirty-Five ........................................................293
Chapter Thirty-Six..........................................................303
Chapter Thirty-Seven .....................................................309
Chapter Thirty-Eight ......................................................317
Chapter Thirty-Nine ......................................................323
Chapter Forty.................................................................331
Chapter Forty-One ........................................................339
Chapter Forty-Two ........................................................349
Chapter Forty-Three......................................................355
Chapter Forty-Four .......................................................363
Our young heroes' journey continues..................................371
Chapter One .................................................................371
Chapter Two .................................................................381
More Books by Andy Peloquin.........................................393
About the Author...........................................................395

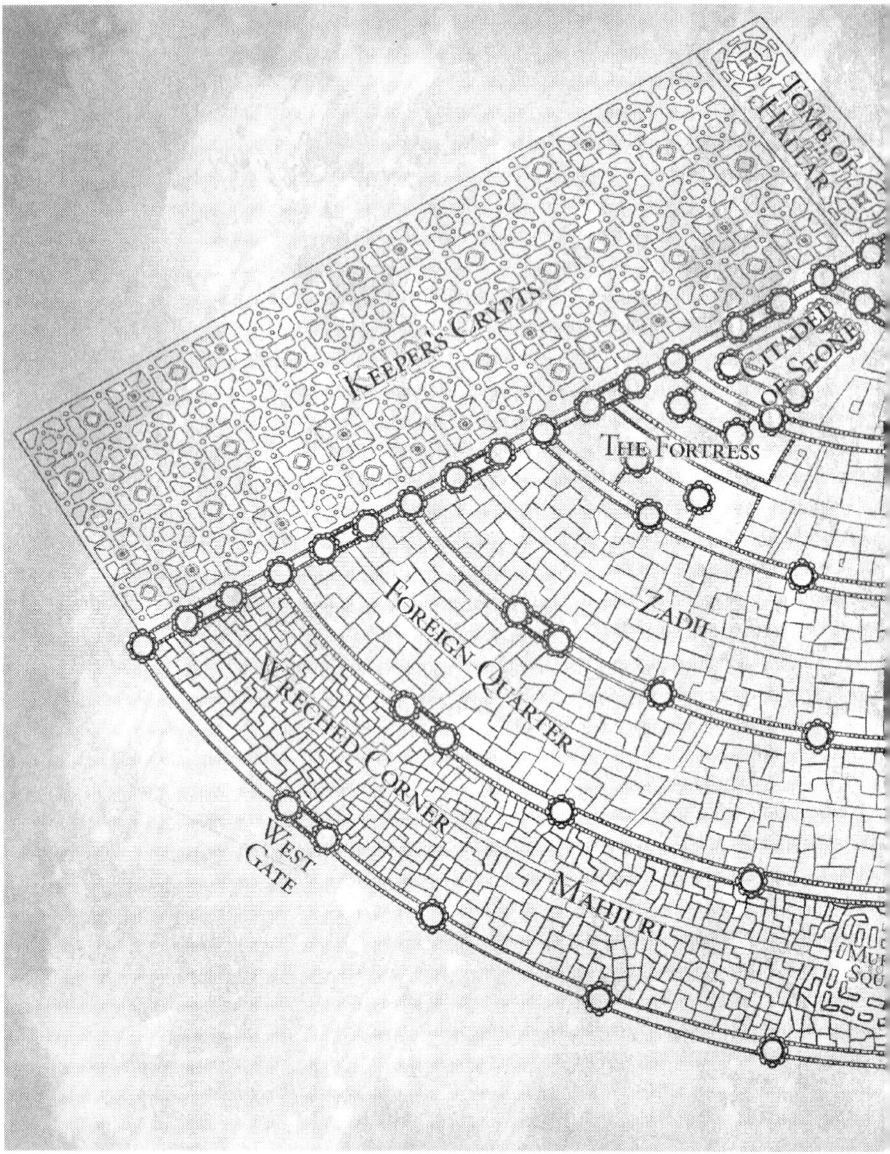
Tomb of Hallar
Keeper's Crypts
Citadel of Stone
The Fortress
Zadii
Foreign Quarter
Wreched Corner
West Gate
Mahjuri

# Shalandra

# Chapter One

*Five years and a day,* Issa thought. *Five years and a day training in Killian's forge for this moment, and this is who I'm up against?*

Her eyes locked on the hulking brute that stood a few yards to her right. His stance, low guard with his right foot shuffled slightly back and to one side, marked him as a student of the Academy of the Silver Sword. Broader in the shoulder than a draftsman's ox, with hands that looked too large for his two-handed blade, he would be a fearsome foe for any contender. The ornate turquoise band of an *Alqati* around his copper-skinned forehead marked him as a member of Shalandra's military caste—with all the training that included.

Yet despite the fear coiling in Issa's gut, she forced herself to stand tall and face her challenger without hesitation. Nervous sweat rolled down the big man's face—he felt as unnerved as she, as daunted by what lay ahead. He, too, knew that his hopes of surviving the trial of steel hinged on his courage, skill, and the strength of his arms.

She could almost read the unspoken question in his eyes: *Am I prepared for this?*

Issa had done everything in her power to assuage those doubts. She'd trained for years in preparation of Hallar's Calling, the yearly tournament that selected only those blessed by the Long Keeper to join the Blades. Five years evading Savta and Saba's questions or lying to them, all in the hope that she could lift her family out of the squalor they were cursed to as *Earaqi*. She hadn't been chosen, hadn't been summoned to the Hall of the Beyond for the trial of the Crucible. That hadn't stopped her, just as this new obstacle wouldn't stop her.

*No meathead is going to get in my way.* She clenched her jaw, determined. *I will claim one of those blades.*

The clarion call of a trumpet snapped Issa's attention away from her immediate foe.

*The time has come.*

Her gaze roamed over the five thousand spectators sitting in breathless silence on the stone benches that surrounded the Crucible, the arena testing grounds where she and her fellow hopefuls would face the Long Keeper's challenge in the hope of being chosen to serve. High golden sandstone walls separated her from the people—from high-ranking *Dhukari* to those *Mahjuri* and *Earaqi* fortunate enough to receive the invitation to witness the spectacle—but their faces revealed the same eager excitement that thrummed through her. They had come to see battle and death, and by the Long Keeper, they would have it!

As the trumpet sounded again, five thousand pairs of eyes turned away from the Crucible and toward the Royal Stands. Amhoset Nephelcheres, Pharus of Shalandra, Servant of the Long Keeper, Word of Justice and Death, sat on a throne carved from the same golden sandstone of the arena. He was a regal figure, tall with broad shoulders and a strong head to bear the ornate golden headdress of his office. A mountain of plush, velvet-covered pillows softened his seat, and servants wearing golden *Dhukari* headbands held fans of ostrich feathers and gold-inlaid wood to shield him from the bright midday sun.

Yet Issa's eyes traveled to the figure sitting beside him. Callista Vinaus, Lady of Blades, sat in a similar throne, yet hers lacked any trace of ostentation and comfort. She didn't so much sit as perch, her posture at once relaxed and wary. Her two-handed Shalandran steel sword of office rested against the side of her chair, and she wore the black, ridged plate mail of a Keeper's Blade.

Though the woman's hard face lacked the Pharus' classical beauty, even from this distance, Issa could see that it had a beauty of its own—the strength and determination that earned her the highest-ranking military office in Shalandra. Like all Keeper's Blades, she wore a helmet—shaped like a snarling mountain lion—rather than a headband, but the stripe of gold on the helmet's forehead marked her as Dhukari.

Issa's gut tightened. If she emerged victorious, she would serve the Lady of Blades directly. It was the highest calling in Shalandra outside of the

Necroseti priesthood, and the only way to give her grandparents a better life. Savta and Saba would finally be able to stop their toiling and enjoy their golden years in the comfort of the Keeper's Tier, the level of the city reserved for the *Dhukari*. Issa fought for them this day.

Tinush, the eldest member of the Keeper's Council and High Divinity of the Necroseti, stood and strode toward the edge of the Keeper's Stands—the box reserved for the highest-ranking of the Long Keeper's clerics. His shin-length *shendyt* was made of linen spun with gold thread, a match for the white-and-gold stole draped over his aging shoulders. Like all of the high-ranking Necroseti, he wore a bejeweled white *hedjet,* a tall, almost conical-looking crown that sat atop his golden headband. Thick bands of *kohl* ringed his eyes and he'd painted on seven large black dots to denote his rank.

"Uncover yourselves." Tinush's voice rang out loud across the Crucible with a strength that belied his age. "Remove all trappings of rank and caste, for today you stand bare before the Long Keeper's judgement."

Issa and the others in the Crucible reached up and removed their headbands, the markings of their caste. Issa's simple red cloth band marked her as *Earaqi,* the laborer caste. Most of those surrounding her wore the bright blue of *Alqati,* white of the *Zadii,* and brown of the *Intaji.* A few wore the gold bands that marked them as members of the *Dhukari,* Shalandra's ruling caste. Only one other person in the arena, a willowy boy two or three years younger than her, wore the red. Two young girls standing off to the side tried to hide the black headbands that marked them as *Mahjuri,* the wretched caste. None of the enslaved *Kabili* would fight bare-headed today.

"The Long Keeper cares not for titles, wealth, or fame," Tinush continued, his voice echoing with strength across the arena. "The god of death cares only for one thing: your courage. Courage alone will mark you as deserving to join the Blades, the Long Keeper's warriors on Einan. Steel your hearts, for only the worthy will come through victorious."

Issa felt the familiar tightness in her gut, the thrill of anticipated battle trembling in her hands. She didn't know if she was worthy—no one did until they faced the test of the Crucible—but she had done everything she could to be ready for this moment. Killian had insisted she wait another year. She hadn't listened, and now it was too late to go back.

She didn't want to go back. More than anything else, she wanted the horn to sound the beginning of the trial. The moment she heard that sound, her life would change.

"*Always know your surroundings.*" Killian's words echoed in her mind. "*Even the slightest bump or dip in the ground, the smallest twig can be turned into a weapon against your enemy.*"

Between hammering heartbeats, Issa drank in every detail of the Crucible. Solid stone walls thirty feet high ran in a circle two hundred feet in diameter. A ring of sand-covered ground surrounded the outer edge of the Pit, with eight wooden plank bridges spanning the deep, ten-foot wide ditch that separated them from the Keeper's Steps at the middle. Wooden platforms built like uneven stepping stones rose thirty feet into the air in the heart of the area. Upon the highest platform stood the stone sheaths that held the five two-handed flame swords of the Blades.

Her fists clenched to still the tremor, to calm her nerves. She would claim one of those weapons today. She *had* to.

The clangor of the horn shattered the breathless silence, accompanied by the sudden roar of the crowd. The signal had been given. The trial of steel had begun.

As Issa expected, the huge ox-sized brute to her right charged straight at her. Sixty-five young men and women faced the Crucible today; no more than five would claim the blades and emerge victorious. But the swords would not fall to the quickest or cleverest. The Blades were warriors, training in the art of battle and conquest. They sought those that could outfight their enemies as well as outrace them.

Issa sized up her bull-rushing opponent. He moved with the grace of a practiced combatant, his sword held steady even as his huge feet pounded toward her. The Academy of the Silver Sword taught their fighters to use size and strength as well as skill. With that huge two-handed sword, a well-forged steel simulacrum of the flame blades he sought to claim, he could cut her in half. Casualties among the tested were high.

But Issa had no intention of being one. Even as the huge boy rushed her, she stepped back into a stance taught at the Academy of the Striking Serpents. She wielded two short blades to his larger one and the pose—right-handed sword held low, left-handed sword poised for a high strike—gave her the speed to combat his strength.

The boy slowed as he came within striking range and swung a testing blow. Issa batted the soft strike aside and chopped at him with her right-handed sword. When her opponent blocked low, she aimed high. She didn't give him time to regain his balance but pushed him hard.

*"Always make your enemy underestimate you,"* Killian had pounded into her daily for their five years of lessons. *"Make them see you as nothing but an Earaqi girl until you're ready to spring your trap."*

Not for the first time, Issa gave silent thanks that Killian insisted on teaching her all the sword styles practiced in the six Academies of Shalandra reserved for the upper castes. She, like all low-caste Shalandrans unable to afford costly private education, attended the Institute of the Seven Faces, the school available to the general public. Her low-caste studies had prepared her to fight like a brawler, but Killian had hammered those tendencies out of her with the same ruthlessness that he hammered the steel in his smithy.

When the huge boy transitioned into the high guard pose favored by Silver Sword students, Issa smiled. She'd trained to defeat this stance and its powerful chopping attacks for more than a year now.

*Underestimate this!*

She stepped in with a low swing meant to bait her opponent, then twisted out of the path of the expected blow. The heavy two-handed sword whistled inches past her face and *thunked* into the dirt. Issa's left handed-blade struck out and carved a thin line across the back of the boy's hand, hard enough to loosen his grip without severing fingers. She drove the tip of her right-handed sword into his thigh until it struck bone. The boy howled, falling to one knee, and Issa knocked him out of the fight with a hard punch to the face–a mercy he likely wouldn't have extended to her.

Before the boy's unconscious body *thumped* onto the sandy soil, Issa whirled to face her next opponent. The melee swirled around her as the young men and women locked in combat—some to the death. Already, the blood of more than a dozen stained the sands. High-caste *Alqati* and *Dhukari* died beside *Earaqi* laborers and *Mahjuri* outcasts.

Instinct and hard training warned Issa of a threat from behind. She whirled and brought up her swords in time to block a powerful cross-body blow from a two-handed sword. The impact knocked her backward and sent her blades wide, but she threw herself into a roll that carried her out of her enemy's reach.

"Not today, lowborn!" snarled the young man facing her. He looked about the same age as her, with long, curling hair pulled into a tight braid at the nape of his neck and features that might have been handsome had they not been twisted by rage and bloodlust. Though he fought bare-headed, the *kohl* ringing his eyes and seven black beauty marks on his face marked him as one of the *Dhukari,* a son of the Necroseti priests.

A hard smile touched Issa's lips. Doubtless the youth's father and mother watched from the stands. *What will they think when they see their son bested by an Earaqi?*

The *Dhukari* shot a contemptuous glance at her short swords. "You got lucky with Lorkal," he said, his eyes darting to the unconscious hulk at her feet. "He never was the Academy's best. Let's see what happens when you face the Silver Sword's finest."

When the youth stepped toward her, Issa did the one thing he didn't expect: she hurled her short swords at him. A quick throw, meant to knock him off-guard and shatter his concentration for a second. The young man batted aside her first blade with ease and grunted as the pommel of the second hit him square in the chest.

Issa was already charging, pausing in her furious rush long enough to scoop up the two-handed sword of her fallen foe. The young man's sneer changed to wide-eyed surprise as he recovered and found her rushing straight at him.

She threw all the force of her arms and shoulders, strengthened by years of training and swinging Killian's hammer, into the blow. The two-handed sword crashed into the youth's with jarring force. Her edge slammed into the flat of his blade. Any ordinary weapon would have bent, but his premium-quality Voramian steel sword simply flew from his hands.

The tip of her blade was at his throat in an instant. "Silver Sword's finest?" She snorted. "Makes me glad I didn't bother."

Before Issa could strike—a blow to wound or kill, she never decided—movement flashed in the corner of her eye. She whipped her two-handed sword up and around to deflect a blow aimed for her neck. The strike, which would have opened her throat, flew wide. Issa didn't bother bringing her heavy, two-handed blade around for a counterstrike against her opponent, one of the two *Mahjuri* girls. Instead, she reached up to grip the edge of the sword just above the crossguard and whipped the pommel around. The heavy steel knob slammed into the side of the girl's head.

The *Mahjuri* girl staggered backward, stunned. Issa whipped around to take down the arrogant *Dhukari* youth, but the boy had scooped up his sword and was locked in combat with a shorter, smaller young man.

In the momentary lull, Issa took in the rest of the combatants. Only thirty of the original sixty-five remained standing, all fighting in twos and threes. Issa's gut tightened as she saw three figures pounding over the wooden bridges and leaping onto the platforms that led up toward the blades.

Killian's words echoed in her mind once again. *"Just reaching the top doesn't guarantee you get a blade. Only the worthy will be able to draw the swords."*

With a growl, Issa turned away from the battle and raced toward the nearest bridge. The wood creaked and sagged beneath her, and it took a conscious effort not to look down into the twenty-foot pit lined with sharp steel spikes. She heard the *crunch* of wood and an agonized scream off to her right as one of the bridges collapsed beneath two racing youths.

The sound of pounding feet echoed behind her and Issa had to throw herself to the side to avoid a sword stroke aimed at her back. She leapt up onto a short wooden platform just as the arrogant *Dhukari* boy made the crossing. But instead of following her, the young man turned and, with a vicious snarl, set about hacking at the bridge.

The *Mahjuri* girl had raced after them and had gotten halfway across before the bridge began to shudder. Issa saw that with two or three more well-placed strikes, the youth would collapse the bridge and the young girl would plummet to a horrible death. She hesitated only a heartbeat before leaping back down and charging the boy. They might be competing for the same five blades, but no one—especially no one that lived a life as hard as the *Mahjuri,* the outcasts and wretched of Shalandra's poorest tier—deserve to die like that.

Issa yelled as she charged, just to get the youth's attention. The young man turned to her and deflected her wild strike, but Issa hadn't intended to kill him. Just distract him for a few seconds.

The *Dhukari* youth didn't share her reservations. He hacked at her with all the strength in his arms, which were heavy with lean, corded muscle honed over his years at the Academy of the Silver Sword. His bare, sweat-covered chest gleamed a golden bronze in the sunlight, his muscles rippling as he tried to kill her.

Issa would be damned if she fell now, so close to her goal. The moment she saw the *Mahjuri* girl's feet touch the Keeper's Steps, she disengaged with a quick swipe of her two-handed blade. The attack forced the *Dhukari* youth to leap back for fear of a debilitating leg wound. Issa felt a momentary satisfaction as he almost stepped off the ledge, his heels dangling on empty air. She didn't wait to see if he regained his balance or fell to his death but turned and scrambled up the nearest wooden platform.

The platforms were arranged like an uneven staircase that rose in unpredictable, erratic patterns. She couldn't just climb straight to the top, but had to leap between platforms and scramble up the wooden walls using the gaps between the planks as finger and footholds.

All this while dodging her opponents. Thirty had dropped to twenty-five that she could see, including the three nearly at the top of the Keeper's Steps. She'd climbed higher than most of the rest, but they would catch up to her. She couldn't let herself be caught hanging on to a ledge or pulling herself up. Her opponents wouldn't hesitate to put an end to her—anything to get those blades. Everything changed the moment the sword was drawn from its sheath.

Issa growled as a sharp, stinging line of pain opened along the back of her leg. She scrambled up just in time to avoid another blow, this one from the short, thin-bladed sword—called an estoc, a weapon favored by the Institute of the Seven Faces for its light weight and ease of use—wielded by the *Mahjuri* girl. Fierce determination shone in the girl's dark eyes as she swiped at Issa again.

Not bothering to block, Issa scooted away from the ledge and leapt to her feet. She had seconds before the girl caught up, so she had to open a gap between them. Her two-handed sword gave her the advantage in proper combat, but the platforms were too narrow for her to swing freely. She didn't want to find out if the *Mahjuri* girl was good enough to defeat her.

A loud bark of laughter sounded from above and ahead of her. Issa's heart stopped as she looked up. Somehow, the arrogant *Dhukari* youth had managed to gain the lead, and he was halfway between her and the uppermost platform. He'd get to those blades before her, or wait until she caught up then take her down.

With a growl, Issa pushed the worry from her mind and focused on her immediate surroundings. Another *Dhukari* youth was on the platform next to her, his back turned. She leapt onto the platform and drove the pommel of her sword into the base of his skull. He collapsed into a boneless heap at her feet with a loud *thump*.

Issa jumped across a broad gap onto a higher platform and scrambled up a plank ladder. Instinct warned her of danger as her head reached the level of the next platform, and she ducked in time to avoid a wild swing of a two-handed sword.

"No you don't, lowborn!" The handsome, arrogant face of the *Dhukari* youth sneered down at her. He held his sword poised to drive into her face, throat, or chest if she attempted to climb. "The blades will go to those worthy, not a filthy mud-eater like yooOAAAH!"

His words cut off in a growl tinged with pain. Issa was surprised to see the *Mahjuri* girl pulling her slim sword free of the young man's back. The wound wasn't fatal, but it would hurt enough to slow down the arrogant youth.

The *Mahjuri* girl ducked his wild backhand swing and snapped off a low-kick aimed at his knee. A dirty street fighting tactic taught in the Institute of the Seven Faces, something the fine blademasters of the Academies would never countenance. The kick caught the young man on the side of the knee and his leg crumpled beneath him. He cried out and sagged to the wooden platform.

Issa seized the opportunity to scramble onto the level, kicked the sword from his hand, then raced on to catch up to the *Mahjuri* girl. The uppermost platform stood just ten feet above her, with only five levels between her and her destination.

But at the top of the Keeper's Steps, the combatants were packed closer together. Ten young men and women had reached the platform ahead of her. Two had managed to draw the two-handed blades, and the battle was over for them.

The other eight, however, seemed determined not to let their failure allow someone else to succeed. They might not have drawn the blades, but they turned to face outward to cut down any of their opponents that hadn't yet reached the pinnacle.

"Hey!" Issa called to the *Mahjuri* girl. She didn't know the girl's name, but right now that didn't matter. "Hey!"

The girl turned to look, and she crouched in anticipation of an attack as Issa bounded onto the platform beside her.

But Issa made no move to strike. Instead, she pointed at the uppermost platforms. "We need to work together if we're going to get to those blades."

"Work together?" The *Mahjuri* girl narrowed her eyes. "We are enemies."

"We were," Issa said, "but right now, our only chance of getting through to the final platform is if we help each other." She grinned. "There are five blades and only two of us. Seems the odds are in our favor, don't you think?"

Suspicion filled the girl's piercing gaze. It was to be expected. The *Mahjuri* lived a hard life, reviled and mistreated by all of the castes above them. Even the *Kabili*, the slave caste, often fared better than the *Mahjuri*. Yet the girl had seen Issa's *Earaqi* headband that marked her as a member of the laborer's caste, barely one step above the *Mahjuri*, the closest to equals the girl would ever find.

"So be it," she said with a nod. "Together."

"Good." Issa tightened her grip on the two-handed sword. "I'll go first, cut a way through for you, then you bring them down from behind. Got it?"

"Got it." Grim resolve filled the girl's voice.

"I'm Issa, by the way."

"Etai," the girl responded.

"Well, Etai, let's do this."

Issa sucked in a deep breath and leapt onto the next platform. Two young men stood waiting for her, their long hand-and-a-half swords held in the close-guarded stance of the Academy of the Darting Arrow. Issa knew one would attack in a flurry of quick thrusts intended to keep her sword occupied while the other waited for a chance to strike.

She didn't intend to give them that chance.

The moment she found her balance, she planted her feet and brought the sword across in a two-handed blow like a woodsman felling a tree. Her sword crashed into their blades and knocked them wide, the force throwing them off-kilter. The momentum of her swing carried her sword across and too wide to recover as well. Had she fought alone, she might have died then and there.

Etai seized the opening, darted around the youth on the right, and drove the tip of her slim-bladed estoc into his back. The youth cried out and crumpled, blood spilling from a wound Issa guessed had hit a vital organ. When the second boy tried to attack Etai, Issa smashed the flat of her blade into the side of his head. The impact knocked the boy off the platform and he landed with a loud *crunch* on the level below.

Issa leapt onto the next platform in time to save Etai from being impaled by a blow from another Silver Sword student, then brought her knee up between the young man's legs. When her opponent crumbled, Etai cut him down with a savage chop to his sword arm. Issa lifted the wailing youth's slim body from the ground and, with the strength in her forge-hardened muscles, hurled him into the trio that stood waiting on the platform above them.

"Why thank you!" called a familiar arrogant, mocking voice. Issa's gut clenched as she saw the *Dhukari* boy leap onto the uppermost platform and reach for the hilt of one of the three blades still in their sheaths. He sneered at her and heaved at the blade. With a whisper of steel on stone, the huge flame-bladed sword slipped free of its sheath.

"Yes!" the youth cried, triumph in his voice. He lofted the blade high, where it glinted in the bright sunlight.

Issa's gut clenched. *Two blades left.*

Even as she thought it, five more figures broke through the youths guarding the platform. Issa wanted to scream in anger and frustration as they fought for the blades. So close, just ten feet away, only to fail!

Yet nothing happened. Try as they might, the five could not pull the swords free. The triumph in their expressions turned to panic, then horror, then devastation as they realized the truth. They had reached the blades but the Long Keeper hadn't found them worthy.

Issa was moving before she realized it. Her long legs carried her up to the last platform, cleared of all opponents. A cry from behind her stopped her in the instant her foot touched the level that held the blades.

Etai was on the ground, clutching a wound in her leg. Behind her, a young man held his short sword raised to strike.

Issa had a moment to act. She was within reach of her goal, the thing that would change her family's life forever. Yet what would Savta and Saba say if they knew she'd abandoned a companion—a friend made in the heat of battle?

With a growl, she whipped around and hurled the two-handed sword at the youth standing over Etai. She didn't bother with technique or precision—Killian would murder her for such a foolish use of her weapon—but instead hurled it with all her force. The heavy blade turned lazily in the air and crashed into the boy's chest. The spinning blade cleaved through the side of his neck and he fell back, blood misting in the air.

Issa raced the three steps toward Etai, scooped up the fallen girl, and raced back toward the platform with the blades. To her horror, she found the *Dhukari* youth standing in her path. His flame-bladed sword, made of the finest, deep black Shalandran steel, was poised to drive into her chest.

Issa's blood turned to ice. *He claimed the blade. He should be out of the fight!*

Yet one look in the young man's eyes made it clear he had no intention of stepping aside. The contemptuous sneer on his face told her precisely what he thought of the two lowborns.

But Issa hadn't come this far to let some arrogant *Dhukari* boy stop her. Right arm clenched around Etai's waist, she could only strike out with her left hand. Her palm slapped the curving, flame-shaped steel blade away from her chest and she barreled straight into the young man.

They went down in a heap of flesh, steel, and clothing, but Issa regained enough control to drive the tip of her elbow into the boy's face. Another dirty trick courtesy of her education at the Institute of the Seven Faces, one they didn't teach at the Academy of the Silver Sword.

"Go!" she shouted, and shoved Etai to her feet. The *Mahjuri* girl took one hopping step then sagged on her wounded leg. Her hands reached out to close around the hilt of one of the remaining blades and, with a cry of mingled pain and determination, she ripped the blade free.

Etai stared wide-eyed at the sword in her hand, tears springing to her eyes, and her triumphant laughter echoed across the Crucible.

Issa was a step behind Etai, her hand reaching for the final sword. Another boy, one of the *Alqati,* reached for the blade at the same time. Her fingers closed around the hilt an instant before the boy's did.

A sharp pain drove into her palm and, for a moment, it seemed nothing was happening. Yet, when Issa hauled on the blade, something inside the stone sheath gave way and the sword pulled free with a hiss of steel on stone.

Issa stood, stunned, filled with triumph as she stared down at the huge flame-bladed sword in her hands. She didn't care about the blood staining her palm or the torn, ripped condition of her simple tunic.

The clarion sound of the trumpet proclaimed the truth for all in the stadium to hear. She had defeated her opponents. She had claimed the sword. Her life, and her grandparents' with her, would never be the same after today.

She lofted the sword high, and the crowd cheered louder.

*I will be a Keeper's Blade.*

# Chapter Two

More than anything else in the world, Evren hated temples. Lofty, massive structures erected in honor of the thirteen gods responsible for the creation of Einan. Buildings adorned with ornate trappings, luxuries, and comforts far beyond those enjoyed by the common people that flowed through their halls.

Then there were the priests. Men and women revered for devotion to their gods, looked upon as wise elders to be trusted at all costs.

In Evren's experience, the lavish decorations of temples screamed of abused wealth. The priests he'd been cursed to encounter were little more than men as enslaved to their own greed, lusts, and passions as the congregations they tended to.

Though he had to admit the House of Need in Voramis appeared to stand as a definite exception.

Unlike the grand constructions that surrounded the Fountain of Piety in Divinity Square, the temple to the Beggar God appeared to be one strong gust of wind away from collapsing. Time and the elements had worn away the façade, leaving featureless and crumbling stone. The crooked wooden roof looked to be the most solid part of the temple, and Evren wouldn't trust it with a feather's weight. He cast a nervous glance at the brick-and-mortar doorframe, but thankfully it didn't collapse on him.

He took a deep breath to calm the racing beat of his heart, despite the instincts screaming at him to flee. The last time he'd been in a temple, a priest had died at his hands, and he'd very nearly killed a fellow apprentice. Even now, just the thought of putting himself in the hands of priests—priests like those that had abused him and forced him to fight to survive—sent a shudder of fear down his spine.

Swallowing the surge of acid in his throat, he entered the temple. The interior was clean, at least. Scuffed and faded wooden pews faced the altar to the Beggar God at the far end of the main room. A statue of the Beggar—a hunched, twisted figure wearing ragged clothing and stretching out a pleading hand—stood in silent vigil over the chamber.

Evren hurried past those watching eyes and down the plain stone corridor that led away from the temple's main room of worship. Few people outside of the Beggar Priests and their Beggared children ever saw this section of the House of Need. Though not fancy, it at least appeared able to withstand harsh weather. The low ceiling and stone floors were as plain as the walls, and the doors looked solid enough to stay closed.

*Definitely a far cry from the Master's Temple in Vothmot.* He'd served as an apprentice to the Lecterns, priests to Kiro the Master, and their temple had reeked of opulence and wasteful luxury. All the gorgeous trappings had concealed the true horrors of the temple from the outside world.

Evren couldn't help a nervous clenching in his gut, an instinctive tightening of his fists, as he strode through the unadorned halls. He had no idea what Father Reverentus, head priest of the Beggar God in Voramis and leader of the Cambionari, wanted with him. Whatever it was, it couldn't be good.

He brightened as a gaggle of Beggared children ran past, laughing, shouting, and jostling each other. The Beggar Priests accepted orphans and raised them in the House of Need. That alone had earned a measure of Evren's trust—it was a far cry from his experience in the Master's Temple in Vothmot, his home city far to the north of Voramis.

His eyes scanned the crowd of children for Hailen but caught no sign of the young boy. *He must be at his morning lessons with one of the priests,* he thought.

"You are Evren?"

The question from behind Evren caught him off-guard. He whirled, fists coming up to defend himself, teeth bared in a snarl of defiance. He'd be damned if he let these priests—

"Oh, dearie me!" The pudgy, middle-aged priest behind him flinched, ruddy cheeks going pale in surprise. "A-Are you…?" He swallowed and struggled to regain his composure.

Evren recovered first. "Yes, I am." He let out a silent breath and lowered his fists. On streets of Vothmot, either you were always on your guard or you were dead. "I was told Father Reverentus is expecting me."

"H-He is." Slowly, the color returned to his cheeks and, with a jerky nod, swept a hand down a hallway. "This way, young master."

Evren hid a grin as he fell in step behind the priest. *Young master. I like that.*

As the priest led him through the plain stone corridors, Evren couldn't help smirking at the way the lantern light played tricks with the contours of the man's wax-shined bald head. This nervous-looking man was a far cry from the cold, dead-eyed Lectern Uman and the others he'd fought to escape in Vothmot.

Finally, the priest stopped at a door as unadorned as the rest around him, raised a hand, and rapped on the wood.

"Enter," came the voice from within. An aged voice, yet a strong one.

Pushing open the door, the priest gestured for Evren to enter.

Evren swallowed a flutter of nerves as he saw Father Reverentus sitting in a stuffed armchair. Father Reverentus had a lined, weathered face with a sharp nose, strong chin, and liver spots dotting his scalp and the skin of his arthritis-twisted hands. He sat with a pronounced stoop to his shoulders, but there was nothing ancient about the sharp intelligence that gleamed in his piercing blue eyes.

"Thank you, Brother Mendicatus." The old priest nodded his bald head. "That will be all."

"Of course, Father." With a bow, the portly Mendicatus retreated and shut the door behind him.

Father Reverentus sat in silence for long moments, his eyes fixed on Evren's face. He might have looked like a kindly grandfather, but the burning intensity of his scrutiny belied his appearance. Life on the streets had taught Evren to size people up in an instant, and everything about Father Reverentus told Evren that this priest was far more than he appeared.

"The Hunter has told me of you," Father Reverentus said. "Of your history with the Lecterns and your escape to freedom."

Evren tried to hide the sudden tension in his shoulders and spine. Only the Hunter and Kiara knew the full truth of Evren's past; he hadn't told Hailen, for the boy was far too young to hear such terrible stories. Now, it seemed, Father Reverentus had learned of it as well. Evren trusted the Hunter had a good reason to relay that information to the old Beggar Priest, but he'd reserve judgement until he found out why he'd been summoned here so early in the morning.

Father Reverentus steepled his fingers and leaned back in his chair. "It might surprise you to learn that I know more about your story than you expect. I was familiar with Lectern Uman, but if I'd known the truth of what went on—Keeper, what might *still* be going on—I'd have done exactly the same thing in your position."

Evren said nothing. No one, not even the Hunter or Kiara, knew that Uman's death had been an accident. The street crews in Vothmot had mostly left him alone once they found out what he'd done, and that nugget of misinformation suited him just fine.

The old Beggar Priest gave a dismissive wave of his gnarled hand. "But that is neither here nor there. What matters now is that the Hunter tells me that you can be trusted." He gave Evren a little smile. "He went so far as to call you capable and reliable. High praise, coming from him."

Evren struggled not to grin. The Hunter had done little more than grunt his approval during their training sessions when Evren turned aside a quick blow or disarmed his opponent. Coming from the Hunter, that truly *was* high praise.

"As you know," Father Reverentus continued, "we have come to a certain…understanding with the Hunter." The words seemed to stick in his throat. "As our goals seem to be aligned, at least in the matter of ridding the world of the threat of demons, it is in all our best interests to cooperate. At least, that is what I have been able to convince my brethren in Voramis to see. As for the rest…" He shrugged his slim shoulders.

Evren nodded. The Hunter, once the most famous and highest-paid assassin in Voramis, had uncovered a terrible truth three years ago: demons, a race of otherworldly, bestial creatures known as the Abiarazi, hadn't been scoured from the world thousands of years earlier during the War of Gods, as most of Einan believed. Instead, they had used their skills at shifting shape to conceal themselves among the humans, impossible to differentiate except for the deep black color of their eyes.

The Hunter had shown him the shape-changing skill, shifting his face from his own hard, dark visage to a handsome youth, an old man, then back to his normal features in the space of a few seconds. Evren had shuddered the first time he saw those eyes, like two pools into nothingness. Had he not known the truth of who the Hunter was—not only a Bucelarii, half-human offspring of the demons, but a man willing to fight his own people to save the ones he cared about—Evren might have fled then and there.

"From what I am given to understand," Father Reverentus said, "the Hunter is away from Voramis at the moment. The Hidden Circle alchemist, Graeme was it?" He scanned a parchment on his desk and nodded. "Graeme informed me that the Hunter had departed to Praamis in search of an Abiarazi he believed to be there."

Evren nodded. "Yes." The Hunter had departed almost three weeks earlier. Given the ten-day journey to the nearby city of Praamis, he ought to return soon.

"A matter of great importance has come to my attention." Father Reverentus sat up straighter in his chair and fixed Evren with that piercing, intense stare. "Typically, I would pass the information to the Hunter, but if his information proves correct and there is a demon in Praamis, I believe his hands will be a tad too full to deal with it himself. And, I'm given to understand you have unique skills. Skills that could prove quite advantageous in this circumstance."

Evren raised an eyebrow. "Skills of a thief, you mean?"

"Precisely." Father Reverentus inclined his head. "When the Hunter mentioned that you were quick enough to lift his purse in the Court of Judgement in Vothmot, I believed I had the right man for the job."

"And what's this job, then?" Evren sat back, trying for nonchalance to cover his burning curiosity and the nervous anxiety roiling in his stomach. He couldn't help wondering what sort of job the Beggar Priest wouldn't handle in-house. One that required a thief, no less.

Father Reverentus stroked the white beard that hung to his emaciated waist. "How familiar are you with the city of Shalandra?"

Evren shrugged. "Never heard of it."

"Ah." The old Beggar Priest's face tightened. He reclined in his stuffed, cloth-upholstered armchair once more and pursed his lips. "The City of the Dead, some call it, an entire city built around the worship of the Long Keeper, god of death."

Evren's eyes widened a fraction. "Worshipping the Long Keeper? Are they mad?" He made the warding gesture that all superstitious Einari knew would keep away the eye of the sleepless god. Where the Long Keeper walked, he left only death in his wake.

Father Reverentus' face twisted into a frown. "Perhaps, and yet that is the god they have chosen to worship." He tapped a finger against his lips. "But the only part of their dark worship that should interest you is the Blade of Hallar, the city's most sacred relic. And, I believe, a weapon much like the Hunter's dagger, Soulhunger."

Evren sat bolt upright. Soulhunger was a magical weapon with a gemstone that consumed the life energy of its victims to feed Kharna, the Serenii trapped in the city of Enarium. Evren hadn't seen the dagger at work, but he'd heard tales of the Hunter recovering from mortal wounds thanks to Soulhunger's blood magic. A weapon of immense power and, in the wrong hands, a truly dire threat indeed.

"The Blade of Hallar is said to have belonged to Hallar, the first Pharus and founder of Shalandra," Father Reverentus explained. "My Cambionari brethren in the Beggar Temple in Shalandra have long been interested in it, but only recently have they been able to ascertain that it is truly one of the *Im'tasi* weapons forged by the ancient Serenii for the Bucelarii to wield."

"So why don't they just nick it, then?" Evren cocked his head. "No one would think to accuse a Beggar Priest of stealing it."

"The thought had crossed my mind." A smile tugged at the old priest's lips. "But, alas, it is out of our reach." He sighed and shook his head. "The Blade of Hallar is kept under constant guard by high-ranking Keeper's Blades, the elite warriors of Shalandra, in the most secure room in the Palace of Golden Eternity. It is only ever brought out of its vault four times a year. Once every four months for the Ceremony of the Seven Faces, and once more for the Anointing of the Blades."

Evren frowned. "Let me guess, one of these ceremonies is going to take place soon, and you want me on hand to nick this blade?"

"Precisely." Father Reverentus nodded. "The next crop of Keeper's Blades will be anointed before the Four-Bladed Storm sweeps over Shalandra. If you are as clever a thief as the Hunter believes, it may be that you are better-suited for the task than even he. After all, his manner is far more…direct."

Evren chuckled. "You could say that." The Hunter's Bucelarii healing abilities, strength, and speed made him impossible to kill—for any who didn't know his secret weakness, of course. The fully human Evren had to resort to cunning, trickery, and stealth where the Hunter opted for a frontal assault.

"Once you have procured the Blade of Hallar," Father Reverentus continued, "you simply need to get it to the House of Need in Shalandra. From there, my Cambionari brethren will smuggle you and the weapon safely out of the city and back here. I will not lie and tell you the job will be easy, but you will have as much assistance as we can offer."

"How much time do I have?" Evren asked. "Before the next time this fancy sword will be brought out?"

Father Reverentus scanned one of the parchments strewn across his desk. "One month, give or take a few days. The Crucible will be taking place now, and those chosen to join the Keeper's Blades will be anointed at the next turn of the moon."

*One month.* Evren frowned and pondered the job. *Not a lot of time to figure out something this complex.*

"The journey to Shalandra should take less than ten days," Father Reverentus said, "giving you almost three weeks to find the way to retrieve the sword."

"Three weeks?" Evren's eyebrows shot up. "Cutting it a bit close, aren't you?"

Father Reverentus' eyes flashed at Evren's disrespectful tone, but Evren didn't flinch. He'd lost his fear of priests the night he killed Lectern Uman. The Lectern had tried to stop his escape from the Master's Temple and Evren had lashed out—in self-defense and protection of a fellow apprentice. The priest had deserved a far less kind fate, given the abuse he'd heaped on Evren's head—and *all* the apprentices. Yet even now, after years had passed, Evren still couldn't forget the wide-eyed horror in Lectern Uman's eyes as the blood leaking from his shattered skull stained the water of his bathing pool a deep crimson. Some memories never truly faded, but left an indelible mark on the mind.

"I have just now received all the information required to undertake this quest," Father Reverentus said after a long moment, his tone sharp-edged with irritation. "Were time not such a constraining factor, I might have waited until the Hunter returned from Praamis."

Evren snorted. "Thanks for the vote of confidence, eh?"

Father Reverentus leaned forward, eyes narrowed. "Do not take this matter lightly, young man. This mission is of absolute importance, not only to us as the defenders of Einan, but to the Hunter. My efforts to gain access to the *Im'tasi* weapons stored in the vaults beneath the Beggar Temple in Malandria have been met with fierce resistance. My brethren in Malandria have not forgotten what the Hunter did to Lord Knight Moradiss, Father Pietus, and the other Cambionari. Their blood still stains the carpets and their spirits cry out for vengeance." Anger tinged his words and blazed in his blue eyes. "Only the fact that the fate of Einan is at stake has held us back."

Evren met the priest's anger with cold calm. The Cambionari, the demon-hunting secret priesthood of the Beggar God, had forced the Hunter's hand, but he wouldn't try telling them that. Better try to turn a stone into wine than change a priest's mind.

Yet, despite the unveiled threat in Father Reverentus' words, Evren knew the priest was right. The Hunter had sworn to aid Kharna, the Serenii locked away in Enarium, in the fight against the Devourer of Worlds, a being of chaos that sought to unmake Einan and all of reality. The Serenii-forged *Im'tasi* weapons were invaluable tools in his mission to feed Kharna the life force required to sustain him.

At the moment, the Hunter had just three: Soulhunger, the long sword he'd taken from the Sage in Enarium, and a third sword that had once belonged to the First of the Bloody Hand. Kiara wielded the First's sword and the Hunter had entrusted the Sage's weapon to Graeme and the Hidden Circle, a group of rogue alchemists and information-brokers, for study. A fourth such weapon would prove vital in the Hunter's quest—perhaps the Hunter would even trust Evren to wield it. Gods knew he'd trained enough hours in the last three years to feel confident swinging such a blade.

"I'll do it," he said in a low voice. "I'll find this Blade of Hallar." It would be damned near impossible to learn his way around a new city, find a way into the palace, and come up with an escape route all in the space of three weeks, yet people had believed escape from the Master's Priests in Vothmot equally impossible. He'd do it, if nothing else to show the Hunter that he was truly ready to aid in his quest.

Father Reverentus' face brightened. "Excellent!" He reached for the little bell sitting on his desk and rang it, a tinny tinkling that echoed surprisingly loud in the small chamber.

A moment later, the same portly priest poked his head into the door. "Yes, Father?"

"Brother Mendicatus, provide young master Evren here with everything he will require to accompany Brother Modestus on his journey to Shalandra. And inform Modestus that he leaves within the hour."

"Of course, Father." Mendicatus bowed to the old Reverentus, then stared expectantly at Evren.

Evren stood and was about to follow Brother Mendicatus from the room, but Father Reverentus' voice stopped him.

"This mission is a heavy burden for one so young to carry, but I trust the Hunter when he says that you are strong enough to bear it." The old priest leaned forward and fixed Evren with that piercing gaze. "Perhaps everything you have endured in your past has been to prepare you for this moment in time. May the Beggar strengthen your arm and guide your steps, Evren. The fate of this world may very well rest on your shoulders."

# Chapter Three

Kodyn cast a last glance over his shoulder at Praamis, the city that had been his home for all seventeen years of his life. He knew Praamis like the back of his hand—from the rooftop planks and rope bridges of the Hawk's Highway to the endless underground tunnels of the Night Guild to the maze-like sewer system to the crowded, filthy streets of Old Town Market—that leaving it felt like tearing a piece out of his soul. He would miss his mothers, his mentor and trainer Master Serpent, his friends in House Hawk, and all of the others he was leaving behind.

Yet he couldn't help feeling excited as he returned his gaze to the road ahead. The long, dusty stretch of cleared ground spread from Praamis' South Gate toward the horizon. Destiny awaited him in Shalandra.

A low growl of frustration echoed from beside him. Kodyn hid a smile as Aisha wrestled with the reins of her horse, a roan mare that had proven to be a handful. No matter how much Aisha kicked, swore, or threatened, the mare seemed determined to go her own way. Once, the horse simply wandered off the road and set about cropping grass, and nothing any of them did could get the beast moving until it decided it had had its fill.

*Just her luck that she, the least experienced rider among us, got the most difficult horse.* He grinned. *I wonder which of them will out-stubborn the other.*

Aisha's umber-colored skin, tight-curling hair, dark lips, silver nose and eyebrow piercings, and deep brown eyes proclaimed her a native of Ghandia, a kingdom of plains and grasslands far to the northeast of Praamis. Yet she cursed with a vehemence that would make any Praamian proud. Anyone who saw her—broad-shouldered, lithe muscles, confident posture, with a short-handled *assegai* spear and long dirk at her hip—would immediately recognize her as a warrior.

Briana, his other traveling companion, stood in stark contrast to Aisha. Her skin was a deep golden mahogany, and she had an oval face, sloping forehead, and arrow-straight nose. But it was her build, the slight, petite frame of a young woman more given to knowledge and academia than battle, that made her stand out. That, and the still-healing bruises and cuts on her face.

"How are you feeling?" Kodyn asked.

"Fine," Briana said with a little smile. "Glad to be getting back to my father and my home. And to be back in the bright sunlight and fresh air."

Kodyn chuckled. "Yeah, the Night Guild's tunnels can be a bit of an acquired taste."

"It's amazing that so many of you live in that underground warren," Briana said. "There have to be what, two or three hundred?"

Kodyn scrunched up his face. "Four hundred and thirty-six at last count."

Briana's eyes shot up. "And *all* of them are thieves like you?"

"No, not all." Kodyn chuckled. "The Hawks are the third-story thieves, while the Foxes run the streets with the Grubbers. The Serpents are assassins, Scorpions the poisoners, and Hounds the bounty hunters and trackers." He jerked a thumb at Aisha. "Aisha and the others of House Phoenix run the brothels and pleasure-houses of Praamis, protecting the working girls and making sure every client pays what they owe. Then the Bloodbears are like the Night Guild's version of the Praamian Guard, maintaining order among the eight Guild Houses and settling disputes. Plus, they serve as my mother's muscle when she needs something done."

His mother happened to be the Master of the Night Guild, the organization that ruled Praamis' underworld. That fact served as a large part of why he found himself on the road south—he had to find a way to step out of her shadow.

*Speaking of shadows,* Kodyn thought as he cast a glance over his shoulder, *it seems Aisha's in trouble again.*

The roan mare had taken shelter in the cool shade of a weeping willow, and Aisha wrestled with the reins, cursing at the stubborn beast. Kodyn would have sworn he saw a mischievous glint in the horse's liquid brown eyes, a subtle mockery in the way its ears twitched. The horse knew *exactly* what sort of violence Aisha threatened yet seemed smart enough to realize that it was a bluff.

Kodyn slowed his horse to wait, but didn't turn to help. Given Aisha's current mood—as dark as the circles beneath her eyes—any offer of help would be dismissed with the same threats leveled at the horse.

"I don't think I ever thanked you properly." Briana shot a sidelong glance at him, her face flushing a pretty pink. "For saving me, and for convincing the Guild Master to let you escort me home."

"You don't need to thank me." Kodyn felt his stomach flutter as he reached out and laid a hand softly on her arm. "It's my pleasure."

He felt foolish for his reaction to her presence, yet something about the slim Shalandran girl made his heart race, his palms grow sweaty, and his tongue trip over his words. He'd felt attracted to other young women in the past—Ria's role as Master of House Phoenix had led to plenty of interaction with the fancy-ticklers, courtesans, and working girls of Praamis—but Briana was different. From the moment he'd heard her voice in that warehouse where she was held captive, he'd found himself drawn to her.

Of course, Aisha's presence made things a bit more complicated. He'd been nursing a crush on the umber-skinned Ghandian girl for the better part of two years, though that had deepened into genuine feelings in the last few months. By the way Ria and Ilanna, his other mother and Master of the Night Guild, treated the two of them, he was almost certain she had similar feelings for him.

*So now what?* The question had echoed in his mind a thousand times in the last week. *How do I choose between two beautiful women?*

Behind him, Aisha's cursing trailed off as the sound of her horse's clopping hooves grew louder. Evidently, the Ghandian girl had won the battle of wills. Either that, or the stubborn animal had finally cracked beneath the barrage of Aisha's oaths.

With a sigh, Kodyn pushed the worry from his mind. He didn't want to have to think about that, not while the sun hung high in the sky and the day was so beautiful.

The land to the south of Praamis was dusty and dry, though not quite as barren as the Windy Plains to the west. Rocky hills and tall, craggy cliffs rose high in the distance, but the landscape bordering the road was mostly flat, with only gentle crests and valleys in the terrain, like waves of yellow dirt and pale green scrub rather than crystal blue ocean.

Aisha's horse went from a stubborn walk to a determined trot, forcing Kodyn and Briana to speed up their mounts to match the pace. Kodyn didn't consider himself an expert rider, but he'd spent enough time on horseback to know the beasts could keep up a steady jog-trot for hours without tiring. With all the jouncing and jolting, it seemed more likely that the riders would tire first.

He was too excited to feel tired. Ahead of him, ten days to the south, waited Shalandra, the city where he would complete his Undertaking and finally earn his place as a Journeyman of the Night Guild.

His mother had fought to keep him a secret from the Night Guild, not wanting him to suffer the same misery and abuse she had during her years of training. Yet when she became Guild Master, she had abolished the cruel methods that had been used to break the spirits of the apprentices.

Kodyn had spent the last nine years training to be a Hawk, the third-story thieves of the Night Guild. He could pick a lock, scale a building, or creep into a sleeping nobleman's bedroom better than any of his fellow Hawk apprentices—better even than some Journeymen. Years spent training with Errik, the Guild's foremost assassin, and Ria had prepared him to use the long sword that hung at his hip and the various daggers secreted about his person.

All that training would finally pay off when he attempted to steal the Crown of the Pharus, the most priceless relic in Shalandra. His mother had earned her place as Journeyman by achieving the impossible, so he'd have to do the same if he wanted to make his own way in the Night Guild. That meant leaving home and traveling to Shalandra.

The journey gave him the chance to escort Briana safely back to her father, Arch-Guardian Suroth, the high priest of the Secret Keepers in Shalandra. He also needed to learn more about the Gatherers, the death-worshipping cult that had murdered dozens of Praamian men, women, and children. He had sworn to stop them from returning to Praamis at all costs.

His eyes once again fixed on the broad, well-muscled back of the Ghandian girl riding in front of him. Ria had insisted Aisha accompany him, both as witness to verify that he'd accomplished his Undertaking and for some other, secret Undertaking of her own. Kodyn ached to find out what. If only he didn't trip over his damned tongue every time he talked to the beautiful young woman!

The sun wheeled by overhead as they rode, until Aisha drew her horse to a halt around noon. Kodyn didn't complain; his sit bones ached and the jolting trot had left his spine stiff. He welcomed the chance to dismount and share a simple meal of fresh Praamian bread, soft white cheese, and olives.

They ate in tired silence, and Kodyn found himself wishing for a tree, bush, even a stalk of tall grass—anything to provide shade from the bright sun and cool the sweltering heat.

To his surprise, Briana was the first to speak. "Aisha, you are from Ghandia to the north, yes?"

Aisha nodded. "Yes, though I am surprised that you know of it. Not many people this far south know of my people."

"Ahh, that is my father's fault." Briana smiled. "I inherited a love of learning from him, which he encouraged by hiring tutors to teach me everything they could: philosophy, politics, the geography of Einan and Fehl, the religions practiced on both continents, even the martial teachings of the Blades and Indomitables. That last, I fear, I know little of, for there are few outside the Academies that learn the strategies of war and battle."

"You said your father was a Secret Keeper, right?" Kodyn asked.

Briana nodded. "Yes."

"Is it true the priests have their tongues cut out?" The words slipped from his mouth before he realized it. He kicked himself as Briana's expression darkened and a shadow passed over her eyes.

"It is," she replied in a quiet voice. "And my father very nearly died when the Temple of Whispers learned of my existence." She lifted her gaze to meet his and sorrow sparkled in her *choclat*-brown eyes. "It is forbidden for Secret Keepers to marry or have children, for fear that the knowledge they obtain might leak out into the world."

"If so, how is it possible that he's still the High Secret Keeper?" Aisha asked.

Briana turned to the Ghandian girl. "Because of who my mother is. Was." She swallowed and dropped her gaze again.

Kodyn's gut tightened. "She's dead?" The question sounded so stupid, but he couldn't think of anything else to say.

Briana nodded. "Died giving birth to me." Her face fell, and for a minute she seemed to be wrestling with tears. Finally, she continued in a quiet voice. "She and my father were the only two Secret Keepers responsible for studying the works of the Serenii in Shalandra. With her dead, my father alone retained the knowledge they'd accumulated over a decade of study. The Secret Keepers couldn't afford to kill him and risk losing their research. They allowed him, and me, to live."

Kodyn reached out and placed a hesitant hand on her shoulder. "I'm sorry for bringing up the painful memories." He had his own share of memories to wrestle with, chief among them the night that strange, sickly blue-green fire nearly killed him and Ria. To this day, even the open flame of a candle made him hesitate.

"No, it's okay," Briana said, and quickly scrubbed at her cheeks. "It is my burden to carry. Mine, and my father's, together. Thanks to you, the both of you, he will not lose me too like he lost my mother."

"I'm glad." Aisha's voice was rough, husky with emotion.

"Yeah, me too," Kodyn said. He gave Briana's arm a little squeeze then pulled his hand away. "We should keep riding. We've got four or five hours left before we reach Rosecliff, and the sun's setting earlier these days."

Briana nodded and, finishing up the last of her meager meal, stood and brushed the crumbs from her blue woolen dress—a parting gift from Ria. Aisha quickly repacked the bags, secured them to her saddle, and mounted up. Kodyn helped Briana climb onto her horse's back before following suit. A heavy silence hung over their little crew as they rode on down the southern highway.

As the hours passed, the landscape began to change. The hills and valleys grew more pronounced, the craggy cliffs pressing closer to the road. Scrub gave way to thicker, greener grass dotted with a smattering of hardy plains flowers—evening primroses, milkweed, clovers, and peas—that filled the world with a hint of color.

Relief pierced Kodyn's weariness as he spotted the highway-side town of Rosecliff in the distance. The town, named for the red sandstone cliff that stood on the opposite side of the caravan route, was little more than a random assortment of stone and wooden buildings clustered around a small freshwater lake. Cattle, sheep, and horses grazed on the lush green grass ringing the water, next to sparse tracts of land where farmers stubbornly fought to grow enough crops to feed the people.

But right now, he felt as if he'd rarely seen anything so beautiful. The light of the setting sun bathed the world in a soft rosy brilliance that seemed to set the red cliff glowing. If he wasn't so tired, he'd have contemplated making the trek up the narrow path to sit and bask in the twilight radiance. It would be a magical, romantic place to take Aisha…or Briana.

Kodyn led them toward the town's one inn, a two-story building of wood and bricks that stood at a precarious tilt, as if one strong gust of wind would knock it over. A faded, dust-covered sign above the door proclaimed "Rosecliff Inn". He dismounted and helped Briana down from her horse, but when he turned he found Aisha still in her saddle, her eyes fixed on something to the north. He followed her gaze until he saw the object of her focus: a graveyard that spread along the south face of a barren hill a few hundred paces north of the town.

Aisha gave a little shudder, her face pale despite her dusky skin. She blinked hard as if trying to clear her vision, then turned away quickly and half-leapt from her saddle. The Ghandian girl didn't even bother to hitch her horse to the post but strode inside in a hurry.

*What the bloody hell?* Kodyn's brow furrowed. *What could there possibly be about a graveyard that makes a fierce warrior like Aisha act like that?*

Perhaps it had something to do with her Undertaking or the secret reason Ria had insisted Aisha accompany him. Whatever it was, he intended to find out.

# *Chapter Four*

Aisha fled into the Rosecliff Inn to escape the spirits of the dead.

She didn't want to hear their whispers carried on the wind, see their pleading eyes. She wanted peace.

But deep in her heart, she knew they would not leave her alone. The spirits had claimed her father, and now they had come for her, too.

"Greetings, greetings!" A portly woman with a flour-stained apron and a broad smile bustled toward Aisha. "Welcome to the Rosecliff Inn. I'm your host for the evening, Rose." She smiled, as if at some great joke. "What can I offer you, young lady?"

"Two rooms." Aisha held up two fingers. "And dinner for three."

"Three?" Rose cocked an eyebrow and glanced around Aisha toward the door. "Ahh, that handsome lad and beautiful lass outside are traveling with you? So young, all of you. What brings you out Rosecliff way?"

Aisha found the woman's habit of speaking without waiting for her questions to be answered beyond irritating, though perhaps she had to write it off at her sour mood. The sight of the graveyard and the spirits hovering above the headstones was enough to ruin anyone's day.

She managed a curt response. "Traveling south."

"South, eh? Lots of south to travel before you hit the coastline." Rose beamed and tucked a stray red curl back under her bright crimson handkerchief. "Anywhere specific?"

Aisha tensed at the question. Perhaps Rose was just trying to make friendly conversation, but life as a slave and a member of the Night Guild had taught Aisha to be wary of everyone.

"Just traveling," she answered with a dismissive wave.

"Always wanted to travel," Rose said, half to herself. "I always told my Gerry, Keeper rest his soul, that we'd take a trip north, tour the wine country outside Nysl. Those parts they let visitors see, of course. But running an inn's a full-time task, especially now that my Gerry's passed on. Perhaps once Braith and Karlyle are old enough to handle it on their own, or they've got wives to tend the stove, I'll have a chance to—"

"What about the rooms?" Aisha asked, brusquer than she'd intended in an attempt to interrupt the ceaseless, aimless meandering of the woman's train of thought.

"Oh, of course, dearie!" Rose beamed and gestured toward the staircase at the back of the common room. "Up the stairs, two doors on your right. Keys are underneath the mats."

For the first time, Aisha took in the interior of the inn. It was a simple place—little more than stone bricks held together with mortar, with an empty fireplace on one wall and a long bar made of weathered wood on the other. Worn chairs stood around the five small tables in the taproom. Only three other people, all wearing rough farmer and shepherd clothing, sat drinking and eating in silence.

"Greetings, greetings!" Rose called out as Kodyn and Briana entered the common room. "Your young companion here was just telling me that you'll be staying for dinner. I've got a fine brace of rabbits on for the stew, and fresh bread a-baking. The finest butter in all of—"

Aisha hurried up the stairs before the chatty innkeeper could draw her into another stream of one-sided chatter.

The Rosecliff Inn was the only two-floor building in the small town. The upstairs held just four rooms—two on each side of the hallway—all smaller than her simple quarters in the Night Guild tunnels. Mats of dyed and woven grass provided the only spot of color in the dull stone and wood hallways, as well as the "hiding place" for the keys.

Not that the keys served much use. Aisha hadn't learned half of what those of House Fox or Hawk learned about locks and even she could pick them in seconds.

The rooms were small, with just one simple wooden cot topped by a mattress and pillow stuffed with prairie grasses. The room's single other item of furniture was a rickety wooden chair. A mirror the size of her hand and a clay chamber pot completed the décor.

Aisha dropped her bags onto the chair with a tired sigh. She'd take the floor and give Briana the bed. Kodyn would have the second room.

Ria and Ilanna had given them more than enough coin to make the journey to Shalandra comfortable, and for once Aisha didn't mind parting with the gold. Here, away from the Night Guild's persnickety bookkeepers, she could afford to spend a bit more on a hot meal for the three of them and a private room for her and Briana.

By the time she'd shrugged out of her pack and stuffed it out of sight behind the room's single chair, Kodyn and Briana made it up the stairs. They both had the look of a pole-axed steer.

*They didn't escape Rose fast enough,* Aisha thought with a small grin. *Let's just hope there are enough people come dinner time that she'll only dish out a small helping of that babble with our meals.*

Briana looked at Kodyn for a moment, hesitant, before stepping into the room.

"Take the bed," Aisha told her. "I'll be more than comfortable on the floor." In the brothel where the Bloody Hand slavers had chained her for two months, she'd had little more than a ratty blanket for a bed. Back home in Ghandia, she'd grown up sleeping on the ground under the open sky or on a pile of twigs and savannah grass.

"Thank you," Briana said with a shy smile.

Aisha nodded. She didn't know quite what to make of the girl Briana. *She'd never survive on the Ghandian plains or in the Night Guild, that's for sure. Too soft and gentle, not enough fight in her.*

Briana looked every bit the scholar—or scholar's daughter—from her soft white hands to her blue woolen dress to her slim build. She spoke in a quiet voice, her manner unassuming, and though she carried herself with the poise of a noblewoman, she lacked the tone of assertive command.

But it wasn't just that. Even the oldest, blindest elder in her village would have seen Kodyn's affections for the girl. As the memories of the abuse and horrors sustained during her captivity faded, Aisha found herself drawn more and more to the handsome young son of the Guild Master. She'd fancied him even back when he'd been a gangly youth, but now that he'd grown into a strong, capable thief, she'd noticed that her fancy changed to something more.

So to see Kodyn falling all over himself to be attentive to Briana grated deep down in Aisha's stomach. She hated herself for feeling that way, but she couldn't help it. She had nothing against the slim Shalandran girl, but it took a supreme effort of will to hold her tongue when she wanted to snap out.

Had she found herself in such a situation back in her village, she would have challenged Briana to a battle of *assegai* and *makrigga*. The two of them would dance the *Kim'ware* until one yielded to the other. The victor would walk away from the fight with Kodyn as the prize, and the loser would find a new male upon which to lavish her attention.

But this wasn't Ghandia. As she'd learned during her years serving as an apprentice Phoenix, the people of Praamis preferred a much subtler approach. They courted through genteel words and polite smiles instead of combat and strength of arms.

Briana was cultured, refined, and educated. Aisha couldn't compete with her, and that thought only soured her mood further.

"Hungry?" Briana asked with a bright smile. "That midday meal barely made a dent in my stomach, and I'm ready for some real food. That rabbit stew and fresh bread smelled amazing."

At the same time, Aisha couldn't despise the young woman. Briana had survived kidnapping, captivity, and beatings at the hands of the death-worshipping Gatherers. The cultists had dragged her hundreds of miles away from her home in order to strong-arm her father into giving them what they wanted. Yet all of that suffering hadn't dampened Briana's bright spirit. She had an innate cheerfulness that Aisha hadn't seen since the last time she'd run through the tail plains grasses with her younger sister the day before the slavers hauled her away. She couldn't hate anyone that reminded her of cheerful, playful Nkanyezi.

"Sure," Aisha said with a sigh. "I could use a meal." To distract herself, if nothing else.

They found Kodyn waiting for them downstairs. He'd claimed a table for them, and moments after they took their seats, Rose bustled out of the kitchens. The tray in her hands bore three bowls and three mugs with watered wine.

Steam wafted up from the bowl, carrying with it the familiar spices of cardamom, cumin, and a hint of something earthy that Aisha recognized as a special red chili pepper she'd loved as a child in Ghandia. The bread seemed to fall apart in her hands, soft with a crispy crust, served with a dish of salted butter. A fine meal, but Aisha's heart wasn't in it.

Kodyn had chosen a table next to the window, and through the filthy oilcloth covering she could see the graveyard. Try as she might, she couldn't keep her eyes away from the sea of headstones. And the spirits that hovered above them, invisible to all but her.

She barely heard Rose's inane chatter, Kodyn and Briana's conversation, even the sound of the people flooding in and out of the inn. A part of her hated her inattentiveness—she ought to be on guard, wary of any threats—yet she couldn't bring herself to focus.

*I need to get away from here!* Her gut clenched, her appetite fled. She almost ran out of the inn and leapt onto her horse. She'd rather sleep under the stars far away from the graveyard if it meant she didn't have to hear or see the spirits.

But that would mean explaining things to Kodyn and Briana. Right now, she had no desire to share her deepest fear with anyone.

She pushed her bowl back and stood. Kodyn and Briana looked up at her with curious expressions.

"You okay?" Kodyn asked. His brow furrowed and genuine concern shone in his eyes. "Feeling sick?"

"Sure," Aisha told him. "I need some fresh air. I'll be back soon."

She didn't wait to hear their answers but strode out of the inn's common room to where her horse stood. Gathering up her reins, she climbed into the saddle and dug her heels into the horse's ribs. The stubborn mount resisted for a few moments, then finally caved to the insistent pounding of her sharp boot heels and set off at a run away from the inn. Away from the graveyard.

Aisha turned the horse's head east, toward the path that climbed to the clifftop. She gave the horse its head, let it set the pace. She just wanted to get away from the waiting spirits.

*Why me?* Her mind whirled as she rode. Sorrow welled up in her chest at the memory of her father's vacant stare and blank expression. She didn't want to be like that. *What have I done to deserve this curse?*

At the top of the cliff, she threw herself from her saddle and dropped to her knees a pace from the edge. She closed her eyes and leaned on her hands, gasping for breath. Tears streamed from her eyes with the realization of what lay in her future.

She could see the *Kish'aa*, the spirits of the dead. A gift, or a curse, given to only a few Ghandians. She was *Umoyahlebe,* a Spirit Whisperer. Just like her father.

She'd seen her first spirit during her captivity. Another young girl, barely thirteen, had died chained a few paces away from her. Aisha had seen the moment the girl died, watched the spirit rise from her body. It didn't matter that the southerners believed in the thirteen false gods—the spirits of the dead cared not about religion or creed.

She had desperately tried to write it off as the hallucinations brought on by Bonedust, the mind-altering narcotic their slavers had used to keep them docile. Yet just two weeks earlier, she had seen the spirit of one of the children murdered by the Gatherers. On her seventeenth birthday, the same day as her father.

The memory of the last time she'd seen her father brought a sick sorrow to her gut. Wandering their village at night speaking to the dead, with nary a word for the living. Not for his wife, his son, or his two young daughters.

Ghandians considered *Umoyahlebe* sacred, wise elders. Their ability to speak with those that had gone to *Pharadesi,* the afterlife, made them special. But Aisha knew better. The spirits had driven her father mad.

*And now that's to be my fate, as well.* It had taken years for her father's mind to fray, yet to Aisha, that madness seemed as inevitable as the sun rising in the morning. *Is there no way to escape?*

Perhaps there was. Ria had sent her to Shalandra in the hope of helping her cope with the gift. Somehow, Ria had known what her father—and perhaps all Spirit Whisperers—knew.

"*In the City of the Dead,*" her father had told her years ago, before the spirits had broken his mind, "*you will find the Kish'aa speak clearest. The reverence of the people of the dead draw the spirits, bring them into closer contact with the living. And the city on the mountain is nearer to the ancestors. There, you will hear their whispers. There, you will find your destiny."*

"I know my destiny," she said aloud. Anger simmered in her gut. "It is to be driven mad by the whispers only I can hear."

Though despair echoed in her thoughts, she forced herself to stand. She was Ghandian, daughter of a chieftainess, and now apprentice in the Night Guild. She was no coward to run and hide. She hunted the enemy and faced them with bared teeth and drawn steel.

The anger burned away at her despondency until only cold, hard resolve remained. She straightened, her fists clenched tight, and turned to stare straight at the graveyard beside Rosecliff. Even from this vast distance, she could see the wispy, ethereal figures hovering in the fading daylight. They turned pleading eyes and begging voices toward her.

Yet Aisha did not flee, did not look away. She stood her ground, unyielding and unbroken by dread of the future.

"I do not fear you!" she shouted as loud as she could. "I am not afraid, *Kish'aa!*"

If she was to find her destiny in the city where the dead gathered, so be it. She would face it, come what may.

Jaw set, spine straight, Aisha strode toward her horse, mounted, and rode back toward Rosecliff. Toward the graves with the spirits that cried in her ears.

And she did not block them out. She embraced their cries.

She was *Umoyahlebe*. The spirits spoke to her, and she listened.

## Chapter Five

Issa felt the eyes of everyone on the Cultivator's Tier fixed on her. Or, perhaps, on the four towering, armored soldiers escorting her along Commoner's Row, the broad avenue that ran east and west along the second-lowest tier in Shalandra.

The Indomitables were silent and stern, their faces as hard as their black-burnished half-plate armor and flat-topped, spike-rimmed helmets. Though they made no move to draw their long sickle-shaped *khopesh* swords, people gave way before their glares and deep blue headbands. All *Earaqi, Mahjuri,* and *Kabili* had long ago learned to fear the wrath of the *Alqati* warrior caste.

The soldiers hadn't given her time to wash the blood off her hands, face, and clothing. Immediately upon the completion of the Crucible, she had been escorted out of the Hall of the Beyond, through the streets of the Artisan's Tier, and down Death Row, the broad avenue that ran along the eastern side of Shalandra from the Keeper's Tier at the top to the East Gate on the lowest level, the Slave's Tier.

Anger and hostility showed in many of the eyes watching their progress. Higher-caste *Dhukari* and *Alqati* welcomed the presence of the Indomitables—the black-armored soldiers kept the lower-caste "rabble" away from their clean streets and fancy homes. But down here, in the lower tiers, the people had grown weary of the hard-fisted treatment by the soldiers. Though Issa had done her best to avoid the clandestine gatherings of dissenting youths and the protests that occasionally sparked up around the Cultivator's Tier, she knew of the unrest simmering in the hearts and minds of far too many *Mahjuri, Kabili,* and *Earaqi.*

Issa walked tall, her head held high, eyes fixed forward, but tight knots had formed in her stomach the moment she stepped foot outside of the Hall of the Beyond. Until then, she'd been so focused on winning the battle in the Crucible that she hadn't given thought to what came next. What it meant to be one of the Keeper's Blades.

All in Shalandra knew that the Keeper's Blades served as Shalandra's elite fighters, leading the Indomitables when Shalandra went to war. Yet listening to her Savta and Saba speak of them, or the way Killian's eyes grew shadowed whenever she mentioned becoming a Blade, Issa knew there had to be more to it.

And she was about to find out. The thought of her future both excited her and sent a nervous fluttering through her stomach.

*This could be my last time on the Cultivator's Tier as an Earaqi.*

The members of her caste farmed the fields south of Shalandra, provided muscle as hired laborers for the *Zadii* and *Intaji*, and served in the homes of the *Dhukari* and *Alqati*. Their education in the Institute of the Seven Faces included only the basics of letters and numbers, but they were considered the unskilled labor of Shalandra.

The buildings of the Cultivator's Tier were as neat and orderly as the *Earaqi* that lived there. They were squat structures carved from the golden sandstone of the mountain, though a handful had earned enough over their years of labor to add a second floor using bricks of sun-baked red clay and prairie grasses. The streets that intersected with Commoner's Row were clean and free of debris, and even the back alleys running parallel to the highway bore none of the refuse and filth common on the Slave's Tier, the city's lowest level. *Earaqi* might not have much, but they took pride in the knowledge that they weren't *Kabili* slaves or outcast *Mahjuri*.

In addition to red headbands of woven cloth, *Earaqi* men wore no shirts, only *shendyts* of rough wool and canvas. *Earaqi* women wore *kalasiris*, knee-length sheath dresses of linen held up by twin straps. Simple, rough clothing for simple, rough people. They wore no eyeliner, and their faces bore only one or two black beauty marks—few could afford the high-priced *kohl*, and the charcoal-and-oil paste favored among the less affluent *Earaqi* wore off after a day of hard labor.

Issa caught sight of Serias, one of Killian's Mumblers, race off toward her home, doubtless carrying word to her Savta and Saba.

Issa's gut clenched when she caught sight of the squat stone building that she called home. The door flew open and out strode Nytano, her grandfather. Well into his seventh decade of life, his beard had gone from dusky grey to silvery-white, but he had the same broad, strong shoulders Issa had loved to ride as a young girl. A familiar fire burned in the dark eyes he fixed on her.

"Issa, *nechda,* what is the meaning of this?" Worry deepened the lines around his eyes and mouth.

"You are the grandfather of the one called Issa?" The man who spoke had a ring of *Alqati* blue with a single line of silver etched into the forehead of his helmet—the mark of a Protector, a mid-ranked officer in the Indomitables.

"I do not know what crime you believe my grandchild has committed," Nytano began, "but it must be some mis—"

The Protector cut him off with a sharp gesture. "No crime has been committed. Your granddaughter proved herself in the Crucible this day and she has been chosen by the Long Keeper for the highest honor that can be bestowed upon any Shalandran. She is to become a member of the Keeper's Blades."

Nytano's face went pale, his eyes wide. "Th-The Keeper's Blades?"

The Indomitable officer ignored the question. "Say your final farewells before your training with the Blades begins." His voice held an impatient edge. "Five minutes, no more. The Trial of Stone begins in one hour."

With a nod, Issa hurried inside her house, her mouth suddenly dry. She'd been dreading the inevitable conversation more than the threat of death in the Crucible.

The home was simple, little more than four stone walls and a thatched roof, with a double-sized cot for her grandparents and a small rush mattress in the corner for her. Their one luxury was the wooden table and chairs Nytano had built before Issa was born.

Her grandfather followed a step behind her and closed the door.

"Issa!" His voice was hard, edged with anger and hurt, and it stopped Issa in her tracks. "What have you done, *nechda?*"

Issa heard the concern in his voice. She'd stolen into the Hall of the Beyond knowing how he and Aleema, her grandmother, felt, and now came the inevitable confrontation.

"I did what I had to, Saba." Issa didn't back down from her grandfather's anger. Perhaps the fact that she'd just defeated some of the best-trained fighters in the city bolstered her confidence, or perhaps she knew she'd made the right choice to enter the Crucible despite her grandparents' wishes. "You and Savta have worked so hard all your lives, and the only way I could improve our station was to—"

"You think either your Savta or I care about living the life of an *Alqati* or *Intaji*?" Her grandfather strode toward her, eyes blazing. "All that matters, all that's ever mattered, is keeping you safe, *nechda*. We would be content as *Mahjuri* if it meant you were with us. In the Blades, you are beyond our reach, our ability to protect."

"As a Blade, I won't *need* you to protect me!" Issa's voice rose to match her Saba's anger. She didn't back down but raised her head, defiance burning within her like the glowing furnace in Killian's forge. "I'll be able to protect you and all of Shalandra. I have been chosen by the Long Keeper himself, an immense honor. I'd think you'd be proud of me."

"Proud of you for what?" The voice of Aleema, her Savta, drifted through the back door, followed a moment later by the woman herself. Age hadn't dimmed her beauty, and she still wore her long, silver hair pulled up in an ornate bun that would have belonged in any *Dhukari* home. Somehow, she made even the red linen headband and the woven rush laundry basket balanced on her hip appear elegant.

"I have been called by the Long Keeper to become a member of the Blades." Issa stood tall, proud. "I was one of the few in the Crucible to claim a blade."

Aleema paled, the basket falling from her grip, and her hands went to cover her mouth. "No, *nechda!* How could you?"

Issa felt the anger boiling up within her. "I did it for you! Look at this." She gestured at their sparse home. "You and Saba deserve better than to serve the *Alqati* and *Dhukari* that lord their wealth and caste status over you. It is not your fault that you were unfortunate enough to be born to the wrong caste. I simply refused to accept it, so I found a way to do what you could not. I found a way out of poverty, a way that I can make a difference in Shalandra by serving the Long Keeper and the Elders of the Blades."

"But *nechda,*" Aleema protested, "the life of a Keeper's Blade is dangerous."

"Walking down Commoner's Row is dangerous!" Issa threw up her hands. "Life is full of dangers, but as a Blade, I will be trained to defend myself and others."

"And who trained you to fight in the Crucible?" asked her Saba from where he stood beside the door, arms folded, a scowl on his face. "Tell me it was not that accused blacksmith!" He spoke the last word like a curse.

Issa whirled on him. "At least Killian believed I could be more than just an *Earaqi* servant or farmer."

Nytano slammed his palm on the table. "I told you to stay away from him! He is the one to blame for this nonsense."

"It is not nonsense." Issa's voice rose to a shout. "I have been chosen by the Long Keeper. I claimed a blade, and I am worthy of service to Shalandra. I am sorry you are too fearful and blind to see the truth."

Both her grandparents looked as if she'd slapped them. Issa regretted her words, but right now, she was too angry to apologize.

"I came to bid you farewell before my training, but it seems we have said all that needs saying." Stiff-backed, Issa strode toward the small space she called her room and seized her bag. She'd packed it that morning before sneaking out toward the Hall of the Beyond. When she turned back, she found her Savta and Saba staring at her with pain etched into their expressions.

"I will see you again," she told them in a quiet voice. "I am sorry you are angry with me, but I have to do this. For me and for you."

Silence hung thick in the hovel for a moment, then Aleema came over and embraced her. "Be careful, *nechda,*" she whispered in Issa's ear. "The greatest threats are rarely those you can see. Beware the blades in shadow."

Issa wrapped her arms around her Savta's broad shoulders and pulled her tight. When she broke off the embrace, tears filled Aleema's eyes. Issa hesitated when she turned to her grandfather. Hurt and anger sparkled in Nytano's eyes, but after a moment, he spread his arms to hug her.

"Strike first, strike true," her Saba said. Once, he would have bent to kiss the top of her head. Now, they were of a height, so he pressed a kiss to her cheek. "A strong heart is worth more than the strongest arms."

A lump rose in Issa's throat as she nodded and held her grandfather tight. She blinked away tears and hurried out the door, to where the four Indomitables stood waiting. When she glanced back, she found her Savta and Saba at the door to their small house, fingers interlaced, worry etched into every line on their aged faces.

Issa drew in a deep breath and forced the worry down. She'd known they wouldn't approve—since her twelfth nameday, the day she was old enough to enter the Crucible, they had done everything to dissuade her from attempting the impossible. Yet somehow, Issa had always known she was destined for more than the life of an *Earaqi*. The Crucible had been the most direct path, so she had been determined to take it.

She'd made her choice, but now she had to live with how it affected her grandparents. They had raised her from a young age—Saba had rarely spoken of her parents, saying only they had died shortly after her birth. She would miss them fiercely.

*My duty is to Shalandra now.*

She had been chosen by the Long Keeper. Being one of the Keeper's Blades meant a life of service, a higher calling than scratching out an existence by the sweat of her brow. She would be worth so much more than just one more laborer and farmer.

News of Issa's acceptance into the Blades traveled fast on the Cultivator's Tier. By the time she and her Indomitables escort covered half the distance to Death Row, she found the streets lined with *Earaqi* onlookers. Some glowered and muttered under their breath, but most cheered and waved, even pressed little gifts of food, clothing, and flowers toward her. She had done what most of her caste could only dream of. She had found a way out.

More people lined Death Row as they ascended, but Issa's eyes sought out the one person she'd hoped to see above all. Killian, a strong-featured man with dark eyes, a thick black beard, and the barrel chest and sloped shoulders of his profession, stood among the throng. His gaze locked with hers for a single moment and a small smile played on his lips. He said nothing, but that little smile spoke volumes. In that instant, she read the pride she'd hoped to see in her grandparents' eyes.

The lump returned to Issa's throat and it proved much harder to banish now. Killian, a member of the higher *Intaji* caste, had seen something in her. She wanted to thank him for the years of training—he'd drilled her in the fighting forms of every Academy in Shalandra, along with street fighting techniques and some he claimed were taught to the Keeper's Blades—and for never pressuring her to become one of his Mumblers.

He'd been the one to show her how to sneak into the Hall of the Beyond with the other entrants. Thanks to him, she had the skills necessary to seize her chance of becoming a Blade. She owed him a great deal, and she would find a way to repay him.

*But not today.* Today, she could only think of the ceremony that awaited her. The Trial of Stone would confirm her acceptance into the most elite fighting force in Shalandra.

*Provided I survive it, of course.*

# Chapter Six

As Evren followed the pudgy Brother Mendicatus through the House of Need, he couldn't help glancing down the corridors they passed, hoping to catch a glimpse of Hailen. If he was to leave Voramis, he wanted to say goodbye to the younger boy.

He'd promised the Hunter that he'd look out for Hailen, but he wouldn't be able to do that from Shalandra. Thankfully, Kiara would remain in Voramis to watch over Hailen while the younger boy continued his secret training at the House of Need.

Evren knew everything about Hailen's past: his childhood in Malandria, the night the Hunter had killed the Cambionari and taken the boy from the temple, his travels with the Hunter, and the truth of the strange *Melechha* abilities he'd inherited from his ancestors, the long-dead Serenii. He also knew that the Cambionari wanted to control Hailen's powers—to protect the world, they said, but Evren's experience with priests in the past made him suspect that they wanted it for their own greedy ends.

The Hunter had agreed to let Father Reverentus and the Cambionari educate Hailen, help him learn how to control the powers that they believed would one day manifest. Evren didn't know what that training involved and neither the Hunter nor Kiara had chosen to share the details with him. He'd have asked Hailen, only the Beggar Priests kept the boy locked up in the House of Need most of the time.

Evren felt a stab of sorrow as he reached the front of the Beggar Temple without catching a glimpse of Hailen. He and Hailen might not share the same blood, but he had come to see the boy as a younger brother. The thought of leaving Voramis without saying goodbye tore at him.

Yet Brother Mendicatus seemed in a rush, hurrying toward a door that led into a small walled enclosure within the temple grounds. There, a wooden cart stood waiting before the closed gate, with an aging draft horse hitched to its traces. Beside the cart stood the man that had to be Brother Modestus. He was grizzled, with skin sun-burned to a leathery brown almost a match for Evren's own and dark green eyes that regarded Evren with distrust.

"He the one?" Brother Modestus' voice was a strange mixture of sounds: half-grunt and half the sound of grinding stones. His tone held as much warmth as a Vothmot winter wind.

"This is young master Evren." Brother Mendicatus swept a hand toward Evren. "A comrade of a certain…acquaintance."

*That's the politest way I've heard anyone talk about the Hunter before.* People cursed his name, spoke in fear, or simply avoided mentioning the assassin altogether. Few people beyond Kiara, Graeme, Hailen, and Father Reverentus knew the man behind the legend.

Brother Modestus grunted and shrugged. "Let's go, then."

Evren cocked an eyebrow. "Just like that? If I'm going to do what you want me to, I'm going to need a few things. Tools and such."

"All has been provided," Brother Mendicatus said, and swept a hand toward the cart. "We spoke to Mistress Kiara before summoning you this morning. She has given her permission to send you off on this mission. With your consent, of course."

Evren nodded. Kiara had become a mix of surrogate mother and older sister to him, and if she'd signed off on the task, it was good enough for him. She took the quest of hunting down and eradicating demons as seriously as the Hunter—more so, given that she lacked the Hunter's inhumanly long lifespan. She'd only sanction the task if it furthered their mission.

As he pulled himself up onto the wagon, Brother Modestus passed him a heavy leather backpack. Within the pack, Evren found dark grey clothing, lockpicking tools, an assortment of daggers, soft-soled boots of the highest caliber, and some of Graeme's fabulous glass lanterns filled with their never-quenching alchemical fuel. Everything he'd need for his task of stealing the Blade of Hallar.

With a nod, he buckled the pack closed and dropped it into the back of the wagon beside the piles of stuffed sacks. All of the sacks bore the trademark of *"Tschanz and Co."*, a legitimate Malandrian transporter of corn, wheat, and rice all around the south of Einan. It would provide suitable cover should anyone question their presence in Shalandra.

Which raised questions in Evren's mind. *Why would the Beggar Priests conceal the truth?* Brother Modestus wore a simple trader's cloak, breeches, and trousers, with nothing to proclaim him a Beggar Priest—though Evren guessed the cloth-wrapped bundle between his feet concealed a weapon. *Why not just ride into Shalandra in the guise of a priest rather than a merchant or trader?*

"May the Beggar smile on you and guide you in your efforts," Brother Mendicatus said as he hauled open the gate.

"And you." With a nod, Brother Modestus snapped the reins to set the horses in motion.

Neither priest seemed interested in whether or not Evren invoked any blessings, so he didn't bother. Instead, he sat back against the straight-backed wooden seat and prepared himself for a jolting, bumping ride.

Traders' wagons lacked the coiled spring suspension common among the fancier carriages of the nobility—Evren had seen many such vehicles rumbling through Vothmot, filled with treasure hunters seeking the Lost City of Enarium. As he'd feared, the steel-banded wooden wheels struck every single rut and cobblestone on the way out of Voramis. By the time they reached the Traders' Gate, Evren's teeth felt ready to fall out from clenching them so hard. He'd take a night in the freezing cold Vothmot rain any day over this.

The company didn't prove much better than the transportation. Brother Modestus had the loquacity, humor, and wit of a boulder, and the temperament to match. He met every one of Evren's attempts to engage him in conversation with taciturn silence and that same suspicious gaze.

Even when Evren tried to pry information on whatever the Four-Bladed Storm was, Modestus was sparing with his answers.

"Big storm, kicks up every year," he rumbled. "Winds sweep through the four mountain peaks and turn nasty." That was it. No explanation on which mountain peaks he referred to or what its significance was.

Evren finally gave up after a few futile minutes and sat back against the seat. His gaze swept across the grassy plains, curving wagon trails, and tall trees that bordered the southern road. As boring as he'd expected, made worse by the unending silence.

It would take nine days to reach Shalandra. Nine days of sitting mute beside the stony Brother Modestus.

Evren stifled an inward groan. *This is going to be fun.*

The hours dragged on in mind-numbing silence broken only by the occasional hail of a passing wagon driver. The landscape was beautiful, but Evren could only see so much blue sky and green-and-brown forest before he grew bored. He'd spent his entire life living in large cities like Voramis and Vothmot, where danger could lurk around every corner. Here, instead of fighting for his life with a rival gang, he fought for his sanity in the endless expanse of nothingness.

He nearly wept in relief when, an hour before nightfall, Brother Modestus broke his silence to grunt, "We camp here for the night."

The taciturn Cambionari pulled the wagon into a small copse of young trees a short distance from the road, and Evren leapt off the hard wooden seat before they'd come to a full stop. He didn't care that his backside was numb and his entire body ached from the incessant jolting. All that mattered was that he could stretch his legs and move around.

*Maybe, if I'm lucky, we'll be attacked by bandits or highwaymen. Anything to break the silence!*

Miracle of miracles, Brother Modestus spoke to him again. "Bed rolls are in the back. Get some sleep. We're up before dawn."

With a nod, Evren scrambled into the back of the cart and set about loosening the canvas covering the sacks of grain. To his surprise, when he stepped onto the canvas, his foot struck something too soft to be grain and too yielding to be wooden crates. That something gave a little yelp and squirmed out from beneath him.

"Bloody hell!" Evren leapt backward off the cart, drawing a dagger before he landed. He crouched in a fighting stance, blade held at the ready, eyes fixed on the now-moving canvas. "Come out of there, hands where I can see them!"

"It's me." The canvas muffled the words, but Evren thought he recognized them.

Sure enough, when he threw aside the canvas, he found himself staring into a familiar face: full lips, cheeks that were just losing their childish fat, a rounded chin, upturned nose, and hair that had darkened to a deep chestnut brown in the last two years.

"Hailen, what in the Keeper's name are you doing here?" Evren asked.

Guilt shone in Hailen's strange violet eyes and he blushed. "I—"

A furious rumble sounded behind Evren, and he whipped around in time to see Brother Modestus whip a sword from his cloth-bound bundle. The priest's eyes were fixed on Hailen, but no sign of recognition shone within.

Evren had an instant to act before Modestus laid into Hailen for being a stowaway, thief, or something worse. He leapt between the wagon and the big priest and threw up his hands.

"He's with me!" Even as he said it, he sized up the priest. Brother Modestus stood a hand's breadth taller and wider in the shoulders, and Evren had no doubt the trader's cloak hid a warrior's build. But Evren wouldn't back down from a fight even if he wasn't certain he could win. He'd taken too many hard knocks to be cowed even by someone like the Cambionari.

Brother Modestus narrowed his eyes. "What do you mean, with you?" His sword remained unsheathed, though he made no threatening move toward Hailen. "Father Reverentus said nothing about two of you."

Evren thought quickly. A lie could backfire, but did he dare tell the truth?

"I'm Hailen." The words, spoken in Hailen's bright, cheery voice, decided it for him.

The Cambionari's grizzled face froze. "The *Melechha?*"

"Yes." Evren nodded. "The one who's been studying in the House of Need under Father Reverentus' direct supervision." He made that last bit up, but he could be fairly confident it was true. From what the Hunter had told him, few knew the full truth of Hailen's heritage. Evidently, Brother Modestus of the Cambionari numbered among those few.

Brother Modestus stared at Hailen for a long moment, then finally grunted and sheathed his sword. "The eyes don't lie." He folded his big arms across his chest and fixed Hailen with an angry glare. "I take it the Father doesn't know you're here."

Once again, Hailen blushed. "Not…really," he admitted. His gaze turned to Evren and his voice turned plaintive. "I heard Father Reverentus talking about sending you away and I had to come!"

Evren groaned inwardly. At eleven, Hailen was more child than Evren had been at the same age. The Hunter had had his hands full safeguarding Hailen during their journeys to Enarium, and he'd let the Beggar Priests take the boy largely out of a desire to keep him out of harm's way. Yet here, in the middle of nowhere, a day's travel from Voramis, he had no one but Evren to protect him.

"Damn," growled Brother Modestus. "That's two days wasted."

"What?" Evren narrowed his eyes. "You're thinking of taking him back?"

"Take me back?" Hailen shook his head. "No, no, no. I hate the temple, and the lessons are soooo boring!"

"Bored's better than dead," Brother Modestus grunted. "Father Reverentus would never let us hear the end of it if the *Melechha* got hurt. Not too many of his kind left."

Evren glanced at Hailen, saw the pleading in the boy's violet eyes. "We don't have time to go back." The words poured from his mouth before he realized it. "Two days' delay could turn any chance of success into guaranteed failure."

Brother Modestus' face drew into a dark frown. "We've got to take the boy—"

"We can't." Evren's instinctive dislike of priests surged to the fore; he argued against Brother Modestus out of force of habit. Yet he poured as much authority as he could manage into his voice. "We've only got a few weeks before the Blade of Hallar is brought out for the Anointing of the Blades, and that's already too little time to plan the job properly. If I want any chance of getting my hands on that blade, I'll need all the time I can get. Two days might cost us that chance."

Brother Modestus scowled, but Evren saw the flicker of hesitation in his eyes. He pressed on, driving the point home.

"Hailen is studying under the Cambionari in the House of Need, right?" He took Modestus' momentary hesitation as agreement. "You're Cambionari, too, so you can teach him what he needs to know. And there have to be Beggar Priests in Shalandra you can turn him over to when we arrive." Hailen protested behind him, but Evren overrode the complaints. "The best thing to do is to stick with the plan. I'll keep an eye on Hailen, keep him out of your way. You have my word that he won't slow down our mission."

He didn't care if the priest thought his word was worth anything, but people had a tendency to take such solemn oaths more seriously. Easier to convince them to do what he wanted. The only promise that mattered to him right now was the one he'd made to the Hunter.

Brother Modestus finally grunted, and Evren knew he'd won.

"The moment we arrive in Shalandra," the priest rumbled, "we get him to the House of Need."

Evren nodded. "That's the best place for him." Another lie, but one he could sell convincingly. "I just want him safe."

This last statement was the full truth. He had no desire to bring Hailen to an unfamiliar city filled with danger, but right now, he had no other choice. He already faced a near-impossible task of stealing the Blade of Hallar, and every hour would count. The delay incurred by returning Hailen to Voramis could spell the difference in their attempt.

And, with Hailen by his side, he could keep an eye on the boy, maybe even learn some of the things the Cambionari were teaching him.

Evren spared a moment of pity for the Beggar Priests in Voramis once Kiara found out Hailen wasn't there. He'd heard a few stories of her days as Celicia, Fourth of the Bloody Hand, and her ferocity, ruthlessness, and tenacity rivaled the Hunter's.

Yes, out here, far away from that wrath, would likely be the safest place for him right now.

Brother Modestus grunted and returned to caring for the horses. Hailen leapt down from the cart and threw his arms around Evren's waist. "Thank you!" Relief flooded his voice. "I couldn't take another day of those lessons."

"What kind of lessons?" Evren asked. "What were they teaching you?"

Hailen shook his head. "Father Reverentus said I'm not to tell anyone."

Evren raised an eyebrow. "I can always convince Brother Modestus to take you back to Voramis, you know."

"No, don't do that!" Hailen begged. "I'll tell you. But you have to promise not to tell anyone else!"

"I promise." Evren smiled at the sight of Hailen's solemn expression.

Hailen leaned forward, a secretive smile on his face. "They're trying to teach me Serenii magic!"

## Chapter Seven

For the fifth time since they rode out of Rosecliff that morning, Kodyn cast a worried glance at Aisha. The Ghandian girl looked tired, likely from lack of sleep. He'd tried to wait up until she returned from wherever she'd ridden off to, but he'd nodded off a few hours after midnight. He'd found her saddling the horses outside the inn at dawn but she hadn't spoken more than a few words to him—never explaining where she'd gone. A shadow still hovered on her face, but something almost triumphant had shone in her eyes every time she glanced at the graveyard.

He wanted to ask her what was going on, but being around her made him feel tongue-tied, awkward.

Instead, he focused his attention on Briana.

"This may sound like a silly question," he said, hesitant, "but if your father is a Secret Keeper, how does he, you know, *talk* to you?"

Briana chuckled. "Without a tongue, you mean?"

Kodyn nodded. "Yeah."

Briana wiggled her fingers in a series of strange gestures, a broad grin on her face.

"What was that?" Kodyn asked.

"It's called hand signing," Briana explained. "You can use your fingers to spell letters and form words. Sometimes, a single gesture can be a whole word. Like this." She placed her thumb on her right temple, two forefingers extended, then bent them once.

"What does that mean?"

Briana gestured to her mount. "It's the sign for horse."

"Let me try." Kodyn repeated the gesture, which earned him a grin and nod from Briana.

"Very good!" She clapped her hands. "Try this one."

She showed him another gesture: all four fingers held together and extended, with a movement of her arm that almost looked like someone painting a rainbow on a canvas. "This means sky."

Kodyn copied the gesture, earning a smile. To his relief, the strange hand signing seemed to arrest Aisha's attention and pull her out of whatever gloom she'd been in for the last few hours. When Briana caught her mimicking the movements, she turned in her saddle to correct Aisha's form.

Over the following couple of hours of riding, Briana taught them nearly fifty different gestures—for words ranging from "sword" to "friend" to "man and woman" to "talk" to "happy"—and the individual signs for the letters of the Einari alphabet. When Kodyn forgot the gestures, Briana corrected his clumsy finger movements with a patient smile.

"Damn!" Kodyn shook his head when he confused the signs for "boy" and "kill" for the second time. "And I thought picking locks was hard!"

Aisha chuckled softly. "It all comes with practice."

Kodyn's eyes narrowed. "It looks like you've had a bit more practice than me, somehow. You've gotten every gesture right."

A shadow passed in Aisha's eyes and she drew in a deep breath. ""Back home, in Ghandia, the village elders use similar hand signs to communicate. My mother and father taught me before…"

Kodyn winced as he saw the pain flash across Aisha's face. "Are the signs the same?" he asked quickly, trying to steer the conversation away from the painful memory of her captivity and enslavement by the Bloody Hand.

"Similar." Aisha repeated Briana's gesture for horse. "We have no horses in Ghandia, so this gesture is used to describe *zabara*, wild beasts of the plains much like horses but with strange green-and-brown striped coats."

"I've heard of those." Briana's eyes went wide. "Or, read about them, more accurately, in one of the many books my father filled the house with. Marvelous creatures, said to be almost twice the size of a horse. Twice as fast, too!"

"Yes." Aisha nodded. "Every child in Ghandia knows to steer clear of the zabara herd during the *Uhamaji* season when they migrate. Stampedes have destroyed villages and slain mighty warriors too slow to get out of the way."

Kodyn smiled. *It's good to have her back,* he thought. She'd been moody, brooding since their departure from Praamis, but it lifted his spirits to see her open up and talk about life before her captivity. He'd hesitated to broach the subject before, but he'd always wanted to know about her culture, customs, everything about the exotic people on the plains of Ghandia.

"My mother believed that the zabara housed the spirits of the greatest warriors and *nassor*—the chieftainesses—of our tribe," Aisha continued. "For only such noble souls could inhabit such mighty beasts."

"Fascinating." Briana fixed Aisha with a curious gaze. "I've heard the people of Ghandia and Issai don't worship the Thirteen like we do. Is that true?"

Kodyn didn't miss the slight stiffening in Aisha's spine.

"Not the same way you southerners do," Aisha said finally. "You believe the gods of Einan to be all-powerful, wise beings that see everything from their halls in the heavens, yes?"

Briana nodded. "Every Einari kingdom has their own variations on the belief, according to my father, but they all share the reverence of the Thirteen."

"In Ghandia, we, too, believe in the Thirteen, but we do not call on them directly," Aisha explained. "They are too far away to hear us, but the spirits of our ancestors—the *Kish'aa,* as we call them—intercede with the gods on our behalf. They were once human, so they understand our human needs far better than any god could."

"I'm sure my father will want to talk with you," Briana said, her eyes sparkling. "His life's work revolves around the study of the Serenii artifacts, culture, and writings, but he loves to discuss the theologies and philosophies that have sprung up around the continent."

Aisha inclined her head. "I'm certain we will have the chance to speak on the matter. However, I doubt I'll be of much use in the conversation unless I learn more of the hand signs."

"Did it make talking with your father difficult?" The words slipped from Kodyn's lips before he realized it. He mentally kicked himself for such an insensitive question.

"I learned to read hand signs before I learned to speak." Briana's face showed no sign of offense or insult. "I have never heard my father's voice, but I have never doubted for a single moment that he loves me. His eyes and hands speak clearly enough."

Kodyn could only nod. He had blundered into sensitive topics with both Aisha and Briana; best he hold his tongue for now.

He turned his eyes back to the terrain—more of the same wide-open, scrub-covered hill country broken occasionally by steep, craggy cliffs of stark stone.

"What about you?"

Briana's question caught him off-guard. "W-What about me?" he stammered.

"I met both of your mothers in Praamis," Briana said with a disarming smile. "I have told you of my father, so what of yours?"

Kodyn's brow furrowed. A tense silence hung in the air for a long moment before he finally said, "I never met my father."

"Oh." Briana's face fell, and her expression turned guilty. "I-I'm sorry for—"

"No, it's fine." Kodyn shook his head. "My mother doesn't like to talk about him much."

He hesitated when he felt Aisha's gaze fixed on him, a burning curiosity in her eyes. She, like all in the Night Guild, had to have overheard the myriad rumors about his parentage, yet she'd never broached the subject with him.

After a long moment, he drew in a deep breath. "She told me he was an apprentice in House Scorpion. Ethen, she said his name was. The first friend she made, the one who made it possible for her to survive the brutal training."

His own training hadn't been without its share of challenges, perils, and even a few beatings by the crueler instructors charged with turning clumsy children into capable apprentices. Yet, from the stories he'd heard of the now-deceased Master Velvet, his mother, Master Serpent, and his father had undergone some truly horrible torments when they first joined the Night Guild.

"He sounds like a good man," Briana said in a quiet voice.

Kodyn nodded. "The few times I've heard Mother talk about him, it was always with a sad fondness. She never said it but I think he died trying to protect her, though from what, she doesn't say."

A tense silence hung in the air as his words trailed off. Kodyn found himself retreating into himself as he always did when the topic came up. He tried to avoid it whenever possible. Mention of his father brought a strange emotion—instead of the pain of losing someone close to him, he felt an emptiness, a vacuum where something important should be. As if he'd been born blind, mute, or deaf. Where he *ought* to feel strongly for a father, he had …nothing.

When he'd tried to ask Master Serpent, her mother's oldest friend, the assassin had refused to give him answers. "Not my place to tell," Errik had said. "Your mother wants you to know, she'll tell you."

Yet, in many ways, Kodyn had enjoyed a far better childhood than most of his fellow Night Guild apprentices. His mother and Ria had done their best for him, and he'd never lacked for love and affection. Many of his mother's friends—including Errik, the hulking Pathfinder Jarl, and even Darreth in his own awkward way—had served as paternal figures.

Aisha rode her horse closer for a moment; just enough to reach out and casually brush a hand across his arm. Her eyes locked with his and he saw quiet reassurance written there. Once again, he found himself at a loss for words, but he felt a surge of gratitude. No matter what happened, no matter what sorrows lay behind or challenges lay ahead, he could count on Aisha's strength. Not only her martial skills—she was almost a match for Ria with the *assegai* spear, and most of the younger Journeymen and apprentice assassins of House Serpent avoided sparring with the young Ghandian woman—but her resoluteness and fortitude of spirit.

They rode in silence for a few minutes. Briana seemed embarrassed that she'd brought up the topic, and Aisha seemed content to keep her thoughts to herself. Kodyn couldn't think of anything to revive the conversation, so he focused on the road. A few hundred paces ahead, the cliffs closed on in the road and huge boulders littered the land bordering the highway.

As they drew closer to the boulders, a sound reached Kodyn's ears. He tensed, every sense on alert. It had been a tiny sound, so faint he almost thought he was imagining it. Yet, when he glanced over at Aisha, it seemed she'd heard it, too. Her eyes remained fixed on the road in front of her, but her hand moved slowly toward the wooden shaft of her *assegai*. Kodyn reached his arms up in a wide stretch and when he lowered them again, dropped his right hand onto the saddle horn, a hand's breadth from the hilt of his long sword.

He pricked up his ears. Years traversing the Praamian sewer tunnels and racing across the Hawk's Highway—a network of ropes, bridges, and planks that spanned the city rooftops—had sharpened his hearing. *There!*

The sound came again, quiet but familiar, one he'd heard a thousand times crawling through the Praamian sewer tunnels with the Hounds and Foxes: the scuff of boots on stone.

His gut tightened as he prepared for—

"Hands high!" A loud voice split the silence of the morning. "Keep 'em away from those weapons, unless you want us to turn you into a prickly pig right now!"

Kodyn's heart sank as he caught sight of the speaker. The man stood between two huge boulders, wearing a cloak the same dull red as the rocks beside him. In his hand, he carried a loaded crossbow, its tip pointed right at Kodyn's chest.

# Chapter Eight

Nervous knots formed in Issa's stomach as she marched up the broad stone steps toward the highest room in the Hall of the Beyond. The temple to the Long Keeper dominated the center of Shalandra's uppermost tier. It was a huge building, nearly a mile long and four hundred paces wide, with seven spire-tipped towers that reached golden fingers into the darkening sky—one for each of the Long Keeper's seven faces.

Enormous columns twice the width of Issa's outstretched arms supported domed ceilings of golden sandstone, but few outside of the Necroseti ever saw what was beyond those columns. The populace was only permitted to enter the western side of the Hall of the Beyond, which was occupied by the enormous arena where the Crucible had been held that day. The center and eastern sections of the temple housed the Necroseti's inner chambers and places of worship.

However, for the ceremony tonight, Issa and the other victors of the Crucible had been summoned to the most sacred chamber in the Hall of the Beyond: the rooftop sanctuary where stood the monument to the Long Keeper, god of death.

The sanctuary rose above all of Shalandra, its height rivaled only by the Palace of Golden Eternity above it. Like the palace, the Hall of the Beyond was said to have been carved from the very stone of Alshuruq, the mountain known as Dawnbreaker, by Hallar himself. Issa risked a look back over her shoulder. The view from the staircase stole her breath. She could see all the way from the Keeper's Tier, down across the four lower tiers with their broad avenues and narrower streets, to the vast expanse of farmlands that spread outward from the base of the mountain city.

But the sight of the frowning Necroseti behind her turned her attention back to their procession. The Keeper's Priests wouldn't allow anyone to delay their ceremony, which *had* to take place just after sunset.

Issa studied the four figures beside her. The *Mahjuri* girl was speechless and wide-eyed, daunted by the grandeur of her surroundings. The arrogant *Dhukari* youth basked in his triumph, head held high, a swagger in his steps. The other winners, twin boys wearing the brown headband of the *Intaji*, seemed too young, too small in the company of the older victors. Their eyes darted around, as if afraid of every shadow.

Fire coursed through her calves as she climbed, but she forced herself onward. If the Necroseti priests could ascend the stairs, she could too.

The sun had just touched the western horizon by the time they reached the sanctuary room at the top of the stairs. An enormous statue carved from golden sandstone guarded the sanctuary's entrance. The seven stern faces of the Long Keeper stared down at her—one each for mercy, justice, vengeance, sorrow, joy, eternity, and change. The stone eyes seemed to follow her as she passed it and strode into the templetop chamber. Her insides trembled beneath that solemn gaze and she swallowed a surge of anxiety.

*I'm meant to be here,* she told herself, steeling her courage. *I won. I was chosen by the Long Keeper.*

A thick wall of incense struck her like a blow to the face as she stepped into the sanctuary. Clouds of too-sweet smoke rose from braziers burning at the four corners of the chamber. Hooded figures filled the room, standing silent vigil. A shudder ran down Issa's spine at the sight of their masks: smooth, featureless white ceramic that made them appear almost corpse-like. The light of dozens of oil lanterns splashed strange, flickering shadows dancing across the midnight black robes the Necroseti reserved for solemn ceremonies.

Within the sanctuary stood another seven-faced statue, the eyes of the Long Keeper fixed on the gold sandstone altar dominating the center of the room. Upon the altar, a horseshoe-shaped cradle of steel glimmered in the lamplight.

Issa's heart hammered a nervous beat. She'd rarely seen so many priests of the Long Keeper this close, and never the Keeper's Council. Yet all six of them, including High Divinity Tinush, stood waiting for them behind the altar. Only they—and the seventh man, who wore the dull brown of a Secret Keeper rather than the black of the Long Keeper—wore no masks. Their solemn miens threatened to unnerve her.

Issa and the others halted three paces away from the altar as they'd been instructed. Upon returning from her visit to her home on the Cultivator's Tier, a pair of Necroseti priests had prepared her for the role she was to play in this ceremony. Now, facing the Keeper's Priests directly, their words flew from Issa's mind.

*Boom, boom, boom!* Issa startled and nearly jumped as the sound of a metal-capped staff striking the stone floor seemed to echo through the chamber. A moment later, a door behind the Keeper's Priests opened and two figures strode through.

Issa sucked in a breath. *The Pharus himself!*

Pharus Amhoset Nephelcheres wore a gold and black *nemes* headdress with an ornamental stole and *shendyt* to match. A ceremonial mask of pristine ivory obscured his features. On his heels came Lady Callista Vinaus. The Lady of Blades wore her full armor of black segmented plate mail with spikes at the shoulders, elbows, and knees. Yet beneath her helmet, she wore a mask depicting one of the scowling faces that adorned the Keeper's Statue—the war mask worn into battle by all Indomitables and Keeper's Blades.

Issa swallowed. *The most powerful people in Shalandra, here to witness this.* A mixture of elation and trepidation thrummed through the core of her being. The eyes of Lady Callista, the Pharus, and the Keeper's Council seemed to judge her every move. She had won in the Crucible, but would she fail whatever lay ahead? This was everything she'd hoped for, yet now that she was here, it took all her willpower to still her expression to hide her unease.

The six High Divinities bowed to the Pharus, who nodded once before moving to join the figures assembled to the right of the altar. The Lady of Blades received no obeisance from the priests, but strode without a word toward the armored, war-masked figures to the left of the altar. The Elders of the Blades, the highest ranking military officers in Shalandra. The ones that Issa would serve once—*if*—she proved worthy.

"We stand here, beneath the all-seeing gaze of the Long Keeper, to bear witness to the second trial of the Blades." High Divinity Tinush's voice rang out in the chamber with a strength that belied his age. He fixed his gaze on Issa and the others in turn. "The first, the trial of steel, proved that you five were worthy beyond the measure of your foes. The blades, forged from the very stone beneath your feet, chose you."

His expression grew stern. "But only those who bear the mark of the Long Keeper may join the Keeper's Blades and serve the Pharus, his representative on Einan. Step forward, worthy ones, and face the trial of stone. May the Long Keeper have mercy on all of you."

Jaw clenched tight, Issa stepped forward first as she'd been instructed and moved toward the sandstone altar. She caught a flash of movement from the corner of her eye. The scowling black steel war mask concealed Lady Callista's features, but the Lady of Blades had leaned forward.

As Issa approached, the seventh man—Arch-Guardian Suroth of the Secret Keepers, she recognized—stepped up to the altar. From within his robes, he drew out a strange-looking object: a metal rod the length of Issa's forearm, tipped with a red gemstone that seemed to glow in the torchlight.

Issa's blood ran cold. *Bloodstone*. The stone numbered among the most toxic substances on Einan. Said to be twenty times more potent than Voramian cinnabar, it could kill a grown man with a touch.

She resisted the urge to flinch, to flee. Her eyes searched the gaze of the Arch-Guardian and, behind the solemnity, found reassurance written there. He never smiled, but there was a hint of kindness written in his strong face. With a barely perceptible nod, he placed the metal rod into the groove cut into the metal horseshoe-shaped cradle.

Drawing in a deep breath, Issa stepped up onto the stair before the altar and, with only a heartbeat's hesitation, bent to place her face into the cradle, as the Necroseti had instructed her. The glowing crimson stone loomed large in her view and she gritted her teeth as she touched her forehead to the stone.

The stone was hot, hotter than her flesh, and the contact made her skin crawl. Heat surged into her face, her cheeks, and her forehead. She could feel the sizzling, crackling of her skin as the glowing stone burned its mark into her. When she pulled away a moment later, she had to clench her jaw hard to keep from crying out at the pain.

The world spun around her in a dizzying chaos of glowing gemstones, flickering torches, and black-robed figures. A strong hand seized her arm to steady her, but Issa reeled from the terrible effects of the bloodstone's toxins. It felt as if a fist of iron hammered against her skull, trying to rip her head from her shoulders and claw its way into her brain.

Something hard struck her knees. She forced herself to focus, to return to consciousness, and found she'd fallen to a kneeling position, one hand clutching the altar. The stone was cool beneath her fingers, an island of peace amid the surging, rushing heat flooding her body. Drawing in a deep breath, she concentrated on that single constant. Even as the room whirled in wild circles around her, she clung to the solid, unmovable object beneath her fingers.

Slowly, one agonizing, sluggish heartbeat at a time, the room swam into focus. Tears blurred her vision and her stomach protested, threatening to empty its contents. But Issa swallowed the acid burning in her throat and, with effort, took one deep breath, then another.

The pain faded, the dizziness receded, and Issa managed to stand. Arch-Guardian Suroth kept a steadying grip on her arm until she could stand on her own. At her nod, he released her and stepped back.

"She still lives," High Divinity Tinush's words echoed through the chamber.

Issa spoke the ceremonial words she'd been taught. "I have been touched by the Long Keeper." Her voice sounded small, weak, faint through the pounding of her pulse, but she straightened her spine and lifted her head. "Am I worthy to serve?"

Tinush stepped forward and squinted at her forehead. After a moment, a smile split his aged face. "The Long Keeper has judged her worthy to stand in his halls, to bear the mark of his favor."

"All praise to the god of death!" the Necroseti in the room echoed in a single voice.

Tinush reached into his robes and drew out a small glass vial that contained a pale red liquid. "This mark proclaims you to be chosen of the Long Keeper." He opened the vial and dabbed a few drops onto Issa's forehead. "Let all who see it know that you are beloved of our god, servant of death."

Issa clenched her fists against the sudden pain in her forehead. The liquid increased the intensity of the throbbing, sizzling sensations, and it took all her willpower to remain upright as the room spun crazily once more. The rest of the priest's words faded into the dizziness. She moved like a corpse, every muscle tense, as she stepped away from the altar toward the waiting Elders of the Blades.

"Welcome, servant of death." The Elder spoke in a sonorous voice, and in his strong hands he held out the flame-bladed sword Issa had claimed in the Crucible earlier that day. "With this sword, you swear fealty to the Long Keeper and the Pharus, his servant on Einan. Do you so swear?"

"I swear!" Issa replied without hesitation.

"With this sword," the Elder continued, "you swear to sever all ties to your past life, to who you once were, and leave behind your old life to become *Dhukari,* an honor bestowed only upon those who are worthy. Do you so swear?"

Issa hesitated. *A cruel thing to ask.* She'd snuck into the arena to give her grandparents a better life, and now she was being commanded to sever all ties with them? *Yet, if it improves Savta and Saba's station, it is worth it.*

"I swear!" The words brought a lump to her throat. She hated the way she'd left her grandparents' house earlier that day. *Will those harsh, angry words be the last they ever hear me speak?* No, she determined. She would find a way to speak to them again. She would make things right.

"With this sword, you swear to heed the commands of your officers, to serve the Lady of Blades and the Elders without hesitation. Do you so swear?"

"I swear!" Issa's voice grew stronger, more confident.

"With this sword," the Elder spoke the final words of the oath, "you swear to serve the city of Shalandra and its people to the best of your ability, until the Long Keeper chooses to gather you into his arms. Do you so swear?"

"I swear!" The dizziness had faded, replaced by elation as Issa repeated the oaths of the Blades—the oaths she'd dreamed of taking for five long years.

"In the sight of the Long Keeper and his witnesses on Einan, so let it be." With those solemn words, the Elder drew the huge blade from its sheath and handed it to Issa hilt-first. "Welcome to the Keeper's Blades, Issa of the *Dhukari.*"

Elation washed over her like a hot bath, drowning out everything around her as she returned to her place in line with the other accepted Blades. She could see only the golden altar in the center of the room, feel the throbbing pain in her forehead. Her mind barely registered when the Keeper's Priest called out the next name.

*I did it!* She found it hard to breathe for the excitement. All her hard work and patience of the last five years had paid off. Her grandparents would be elevated to the Dhukari caste, their lives improved. Yet it was more than just the promise of a better life. Through her toil, blood, and sweat, she had won the right to serve the Long Keeper and her city.

A piercing cry shattered her thoughts. Her eyes refocused, snapped toward the sandstone altar in time to see one of the two *Intaji* twins crumbling to the stone floor. He writhed and jerked, his body gripped in a paroxysm of agony. His shrieking cries echoed off the walls around him.

Issa's heart stopped, her breath trapped in her lungs. She could only watch, frozen in horror, as the youth convulsed at the foot of the sandstone altar. No one moved to help him—not the Secret Keeper with the kind eyes, the masked Keeper's Priests, or the Elders of the Blade. Silent and stern, they waited until his fate was determined by the trial of stone.

Slowly, one heart-rending breath at a time, the *Intaji*'s spasm quieted to a few weak jerks, a twitch, and finally one quiet shudder. Pale-faced, eyes wide, he lay staring up at the roof, silent and deathly still.

* * *

Issa wanted to be sick. She didn't know the fate of the twins. Both *Intaji* boys had collapsed after their trial of stone, and the Necroseti had carried them away on stretchers. The grave expression on Arch-Guardian Suroth's face told her that the boys' future still hung in the balance. Not all survived the touch of the bloodstone. Some were claimed by the Long Keeper before they could be accepted into the Blades.

Yet that horror only dimmed the triumph within her, but couldn't extinguish it altogether. She felt as if she walked in a dream, yet she repeated in her mind that it was true. She had passed the trial of steel and the trial of stone. She had taken the oaths of the Blades and received her sword, the flammards with their strangely undulating blades. Now, she followed the Elders of the Blades down the broad stone stairs and onto the Path of Gold, the broad avenue that spanned the uppermost tier of Shalandra. From there, they would take her to the Citadel of Stone, home of the Keeper's Blades.

Beside her, the slim *Mahjuri* girl seemed incapable of taking her eyes off the huge sword in her hand. Even the *Dhukari* youth had lost his arrogance in the wonder of his acceptance.

The Citadel of Stone appeared exactly as its name suggested: a vast stronghold carved from the golden sandstone of the mountain. Towers, turrets, and a parapet ringed the upper heights, but Issa's eyes were fixed on the enormous bloodwood gate before them.

The Elders of the Blades stopped at the entrance and pounded on the gate. The rattling of chains and the *thunking* of huge bolts being drawn echoed through the heavy wood. Slowly, the gate rose and Issa caught sight of the Citadel's interior.

Fifty Blades in full armor, helmets, and scowling war masks lined the Citadel's courtyard. They stood in perfect silence, ranks as neat as a bookkeeper's sums, flame-bladed swords raised in salute.

A huge man with the gold-and-black stripe of a high-ranking officer stepped from the front of the ranks. "Who goes?" came his challenge.

"The chosen of the Long Keeper," Issa and her two companions echoed in unison.

"Do you bear the mark of his touch?"

"We do." Issa's voice rang out loudest.

"Then enter the Citadel of Stone, beloved of death." The Blade gave a salute—right fist to left shoulder—then marched back into his place at the head of the men lining the courtyard.

It took Issa every shred of willpower not to let a smile broaden her face as she took her first steps into the Citadel of Stone and the new life of a Keeper's Blade awaiting within.

## Chapter Nine

Adrenaline thrummed within Aisha's muscles as she heard the bandit's call. From her position, she could make out the rounded outlines of at least five more bandits, each wearing the same rust-red cloak as their leader—a weather-beaten fellow with a hungry expression and greed written in every line of his pock-marked face. Only two carried crossbows, but she had little doubt the rest carried weapons of their own.

With Kodyn by her side, she could take five armed men any day. The crossbows complicated things. Worse, they had Briana to protect, and Briana was clearly no fighter. The Shalandran girl let out a yelp of surprise, setting her horse skittering and dancing beneath her.

Kodyn, however, remained calm, exuding confidence, his right hand hovering close to his sword.

"Hello, friends!" he called out in a jaunty tone that bordered on mocking. "A beautiful day to enjoy the shade of those fine boulders, isn't it? I almost find myself tempted to get out of the heat and join you. Alas, we've got a lot of ground to cover, so we'll have to decline your kind invitation."

Aisha stifled a groan. *Watch him go and get us all killed!* Kodyn had definitely inherited his mother's wit and sharp tongue.

She scanned the rocks and found two more red-cloaked men she hadn't spotted before. That made seven—still decent odds, but not with those crossbows pointed at Kodyn.

Back in Praamis, Kodyn had convinced his mother, the Master of the Night Guild, that the Gatherers might attack Briana—intending to either kidnap or kill her, anything to gain leverage over her father. Unless these men wore the world's cleverest disguise, they looked too rough to be hired assassins. Everything about them—from their ragged clothing, patchwork leather armor, and rust-dulled weapons to their lean, hungry faces—screamed bandits.

"Quite the jaw on you, pup," snarled the man that had spoken. "Get you into trouble, so 'twill."

Aisha's gut tightened as the bandit's finger twitched toward the trigger of his crossbow. Not even Master Serpent could dodge a crossbow bolt fired from that range.

"Easy, now." Kodyn's voice turned placating. "I'd hate for any of us to go and end up dead, myself and my companions most of all. What say we chalk this all up to a misunderstanding, have a good laugh at ourselves, and go our separate ways?"

"Shut yer mouth," the bandit growled. His face turned an angry shade of red. "We're the ones'll be doing the talking here. Empty yer saddlebags and give us the gold."

"Gold?" Kodyn cocked his head. "I think you might have us confused with another, richer group of travelers. I saw them when we were riding out of Rosecliff. They ought to be along shortly, just in time for you to relieve them of their valuables."

Aisha couldn't believe Kodyn. She'd always known he was cocky, but this bordered on glib insanity. She wanted to reach out and grab his arm, smack him up the back of his head—anything to get him to shut up before he got himself skewered by a crossbow bolt—but didn't want to risk setting off the trigger-happy bandits.

Another man sidled up behind the speaker. "Boss," the second man muttered in a voice far too loud to be a proper whisper, "I don't think they're the ones."

"What do you mean?" hissed the bandit leader, again loud enough for Aisha to hear clearly. "We got the word that they'd be coming this way today. A small company of three, without a Blade to guard them." He gestured at Aisha and Kodyn with a wave of his hand. "Do any of these three look like a Blade to you?"

"No, but—"

"Shite!" The loud curse came from Aisha's right. Out from the rocks popped another man she hadn't spotted. Fear covered his dust-stained face. "Boss, incoming!"

The sound of drumming hooves echoed from behind them. Aisha turned in her saddle to see a mounted rider charging toward them. The wind streamed through his cloak, pulling it back to reveal heavy black plate mail armor and helmet to match. His horse was huge, the largest warhorse Aisha had ever seen. The rider swung an enormous two-handed sword with a strange flame-shaped blade above his head.

"Keeper's Blade!" cried the man that had spotted the rider.

The bandit leader cursed. "Our man insisted there wouldn't be an escort."

"We need to run, now!" said the second man. The others had already begun to scramble away, down the rocks and out of sight.

It took the bandit leader a long moment to make up his mind, but finally he turned and fled after his companions. Within seconds, the bandits disappeared among the boulders and rocks.

Aisha quickly turned her horse to face the charging newcomer. He might have scared the bandits off, but that didn't mean he was friendly. He could be a worse threat than the ragged highwaymen. He was alone against the two of them, but one look at his armor, warhorse, and huge sword told Aisha they'd be in for a vicious fight if the warrior turned out to be an enemy.

The warrior reined in a few paces away from them, his eyes fixed on the rocks to the east. "Any of you hurt?" He spoke in a voice at once gruff and polite, as deep as a rumbling zabara bull.

"No," Kodyn replied. "We had it handled, thank you very much."

The bronze-skinned warrior ignored the response until he seemed content that the danger had passed, then he sheathed his huge flame-bladed sword in the scabbard that hung from his saddle and turned a stern gaze on Kodyn. "Don't they teach you any manners in Praamis, young man?"

Kodyn bristled, but the comparison was apt. The man—the bandits had called him a Keeper's Blade—had to be closing in on forty, with broad shoulders, strong hands, and the confident posture that only came with years of training and experience. His eyes were as dark as Briana's, set beside a strong nose, and he wore his beard pulled into a tight braid at his chin, oiled to keep it tight, with shaven cheeks and moustache. His accent also matched Briana's—a mellifluous rhythm that emphasized harder syllables while softening the vowels.

"Yes, they do," Aisha said. She used her hips to push her horse into motion and walked it forward until she was between Kodyn and the armored warrior. "You have our thanks, sir…?"

"Ormroth, *Ypertatos* of the Keeper's Blades of Shalandra." The warrior bowed in his saddle. "I am surprised to find you traveling in such a small company. I'd thought even Praamians and…" He looked her over curiously, as if trying to decide where she was from. "…and others knew that this area is notorious for bandits and highwaymen."

"We are unfamiliar with these roads." Aisha shook her head. "But, as you can see, we are capable of taking care of ourselves." She gestured to Kodyn's sword and her weapons.

"Perhaps you are." Ormroth pursed his lips, which tugged the corners of his mouth up and pulled his oiled beard tight. "All the same, more dangers may lie down the road you travel. I suggest you turn back and return to Praamis unless you have business in the south."

To Aisha's surprise, Briana spoke up. "They do." The Shalandran girl kicked her horse forward and moved toward the warrior. "You say you are an *Ypertatos* in the Keeper's Blades? Show me your mark, *Dhukari*."

Ormroth fixed Briana with a stern glare. "Who are you, *taltha*? Where is your headband?"

"Taken from me by the same men who held me prisoner." Briana sat straighter in her saddle. "You bear the armor and carry the sword of a Blade, and I see the gold on your helm. But I demand you show me the Keeper's mark."

Aisha exchanged a glance with Kodyn. Beneath his outward bravado, she saw confusion that mirrored hers. Neither of them understood Briana's words, yet something about the girl's manner indicated that this warrior was more friend than foe.

But life in the Night Guild had taught Aisha to be prepared. She flashed Kodyn the silent hand signal for "*sword*" and "*fight*"—both gestures Briana had taught them. Kodyn gave her an almost imperceptible nod, his hand creeping toward the hilt of his sword. Aisha made no outward move, but inside, her muscles tensed, ready to fight if need be.

After a long moment, the warrior reached up and removed his helm—shaped like the head and snarling fangs of a lioness. On his forehead, he bore a circular scar as thick across as the tip of Aisha's finger.

Relief filled Briana's expression. "Thank the Long Keeper! I am Briana, daughter of Arch-Guardian Suroth."

Ormroth's eyes widened a fraction. "My lady!" He bowed in his saddle again, deeper this time. "I had no idea you were away from Shalandra."

Aisha allowed the tension to drain from her shoulders and her muscles relaxed. There was no mistaking the deference in the man's tone—he would be no threat, at least not to Briana.

"As I said, I was taken from my father's house. I'm certain he will look favorably upon the man that returns me safely to his arms." Briana's voice grew solemn, almost ceremonial. "As a member of the *Dhukari,* I insist that you accompany us back to Shalandra and offer the protection of your sword and skill."

"It would be my honor, my lady." Ormroth hesitated. "However, I must inform you that I am already on a mission for my Lady of Blades. That must be my first priority. I trust that your companions will aid me in protecting you and, by the grace of the Long Keeper, together we will reach Shalandra without further mishap."

The exchange, too, puzzled Aisha. She'd known that Briana was the daughter of Suroth, the highest-ranked Secret Keeper in Shalandra. But Ormroth's deferential treatment and the way Briana commanded his service made it sound like she was royalty.

"If you will wait for me here," Ormroth said, turning his horse around, "I will return shortly."

"Of course." Briana nodded.

With a click of his tongue, Ormroth set his horse into a gallop. Up the road, at least a quarter-league to the north, Aisha caught sight of two figures on horseback.

The three of them watched in silence. The moment Ormroth had ridden out of earshot, Kodyn rounded on Briana. "What in the bloody hell just happened?"

"What do you mean?" Briana's brow furrowed in confusion.

"He just did what you told him!" Kodyn shook his head. "Believed that you were who you said you were without question. If it was me, no way I'd have taken you at your word just like that."

"Life in Shalandra is not the same as you are used to," Briana explained. "Our city is divided into seven castes. The *Mahjuri* are the outcasts, the *Kabili* the slaves, and the *Earaqi* the servants, farmers, and unskilled laborers. Then there are the *Intaji,* the artisans, smiths, cobblers, and any others who build or craft with their hands. The *Zadii* are the intellectuals, the healers, philosophers, architects, engineers, and teachers, along with the priests of the twelve gods, all but the Long Keeper. His priests are among the *Dhukari,* the highest-ranking caste in Shalandra."

"You called him *Dhukari,* right?" Aisha said.

"Yes." Briana smiled at her. "The Keeper's Blades are specially chosen by the Long Keeper, and that honor elevates them from whatever caste they were born into. They are higher than the Indomitables and the rest of Shalandra. Only the Necroseti, the Long Keeper's priesthood, and the high councils—the Elders of the Blade and the Keeper's Council—outrank them."

"You said seven castes." Kodyn frowned. "I counted six."

Briana nodded. "The *Alqati* are warrior and military caste. The Indomitables, Shalandra's army, and their families. They are second only to the *Dhukari* in standing."

"But why did he just accept that you were who you said you are?" Kodyn insisted.

"In Shalandra, the caste society is rigid," Briana explained. "When one is born into a caste—be it slave, outcast, artisan, or warrior—it is nearly impossible to rise above their station. No Shalandran would claim to be of a higher caste; it is an unfathomable, unforgivable deceit."

Aisha found this concept unnecessarily complex. In Ghandia, every villager had their own purpose, but there were no ranks like the Praamian nobility or the Shalandran castes. The village elders were chosen according to their age and standing among the tribes, but blood and wealth never came into play in Ghandian society.

"So you're telling me that he accepted that you were of this *Dhukari* caste just because you said you are?" Kodyn sounded incredulous.

"Yes." Briana said it as if were the simplest thing in the world.

Aisha spoke up. "Before he recognized you, he called you *taltha*."

Briana gave her a little smile. "It is the Shalandran word for 'little sister'. Sort of like how a Praamian elder calls a youth 'lad', only more polite and reserved for young women."

The sound of drumming hooves grew louder and the three of them turned to find Ormroth and the two other figures riding toward them. The two wore simple, dust-covered travel garb and rode horses that were sturdy but lacked the raw power of the Blade's warhorse. A single spot of color stood out from their dull outfits: headbands made of gold-colored thread.

"They are *Dhukari* as well," Briana whispered to the two of them. "That, and the fact that they travel in disguise in the company of a Blade means they are returning from the sale of Shalandran steel."

Aisha sucked in a breath. Shalandran-forged steel, made using the special shalanite ore found exclusively in the mountains around Shalandra, was considered the best-quality steel on the world of Einan. The city only permitted a fraction of the steel to be traded, always at an exorbitant rate. If these men had just returned from selling a shipment, they would be loaded down with a fortune in gold.

Suddenly, the bandits' words made sense. *Somehow they knew these Shalandrans were coming, so the ambush was for them.* She, Kodyn, and Briana had simply been unlucky enough to arrive first.

Ormroth and his companions reined in before Briana. The Blade introduced the two as Arhin and Feasah. Immediately upon learning Briana's name and parentage, Arhin dug into his pack and produced a golden headband.

"It would be my honor to present this to the daughter of Arch-Guardian Suroth," he said, and bowed low in his saddle. The strip of woven-gold cloth bore a trio of bright blue gemstones—clearly of great value, yet he offered it without hesitation.

"Thank you." Briana gave a little bow of her own and accepted the headband. She let out a little sigh as she wrapped it around her forehead, as if someone had just restored her sight or replaced a lost limb.

"Come, my lady," Ormroth said. "We must hurry. I doubt the bandits will return, but I would not risk your safety and that of my companions."

"Of course." Briana turned her horse back toward the south. Aisha kicked her horse into motion beside the Shalandran girl, and Kodyn moved to ride on her far side.

Ormroth took the lead on his huge warhorse, and the two *Dhukari* nobles rode behind him, with Kodyn, Aisha, and Briana bringing up the rear. Aisha's hand never strayed far from the shaft of her short-handled *assegai* spear and she found Kodyn remained vigilant, ready to draw his sword at a moment's notice.

Jagged cliffs pressed in around the road, rising high to the east and west and blocking out the sunlight. A chill fell around them as they rode through the bluffs. A nervous tension thrummed within Aisha—if more bandits were to attack, this would be the place.

At the head of their little column, Ormroth drew his massive two-handed blade.

Aisha's heart stopped. The steel, black as midnight, seemed alive with blue-white energy, as if lightning sizzled along the length of the blade. To her horror, dozens of transparent, ethereal shapes clung to the sword's curving edge. Men and women, spirits of the dead, all bound to that strange sword. Pleading eyes turned toward her, and ghostly mouths opened to voice a whispered plea.

Last night, on the bluff overlooking Rosecliff, Aisha had decided to face the spirits. Now, seeing them so close, she nearly recanted her decision. She could feel them pressing at her mind, could almost taste the energy crackling from the dead.

Long ago, during one of his more lucid moments, her father had tried to explain it to her. "Within us all is a spark of life. It burns brightest at our birth and slowly fades as we age, until it is exhausted out at the end of our lives. But for those lives snuffed out too early, the spark does not fade, does not die. It remains all around us in the form of the *Kish'aa,* the spirits that only a Spirit Whisperer can see and touch. Some few, those with the favor of the *Kish'aa,* can even learn to control those sparks."

Her father had tried to control the sparks, to channel the energy of the *Kish'aa,* and it had cost him his sanity. She'd lost her father to the spirits, and now they had come for her.

Somehow, impossibly, these strange swords managed to collect the energy of the dead. The energy sizzling along its length would, in the right hands, make it a truly powerful weapon.

And only Aisha could hear the wailing of the spirits tethered to the blade.

# *Chapter Ten*

Issa leapt out of her simple cot the moment the door to her room—little more than a stone cell with a bed and chair, really—opened.

The newcomer was a well-built man a year or two her senior, with a broad, handsome face, dark eyes, and hair that hung in a braided tail down to the small of his back. Though heavier than her, they were a match in height and the width of their shoulders.

He smiled at the sight of her fully-dressed, flammard gripped in her hand. "Not even dawn yet, but you're already eager to begin your training, I see."

"Very." Issa nodded and returned his smile.

"My name is Hykos." The man extended a strong, calloused hand. "I'm to be your instructor for the duration of your training in the Citadel. In public, you may address me as *Archateros*."

"Issa." Issa shook his hand. His grip was firm, confident, with force that Issa thought could crush stone.

"I expected you'd need a few moments to dress," Hykos said, grinning. "But if you're prepared, we can depart for the training yard at once."

Issa fell into step behind Hykos and followed him out of the small room she'd been assigned the previous night. The man wore the full plate mail of the Blades, yet he moved with an easy, relaxed step. His armor made virtually no sound, a far cry from the clanking metal plates of the Indomitables' breastplates, backplates, and shoulder guards.

"To everyone else in the Citadel of Stone," Hykos said, "your name is not important. Until you are confirmed into the Blades at the Anointing in a month's time, you will simply be referred to as *Prototopoi.*" He shot her a little smile. "It means 'novice', but the way some of those here say it, it sounds more like 'idiot' or 'incompetent'."

Issa nodded. "I'll try not to take it personally."

"Those accepted into the Blades are *Defteteros* for the first six months after confirmation. The training and duties remain the same, though there is far less mockery from the higher-ranked *Katoteros*. It takes four years of training to reach the rank of *Archateros*, ten to become an *Ypertatos* and twenty to reach *Invictus*. All of the Elders of the Blades are *Invictus*, and only Lady Callista herself is *Proxenos*."

"If you're *Archateros*," Issa asked, "that means you've been here four years?"

"Five," Hykos corrected. "I was fourteen when I was chosen by the Long Keeper."

Issa glanced up at his forehead. He wore no helmet, but instead a golden headband with a silver disc in the center of his forehead—a sign of his rank and status as *Dhukari*—which covered the mark left by the trial of stone. Her fingers went to her own forehead and found the skin still sensitive to the touch. The burning pain had gone, but it would likely be tender for a few more days.

"Piece of advice," Hykos said. "Don't bother with a headband until the pain goes away. Friction with the silver can rub it raw."

"Thanks." Issa nodded.

In the pre-dawn light, the Citadel of Stone seemed a cold, forbidding place. Carved from the golden sandstone of the mountain, it was as solid, blocky, and practical as a fortress should be. The walls were bare of ornamentation or color. The closest the Citadel came to any form of décor was the myriad of weapons hanging on the wall—bladed weapons, polearms, daggers, axes, and hundreds more Issa didn't recognize.

"I saw you fight in the Crucible." Hykos shot her a sidelong glance. "When you walked in with those two short swords, I thought for sure you'd end up dead. The way you brought down that ox proved me wrong. Then you saved Etai from Kellas, and I knew there was no way I'd let *Archateros* Byrach ruin you. I claimed you as my *prototopoi* before he could." He dropped his voice to a conspiratorial whisper. "Byrach fights with the grace of a bull in heat."

Issa chuckled. "Then I'm definitely glad you chose me."

"Answer me this, though." Hykos stopped and fixed her with a stern glare. "You weren't chosen to fight in the Crucible, were you?"

Issa's stomach bottomed out. Every year, the Necroseti visited the Academies and Institutes of the Seven Faces of Shalandra to test the youths. Their testing revealed those chosen by the Long Keeper to enter the Crucible and attempt to claim one of the blades.

Issa hadn't been tested, hadn't been chosen. She'd dreaded this moment since she first stepped out onto the sands of the Hall of the Beyond. With Hykos' dark eyes boring into hers, she had to tell the truth.

"No," she replied in a quiet voice. "I wasn't."

"I didn't think so." Hykos folded his arms over his chest, his gaze piercing and his scrutiny intense. "There were only supposed to be sixty-four candidates. How did you get in?"

Issa hesitated. If she told the truth, she could get Killian in serious trouble. He'd been the one to show her the hidden way into the temple's tunnels, had told her what she needed to do to blend in with the other candidates.

"Did you use the secret tunnels?" Hykos asked.

Issa stiffened. "Y-You know about the tunnels?" Killian had called them one of Shalandra's best-kept secrets.

"Of course." Hykos snorted. "Every Blade learns the hidden ways around Shalandra, though that's not something we like to publicize. I'm certain the Indomitables, Necroseti, and the rest of the priesthoods wouldn't look favorably on our being able to get into their strongholds without their knowledge."

Issa felt her gut twist into knots. Hykos had discovered her secret; the only question remained what he'd do.

The Blade narrowed his eyes. "The Necroseti testing would have marked you as worthy, which means you didn't undergo their tests. Why not?"

Issa's eyes slid away. "My grandparents refused to allow it."

Every year, Savta and Saba locked her inside her room on the day the Necroseti visited the Institute of the Seven Faces on the Cultivator's Tier. When she tried to sneak out, Saba would be waiting for her. She'd never seen her grandparents so determined in her life. She hadn't understood it, but resented them for it.

"And yet you entered anyway." Hykos stroked his shaven upper lip. "Somehow managing to sneak in through the secret tunnels—tunnels an *Earaqi* should have no knowledge of—and getting into the Hall of the Beyond without being caught." A smile broadened his face. "Just the sort of resourcefulness that makes for a good Keeper's Blade."

His words caught Issa off-guard. She'd expected recrimination, anger, even denouncement and punishment. Hykos' approval left her speechless.

"Truth be told, I've never seen anyone fight the way you did," Hykos continued. "The dirty tricks and ruthless cunning of an Institute-trained fighter, but with the grace and skill honed over years at any of the Academies. Hell, the way you took down the Silver Sword with a Striking Serpent guard, then took down those Darting Arrows with what was clearly a Silver Sword attack, that's the sort of skill that takes years to master."

He fixed her with an expectant look, as if waiting for her to divulge her secrets. Issa remained silent. Killian had made her swear that she would *never* speak of where she'd learned to fight. For her protection as well as his, he'd insisted.

Hykos gave a dismissive wave. "There are a few bad habits I'll have to hammer out of you, but you've got the foundation well enough. Best of all, you know how to do more than just swing that blade of yours around."

Issa stared down at the huge two-handed sword in her hands. Killian had made her train with a flammard—one he'd forged in his own smithy from premium Voramian steel—daily, hammering the movements into her until her arms ached and her lungs burned. She was here thanks to him. She just hoped she'd get a chance to tell him that.

Hykos seemed not to notice her sudden somber mood. "Until the ritual that confirms you as a full-fledged Keeper's Blade, that sword is just another weapon—a good one, made of the finest Shalandran steel, but as lifeless as a wooden spear or a chunk of stone. But all that changes after the Anointing."

He drew his own two-handed blade from its sheath on his back and held it with reverence. "You will be bonded with your blade. The steel chose you, recognized something within your soul that makes you worthy to wield it." His eyes returned to her and his voice filled with wonder. "With that bond, the sword will give you power like you could never imagine."

Excitement fluttered in Issa's stomach. Everyone in Shalandra had heard tales of the Keeper's Blades and their legendary abilities. She doubted most were fabricated or exaggerated out of proportion, but if even a fraction held a grain of truth, the Blades were warriors to be feared. And she was going to become one of them.

Hykos sheathed his sword. "But until the Anointing, you will undergo the Blades' training regimen. I warn you now, it will be more difficult, more demanding than you could expect. It's not too late to walk away."

Issa shook her head without hesitation. "Not a damned chance!"

"I was hoping you'd say that." Hykos smiled. "Then our training begins now with a visit to the armory."

He led her through the stone hallways and corridors of the Citadel of Stone. Thankfully, Issa had a good sense of direction, and the layout of fortress was organized.

The center of the Citadel of Stone was dominated by an enormous training yard—doubtless it would double as a staging ground in times of war. All Issa had to do to get around the Citadel was cross the yard and find an entrance that led toward her destination.

Hykos, however, took her on a more circuitous route to introduce her to the rest of the Citadel. Her room had been located along the western side of the Citadel, on the second floor. After descending to the ground level, Hykos led her around the interior and pointed out the important areas she needed to know: common room, kitchens, a library, classrooms where she'd receive her academic lessons, Grand Chapel with its statue of the seven-faced Long Keeper, and, finally, the armory and smithy on the southern side of the training yard.

Issa's jaw dropped as she strode into the armory. The first chamber she entered was easily fifty feet wide and thirty across, lined from floor to ceiling with swords of every conceivable size and shape. The entire western wall held row after row of two-handed training swords, both wooden wasters and dull-edged metal blades. The three chambers beyond contained axes, polearms, bows, crossbows, daggers, and more weapons she'd never dreamed of—every conceivable tool of killing from every part of Einan and even Fehl across the Frozen Sea, Hykos explained.

The sound of *clanging* hammers brought a smile to her face. She'd spent hours in Killian's smithy, both to learn how to maintain her weapons and equipment and to strengthen her arms. The tang of hot metal, the loud hiss of quenching steel, and the rhythmic pounding of mallets were as familiar to her as sun and rain.

Her heart sank as she saw a familiar face in the smithy. *Not him!*

"If it isn't the lowborn?" The *Dhukari* youth—*Hykos called him Kellas*—sneered at her. "I thought I smelled dung." He stood clad in a full set of black, spiked armor, complete with a snarling lion helmet, his two-handed sword in a sheath on his back.

Issa gave him a sweet smile. "That's what happens when you wipe your face and arse with the same hand." She had no need to fear him; they were both Blades-in-training, chosen by the Long Keeper. And, she noticed for the first time, he stood a few inches shorter than she. When she drew herself to her full height, he had to look up at her.

Hykos chuckled, as did the hulking Blade beside Kellas—Issa guessed he was the one Hykos had called Byrach. Kellas, however, bristled and turned a bright shade of red.

"Listen here," he snarled, "you were lucky in the Crucible. But just because you're a Blade doesn't make you a true *Dhukari,* just as wearing this armor doesn't make you a true warrior. You don't have the skill!"

Issa cocked her eyebrow. "That's not what I remember." She stepped closer and shot him a mocking smile. "I distinctly recall *you* kneeling in the sand waiting for my blade to take off your empty head."

"You little—!" Kellas roared and lunged for her.

Issa tensed, ready to deflect his attack, but the huge Blade moved first—snagging the collar of Kellas' armor and hauling him roughly backward.

"Save it for the training yard," Byrach barked. "Once she's armored up, you'll be free to take out your hostility on each other."

"I'll be looking forward to it!" Kellas, once free of Byrach's grip, gave her a smug smile. "We'll see how lucky you are when there's no one to save you from my blade." He followed Byrach out of the smithy but shot one last sneering glance over his shoulder as he left.

Hykos gripped her shoulder and turned her to face him. "Insecurities always shout the loudest. A confident warrior is silent. Let your blade do the talking."

Issa nodded. She couldn't wait to get in the training ring and wipe that smug arrogance off Kellas' face.

"Let's get you that armor." Hykos led her through the smithy. The familiar smells of coal smoke, heating metal, and burning beeswax washed away her irritation at Kellas. She welcomed the oppressive heat of the furnaces, the repetitive *whoosh* of the pumping bellows. To her, the smithy had been a place where she could forget about the world and focus on pounding steel into its proper shape.

"I believe this belongs to you," Hykos said with a grin.

Issa's drew in a sharp breath. "Keeper's teeth!"

There, on an armorer's dummy, hung the most beautiful suit of armor Issa had ever seen. Made of black Shalandran steel, it was comprised of segmented plates that had been fitted together with the skill any artisan would envy. Even before she put it on, Issa could see that the articulated plate mail would offer incomparable freedom of movement, yet provide more effective protection than even the Indomitables' solid steel breastplates.

Hykos helped her put it on—a surprisingly complex task involving nearly twenty buckles, belts, and straps that had to be secured just so—and stepped back. "How does it feel?"

Issa took an experimental step, then picked up her blade and swung. "Amazing! It's so light and moves so easily." Every joint, from the shoulders to the knees, had enough flexibility to allow a full range of motion without sacrificing the ability to repel her enemies' attacks. The spikes on the shoulders, elbows, and knees would serve as offensive weapons in close-quarter combat. The flat design of the breastplate made it suitable for men and women alike, providing ample cushioning and protection without crushing her breasts.

Hykos nodded. "Only the finest Shalandran steel is used for the armor, just as with the blades. It's strong enough to deflect a crossbow bolt and the thrust of a sword, yet weighs less than Voramian or even Odarian steel. With that armor, you are as unstoppable as death itself."

Issa marveled at the armor. "It's truly a work of art!" She knew firsthand just how much effort went into crafting every piece—Killian had insisted she learn the basics of blacksmithing so she'd have the skills necessary to repair her own weapons and armor. Swinging his ten-pound hammer had strengthened her body and lungs. He truly *had* given her everything she needed to be ready for this moment.

*But why?* The question had plagued her for the last two years. Killian was *Intaji,* above her caste, and had no relation to her grandparents. He had no reason to help her. Yet he had, never asking anything in return. When she'd posed the question, he'd answered by saying, "The time will come when you understand. When that day arrives, we will speak of this again."

Hykos clapped her on the shoulder. "Ready?"

The impact snapped her from her thoughts. "Yes."

A small smile played on Hykos' lips. "Then I think it's time you teach Kellas the lesson he's been begging for."

## Chapter Eleven

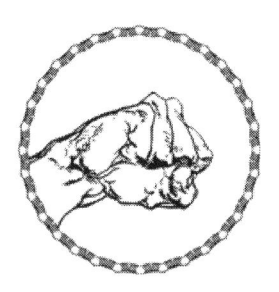

From his perch atop the driver's bench, Evren tried to overhear what Brother Modestus was saying to Hailen. The Cambionari priest spoke quietly, his rumbling tone too quiet for Evren's ears to pick up over the clatter of the wooden wagon wheels and the steady *clop, clop* of the horse's hooves.

With a frustrated sigh, he settled against the wooden seat back and resigned himself to a long morning of traveling through the rocky, boulder-strewn landscape. At least the myriad of stones, many larger than a Voramian house, provided something to look at, perhaps even take his mind off his worries.

He'd had a fitful night of rest, his sleep plagued by dreams of Hailen being consumed by fire or screaming as Soulhunger devoured his life force. When he'd awoken covered in sweat and breathing hard, the gruff Modestus had already been awake and tending to their small fire. The meager breakfast of trail biscuits and dried cheese hadn't lifted Evren's spirits.

*What the hell does it even mean, using Serenii magic?*

He'd heard Hailen's stories of Enarium, from the strange glowing Keeps to the crystals lining the walls of Khar'nath to that eerie swirling void of blackness at the uppermost room of the Illumina. The magic of the Serenii was said to be as old as Einan itself, enabling the ancient, immortal beings to shape the world to their wills. The thought of Hailen using power like that sent a shudder down Evren's spine.

He had no true understanding of how it worked—few on Einan understood the Serenii relics, weapons, language, or constructions—but he had little doubt that using the power came at a price. Just the fact that it relied on

Hailen's blood was bad enough. The Hunter had shown him Soulhunger's magic, the way the steel devoured blood, the brilliance of the gemstone as it fed. What if the Serenii magic consumed Hailen? Could wielding that power ultimately kill him?

He doubted Hailen knew, and couldn't be certain if the Cambionari knew either. No one had wielded this magic on Einan for thousands of years, it was said. His years spent as an apprentice Lectern in the Master's Temple had exposed him to some of the oldest histories and written records in existence, and he'd heard of none that contained more than a few threads of information, the barest hints and allusions, on the Serenii power.

The Hunter's time in Enarium made him the closest thing to an expert. Even Graeme and the information brokers in the Hidden Circle knew less than what the Hunter had learned during his brief contact with the Serenii being known as Kharna. If he knew that Hailen was learning to wield the power of that ancient race, would he let the boy continue his education with the Cambionari?

Right now, the Hunter wasn't here, so it fell to Evren to protect Hailen. He'd talked Brother Modestus into bringing Hailen along to Shalandra, in part so he could keep an eye on Hailen but also so he'd have company on this journey into the unknown.

Brother Modestus would keep Hailen safe in the House of Need in Shalandra so Evren could be free to focus on his task. When it came time to flee the city with the stolen relic, Hailen would return with him. Evren would be able to visit Hailen during his stay in Shalandra—an occasional relief for the inevitable loneliness.

*What happened to me?* Evren shook his head. *When did I go soft?*

Life on the streets of Vothmot had tested his limits, forced him to make hard choices and take actions he'd regretted. He'd preferred to be alone; no one to use against him, no weakness for enemies to exploit. Yet over the last three years, Evren had grown accustomed to their odd little family. The Hunter, Kiara, Hailen, and even Graeme—in the role of the quirky uncle—had come to replace those he'd left in Vothmot long ago.

He'd accepted the challenge of stealing the Blade of Hallar so he could prove his worth to the Hunter and Kiara. Having Hailen on hand made him feel a little less alone on what could prove a truly challenging endeavor.

A smack on his shoulder snapped Evren from his thoughts.

"Seven!" called Hailen.

Evren shot a glance over his shoulder. Hailen, who appeared to either have finished his lesson or grown bored of Brother Modestus, had climbed up onto one of the grain sacks and now sat behind Evren like a cat perched on a comfortable sofa.

"You sure about that?" Evren asked.

A grin split Hailen's broad, flat-nosed face as he nodded. "Seven, definitely."

"You *really* sure?" Evren placed extra emphasis on the word. "You know what happens if you're wrong."

"Seven, seven, seven!" Hailen bobbed up and down eagerly.

Evren's face grew serious. "Seven it is, then." After a moment, he smiled and shook his head. "Damn, you just got lucky!"

"Not lucky," Hailen insisted. "I know you, Evren."

He pointed to the knife in Evren's belt. "One." His finger indicated Evren's right forearm, left forearm, and both boots. "Two, three, four five." After a pensive pause, he tapped the wooden seat behind Evren's lower back. "Six, for sure. I know you've got seven, but I can't decide if it's—"

With a flick of his right wrist, Evren produced two daggers from his forearm sheaths. "Close enough." He slipped the throwing knife back into its sheath and handed the straight, double-edged stabbing blade to Hailen. "You win."

Hailen took the blade with a triumphant expression and held it up. "I'm getting better at this." He scrambled up onto the seat beside Evren, while Brother Modestus settled into a relaxed position in the back of the wagon.

"Or I'm getting predictable." Evren grinned. "I'd better change things up for next time, or else I might run out of knives."

The game was a favorite of Hailen's. Perhaps his enjoyment stemmed from the fact that the Hunter and Kiara strenuously objected to the prize. They'd made it clear that they'd rather the boy didn't carry bladed weapons, not until Hailen had some training. Both the Hunter and Kiara had been too busy for Hailen, so Evren had taken to teaching the boy what he knew. Mostly bareknuckle boxing and the sort of dirty knife-fighting tricks common in street brawls, but also a few of the sword skills pounded into Evren over the last few years of training with the Hunter and Kiara. Hailen was far from holding his own in a fight, but at least he wasn't the same helpless, terrified young boy he'd been when Evren first met him.

The boy had changed a great deal since that first day on the trail to Vothmot. Then, he'd been losing his mind to the *Irrsinnon,* the madness inherited from his Serenii ancestors. The Hunter had found a cure for Hailen in Enarium, freeing him from the curse's grip. It had also wiped away the extreme innocence and naiveté that had marked Hailen as *Melechha.* Now, Hailen could almost pass for a "normal" eleven year old—all except for those strange violet eyes and the fact that his blood could be used to wield world-shaping magic.

"How does it work?" he asked Hailen. "How does your blood, or any blood for that matter, activate the magic?"

"I don't know!" Hailen threw up his hands, temper flaring. "Father Reverentus and the other Cambionari are convinced it works so they're teaching me a lot of what they call 'magic words' that should help. But it's so much to remember, and I never get to have any fun. Ever!" He slapped a hand against the wooden bench in frustration.

"You're very possibly the most important person alive on Einan right now," Evren told him. "I know that's a big burden, but imagine what you could do once you learn how to use the Serenii magic properly."

"Yeah, the Hunter says the same thing all the time." Hailen sat back, arms folded across his chest. "It's like everyone's expecting me to do something amazing just because I *happen* to have some weird, old blood."

"Don't you *want* to learn to do magic?" Evren's eyes widened. "If I could do what you can—"

"I want to learn," Hailen said, his tone bordering on plaintive, "but I'm sick of being locked up all day in that stuffy temple. I want to run around and be free like you."

Hailen's words surprised Evren. Were their roles reversed, Evren was certain he'd throw himself into learning magic with the same intensity he'd dedicated himself to his training with the Hunter. For years, he'd only had his skill, wits, and strength to keep him alive. A hard life on the streets had taught him to value every tool and weapon at his disposal.

Yet Hailen had a point. The boy had spent the first six years of his life cooped up in the House of Need in Malandria. During his travels with the Hunter, he'd suffered more than Evren could imagine. Then, upon his return to Voramis three years earlier, his time had been divided between the Hunter's safe houses and the Beggar Temple with Father Reverentus. He hadn't had anything close to a happy childhood.

"You've a responsibility, boy," Brother Modestus' gravelly voice echoed from the back of the wagon.

Evren shot a glance over his shoulder at the Cambionari.

Modestus' eyes fixed firmly on Hailen. "You've the power to change the world, make it better. That's a gift and a burden." He sat up straighter and drew his sword from the cloth-wrapped bundle he carried everywhere he went. "My knowledge and training makes it my duty to safeguard the world from demons. I don't know what your gift is intended for, but there's no doubt about it, you've a responsibility to protect those who need you."

Evren had heard those words, or something similar, from the Hunter. The assassin was the last of the Bucelarii, half-human and half-demon. He had accepted the burden of protecting Einan by ridding it of his demonic Abiarazi ancestors. That responsibility had taken him to Praamis, which explained why Evren found himself traveling to Shalandra in the Hunter's place.

Hailen's expression had grown solemn, his shoulders slumped. "But it's so much!" he whispered, almost a whimper, and tears glimmered in his eyes. "So much that could go wrong if I mess up."

"That's why you learn," Brother Modestus replied. A hint of compassion slipped into his usual gruff tone. "A swordsman practices so he doesn't mess up the next time he fights an enemy. Knowledge is power, and power keeps you and those you love alive."

The taciturn Modestus' sudden talkativeness shocked Evren. The Cambionari had spoken more words in the last minute than he had the entire previous day.

"Drop that sword, old man, and get yer hands up high!" A voice called from the boulders on the side of the road. "You, boy, pull those horses to a stop."

Evren whipped toward the sound and found himself staring down the length of a crossbow bolt. The steel tip pointed at his face, and though its owner—a lean, rangy man clad in rust-red clothing, with a face pitted and scored by pockmarks—stood more than thirty paces away, Evren doubted the shot would miss him. If it did, it could strike Hailen. He'd never take that risk.

Brother Modestus climbed to his feet in the back of the wagon. "We've little of value to steal. Just grain to sell in Shalandra, but nary a copper bit between us."

"That sword's mighty fine," said the man, evidently the leader. Greed sparkled in his hungry eyes. "Hand it over and half the grain, and we'll let you go."

The word "we" set Evren's heart hammering. He scanned the boulders for any more enemies. Red cloaks the same color as the sandstone concealed them, but not as well as they imagined. Evren counted four, two with crossbows, but there could be more.

"The grain is yours." Brother Modestus waved at the sacks piled on the back of the wagon. "But not the sword."

The bandit leader's eyes narrowed. "You stupid or something?" He swung his crossbow around to point at Brother Modestus' chest. "You've one sword, old man, and we've more than a dozen blades between us."

"Which is why I'm happy to part with the grain." Modestus' face could have been carved from stone for all the fear he showed. "The sword's priceless."

"Even more reason for us to take it!" the bandit snapped, and the second crossbow pointed at Modestus. "Hand it over now, *and* the grain with it, and consider yerselves lucky we let you live, you crazy old bastard."

"No." Modestus shook his head.

The bandit leader's expression grew confused, as if he couldn't understand why his threats had proven ineffective. "Don't mess with us! We've already had our big score stolen from us. You don't give us what we want, we'll leave yer body for the crows and dune jackals."

Brother Modestus said nothing but made no move to hand over the sword.

"Drop him!" shouted the bandit leader.

The crossbow strings *twanged* in unison and two steel-tipped bolts flew through the air, straight toward Brother Modestus' head.

# Chapter Twelve

The sound of clashing steel set Issa's heart pounding, a thrill of excitement coursing through her. She'd spent so many years training and practicing in the secret of Killian's forge—to be in the company of warriors, the most renowned in Shalandra, set her pulse racing.

The heat of the smithy faded behind her as she stepped out into the broad training yard. The sun had just begun to peek its brilliant face over the horizon, and a welcome chill hung in the dawn air. Solid walls of golden stone surrounded the yard, like sentinels bearing witness to the prowess of the newest Keeper's Blades.

In the middle of the cleared space, two armored figures struck at each other with massive two-handed swords. Even with his helmet on, Issa instantly recognized the swaggering arrogance of Kellas. She guessed the second, smaller figure being battered around the training ground was Etai.

The *Mahjuri* girl had wielded an estoc in the Crucible, and she looked ill at ease with her huge flammard. It weighed twice as much as her shorter, lighter sword, the blade alone nearly her height. She deflected rather than blocked Kellas' blows, but her smaller frame couldn't absorb the punishment from the *Dhukari* boy's blade. Within seconds, Etai's sword lay in the dust, Kellas' tip at her throat.

Issa felt a stab of pity for Etai. Kellas' victory would only feed his hubris and likely eat away at the *Mahjuri* girl's confidence. Next time they clashed, Etai could already be half-defeated in her own mind before they ever crossed blades.

*Not if I take Kellas down a peg.*

Etai's *Archateros* trainer, a stern-faced woman even taller than Issa and Hykos, clucked her tongue and barked an order for Etai to retrieve her sword.

"Not bad," called Byrach, Kellas' trainer, as he lumbered out onto the training field. "But you're an idiot if you think toying with your enemies is the way to win."

Kellas ripped off his helmet. "I wasn't toying with—"

The towering Byrach seized Kellas' gorget and pulled him close. "Shut your mouth and open your ears." His expression grew stern, his voice a growl. "Showing off gets you dead. You fight to finish the battle as quickly and brutally as possible."

"Yes, *Archateros*." Kellas colored, a mixture of ashamed red and infuriated purple.

Issa couldn't help smiling at the sight of the arrogant *Dhukari* youth humiliated. *He deserves that and more.*

"Byrach, think your *prototopoi's* up for another challenge?" Hykos called.

Issa heard the scorn in the word, a cross between "village idiot" and "constipated dog".

"Aye." Byrach released Kellas' gorget. "He could use the practice."

Kellas straightened his armor, face flushed, and glared at Issa. "You're putting me against another *lowborn?*"

"Mouth shut, sword up!" Byrach growled and cuffed Kellas with a gauntleted hand. "Your enemy's heritage doesn't matter; all you need to care about is the cut of their blade."

Hykos laid a hand on Issa's arm and pulled her to one side of the training yard. "Listen to what Byrach told Kellas. Fight to finish it."

"Yes, *Archateros*." Issa nodded and slipped on her mountain lion-faced helmet. The steel weighed far less than she expected and the thick padding made the helmet sit comfortably on her head. Without the scowling war mask, her field of vision remained unimpeded.

"First to lose their sword or hit the sand runs ten laps around the Citadel," Byrach barked out.

Hykos grinned. "Make it fifteen."

Issa turned her attention away from her *Archateros* and focused on Kellas.

"Let's do this!" the *Dhukari* youth snarled and stalked toward her. "Nowhere to run this time, *Earaqi*."

Issa studied his posture, movements, everything down to the placement of his hands. Though the war mask hid his expression, he moved with the confidence earned through years of training. She'd caught him off-guard in the Crucible, but now he was ready for her.

*Or so he thinks.*

She adjusted her stance to the low guard taught at the Academy of the Windy Mountain. A solid position, with her feet planted and her sword held low, ready to ward off the first-contact rush they taught at the Academy of the Silver Sword. Kellas seemed to recognize her stance and adapted accordingly, raising his sword to a high-guard position.

Issa waited, forcing him to attack. He obliged by stepping forward and striking out with a quick blow meant to test the range of his sword. Issa batted it aside, knocked away a thrust aimed at her gut, then quickly leapt to the right with a high block that led into a counterattack. The technique, courtesy of the Academy of the Darting Arrows, nearly won her the battle. Kellas barely managed to turn away the blow and had to lean back to avoid the tip of her blade. The blow, that would have rung off his helmet with jarring force, *clanked* against his pauldron.

Kellas recovered quickly and came after her with powerful, sweeping blows of his two-handed sword. Issa recognized the tactic; he'd used it to overpower Etai. But her muscles, hardened by years of swinging swords and smith hammers, could take the battering. She knocked away the blows and responded with a quick thrust of her own.

The tip of her flame-bladed sword slammed into Kellas' breastplate hard enough to stagger him. He stumbled back, his heel catching on a clump of sand, and his arms flew wide as he tried not to fall. Issa seized the advantage to charge. Two steps brought her within striking range and her backhanded blow rang off Kellas' helmet. The attack, the equivalent of a jab in bare-handed combat, set her up for the true finishing strike: a downward chop aimed at his neck, where his armor was weakest.

The blow would have killed Kellas had she followed through. Instead, she turned the strike aside at the last moment and let the blade ring off Kellas' pauldron. The impact was enough to numb his left shoulder, and Issa thought she heard a grunt of pain through his steel war mask. Issa brought her sword around and rapped him on the knuckles. His Shalandran steel gauntlet protected his fingers but couldn't dull the force. Kellas actually yelped as his two-handed sword fell from his fingers and *thumped* to the sand.

"Hah!" Hykos cried, and applause broke out around the training yard. "Seems like your—"

He never finished the sentence. With a roar, Kellas bent, scooped up his sword, and charged Issa. Issa, believing the fight finished, had stepped back and lowered her blade. The sudden rush caught her by surprise. She barely had time to bring up her sword to block.

The blow never struck. Instead, a third flame-shaped blade crashed into Kellas' sword before it made contact with Issa's. Sparks flew and Issa heard a loud *crackling* sound as the two met. Kellas was thrown backward and collapsed to the ground, his flammard once again flying from his hand.

Hykos didn't sheathe his sword as he bent, seized Kellas' gorget, and lifted the stunned youth to his knees one-handed. He ripped the helmet from Kellas' face and glared down at the *Dhukari* boy.

"It is over!" he growled. His face, so friendly and welcoming to Issa mere moments earlier, had changed to a mask of fury. "The battle is done."

Kellas paled, his head hanging.

Hykos rounded on Issa. "Your enmity dies here and now. You, and you!" He thrust his sword at Etai, who had taken a seat on a nearby bench. "We are not like the Necroseti. We do not bicker, betray, deceive, or denigrate each other. We are Blades, chosen by the Long Keeper, sworn to the service of our fellow Blades, our Elders, our Pharus, and our people. We serve with strength, courage, and honor."

He turned his glare to Kellas once more. "No more bad blood, understood?"

"Yes!" The word tore from the young man's mouth.

Hykos glanced at Issa and Etai, who both answered in turn. "Understood."

"Good." Hykos released Kellas' gorget and replaced his two-handed sword in its sheath on his back. "Now stand and face each other, the three of you."

The commanding tone in Hykos' voice galvanized Etai into action, and she hustled over to Issa. Issa stepped forward and held out a hand to Kellas. For a moment, the *Dhukari* boy glared up at her, disdain etched into his eyes. Yet, beneath Hykos' stern glare, he had no choice but to accept Issa's help.

The three of them faced each other: noble *Dhukari*, toiling *Earaqi*, outcast *Mahjuri*.

"Swear now," Hykos commanded, "before the Long Keeper and his Blades, to honor each other, to treat the ones before you as brothers and sisters, to fight and, if necessary, die for each other."

"I swear!" Issa said.

"I swear," Etai echoed.

After a moment, Kellas added his voice. "I swear."

"So be it." Hykos nodded and stepped back. "From this day forward, you are no longer *Dhukari*, *Earaqi*, or *Mahjuri*. As you swore to the Elders, your past life is behind you. You are now the Keeper's Blades, one body, one mind."

"Yes, *Archateros*," Issa said.

"Yes, *Archateros*," the other two repeated.

"Good." Hykos turned and shot Byrach a pointed look. "Now, I believe there's the little matter of the loser running laps."

\* \* \*

Issa tried hard not to grin as she glanced at the puffing, heavily-sweating Kellas circling the training yard. Their new suits of armor were far lighter than Voramian steel, but they still weighed at least twenty pounds. Add to that the weight of Kellas' sword and the exhaustion of the battle, and he'd be feeling the burn.

"Again, you prove yourself clever and skilled." Hykos' voice snapped her back to her training. "But you got sloppy. You had three chances to take him down before he transitioned through that first blow, and ten more before you finally finished it."

Issa frowned. "So many?"

Hykos nodded. "The fact that you did not see those openings speaks to your inexperience rather than a lack of skill. Over the next weeks, it will be my task to hammer that experience into you. If you survive, by the time you are confirmed in the Anointing, you will be on your way to becoming one of the best of the Keeper's Blades."

Issa glowed beneath the pride, a smile tugging at her lips.

"*If* you survive," Hykos emphasized.

The words sent a little flash of anxiety through her. *That sounds ominous.*

The somber look in Hykos' eyes told her she was in for training that made Killian's demanding regimen seem like a walk in the Keeper's Gardens.

"Start with the basics," Hykos commanded. "Set up in that same Windy Mountain stance you chose to open the fight. A good, solid stance, but with too many weaknesses to be practical in real battle. See, when you plant your feet like that, you open yourself up to a counterattack. Like this…"

The next two hours passed in a blur. Hykos pushed her hard, forcing her to repeat mistakes and transitioning between offensive and defensive techniques so quickly she hardly had time to learn one before he threw another at her. When she mastered a sword stroke, he showed how that attack could be turned against her, and how to counteract those counterattacks.

Sweat soon streamed down her face and soaked into her under-tunic. The weight of her armor and sword dragged on her until it felt like she fought with millstones hanging from her arms and legs. Her muscles burned and her lungs begged for air, and still Hykos continued.

Finally, the *Archateros* stepped back and nodded. "Good enough for now."

Issa gasped and let her arms fall by her sides. All of her strength and willpower went into keeping a firm grip on her sword when she wanted nothing more than to drop it, and the armor with it, to the sands.

"After breakfast," Hykos began, "we've got lessons with—"

"*Invictus* Tannard, sir!" Byrach's voice echoed from behind Issa, ringing with a note of respect. Hykos immediately snapped to attention, his stance rigid and upright, and his fist came up in the Blades' salute.

Issa whirled and saluted as well. Her eyes fell on the newcomer to the training yard: taller than even the hulking Byrach, with sloping shoulders, thick arms, and hands that looked capable of crushing skulls. He wore no helmet, his bearded, angular face as hard as the steel of his black plate mail. The Invictus fixed his gaze on her, and Issa shuddered at what she saw in his eyes. Nothing. They were the cold, dead eyes of a killer.

"*Archateros.*" Tannard's voice rumbled like thunder. He spoke without looking away from Issa. "This is Issa?"

"Yes, *Invictus*," Hykos responded.

"Then you are relieved, *Archateros.*" Tannard's hard eyes went to Hykos. "I have decided to oversee this one's training personally."

Hykos' eyes widened a fraction. "You do her honor, *Invictus*. But surely you—"

"Surely you weren't about to question my order, *Archateros* Hykos?" Tannard's face looked as if it had been carved from the very stone of the Citadel, with the emotion to match.

"No, sir!" Hykos stiffened.

"Good." Tannard nodded. "Though, perhaps it is best that you remain. From what I hear, she has already bested the other *prototopoi*. She will need a true Blade to help her in her lessons." He gestured to Hykos without looking away from Issa. "Draw your sword."

"*Invictus?*" Confusion echoed in Hykos' voice.

"Draw your sword, *Archateros*," Tannard rumbled. "You will administer her first lesson."

Hykos hesitated a single heartbeat, then reached up and drew his sword from its sheath.

Issa reached for her own sword but stopped at Tannard's nod.

"Blades must be able to defend themselves from any threat." Tannard gestured to her gauntlets. "Even without a weapon in hand."

Issa sucked in a breath. She had little doubt Hykos could defeat her in even combat, but bare-handed? After two hours of intense training? She had no hope of victory.

"Now!" Tannard growled. "Defend yourself, *Prototopoi.*"

With an apologetic look, Hykos brought up his huge sword and attacked.

# *Chapter Thirteen*

Brother Modestus moved faster than Evren thought possible. Before the crossbows had even released their deadly missiles, the Cambionari knight leapt over the edge of the wagon and dropped to the ground. One bolt *thunked* into the wagon's side where the priest's groin had been. The second flew high and clattered off a boulder beyond the road.

Suddenly, Modestus charged out from the shelter of the wagon, right at the bandit leader. Sunlight glinted off the razor-sharp edge of his sword and the pounding of his boots echoed loud in the stillness.

The bandit leader, caught off-guard, never had time to reload his crossbow. With a yelp, he half-dropped, half-hurled it at the charging priest. Brother Modestus lashed out with a quick sword stroke that severed the crossbow string and knocked the weapon out of his path. Before the bandit leader had time to clear his sword from its sheath, the priest was on him.

Evren didn't bother to watch—the outcome was inevitable. Instead, he spun toward the bandits on the opposite side of the road. With a flick of his wrist, he dropped the throwing knife from its place in his wrist sheath and into his hand. His arm whipped up and forward, his fingers releasing the slim blade at just the right moment. The knife spun end over end, the blackened blade a dark blur in the bright morning sunlight, and buried to the hilt into the chest of the second crossbow-wielding bandit. The man gaped, mouth hanging slack, and stared down at the blood gushing down his tunic. His crossbow fell from numb fingers and tumbled into a crack between the boulders.

"Get down!" Evren shouted and shoved Hailen to the floor of the wagon's driver box. "Stay here!"

He leapt down from the wagon and charged the two bandits clustered nearest him. One wielded a rusted sword, the other a pair of single-edged daggers as long as Evren's forearm.

Evren whipped out his own daggers—two long, inward-curving, double-edged blades with thick medial ridges called *jambiyas,* weapons native to Vothmot. They were the perfect knives for his compact size and well-honed muscles: long and heavy enough to knock aside the clumsy thrust of the bandit's long sword, with a curving edge that gave him the power to punch it through the man's patchwork boiled leather armor. Blood sprayed as he pulled it free and swung around to block a dagger strike from the second bandit. With the quick, ruthless efficiency the Hunter had drilled into him, he opened his opponent's throat.

He spun back toward his first opponent and found the man on his knees, staring stupidly down at the crimson spilling from his chest. Evren paused long enough to kick the sword out of his hands—no sense risking a blow from the dying man—then raced back toward the wagon and the bandits on the far side of the road.

Brother Modestus had already brought down the bandit leader and a second bandit, and was now carving his way through the three remaining men. To Evren's horror, he saw three more bandits slinking between the rocks. In seconds, they'd reach Modestus and fall on him from the rear.

"Watch out!" he shouted. "Behind you."

Brother Modestus leapt backward and spun to face the new threat, just in time to block a savage thrust aimed at his spine. The bandit stumbled, off-balance as his blow was knocked wide. Brother Modestus brought him down with a quick chop.

Evren raced around the front of the wagon and attacked the bandits that had been tangling with Modestus moments earlier. The first to face Evren fell beneath a horizontal blow that laid open his throat. Evren knocked aside two quick swipes of the next bandit's long sword, dodged a dagger strike from the third, and nearly died as his back struck hard stone. Only his quick reflexes, honed through years as a thief and his training with the Hunter and Kiara, kept him alive. He managed to throw himself to one side. The blade *clanged* off stone a finger's breadth from his head.

As he moved, he lashed out with the blade in his right hand. The razor-sharp edge opened a deep gash in the man's leg, just above the knee. The wound did little real damage but slowed the man down long enough for Evren to regain his balance. He met the bandit's wild swing with a cross-body blow that slapped the sword aside. His right-handed thrust punched the tip of his *jambiya* into the bandit's gut. A quick flick of his wrist sent the tip slicing to the right, opening more flesh, muscle, and organs.

The bandit screamed and fell, his body tripping up his companion. In the instant the man looked down to avoid trampling his fallen comrade, Evren leapt forward and drove both daggers into the man's chest and throat. The bandit died with a wet gurgle.

A piercing wail of pain sounded behind him. Evren's heart stopped. *Hailen!*

The cry came again, too deep and growling to have come from the eleven year old's throat, accompanied by a stream of curses.

Evren whipped around to find Hailen standing atop the wagon, knife held in the defensive grip Evren had drilled into him. Blood stained the tip and edge of the blade. One of the bandits had tried to scramble onto the wagon and earned a slash across the face for his efforts. Hailen attacked again with the short, quick thrust of a knife fighter. The man fell back with a grunt, pulling the blade free from his chest, and fell to the ground beside the wagon.

Five sprinting steps brought Evren to the bleeding bandit and his boot *crunched* into the man's face. Shielding his movements from Hailen with his body, Evren drove his dagger into the unconscious bandit's chest, just next to the wound Hailen had inflicted. His thrust, however, drove between the man's ribs and sliced smooth heart muscle. The bandit didn't move as his blood pumped onto the dusty road.

Silence.

Evren's lungs burned, his heart raced, and his fingers clutched the hilts of his daggers in a vise-grip. Everything around him had gone dead still, the only sound the snorting of the horses and his own gasping.

Then came a pained grunt from ahead. He looked up to see Brother Modestus on one knee, left hand gripping the hilt of a dagger protruding from his side. With a rumbling growl, the priest tore the blade free and hurled it away. Wincing, he cleaned his sword on the fallen bandits' clothing then sheathed it.

The priest turned toward them. "Either of you hurt?"

Evren shook his head, his eyes fixed on the wound in Modestus' side. "That looks bad."

"I'll be fine." Modestus gave a dismissive wave with his right hand. "No major organs or blood vessels hit." He strode back to the wagon with a determined step, his face once again that expressionless mask. Yet, when he tried to pull himself up onto the driver's seat, he growled at the pain of his wound.

"Ride in the back," Evren told him. "You need to rest and heal."

Brother Modestus looked ready to protest, but the pain seemed to make him reconsider. "Just a short rest," he rumbled. "Then I'll spell you at the reins."

Evren shook his head. "We can handle the driving." He turned to Hailen. "Spread some blankets in the back, right there."

Hailen scrambled over the seat into the back of the wagon. It took Modestus two tries to pull himself into the back and onto the makeshift bed, but he refused Evren's offer of help with a growl.

"I'll be fine," he rumbled again. "A bit of rest, and I'll be right as rain in a few days."

\* \* \*

Brother Modestus' wound *didn't* heal. Instead, it worsened.

Evren changed the bandages frequently, ripping up two of his own tunics for dressings, but still infection set in. Much of their limited water supply went into bathing the wound to no avail. Evren had no salves or unguents to use, no knowledge of the plants in this part of Einan to find something for a remedy. By the end of the first day after their encounter with the bandits, Brother Modestus had slipped into a feverish state. The priest moaned, muttered, and mumbled incoherently.

Brother Modestus lived for three more days, in and out of consciousness, sweat dripping down his pale face and soaking his clothes. On the morning of the fourth day, their sixth out of Voramis, Evren awoke from a fitful night of rest to find Brother Modestus awake and staring at him.

"Listen," rasped the grizzled priest. "There's something…you must know!"

Evren scrambled over to the wagon and Modestus' side.

"You must…continue the mission." The priest fixed fever-bright eyes on him. "Must retrieve…the Blade of Hallar. The prophecy…cannot come to pass."

Evren's brow furrowed. "Prophecy?"

*What's he talking about?* The priest appeared lucid, but he'd been in and out of fever dreams for the last day. *Is he even coherent?*

"The Prophecy…of the Final Destruction!" Modestus struggled in vain to sit upright, but slumped back to his blankets, too weak to lift himself. "Reverentus…didn't tell you?"

"No." Evren shook his head. "He said nothing of any prophecy, and definitely none that involved the Blade of Hallar or any Final Destruction."

"Find the sword!" Modestus cried in a hoarse voice. "Stop the prophecy…and save the world."

He slumped back, his eyes falling closed.

"Hey!" Evren grabbed the priest's collar and shook him. "Hey, wake up."

Modestus' eyes fluttered open for a moment, but closed once more.

"How am I supposed to do anything if I don't know about this prophecy?" Evren shouted, trying to wake up the priest. "Tell me what I need to know!"

But Brother Modestus was beyond hearing. The Long Keeper, god of death, had gathered the priest into his arms.

\* \* \*

Evren buried the priest a short distance from the road. The soil was rocky and bone-dry, and Evren had only Modestus' sword to use as a shovel. The sun had risen high into the sky by the time he rolled the priest's heavy body—stripped of its armor and weapons—into the shallow grave and covered it up.

Hailen helped as best he could, somber and silent the entire time. His eyes were wide and rimmed with tears.

Evren knew the boy had seen more death in his short lifetime than most people. Though the Hunter, Kiara, and Evren had tried their best to shield him from more, there was no way to escape reality now.

He glanced over at Hailen. "We should say something for him." What to say, he didn't know.

Hailen knelt beside the mound of dirt and closed his eyes. "May the Beggar God smile on you," he said in a quiet voice, "and guide you on your journey to the Long Keeper's arms, where you will know peace and joy forever more."

Evren bowed his head and repeated the words in his mind. He knew the truth—there was no Beggar God, no Long Keeper, just a handful of ancient Serenii that primitive humans worshipped as gods—but the fallen priest deserved better than a silent burial. The words were for Modestus' sake, not his.

But, as he finished, he felt a new burden weighing on his shoulders. He and Hailen were alone in the middle of nowhere, too far from Voramis and too low on food and water to turn back now. Their only hope lay in going forward to Shalandra. Thankfully, he needed no map to find his way—as long as he kept traveling south on the road, they would reach their destination.

*And what happens when I reach the City of the Dead? The Cambionari have no idea we're coming, and we have no way to prove who we are.*

He'd have to do it on his own. He'd steal the Blade of Hallar and keep Hailen safe. He'd learn about this Prophecy of the Final Destruction and find out what, if anything, could be done to avert it.

Somehow.

He had no choice. If a dying man's words were to be believed, the fate of the world now rested on his shoulders.

# *Chapter Fourteen*

Issa refused to cry out as Hykos landed blow after blow on her arms, legs, sides, shoulders, and back. Hykos struck with the flat of his blade, yet even through the protective layer of her armor, Issa could feel her muscles pounded like steel beneath Killian's hammer. Pain radiated through every fiber of her being, turning her body sluggish, slowing her attempts to dodge, evade, or block the blows. Her gauntleted hands had long ago gone numb.

And all *Invictus* Tannard shouted was "Harder! Faster!" He looked on with the dispassion of a butcher studying a block of meat, watching Hykos carve her to pieces.

Hykos' expression revealed nothing, but remorse filled his eyes. He dared not hold back his blows, Issa knew, dared not disobey his commander's orders. The *Archateros* struck and struck again until Issa fell to her knees, her hands, and finally her face.

"Enough!" The single word, barked like the cracking of a whip, echoed faint through Issa's all-consuming agony. It took her a moment to register the cessation of blows.

A shadow hovered above Issa. "On your feet, *Prototopoi*."

Issa wanted nothing more than to lose herself to unconsciousness, to drown in the torrent of suffering that washed over her. Yet she could not, would not, give Tannard the satisfaction of victory. She forced herself onto one pain-numbed arm, then the other, until she pushed herself up to one knee.

Even the slightest movements proved agonizing, but she forced herself to lift her head, straighten her back, and finally stagger upright to her feet. She stood, swaying, her jaw clenched so tightly she feared she'd snap her teeth or shatter bone.

Tannard came to stand in front of her, his hard, bearded face inches from hers. "Pitiful," he snarled. "And you dare to call yourself a Keeper's Blade?"

Issa gave no reply. She knew his type—she'd encountered many such among the Indomitables that patrolled Shalandra's lowest tiers—he simply expected her to stand there and take the abuse. She could take as much as he dished out. He could knock her down but she would always get back up.

Tannard spat to one side. "To your chambers."

Hykos stepped forward, but Tannard whirled on him. "She goes *alone!* A Keeper's Blade must learn to fight through the pain, to welcome it, to use it to become stronger. If she cannot stomach one simple beating, she does not deserve her place in our ranks."

Issa clenched her fists; the movement brought a fresh wave of pain. Her palms felt swollen, and she guessed at least one finger had been broken or dislocated. But, even with everything that screamed at her to collapse, to crumble, she took a step.

A small step, barely lifting her foot off the ground. Another shuffling, scraping step.

Her eyes met Etai's. The *Mahjuri* girl stared at her with pity.

Another step, then a second and third.

Kellas watched her go. His perpetual arrogant sneer had given way to stunned surprise, perhaps even a hint of grudging respect.

More steps. Slow, painful, her body dragging, her muscles protesting. Yet forward, always forward.

The stone archway into the western wing of the Citadel of Stone seemed an impossible distance away. Sweat streamed down Issa's face as she moved, soaked through her tunic, turned her palms slick. Her armor and sheathed flammard threatened to drag her down.

Yet still she moved. One torment-riddled, stiff step at a time. Through the archway, into the shadows of the Citadel, and toward the nearest staircase.

Climbing the stairs to the second floor proved agony. She rested every second step, her muscles crying out for rest. Issa fought on, one golden stone stair after another. She refused to give Tannard the satisfaction of seeing her fall.

She nearly wept in relief at the sight of her doorway. Her fingers, numb from the repeated pounding of Hykos' blade, struggled to grip the door knob. Finally, she grabbed it in a clumsy two-handed grip and twisted. She staggered as the door swung inward. Every part of her wanted to collapse as she staggered into her room, but a huge frame in the entrance cast the room in shadow. When she managed to turn, she found *Invictus* Tannard behind her.

"You are strong, talented even, but strength and skill are useless without discipline." Tannard's stony expression somehow grew even harder. "And by the Keeper, discipline's what I'm going to teach you."

"Yes, *Invictus*!" Issa managed through clenched teeth.

*Invictus* Tannard remained silent for a long moment, eyes locked on her. "You are forbidden to rest. Do not sit or lie in bed until the sun sets."

Issa wanted to cry, to shout at him, to reach for her sword and hack him down. She did nothing.

"Here, if you want food, you must find it, take it, but without being seen," Tannard told her. "A Blade must be clever and stealthy, even in unfamiliar surroundings. If you cannot steal your meal in the Citadel of Stone, you will not eat, *Prototopoi*."

"Yes, *Invictus*." The words, edged with anger, burst from within Issa's chest.

*Invictus* Tannard stepped forward to loom over her. "The Keeper has no need of fat, lazy soldiers that cannot fight on empty stomachs. A true Blade can do battle even as they die of starvation." He whirled on his heel and strode toward the door. "We will see if you have what it takes to be a true Blade." With those words, he left her alone with her pain.

Issa waited until she was certain that he'd gone before letting out an explosive breath, half-sob and half-shout. *Why in the Keeper's name is he doing this?* She'd never seen the *Invictus* in her life, could think of no reason for his enmity. It didn't matter. He'd singled her out for punishment, determined to break her spirit. Killian hadn't prepared her for this.

But her grandparents had. Savta and Saba had lived a hard life, yet never once complained. Issa had learned the meaning of work, endurance, and longsuffering from them. Life as an *Earaqi* could not break her grandparents; life as a Keeper's Blade would not break her.

She had endured her first lesson. Now came the second. She'd endure that, too.

Theft was common enough in Shalandra that merchants on the Artisan's Tier hired guards to watch their stalls. Thieves and pickpockets unlucky enough to get caught suffered the removal of their right hand on their first offense, right leg on their second, and head on their third. Issa had rarely tried stealing—she was too big to slip easily among the crowds like Killian's Mumblers—but this wasn't Commerce Square. She'd have to figure out how to defeat this challenge based on the specifics of her surroundings.

First, she needed to get out of her armor. She'd move more easily without the weight of her heavy plate mail dragging on her.

It took her the better part of half an hour to remove the black-steel armor. Every movement brought a fresh stab of pain, reminded her of another blow that had slipped past her guard. The buckles on her back and sides proved most difficult. Finally, she simply pulled the armor over her head—sending more agony radiating through her body—and threw it onto the bed.

She slipped off the padding until she stood clad only in the thin tunic she'd found in a neat pile on her bed the previous night. Next she removed her boots and stockings and stood in bare feet. The stone floor was cool beneath her toes. The sensation came as a welcome relief from the heat that coursed through her battered body.

She waited a few minutes before putting her boots on again. Gritting her teeth, she forced herself to move toward the door. If she stopped and let her body cool down, the aches and pains would intensify a thousandfold. She had to keep going until she succeeded at her mission or collapsed from exhaustion.

The few Blades she passed eyed her with a curious mixture of pity, amusement, and curiosity. Their conversations stopped at her approach, then resumed in whispers once they passed her. She had little doubt word of her humiliation on the training ground had spread through the Citadel of Stone like mice through a granary.

To her pain and exhaustion-blurred eyes, the bare stone hallways all looked the same. Yet she knew that she had to head north, then east and down a flight of stairs to reach the kitchens on the ground floor.

Hope surged within her as the smell of baking flatbread drifted up to the second floor. She hadn't eaten since the previous morning—hunger gnawed at her stomach as she stumbled toward the kitchens.

But the direct route wouldn't be the way to get what she needed.

Tannard's words echoed in her mind. *"You want food, find it, take it, but let no one see you. A Blade must be clever and stealthy, even in unfamiliar surroundings. If you cannot steal your meal in the Citadel of Stone, you will not eat, Prototopoi."*

She couldn't enter the common room; Tannard would likely be waiting or have watchers set up to spot her. Her only hope lay in stealing food from the kitchens.

*The question is how many watchers will be between here and there?* Too many, that much she knew without a doubt. Tannard had proven that his lessons had real teeth—he'd ensure his orders were enforced, no matter what.

But one thing she'd learned from her grandmother was that all kitchens had a back way in. Once, when she'd accompanied her Savta to the *Dhukari* mansion where she served, Aleema had explained the building's layout. The kitchens *always* stood placed on the first floor, well away from the areas the *Dhukari* frequented. The upper-caste never wanted to see how their food was made; they simply expected it to be served on time.

But the kitchens also were placed close to a rear entrance. This allowed merchants to deliver food to the rear or side access gates without cluttering up the grand front entrance. And it provided an easy way to dispose of the waste generated by the cooks.

The Citadel of Stone had to have a rear or side entrance that led into the kitchens, just like every other grand building on the Keeper's Tier. Instead of heading through the common room, she could use the alternate route to slip in the back—in the way the garbage went out. It was a desperate plan, as desperate as she felt at that moment. Pain, fatigue, and hunger warred within her; if she could at least solve one, she'd be able to stubborn out the others until sunset.

She half-stumbled down the staircase toward the first floor, but instead of heading east along the stone corridors, she looked for a passage that headed north, outside the rear of the Citadel. Her heart leapt as she caught a glimmer of daylight down a narrow passage.

To her relief, the passage led outside. The stink of refuse and rotting veggies told her she'd made the right choice.

*Thank you, Savta!*

Raw animal carcasses, sodden flatbread, and putrid vegetable and fruit rinds squelched beneath her boots, but she was beyond caring. She moved in a low crouch, biting her lip to avoid crying out, and crept toward the rear door of the kitchens.

The door stood open, and Issa's heart sank as she heard quiet voices coming from within the kitchens.

"No way she's smart enough to go through the refuse heap," said a man's voice.

"You didn't see her at the Crucible or out in the training yard, did you?" asked the second, a woman.

"Barrett certainly painted a picture of her." The man snorted. "Made her sound like Hallar reincarnated, the way he went on."

Despite the torment in her ribs and spine, Issa couldn't help grinning. *They're talking about me.*

"Is it just me, or is it bloody insane the way *Invictus* Tannard is handling her training himself?" the woman asked.

"Definitely not just you, Talla," the man replied. "When the second-in-command to Callista herself steps in, you know a *prototopoi's* either the child of the Pharus himself, the greatest warrior in Shalandra, or the unluckiest piece of shite in the world."

"The way he had Hykos whale on her today, that was cruel, even by his standards," the woman, Talla, said.

*Glad to see I'm not the only one who thinks that.*

"At this rate, she'll be lucky to reach the Anointing alive, much less with all her limbs attached."

"Maybe that's his intention," the man said. "Maybe he's planning to recruit her for his special crew of killers hunting down the Gatherers."

"That's just a rumor and you know it, Gerrad," the woman replied.

"You hear it from enough lips, it's bound to have some truth in it. The way the Gatherers have been ramping up their activity lately, there's no way the Lady of Blades is going to let them continue unchecked. Even if the Pharus is too blind and stupid to move against them."

"Careful," Talla warned. "We serve the Pharus as well as Lady Callista."

"Sure, just like we serve the Keeper's Council and the Necroseti." Gerrad gave another snort of derision. "It's words, nothing more. The Lady of Blades and the Elders are the only ones who deserve—"

"She's not coming in this way." A new voice, a familiar one, interrupted the conversation within the kitchens. "I spotted her heading down toward the deep storage where Fiaugh ages the cheese and hams."

*Hykos?* Confusion furrowed Issa's brow. *What is he doing?*

"Rannus and Churia are waiting for her there," Talla replied.

"They're waiting by the main stairs, but something tells me they're not clever enough to expect Issa to take the stairs beside the library."

"Watcher's beard!" Gerrad cursed. "Of course they won't."

"Go," Hykos told them. "I've yet to eat, so I'll stay here and keep watch while I break my fast."

Issa couldn't make out Gerrad's response, but the conversation died out, leaving only silence. A moment later, the window opened and a small cloth-wrapped bundle flew out. Issa caught it before it landed in the rotting mess of garbage.

"I'm sorry." Hykos' words drifted through the open window. "I can't go against an *Invictus*, especially not Tannard. I'll do what I can to help, but now it's up to you to survive this." His voice grew solemn. "And you *have* to survive this. You're too good to fail. The Keeper's Blades need you."

The window closed, leaving Issa alone in the refuse heap. Opening the bundle, she found a small chunk of soft goat cheese, a quarter of flatbread, and a handful of dried dates. A pitiful meal, but far more than she could have hoped for.

Tears of gratitude welled in Issa's eyes as she devoured the food. How Hykos had known she was coming this way didn't matter at the moment. He had helped her, a quiet gesture of defiance toward the *Invictus'* cruel treatment.

Grim resolve hardened into a ball within her as she slipped back toward her room. She had little doubt that a great deal more suffering lay ahead; Tannard had proven himself a cruel, ruthless trainer, and he'd taken a special interest in her.

Yet she wouldn't face it alone. That small glimmer of hope was more than enough to keep her from giving up.

*He won't break me,* she swore in her mind. *I've come this far, and nothing's going to stop me from becoming a Keeper's Blade.*

# *Chapter Fifteen*

Nervous tension tightened Evren's shoulders as the wagon rattled the last few paces toward Shalandra's West Gate. The gate was a massive construction of steel-banded stone easily forty feet tall, suspended from iron chains thicker than his arms, and set in the seventy-foot stone wall that surrounded the base of the city. The wall, like the rest of Shalandra, appeared to have been hewn from the golden sandstone of the mountain upon which it sat.

Shalandra looked like someone had cut the circular mountain like a pie and built a city into the removed slice. It was constructed into six levels: the largest at the bottom, and each growing progressively smaller as they rose toward the enormous building—Evren guessed it was the palace—at the pinnacle. The city faced due south, with both the western and eastern edges marked by sheer cliffs that rose hundreds of feet above the golden stone buildings.

A company of eight guards stood at the gate. All wore heavy black-burnished armor—a strange type of half-plate mail that encased their upper bodies in solid steel while leaving their legs free for quick movement—and carried long sickle-shaped swords. Their helmets were flat on the top but rimmed with spikes, bearing a strange blue ring around the forehead. Even stranger, they wore dark *kohl* around their eyes, and their faces bore five black dots like beauty marks painted onto their skin. An unusual affectation, similar to the way Voramians painted their cheeks with beet juice to add color to their pale skin.

One of the guards studied him through narrowed eyes, as if trying to decide what to think of the young man driving a wagon. His goods bore the mark of a Malandrian merchant, yet he could almost pass for Shalandran.

Over the last day, as traffic on the road had increased, Evren had noticed that the people of Shalandra bore strong similarities to the people in his home city of Vothmot. Voramians, Praamians, and Malandrians tended to be pale, but Shalandrans had skin of a deep, golden bronze—a shade lighter than the people of Vothmot, colored like almond peels. Their eyebrows were thinner, their eyes smaller and rounder, but with similar tight jawlines, prominent noses, and dark, wavy hair.

"What is your business in Shalandra?" the guard demanded. It seemed he'd decided that Evren was a foreigner. That might have to do with the fact that Hailen sat on the wagon seat behind him—with his brown hair and cream-colored skin, he stuck out among the sea of Shalandrans. The accent reminded Evren of his own home in Vothmot far to the north, though slightly harsher, hardening the syllables and making the vowels rounder, more musical.

"Hauling a load of grain for my father." The lie came easily; Evren had rehearsed it in his mind the last two days. "He took ill the day we had planned to leave Voramis, so it falls to me to bring it."

"Alone?" The soldier raised an eyebrow. "Don't you know there are bandits on the road?"

*There are at least ten fewer now,* Evren thought. Outwardly, he forced a grin and jerked a thumb at Hailen. "I've got him along for protection."

Hailen gave the guard a bright grin. "Hello!"

The guard snorted and shook his head. "I'll need to inspect your goods."

"Of course." Evren reached back and twitched aside the tarp. His eyes went to Brother Modestus' bloodstains still on the wooden walls and floor of the wagon. They hadn't had the water to scrub it out; he could only hope the guard didn't care enough to question the sight.

The armored man eyed the bloodstains curiously for a moment, then hopped up onto the wagon and poked around among the sacks and crates. A few seconds later, he jumped down and strode alongside the wagon to stand in front of Evren.

"Follow the eastern road, the Path of Sepulture, up to the Cultivator's Tier," he instructed. "From there, take the Commoner's Row eastward, toward the Trader's Way. That road will take you up to the Artisan's Tier. There you'll find Commerce Square, where you can sell your wares. If you plan to spend the night in Shalandra, you'll find lodgings in the Foreign Quarter on the western edge of the Cultivator's Tier."

"Got it." Evren nodded. He had no idea what those street names referred to, but he'd figure it out.

"*Only* in the Foreign Quarter." The guard's expression grew severe. "We have opened our city to your kind, but Shalandra is not yours to roam freely. If you're found outside the Foreign Quarter after dark, you will be detained and questioned." The tone of his voice made Evren suspect that there would be few questions involved, but an abundance of beatings and incarceration.

"Understood!" He kept a smile on his face, but inwardly he cursed. He'd have a hard time sneaking up to the palace to steal the Blade of Hallar if he couldn't move around Shalandra unhindered.

*Lucky for me, I could probably pass for a local. Even the accent's not too hard to manage with a bit of practice.*

"A word of warning," the guard said as Evren gathered up the reins. "Cover your heads."

Evren frowned in confusion.

The guard tapped the blue band on his helmet. "Only the *Kabili* go bareheaded in Shalandra. If you don't want someone thinking you're a slave, cover up."

"Thank you," Evren said, though he still didn't understand the meaning.

"You can find headbands and headdresses in Commerce Square." The guard pointed to Hailen. "You'll want to get him one first before someone mistakes him for a slave escaped from a *Dhukari* or *Alqati* household."

"I certainly will." With a nod, Evren flicked the reins and set the horse in motion.

As he drove through the gate, he was surprised to find himself in a broad tunnel. The city wall was at least thirty feet thick and made of solid stone. The passage had been carved wide enough for two wagons to pass at once, but Evren's keen eyes spotted multiple slits and openings in the wall, ceiling, and ground. Clearly this passage had been built for defense first and commerce second. If the gates were ever sealed in time of war, it would take more than an army to get through.

Through the gate, Evren found himself riding into a world of gold and dust.

Every building on the lowest tier of Shalandra had been carved from the gold-colored rock of the mountain. Most were squat single-story constructions, barely better than stone boxes with openings for windows and doors. The morning sunlight seemed to set the sandstone aglow with an almost enchanted luster, yet there was nothing magical about the crumbling walls and the thick layer of dust that covered everything.

The people had the same crumbling, weathered look of the buildings they called home. All wore black headbands, little more than cords of rope or strips of faded fabric. Their clothing hung in tatters from their gaunt shoulders and bony ribs. Their bronze skin was darkened by the sun and cracked with lines of age and weariness.

A pall of listlessness hung over the people around him—few moved about, and those that did shuffled along, stooped, gazes downcast. Most simply remained where they sat or lay in the pitiful shade of their crumbling houses. Conversations were held in quiet, furtive voices.

Evren had seen hard conditions—both on the streets of Vothmot and the Beggar's Quarter in Lower Voramis—but they paled in comparison to this. At least in those cities, people made an effort to break out of their poverty. They fought, stole, even killed each other, but they *tried* to survive. Here, it seemed the poorest simply abandoned all hope and waited for death to claim them.

For some, that wouldn't be long. A few of the people lying in the rubbish looked three breaths from the Long Keeper's arms. While all around him were emaciated, haggard even, a handful had found a new threat to their existence: disease. Blue blisters dotted their bodies, most crusted over but with pus oozing from the worst of them. Those affected lay where they'd fallen, too weak or ravaged by illness to move, get into the shade, or even cover up.

Sorrow and pity panged in Evren's chest. *This is no way to live,* he thought. *No one should be condemned to such a miserable existence as this.*

The avenue, which the guard had called the Path of Sepulture, ran straight north from the gate, up the hill that would lead him toward the higher tiers. Another wide thoroughfare ran along the lowest tier from east to west. The streets were littered with rubbish, crumbled stone, shattered bricks, and thatch blown free of the roofs. More than a few of the ragged people simply lay on the piles of garbage, drunk, unconscious, or perhaps even dead.

As his carriage rumbled up the Path of Sepulture toward the higher tier, he caught sight of a patrol of the black-armored soldiers marching past. He couldn't help noticing the marked effect of the guards' presence.

The hushed conversations stopped and people hustled out of the patrol's path with frightened expressions. But beneath the fear he sensed an undertone of anger. Glares followed the retreating backs of the marching soldiers. Some brazen men and women even spat—long after the guards had passed, of course.

Evren had lived on the streets, and he'd grown adept at reading the mood of the individuals that made up large crowds. Happy, distracted people made easy marks, but angry throngs were more likely to turn violent, and woe to the pickpocket or thief that made the mistake of getting caught in the middle. He'd have to be blind to miss the subtle undercurrent of discontentment and hostility directed at the guards.

*Maybe the people aren't as content with their terrible lot in life as they seemed.* That never boded well. Once, nearly a decade earlier, the citizens of Vothmot had revolted in response to the Caliph's harsh treatment. It had taken the better part of a year for the Wardens of the Mount to restore order, even after the cruel Caliph had been dragged out of his palace fortress and stoned to death in the Court of Judgement.

Something on a nearby wall caught his attention. The words "Child of Secrets" had been painted onto the golden sandstone in bright red—paint or blood, he couldn't tell from this distance. As his wagon rumbled up the road, he found the same words twice more.

A fifty-foot wall separated the first tier from the second. The gates stood open, with only a quartet of black-armored guards on watch. They let him through with barely a cursory glance at the contents of his wagon. He guessed that they were stationed there to keep out the wretches in the lowest tier—anyone else could come and go as they pleased.

The Path of Sepulture continued up to the third tier, but Evren turned east as the guard had instructed. The second tier—*the Cultivator's Tier, the guard called it*—was arrayed in the same precise layout of streets: the broad avenue known as Commoner's Row running east to west, with smaller streets intersecting. *Good.* He smiled. *If the three higher tiers are laid out the same, it'll make getting around a whole lot easier.*

On the second level, however, the buildings were far better-preserved than those on the lower tier, with whitewashing to cover the stone. Some even had second-floor additions built with sun-baked clay bricks. The roofs were still simple thatch, but in good condition. Hundreds of women and children wielded brooms, filling the air with the dust they swept out of their stone-floored houses. All along the avenue stood cloth-covered shops and stalls built from whatever scraps of wood, brick, and stone the people could cobble together.

As Evren traveled east along Commoner's Row, he found the streets cleaner and neater as well, free of the debris that clogged the lowest tiers. People wore simple clothing—the men wearing skirt-like garments of wool and canvas, the women clad in knee-length dresses that clung to their bodies like a sheath. All wore red headbands of woven fabric or wool—the bright cloth a sharp contrast to the dull colors of their garments. A few even had those strange black dots painted onto their face, though no eyeliner.

A few lighter-skinned Praamians, Voramians, and even Malandrians moved among the people. They dressed in clothing native to their city, but to Evren's surprise, he found they all wore green headbands.

Suddenly, Evren understood what the guard had meant about covering up. Everyone in Shalandra wore some sort of headband or scarf covering on their foreheads. *And color has something to do with status in this city,* he realized.

Those on the lowest level wore black headbands, with green marking foreigners and red marking the people of the Cultivator's Tier. One man wearing a brown headband had the calloused hands of a stonemason, while a man with an elegant white feathered headdress wore a fancier version of the men's skirts, complete with a loose cloak draped over his shoulders.

*Perhaps, if I get the right headband and clothing, I can trick my way into the upper levels to get close enough to the Blade of Hallar.* There was little doubt in his mind that the enormous building on the uppermost tier of Shalandra would be the Palace of Golden Eternity—the place where Father Reverentus had told him he'd find the Blade of Hallar.

Hailen, however, would have to get one of those forest green bands. No sense trying to pass off the pale-skinned boy as a Shalandran.

Again, he spotted the strange words "Child of Secrets" painted on the wall of a house set into a back alley. A short distance away, just as he approached the broad avenue the guard had called Trader's Way, he caught sight of a new one.

*Child of Spirits?* He arched an eyebrow, curiosity burning. Given how carefully the people on this tier cared for their homes, it seemed strange that they would allow such defacement. *So what does it mean? It has to be important.*

The sounds of booted feet marching toward him snapped his attention back to the road. A twenty-strong patrol of the black-armored guards approached, and from their purposeful stride, it was clear that they had no intention of moving out of the road. Evren was forced to quickly steer his wagon to one side to make way for the patrol. One of the guards even snarled a curse at him for not moving fast enough.

He snorted. *Quite the friendly lot, aren't they? Then again, what city guards ever are?*

Trader's Way was a massive avenue—wide enough for four full-sized wagons—that ran north to the third tier and south to the gate on the lowest tier. It seemed to provide the most direct route from the marketplaces on the upper tier to the vast swaths of farmland and grazing pasture that radiated southward outside the city wall.

On the Artisan's Tier, the mercantile establishments seemed more permanent, with countertops of solid stone, strong brick pillars, even the occasional clay-tiled roof among the sea of thatch. The quality of the wares on the Artisan's Tier far exceeded that of the goods sold on the lower tier. No woven rush baskets or clay pottery and cookware up here.

To the east, Evren caught sight of quality steel tools, knives, and farming tools mingled with wrought-iron decorations and ornate painted ceramic pottery. Massive wheels of white cheese sat beside man-height piles of fresh-baked flatbreads. The smell of cinnamon, cloves, and other sharp spices drifted up from a stall heaped high with pastries covered in bright-colored, elegantly swirled frosting. Jewelry of gold, silver, and precious metals studded with twinkling gemstones hung from metal stands, under the watchful guard of stern-eyed men clad in padded jerkins and carrying iron-studded truncheons. Everything that could be crafted by an artisan's hand, heart, and mind stood on display for the people of Shalandra.

The marketplace to the west was filled with fresh fruits, vegetables, nuts, seeds, spices, grains. The entire southern edge of the market was dedicated to butcher's stalls, where the shadow of the wall provided a modicum of shade to keep the raw meat cool. Another section was dedicated to fabric of every conceivable hue and texture, bolts of wool, cotton, and linen, even powdered dyes ground from beetle shells, berries, and minerals.

Traffic was heavy as the sun approached high noon. A sea of men, women, and children flowed in through the twin marketplaces in a steady stream. Here, the disparity between the classes of Shalandrans became painfully obvious.

Those in red headbands wore clothing of roughspun wool, linen, and faded cloth. White and brown headbands indicated a higher level of wealth, though many still had the hard hands and broad shoulders of laborers or the perpetual stoop of intellectuals that dedicated their lives to hunching over books and scrolls. Evren saw few headbands of solid gold or blue; instead, people wore headbands with gold or blue braided with the other colors. These wore better-quality skirts and longer dresses, made of finer quality fabrics. Some even bore symbols or markings—an educated guess told Evren they proclaimed them servants of one of the upper-tier households.

Evren turned his wagon into the western market. He had no desire to waste time selling the grain, but he needed the coin. Brother Modestus' purse had been dreadfully light, and he'd only had a few copper bits on him when he'd met with Father Reverentus. A bit of gold would go a long way toward facilitating his task of finding the Blade of Hallar.

*Hopefully I can find a merchant or the servant of some nobleman to take it off my hands.*

Farther to the west, beyond the marketplace, Evren caught sight of towering buildings that bore a strong resemblance to the temples of the Thirteen in Vothmot, Malandria, and Voramis. The architecture and decorative flourishes differed from city to city, but there was no mistaking the lofty grandeur of a building erected to worship one of the gods of Einan.

Evren's heart leapt as he found an empty stall—four brick pillars supporting a terracotta tile roof, with a stone counter at the front. *That'll do nicely.*

He pulled his wagon into the small space next to the stall and set about unloading his grain. Hailen tried to help, but the eleven year old wasn't yet strong enough to lift the eighty-pound sacks.

Evren had just dropped the second sack of grain onto the counter when an angry voice echoed behind him.

"Hey! That place is not yours to claim, *lowborn*."

Evren turned to find a man stalking toward him. Anger blazed in the man's dark eyes, and his three chins wobbled in time with his belly, which drooped disgustingly low over the hem of his white-and-blue skirt. A golden headband soaked with sweat encircled his heavy forehead.

"What's that, now?" Evren cocked an eyebrow at the man. "What did you just call me?"

"Silence, Kabili!" The fat man drew himself up to his full height. "Your kind has no place in this market. This space is reserved for *my* enterprises. You cannot simply install yourself here, among your betters." He waved a pudgy finger at Evren's face. "I will be gracious enough to allow you to move your cart and get out of here. If not, I will be forced to summon the Indomitables to haul you away."

Evren's gut tightened. "Yeah, that's not happening." A part of him knew he was only making trouble for himself, but he had no desire to put up with this arrogant prick's tirade.

"Do not speak to your betters with such disrespect, *Kabili!*" The man raised a hand to slap him.

Evren's instincts, honed over years of bareknuckle boxing in the Master's Temple in Vothmot, kicked in before he realized it. He smacked aside the open-handed blow with contemptuous ease and brought his right hand around for a powerful cross punch right into the man's jaw.

The fat man reeled like a drunken sailor, hand clapped to his face. "You dare?!" His eyes flew wide as his round face purpled in anger. "You dare strike a *Dhukari,* slave?"

"I'm no slave," Evren spat back.

"Bareheaded wretch!" The man glared at Evren. "I will have you whipped in Murder Square as a lesson for any of you accursed *Kabili* that raises a hand to your betters."

Evren's gut clenched as he saw the flat-topped, spike-rimmed helms of a guard patrol moving through the crowd. *Keeper's teeth!*

The fat man saw them, too, and his eyes lit up. "Guards!" he shouted, his voice plaintive and shrill. "Guards! Arrest this slave for—"

Evren leapt forward and drove his fist into the man's face. The fat man sagged on wobbling legs and hit the ground with a jarring *thump*.

Evren whirled toward Hailen and held out a hand. "We need to go, now!" The fat man's plaintive cries had attracted the guards' attention.

Hailen jumped down and seized his hand. "Where?"

"Away from here!" Without hesitation, Evren darted into the crowd, dragging Hailen along behind him.

Years as a thief had trained Evren to slip through even the thickest throng with the speed of a serpent. The black-armored soldiers were coming from the west, but Evren knew the best way out of the marketplace was to the east. He ducked under a hanging roof, darted between stalls, and slithered around the press of people. The guards' shouts echoed behind him, but he left the armored men in the dust in seconds.

He just had to get out of the marketplace and back onto Trader's Way. From there, he'd have plenty of escape routes to choose from: up, down, or farther west.

To his dismay, another patrol was marching up from the Cultivator's Tier below. More guards stood at the entrance to the higher tier. No chance he'd have time to talk his way through those soldiers before his pursuers caught up.

His only way out was east, through the artisans' marketplace. He just had to avoid the jewelry stands with their sharp-eyed guards. Gripping Hailen's hand, he raced across Trader's Way and dove into the bustling traffic.

With Hailen in tow, he darted through the press of people, ducked beneath stall awnings, and squeezed through narrow gaps in the shops. He still retained the quick reflexes that had kept him alive on the streets of Vothmot, but his training with the Hunter had broadened his shoulders to the point that he found himself bowling people aside rather than slithering through them. That only made things worse; the shouts of angry, jostled shoppers would call the guards' attention.

He risked a glance over his shoulder and cursed as he spotted the spiked, flat-topped helms bobbing along behind him. He'd gained a few paces on the guards but he was a long way from outrunning them.

As he ran, he snatched a handful of scarves from the stalls he passed—a green one for Hailen, and red, blue, and brown for him. The guards were searching for a two bare-headed youths, but the headbands would give them cover. He just had to get Hailen out of sight long enough for the commotion to die down.

Luck turned against him as he snatched a white headband. "Thief!" the stall's owner shouted. "Runaway slave!"

Evren's heart sank. *No way I can go back through there now.* He'd just have to keep running farther west until he could find someplace to hole up.

He burst free of the press of people crowding the marketplace and raced up the broad avenue that spanned the longitude of Shalandra. An intersection stood twenty paces ahead, opening up onto a row of grain mills to the north and lumber mills to the south. Wood and wheat dust thickened the air as Evren ran past, but he could see nowhere to hide from the pursuing guards.

At the next intersection, the stink of potash and other foul tanning chemicals twisted Evren's nose and set his stomach churning. He raced on without hesitation. If he got that reek on him, the guards would be able to find him just by smelling him.

The third intersection offered him hope of concealment. The clangor of hammers and the reek of burning metal hung heavy. Smithies and forges *always* had darkened corners and storage rooms where a pair of fleeing thieves could hide.

"This way!" He hauled Hailen down the side street that led north.

He scanned the forges as he ran. The blacksmiths paid him no heed, but he had little doubt they'd raise a fuss if he entered their premises. To his horror, he saw the northern edge of the tier—a solid stone wall that rose nearly a hundred feet—looming closer. He was running out of somewhere to run, so he had to find a place to hide.

His heart leapt as he saw a brick wall a few dozen paces up the road. He had no idea what lay beyond, but the wall was short enough for him to scramble over yet tall enough to provide him concealment from his pursuers. Without hesitation, he raced toward it.

"Here!" He helped Hailen scramble up onto the wall, then pulled himself up after the younger boy. Relief flooded him as he saw an open expanse of dirt—some sort of courtyard, he guessed—at the rear of a smithy. Heart hammering, Evren tried to control his breathing as he listened for any signs of pursuit. If the guards had spotted them leaping over the wall, they'd be in trouble. He could only hope they'd been fast enough.

Something sharp pressed into his back, just between the discs of his spine. "Make any sudden moves," said a low, cold voice, "and you'll never walk again."

# *Chapter Sixteen*

Kodyn had to admit Shalandra was as breathtaking as Briana had said.

From the massive stone wall surrounding the city to the monolithic buildings of the uppermost tiers, it radiated a golden brilliance in the morning light. The towering cliffs to the east and west and the broad expanse of green pasture and wheat-heavy farmlands to the south served to frame the city's beauty.

Since they'd passed the shalanite mines hours earlier, Kodyn had felt the nervous excitement mounting within him. The reality of his situation had begun sinking in: he was about to enter a new, unfamiliar city, with no one but himself and Aisha to count on. He'd come hoping to do the impossible—steal the Crown of the Pharus and bring down the Gatherers that had kidnapped Briana—and now the scope of his task settled in his mind.

To prevent himself from feeling overwhelmed, he focused on studying the people flowing past him. Most wore simple skirt-like garments and tight-fitting dresses—*shendyts* and *kalasiris*—made of linen, wool, and cloth, but he'd seen more than a few people clad in elegant robes dyed bright blue, red, green, and black, threaded through with gold and silver strands. These were conveyed around on covered litters, boxes suspended from wooden poles carried by servants wearing simple clothing. According to Briana, their ornate gold headbands and headdresses marked them as *Dhukari*, the Shalandran equivalent of the nobility.

Briana had also schooled him and Aisha on the basics of life in Shalandra. Control of the city was divided in two—Pharus Amhoset Nephelcheres was the monarch and the final authority on all things legislative and judicial, while

Callista Vinaus, the Lady of Blades, served as the second ruler, commander of the Shalandran armed forces, the Indomitables that doubled as their army in times of war and law enforcement in time of peace.

The *true* power in Shalandra was the Keeper's Council—the six most powerful priests of the Necroseti, the servants of the Long Keeper, and Briana's father, Arch-Guardian Suroth of the Secret Keepers. The Keeper's Council propped the Pharus up as their figurehead while using their wealth and authority to manipulate the city to their whims.

The seven castes of Shalandra lived on five tiers: the *Kabili* and *Mahjuri* on the Slave's Tier, the *Earaqi* and foreigners on the Cultivator's Tier, the *Intaji* and *Zadii* on the Artisan's Tier, the *Alqati* on the Defender's Tier, and the *Dhukari* on the Keeper's Tier. Above them all, built into the highest point of the city, stood the Palace of Golden Eternity, home to the Pharus of Shalandra and the place where Kodyn would find the Crown of the Pharus. How he'd get there remained to be seen. His Undertaking began by returning Briana safely to her father's home on the Keeper's Tier.

The black-armored Indomitables at the gate reminded Kodyn of the Duke's Arbitors: a highly-trained fighting force that took its job seriously. Their spiked helmets and half-plate mail were meticulously cared for, their hooked sickle-swords well-oiled and sharpened to a razor edge.

One of the Indomitables, a man whose helmet bore two strips of silver in the blue band emblazoned on his forehead, snapped a smart salute to Ormroth. "Welcome home, *Ypertatos*."

According to Briana, the title of *Ypertatos* marked Ormroth as a higher-level member of the Keeper's Blades, with more than ten years of service under his belt. Not quite the highest echelon but certainly a well-respected figure.

"Sentinel Mahesh." Ormroth inclined his head.

The ranks in the Indomitables were similar to the martial ranks of the Praamian Guard: Executors were the Commanders, Protectors the Lieutenants, Dictators the Sergeants, and Neophytes the Privates. Mahesh's title of Sentinel proclaimed his rank the equivalent of Captain.

Mahesh bowed to the Blade's two companions and Briana. "Honored *Dhukari*. I trust the Long Keeper favored you in your travels." Mahesh's eyes roamed toward Kodyn and Aisha. "New offerings for Auctioneer's Square?"

"Traveling companions and guests," Ormroth corrected.

"Of course, *Ypertatos*." With a nod, the Sentinel stepped aside to make way for them. "May the Three Faces of Justice, Mercy, and Joy smile on you."

Ormroth led them through the gate, and Kodyn was struck by the immensity of the wall—fifty feet tall and thirty feet thick. *That crumbling thing we call the Praamian Wall has nothing on this.*

Through the gate, the road opened up onto a broad avenue. Death Row was a strange name for the one highway that ascended from the lowest tier to the Palace of Golden Eternity. *Then again, we are in a city that worships the Long Keeper, god of death.*

Death Row ran straight and flat for a few hundred paces before it was joined by the Way of Chains, the road that stretched east to west across the city. Most of the traffic leaving through the eastern gate went in the direction of the shalanite stone mines, though traders and the *Dhukari* traveling north to Praamis and Voramis preferred to use the gate—anything to keep them away from the west.

That was another of the strange things about Shalandra. The city's worship of the Long Keeper meant they treated death with far more reverence than the most superstitious Praamians.

Kodyn's gaze traveled toward the cliff face bordering the western side of Shalandra. He was too far away to see the arched entrances Briana had spoken of, but he could imagine them. Unlike the eastern cliff, the mountain to the west was hollowed out, the space within serving as the final resting place of dead Shalandrans. The city had earned its name "City of the Dead" because of its treatment of their deceased.

Rich Shalandrans spent a fortune to carve ornate tombs and crypts out of the golden sandstone of the mountain. Poorer citizens tried to scrape together enough coin to hire an artisan to craft a simple resting place. No casket burials or funeral pyres here—people went to the Long Keeper's embrace surrounded by solid stone. Some low-caste citizens spent their entire lives saving up for their deaths.

Kodyn glanced at Aisha and found her eyes fixed in the same direction. Her face had taken on that same strange look she'd gotten every time she glanced at Ormroth's sword. Kodyn didn't understand it—he had no idea what was happening with the Ghandian girl—but he hadn't had a chance to ask

Aisha about it. The last few days of their journey had been consumed by Briana, Ormroth, and the two *Dhukari* filling them in on details of life in Shalandra.

As they approached the Way of Chains, the sound of shouts and cries reached Kodyn's ears. He tensed, hand dropping to his sword. Yet after a moment, he realized they weren't cries of pain. Instead, it was the loud patter of an auctioneer shouting out his wares.

Anger burned within Kodyn's chest as he saw what was on the selling block: a short, stocky young man, roughly the same age as him but with the golden bronze skin of a Shalandran. Chains hung from his wrists and neck, and a thick iron band encircled his throat. The slave's chest was as bare as his head. He wore only a loincloth, his muscles on display like a painting in a nobleman's mansion.

A crowd gathered around the auctioneer's platform—men and women wearing headbands of every color, clad in robes ranging from priestly drapes to *Dhukari* silks. They shouted, jostled, and hurled insults at each other, the auctioneer, and the slave.

Fury set Kodyn's hands trembling so hard he had to grip his sword to still them. His eyes wandered across the open-air plaza—Auctioneer's Square, Briana had called it. Nearly twenty such platforms dotted the space, each holding an auctioneer and his human wares. Slaves—not only Shalandrans, but men, women, and children from Malandria, Praamis, Voramis, Nysl, Drash, Ghandia, Vothmot, and even blonde-haired Fehlans from across the Frozen Sea—stood chained to the huge stone pillars that dotted the square.

An image flashed through his mind: Aisha, his friend and companion, or Ria, his mother, shackled and on sale before the vile men and women crowding Auctioneer's Square. The thought only fanned the flames of his rage.

He whirled on Briana. "You have slaves here?" The words came out in a low, angry hiss.

"Yes." Briana spoke as if it was no great deal—to someone who'd grown up in such a society, slavery had to be the most commonplace thing. "Who does all the heavy labor in your city?"

"Servants, but they earn a wage for their work." Outrage laced his tone; hearing the stories of Ria and Aisha's captivity by the Bloody Hand had filled him with a strong hatred of slavery.

"So do the *Kabili*." Briana seemed surprised by Kodyn's reaction. "The Chained Ones offer themselves up in service to the city for seven, fourteen, or forty-nine years. They are needed to mine the ore used to make Shalandran steel and quarry the shalanite stone. When their term ends, the Pharus pays them fair wages. Those who serve for the life term, all forty-nine years, are elevated to *Intaji*. It is the only way many *Earaqi* and *Mahjuri* can raise their status or that of their descendants."

During their journey, Briana had explained the seven castes of Shalandra, from the wretched *Mahjuri* to the martial *Alqati* to the *Dhukari*, the Shalandran equivalent of Praamian nobility. The concept of such a rigidly structured society struck him as strange. Worse, it seemed the people of Shalandra actually *allowed* themselves to be limited by something as arbitrary as their castes.

In Praamis, anyone with enough gold could purchase a patent of nobility. Only a select few, the families of Old Praamis, would actually wield any power in King Ohilmos' Royal Council, but even the poorest Praamian could dream of being a lord or lady.

Not so in Shalandra. People were born, lived, and died in the same caste, with only the barest hope of elevating their status or that of their children and grandchildren. Intermarriage between the higher castes was almost nonexistent, considered taboo. Those born to the wrong parents were condemned to a life of abjection and misery.

*Maybe that's why these low-caste people are so angry,* Kodyn thought.

Tension simmered beneath the surface of the lower-caste men and women they passed. Quiet, barely discernible, yet deep-rooted and burning hot within the people. Angry glares followed them on their way, most directed at the three wearing the elegant golden headbands of the *Dhukari*, but more than a few aimed at Ormroth. When a patrol of black-armored Indomitables marched past, the low-caste populace gave way with reluctance. A few young men wearing red headbands—marking them as *Earaqi*, the laborer caste—waited until the last second to clear the road, a subtly taunting defiance. The same men spat toward the retreating backs of the guards.

The Indomitables were Shalandra's equivalent of the Praamian Guard combined with Voramis' standing army, the Legion of Heroes. They had proven instrumental in the Eirdkilr Wars fought on the continent of Fehl. Yet that war had ended decades earlier. The ten thousand soldiers sent off to slay savage barbarians had returned home to a city gripped by peace. With no war to fight, no loot to bring home to enrich the Pharus' coffers, they had begun to strain the city's resources.

Worse, there were simply too many of them, far more than needed to maintain order in the city. Bored soldiers with no enemy to face often sought excitement and battle in their own homes. The populace of Shalandra had suffered for that boredom.

The *Earaqi* youths muttered among themselves for a few minutes, then turned and hurried away with furtive glances at the Indomitables. They paused beside a wall and each in turn pressed two fingers to the words painted there before moving on.

*Child of Gold*, Kodyn read. *I wonder what that means.*

His curiosity mounted when he saw those same words painted onto four walls—not only in the Slave's Tier, but on the neat, whitewashed walls of the Cultivator's Tier as well. Once, he could write it off as nothing more than the sort of defacement common among the poorer sections of cities like Praamis and Shalandra. Yet seeing that strange gesture from the young men and the repetitions, he knew it wasn't simple graffiti. He resolved to ask Briana later.

The crowds grew thick as they reached the Artisan's Tier, but people gave way before Ormroth's huge warhorse—not graciously, to be certain, most with a muttered curse and a glare. Yet only fools would hold their ground in the face of the heavily-armored Keeper's Blade riding a black charger large enough to crush them beneath its hooves.

The guards at the gate to the Defender's Tier bowed to Ormroth, Briana, and the *Dhukari* and stepped aside to let them enter. Kodyn immediately noticed the differences between the fourth tier and those below it.

The Defender's Tier was home to the Indomitables and their families. Most of the houses stood two or three stories tall, many with gardens filled the streets with color and life. The people on this tier were soldiers, trained for war, with the hard eyes and grim faces that marked their profession. The majority had seen battle during the Eirdkilr Wars and bore the scars—of mind and body—to prove it.

The guards holding the gate to the Keeper's Tier let them through, but Kodyn felt their eyes on him and Aisha. If he hadn't been in the company of Briana, the *Dhukari*, and the Keeper's Blade, he was certain they would have been denied entrance.

With good reason. He let out a low whistle as his gaze roamed the easternmost mansions on the Keeper's Tier. Though not as tall as the six and seven-story mansions of The Gardens or Old Praamis, they covered a far broader surface area—some twice as vast as the sprawling estates of the wealthiest Praamians. Marble and granite accented the golden sandstone, giving everything an air of timeless solidity and incalculable wealth.

The Hall of the Beyond, the massive temple to the Long Keeper, dominated the center of the Keeper's Tier, rivaled only by the Palace of Golden Eternity above it. Kodyn had caught a glimpse of a fortress carved out of the stone of the western cliff face—the Citadel of Stone, home to the Keeper's Blades.

Death Row soon intersected with the Path of Gold, the east-west running highway on the Keeper's Tier. There, Ormroth led them east, toward the largest, most opulent mansions on the highest level. The farther west one traveled, the smaller and simpler the mansions. Though, compared to the dwellings on the lower tiers, there was nothing "small" or "simple" about them.

Kodyn's jaw dropped as Ormroth rode toward a three-story mansion on the southern side of the Keeper's Tier. High golden walls ringed the property, and guards wearing gilded breastplates stood watch at the front gate.

Kodyn couldn't help gaping. "That's *yours?*"

Briana smiled. "My father's, but yes."

"Watcher's teeth!" Kodyn whistled. "That's fancier than half the mansions in Old Praamis."

"Is it?" Briana seemed to find his surprise curious. "I guess I never really noticed."

"Never noticed?" Kodyn shot her an incredulous look. "You live in a palace. How could you *not* notice?"

"It is nothing compared to the splendor of the Pharus' palace," Briana said.

"Damn!" Kodyn breathed. He suddenly saw the Shalandran girl in a new light.

Secret Keepers served the Mistress, goddess of trysts and whispered truths. From his experience, the brown-robed priests were silent, enigmatic men and women that spent their lives holed up in the Temple of Whispers. The stories his mother had told him about their massive underground vaults and storage chambers made them sound like collectors of rare and exotic items, seekers of knowledge, and alchemists like the Journeymen of House Scorpion.

Yet this screamed of luxury and opulence that every Praamian noble would envy. He'd known that her father, Arch-Guardian Suroth, was the highest-ranking Secret Keeper in Shalandra and a member of the Keeper's Council. It finally sank in just what that meant.

"Damn!" he said again.

Despite his surprise, he couldn't help feeling a sense of validation. He'd been correct to return Briana home—not only because reuniting father and daughter was the right thing to do, but because the man who owned a mansion like this *had* to have the sort of connections that could get Kodyn close enough to steal the Crown of the Pharus.

At the sight of Briana, the guards hurried to open the gate for them. Kodyn's incredulity mounted as they rode through the gate into the mansion grounds.

A broad walkway of gold-and-silver tiles was flanked by expansive lawns of meticulous green grass. To the east, in the shadow of the cliff, Kodyn caught a glimpse of smaller buildings—likely stables and all the other additional structures required by a noble household. He guessed the back entrance to the kitchens would be somewhere along the northeastern perimeter of the property.

But the mansion itself was a true masterpiece. Golden pylons carved from sandstone supported arches featuring ornate carvings—images of Shalandra's history were depicted across the face of the three-story building, intersected by decorative whorls that resembled animals, constellations, flowers, trees, and a thousand more pictorials. The construction was almost a perfect rectangle, with sharp corners and perfectly straight lines that would make any Praamian carpenter envious. Yet it hadn't been built, but carved from the mountain's stone.

The double doors at the front of the mansion flew open and a grey-haired woman hurried out to greet them. "Greetings, *Ypertatos,*" she said with a bow that showed no trace of stiffness or discomfort despite her advanced age.

The woman wore an ornate headband of white silk woven with bright peacock feathers on her forehead, her dress a mid-calf-length sheath of white and gold linen suspended by twin white leather straps. Dark lines rimmed her eyes and four black beauty marks dotted her face—another mark of caste, according to Briana. Her voice held the strength of one accustomed to command, yet the humility of a servant greeting honored guests. Kodyn guessed she'd be the Shalandran equivalent of a nobleman's majordomo.

"Honored *Dhukari*, I bid you welcome to the house of–" Her voice trailed off and her dark eyes flew wide as her gaze rested on Briana. A hand flew to her mouth. "Keeper's mercy!"

"It's me, Nessa." Briana's voice was thick with emotion. She scrambled down from her saddle and raced toward the woman. "I'm home."

"Briana!" Nessa threw her arms wide and pulled Briana into a tight embrace. "The Keeper has answered our prayers." Tears streamed down her wrinkled cheeks and she buried her face in Briana's hair, pressing kisses to the top of her head.

Kodyn smiled at the sight. A lump rose to his throat as a memory flashed through his mind: *running toward his mother, being scooped into her strong arms and crushed against her chest. Her tears hot on his face as he threw his arms around her neck. "I knew you'd find us, Mama!"*

Even now, eleven years later, that was a memory he cherished. The memory of being reunited with the mother he'd believed dead in the fire that had burned down their home.

"Thank you, *Ypertatos!*" Nessa ran toward the mounted Blade and pressed her forehead to his foot. "You will have the Arch-Guardian's undying gratitude for rescuing his adoptive daughter."

The word caught Kodyn by surprise. *Briana didn't say anything about being adopted.*

"I am not deserving of thanks, Steward." Ormroth shook his head and gestured to Kodyn and Aisha. "It is these brave warriors that rescued Lady Briana. It was simply the Long Keeper's good fortune that brought us together on the road south."

Nessa turned toward Kodyn and Aisha and surprise registered on her face. It disappeared a moment later as she hurried toward them. "Please, be welcome in the home of Arch-Guardian Suroth. He will want to hear everything."

"Is he here?" Hope tinged Briana's words.

Nessa nodded. "He's in his garden. Go to him. I will see to your companions."

Briana raced into the house, her blue woolen dress flying, hair streaming behind her.

"With your permission," Ormroth said, turning his horse toward the front gate, "we have urgent business elsewhere."

"Of course." Nessa bowed again to the Blade and the two well-dressed *Dhukari*. "May the Long Keeper smile on all of you."

"And you, revered *eema*." Ormroth glanced up at Kodyn and Aisha. "I hope the next time our paths cross, it is under more pleasant circumstances."

"Thank you," Kodyn said with a nod. "Things could have grown ugly if you hadn't showed up when you did." He moved his horse closer to the Keeper's Blade and held out a hand. "I owe you one."

"It is my duty." Ormroth gripped Kodyn's hand with a small smile. "But perhaps there may come a day when you will have a chance to aid another in need. Consider that my repayment."

"As you say." Kodyn inclined his head.

With a farewell salute to Aisha, Ormroth rode away from the mansion, his *Dhukari* charges a few paces behind.

"Please," said Nessa once the *clopping* of horses' hooves had faded into the dull hum of the street outside, "my people will see to your mounts and gear. Allow me to take you to the Arch-Guardian at once. He will want to show his gratitude in person."

Kodyn exchanged a glance with Aisha, who shrugged and nodded. Together, they dismounted and followed Nessa into the house.

The interior was even more opulent than the exterior. Platinum and silver filigree illustrated marvelous patterns on the golden sandstone walls, with yellow-and-white marble tiles on the floor. Carpets and rugs from distant Al Hani added bright splashes of color, with oak and bloodwood furniture standing silent testament to the wealth of Briana's father.

The mansion opened onto a broad hall, which was joined by another short corridor that led into a dining hall and a staircase. Kodyn caught a glimpse of a blue dress disappearing through the arched doorway at the top of the stairs and smiled as he followed the Steward to the second floor. Ornate tapestries and bright paintings hung on the walls, and three corridors led to additional rooms on the western, eastern, and southern wings of the mansion.

But Nessa led them up the stairs to the third floor. *No, not the third floor, but a rooftop*, Kodyn saw. *A rooftop garden.*

He followed Nessa along the marble walkway that led through the garden, marveling at the green life around him. He recognized perhaps three or four of the plants—a creeping ivy here, a fern there. The rest he'd never seen in his life. Flowers with petals of bright purple or flaming orange. Bushes laden with berries of a blue as light as the sky or fruits of a brilliant yellow. Trees that drooped like weeping willows, yet held the soft pink petals of a Voramian Snowblossom. Such exotic flora that shouldn't exist on the third floor of a stone-carved mansion, yet there was no denying the view before him.

In the heart of the garden stood a stone gazebo with a gently-curving domed roof. There, a happy sight greeted Kodyn. An older man clad in the simple brown skirt of a Secret Keeper had his arms wrapped around Briana, an enormous smile on his face and tears of joy streaming down his cheeks. Briana held him tight, face buried in his chest.

When they broke off the embrace, the Secret Keeper's hands flashed in those strange, silent hand signs far too fast for Kodyn to understand. Briana's fingers flew as well, and Kodyn recognized the sequence of gestures that spelled out his name, Aisha's, and the city of Praamis. The Arch-Guardian's face hardened as Briana continued what Kodyn assumed was the story of her captivity at the hands of the death-worshipping Gatherers. He'd spent the last eight days of their journey learning the sign language, enough to communicate clearly, even some of the more complex concepts and words. Yet there was no way he could keep up with the intricate dance of flashing hands and silent signs.

Kodyn and Aisha waited in silence as long minutes passed in this unusual communication. Finally, Arch-Guardian Suroth turned to face him for the first time. He had the same oval face, almond-colored eyes, and thick nose as Briana, though his jaw was more pronounced, the edges of his cheekbones and nasal bridge sharpened by his dark eyeliner and six black dots. To Kodyn's surprise, the Secret Keeper's bare chest rippled as he moved and his shoulders were broad, his abdomen free of paunch. Thick bands of muscle corded his forearms and his hands bore calluses rather than ink stains.

"Thank you," the Arch-Guardian's strong fingers said, albeit at a far slower pace than his conversation with Briana, "*both of you, for bringing my Briana home to me."* His right arm went around his daughter's shoulder and pulled her tight against him once more. "*When I first found her missing, I thought—*"

"Hush, Father." Briana laid her head against her father's chest. "I am home now. That is all that matters."

"*I wish it were so.*" The Arch-Guardian's face grew somber. "*I fear your return may only make things worse.*"

# Chapter Seventeen

The Arch-Guardian's statement caught Aisha by surprise. "Worse?"

Suroth exchanged a glance with Briana.

*"They know everything, Father,"* the girl's fingers said. *"They can be trusted."*

After a moment, the priest let out a slow breath. *"A lifetime's habit of keeping secrets is not easy to break."* His lips quirked into a wry grin and he tweaked Briana's cheek affectionately. *"A habit my daughter has not yet mastered."*

Briana swatted at her father's hand. "Stop that!" she said aloud.

Arch-Guardian Suroth smiled, but his expression quickly sobered. *"So Briana has told you of the reason she was taken?"*

Kodyn nodded. "The priest, Necroset Kytos, took her so they could have leverage on you."

*"That is half-correct."* Suroth frowned. *"Kytos was a member of the Necroseti, a priest of the Long Keeper. Until he was Purged six months ago."*

"Purged?" Kodyn cocked his head. "You mean they kicked him out of the priesthood? What for?"

*"My sources among the Necroseti have remained silent on that,"* the priest replied in the silent hand language. *"But it is whispered that he had joined the Gatherers in their strange worship."*

"He was the leader of the Gatherers in Praamis," Aisha confirmed.

Suroth's expression darkened. *"If those rumors are true, then our situation is dire, indeed."* He pursed his lips. *"When Briana was first taken, I received a message saying that if I did not follow the instructions I was given, she would die. Though it bore no name, I knew it had come from within the Necroseti. As I waited for the next message and the instructions of what they wanted from me, I set my contacts within the Keeper's priesthood to find out what had happened. No one in the priesthood seemed to know, and when no instructions followed, I feared the worst."* He squeezed Briana's shoulder with a strong hand, as if confirming that she really was standing beside him.

"*But if Briana was taken by the Gatherers, it would explain the silence.*" His expression grew grim. "*The Necroseti had her abducted to use against me, but somehow she fell into the hands of Kytos and his cultists.*"

"Which could be why he came to Praamis." Kodyn exchanged a glance with Aisha.

The same thought had just occurred to her. "If the Gatherers stole her from the priests, they'd want to get her far enough away that they couldn't just snatch her back."

Briana's face had gone pale. Aisha felt a momentary stab of pity for the girl. Briana's captivity hadn't been kind, and though the girl had recovered some, it would take far longer than a few weeks for her to recover. Aisha herself still struggled to deal with the aftermath of her own enslavement by the Bloody Hand. She'd spent much of it in a mind-numbed fog induced by Bonedust, a powerful narcotic, so she remembered little of the ordeal. Yet those few memories she retained were vivid enough to wake her up at night. The physical scars might have healed, but emotional and mental scars took longer.

"*But now that she has returned,*" Suroth continued, "*the Necroseti will learn of her presence. They have eyes and ears everywhere in this city. Even in my own household.*" He turned a sorrowful gaze on Briana. "*I believe Eldesse aided in your abduction.*"

"E-Eldesse?" Briana's face went white.

Suroth nodded. "*She, along with two others, is still missing. Four more have been found dead.*"

Briana clapped a hand to her mouth. "But she-she wasn't just my maidservant. She was my friend!" Tears filled her eyes. "Since I was a little girl…"

"*Which made the betrayal all the more surprising.*" Suroth pulled Briana close. "*Yet, the fact that she disappeared the same night you were taken proves beyond a doubt that she was a pawn of the Keeper's Priests. And not the only one, I am certain.*"

"So you're worried that these Necroseti priests are going to try to take Briana again?" Kodyn asked.

*"I would not put it past them."* Suroth's lip curled into a disgusted grimace. *"They have done far worse to others of the Dhukari, though this is the first time that I know they have moved against a member of the Keeper's Council. I am the only member not of the Necroseti, and I am outside their control. I have no doubt they would use my only child against me, even though I have convinced the world that she is only my* adoptive *daughter."*

Aisha's brow furrowed. She'd noticed when Nessa emphasized the word "adopted" upon their arrival. "Why the ruse?" she asked. "Why is it important that she is not your child by blood?" By Kodyn's curious expression, she could tell he'd been wondering the same.

*"Secret Keepers are not permitted to bear children."* The Arch-Guardian shook his head. *"The Temple of Whispers can guard the secret of her heritage, but if it became known around Shalandra that Briana was my daughter by birth, it would eventually leak out to the other cities and the other Secret Keepers around Einan. My friends here in Shalandra might be able to overlook it, but the rest of my order would see it as a violation of our sacred oath to the Mistress."* His expression grew solemn. *"Which, truth be told, it is. Yet, even though it took my beloved wife from me, I have never once regretted my decision."*

He pulled Briana tight and held her for a long moment. When he broke off the embrace, moisture filled his eyes. Aisha pretended not to notice as he wiped his cheeks.

*"For the sake of my daughter, I must not be her father by blood,"* Suroth signed. *"Yet that will not stop the Keeper's priests from trying to use her against me. If they have inserted more spies into my household, they will receive word of Briana's return before the day is out. I fear they will come for her again."*

"Don't you have guards?" Kodyn asked. "People you can trust to protect her?"

*"Until Eldesse, I would have said yes."* Suroth's face grew grim. *"Yet Eldesse's husband, one of the highest-ranking members of my household guard, also played accomplice in Briana's abduction. I can trust Nessa and a few select staff, as well as Rothin, the head of my guard. As for the others..."* He shook his head. *"I have tried my best to inspire loyalty in the Intaji, Zadii, Kabili, and Earaqi that serve me, but the Necroseti's coffers are far deeper than my own."*

The answer struck Aisha like a bolt of lightning to the forehead. "We'll protect her."

Kodyn turned to her, his expression curious. Suroth and Briana's eyes widened—the expressions accented the startling similarities in their features.

"*You?*" Suroth signed.

"Yes, us." Aisha gestured to her *assegai*, strapped to her back, and the sword hanging at Kodyn's hip. "We're more than capable of protecting her if it comes to a fight." She met the Secret Keeper's gaze steadily. "And, most important of all, you can be damned certain that we're not Necroseti spies. Which is a lot more than you can say for most of the people around you."

"*You are clearly not Shalandrans.*" Suroth frowned. "*You, perhaps, could pass for one of us, with the right clothing. As for him.*" He gestured to Kodyn. "*He will stand out like a behemoth in a poppy field.*"

"Is that a problem?" Aisha couldn't help grinning at the comparison. "Is it so uncommon for Shalandrans to hire outside protection?"

"*Uncommon, yes.*" Suroth nodded. "*Unheard of, no. He will draw plenty of attention, that much is certain.*"

"Aisha, can I talk to you for a moment?" Kodyn asked, a pointed look in his eyes.

Aisha followed him a short distance into the garden, away from the gazebo and out of earshot of Arch-Guardian Suroth and Briana, who had begun an animated conversation of dancing fingers.

"We're here for a very *specific* reason," Kodyn told her. "I'm here for the crown, and you're here for…" He trailed off. Evidently Ria hadn't told him her *true* purpose for coming. "Then there's the matter of the Gatherers. I promised my mother we'd make sure they don't come back. It's going to be hard to do all of that if we're playing bodyguard day and night."

"We can do that. All of it." Aisha told him. "And keep Briana safe at the same time."

Kodyn snorted. "Seems a tall order!"

Aisha cocked an eyebrow. "Not up for the challenge?"

Kodyn glared. "It's not that. It's—"

"Listen, you've got almost a year to complete your Undertaking," Aisha insisted. "More than enough time, even for such a tall order as sneaking into the palace and stealing the Crown of the Pharus."

Kodyn's eyes darted around, nervous that someone would overhear them.

"But you know as well as I that the Arch-Guardian is the best one to get you in the right place to get your hands on that crown." Aisha fixed him with a meaningful glance. "And I'd say there are few people better-suited to helping us dig up the secrets of the Gatherers than a Secret Keeper. You heard him talk about his 'contacts within the Keeper's priesthood'. He's one of the most powerful people in the city, and we've got the perfect way to get in his good graces. This is the best way to get what we came here for!"

Kodyn's expression grew pensive. She recognized the stubbornness in his eyes—she'd seen its match during her few encounters with Ilanna, Kodyn's mother and Master of the Night Guild. Yet, as Ria had always emphasized, even the most stubborn person—mother and son—could be convinced to see reason with the right approach.

After a long moment, Kodyn nodded. "You're right. It *is* our best play."

"We can make it work," Aisha told him. "We always knew Briana was our way into the palace. Now, with her father on our side, you've got a real shot of actually pulling off the crown job."

"The way you say it almost makes it sound like you doubted me." A shred of hurt seeped into Kodyn's voice and eyes.

"There's a difference between doubt and common sense." Aisha grinned, but Kodyn didn't return the smile. "I've known you long enough to know that once you set your mind to something, you'll do it. But figuring out *how* to do it is the tricky part, the part that a lot of people don't get right. Now, with the Arch-Guardian's help, we're closer to sorting out the *how* than we were when we left Praamis."

Her words seemed to mollify Kodyn, and his frown faded. "So be it. Looks like we're going to play bodyguard."

Together, they strode back to where Arch-Guardian Suroth and Briana stood.

"We'll do it," Aisha said. "We'll keep your daughter safe."

Suroth's expression darkened to a grim, glowering anger as his fingers signed, *"And why in the Mistress' holy name should I trust you, two thieves, that have come here to steal the Crown of the Pharus?"*

# *Chapter Eighteen*

"This is bloody insane!"

Issa couldn't argue with the trainee's assessment. *These odds are damned impossible!* She and her ten Indomitables-in-training faced nearly five times their number across the training yard. *Another of Tannard's little "lessons".*

Her first week as a *prototopoi* had been a blur of beatings, torments, and humiliations under the *Invictus'* stern gaze. The *Igogi,* the rigorous training regimen that turned raw recruits into disciplined Keeper's Blades, had been made even more challenging by Tannard's determination to break her body and spirit.

The *Invictus* awoke her a full hour before the other trainers roused Kellas and Etai from slumber. By the time they emerged into the training yard, Issa had already been running in full gear for an hour. The *clanking* of their armor as they ran laps distracted her from her meditation, making the brutally challenging task of standing one-legged on a wooden fence post all but impossible.

Breakfast was the closest she came to a moment's peace, but a moment was all she had. Tannard gave her less than five minutes to devour her meal before sending her off to her lectures with *Invictus* Dyrkton, one of the Elders of the Blades. There, she had an hour to absorb as much of the history of Shalandra and the Keeper's Blades as possible—the punishment for failing the *Invictus'* test ranged from beatings to another half-hour run in full gear.

Combat practice and battle training occupied the rest of her morning. Inevitably, Issa found herself at a disadvantage, often facing two or three times the number of opponents, sometimes with inferior weaponry and handicaps imposed on her by Tannard.

The meager lunch of rough-ground grain flatbread and watery soup barely quenched her hunger and failed to give her the energy required to muscle through the intense hour of strength training that followed. By the time she got through her afternoon lessons of statecraft, survival skills, herbology, or ethics—all vital for a Keeper's Blade, according to *Invictus* Tannard—her stomach would be in knots and she'd barely manage to choke down another meal of hard bread and soup, this time accompanied by a single strip of salted meat.

Dinner gave way to sparring sessions. She faced her enemies empty-handed, with daggers to their two-handed swords, or, on those rare occasions when Tannard allowed her the use of her flammard, pitted against two or three *Archateros* under strict orders to show her no mercy. By the time the sun set, she was too tired to do more than collapse into bed. She'd be roused less than half an hour later for the evening task of stealing treats, food, and trinkets hidden in the rooms of the older, more experienced Blades. Failure, as ever, was rewarded with a beating.

Yet the sort of beating she'd take today would far exceed her usual punishment. Worse, the ten Indomitable trainees would suffer with her.

"The object is simple," *Invictus* Tannard rumbled. He thrust a finger toward a bright blue pendant that hung at the far end of the training yard. "The trumpet rings the moment you claim the flag. That sound means victory is yours. Fight until you hear it or you can fight no longer."

Issa stifled a snort. *Easier said than done.* Four battle lines—six wide and two deep—stood between her company and their objective. The enemy wore heavy Indomitable armor while those with Issa wore only padded jerkins. She and her Indomitables—six young women, with four men barely into their mid-teens—carried wooden batons and shields but faced steel swords.

"A Keeper's Blade must always be prepared to face the impossible." The *Invictus'* voice was hard, cold. "A servant of death should know no fear, even against insurmountable odds. If the Long Keeper has marked you, the largest army on Einan will not stop you from dying. Until that day, you are invincible."

Issa had one consolation: the steel swords had no edges. She and her company of trainees wouldn't be hacked to pieces by sharp blades. Death by bludgeoning was still very much a potential outcome.

*Eleven of us against forty-eight of them,* Issa thought. *How in the Keeper's name are we going to do this?*

If she charged in a sharp-tipped spear formation, she might actually punch through the first, even second battle line. But she'd get bogged down at the third line, then quickly surrounded and slaughtered. She'd fail before reaching the halfway mark.

Her mind raced. She couldn't win this with brute strength or superior skill. This was a time to outthink rather than outfight the enemy.

She studied the ten trainees assigned to her. All smaller than their enemies, weaker, doubtless far less skilled. Yet Killian's words, the words that had carried her to victory in the Crucible, echoed in her mind.

*"Always make your enemy underestimate you. Make them see you as nothing but an Earaqi girl until you're ready to spring your trap."*

She wasn't the only low-caste warrior in their company. All of those assigned to her wore *Earaqi* red or *Mahjuri* black, with only one white *Zadii* headband. None of them would have the extensive martial training common in the Academies. Instead, they'd know the brutal, efficient tactics—little more than street fighting with bladed weapons—taught at the Institutes of the Seven Faces. That, and any skills they'd picked up during their years roaming the streets of the lower tiers.

"They know there's no way we're getting through," Issa told her company, "but with the *Invictus* watching, they know we're going to have to try. So we'll give them what they want. We're going right through the middle, spear formation."

"Fastest way to get killed!" snorted one of the young men, a *Mahjuri* by the name of Nysin. "We'll get through one, maybe two lines before our momentum runs out."

Issa nodded. "Exactly." Nysin had come to the same conclusion as her; he might have a better understanding of tactics and strategy than the others. "But we're not going to try to cut our way through to the pennant. We're not going to fight like the *Dhukari* and *Alqati* we face. We're doing this street-style."

She looked at each of them in turn. "Which of you is the fastest runner?"

Two of the *Earaqi* girls exchanged glances. The taller, a slender young woman by the name of Rilith, pointed to the other. "Enyera, probably."

"Good." Issa turned to the shorter of the two. "I want you at the rear of our position and ready to run like your life depends on it."

"I can do that." Enyera, a short girl just on the well-built side of petite, raised an eyebrow. "But there's no way I can get around four lines."

"Think you can get around two?" Issa asked. "No shield or armor to weigh you down, just that club to defend yourself?"

Enyera glanced down at the truncheon in her hand, her expression skeptical. After a moment, she shrugged. "I suppose we'll find out."

"Then watch for your opening. There will be a moment after we get bogged down, before they surround us, that you'll have a gap to slip through. If we can punch through to the third line before they stop us dead, you've just got one line to get around. That fourth line may be so focused on moving forward to encircle us that they won't notice you skirting the third line. You're our best chance of getting that pennant."

Enyera's lips tugged upward. "I'll do what I can."

"As for the rest of us," Issa turned to the other nine trainees, "it's our job to hit them with everything we've got and keep their attention on us long enough for Enyera to get through. It's going to be brutal, but if there's one thing we can do, it's take a beating!"

She saw agreement etched into the eyes of her company. The *Mahjuri* had it worst of all, but life as an *Earaqi* was hard, often more so than the *Kabili* that served in Shalandra's mines. Judging by the scars crisscrossing the *Intaji* youth's hands, he knew the meaning of toil and suffering. The well-fed, well-dressed, pampered youths of the *Dhukari* were soft. Even the *Alqati* lived comfortable lives by comparison to the lower castes. The *Invictus* had done her a favor when choosing her company.

"For the first time in our lives, we're not only *permitted* to strike a member of the upper caste, we're required to." A savage grin split Issa's face and she spoke in a low growl. "Make them hurt."

Answering smiles blossomed on the faces of her company. Rilith even laughed as she hefted her baton. "With pleasure."

"Spear formation," Issa called. "Hit them hard and don't stop until we're through to the third line."

Her company formed up, and Issa's gut tightened as she took her place at the tip of the spear.

She tightened her grip on her two wooden batons—Tannard's idea of magnanimity—and rolled her shoulders in anticipation. Her eyes darted toward the *Invictus*, who stood watching from the sidelines.

*You won't break me,* she swore silently. *Throw everyone in Shalandra at me. It won't stop me.*

With a deep breath, she raised her right-handed weapon and shouted, "Charge!"

She raced toward the enemy, her small company thundering on her heels. Her long legs carried her across the cleared space in a matter of seconds and, with a roar, she slammed into the front rank of trainees.

Her wooden batons flashed out to block a high chop and a thrust from the two combatants in front of her. Her momentum carried her through the first rank, then the second, but she had enough time to lash out with powerful blows of her truncheons. Wood struck flesh with dull *thumps* and two of the enemies sagged, only to be knocked aside by the trainees charging behind Issa.

*First line!*

Triumph surged within her chest as she pounded the five yards toward the second battle line. She poured as much speed into her legs as she could manage and crashed into her enemies with the force of a runaway carriage rolling down Trader's Way. She grunted as a dulled steel blade clipped the side of her head, another striking off her collar bone with jarring force. Her answering blows smacked into the skull and forearm of the enemies in front of her. She winced at the *crack* of bone but had no time for pity. Even as the blunt steel sword dropped from her enemy's hand, she hurled her right-handed truncheon at another foe and scooped up the falling blade before it struck the sand.

Then she was through the second line and racing toward the third. She heard cries of pain from behind her, but the boots of her comrades pounded along to her right and left. Shouting her defiance, Issa raised her sword and brought it down hard onto the blade of the young *Alqati* man directly in front of her. The blow battered through his defenses and slammed into the side of his head. He sagged on wobbling legs, stunned.

Issa's triumph turned to defeat in that moment. The staggering youth stumbled forward, right into her. She caught him and hurled him aside before he could lock arms blindly around her, but that moment cost her dearly. Her charge slowed, momentum gone, and now she faced a full line of twelve armored Indomitables wielding steel swords.

"Now!" She could only hope Enyera caught the command as her signal, but she had no time to look back. Three opponents surged toward her, steel blades singing in the bright morning air.

Issa batted aside the first two strikes with quick parries, but the third slipped through her guard and struck her chest hard enough to send pain flaring down her breastbone. The blow knocked her back a half-step and, before she could recover, two more attacks struck her right leg and left forearm. Her truncheon dropped from nerveless fingers.

Issa gritted her teeth against a cry of pain. She whipped her sword up and around to deflect a powerful strike aimed at her head, but that exposed her stomach to a low, horizontal chop. She doubled over as the blow knocked the breath from her lungs. Desperate, she lashed out in an attempt to drive back her enemy.

But there were too many—in front, behind, and now closing in from their flanks. Her company would be overrun in seconds. If Enyera didn't reach the pennant now, she and her trainees would fall.

The clash of steel, the *thump* of wood striking flesh, and the grunts of fighting men echoed loud in Issa's ears, but no trumpet to signal the halt of battle.

Then Kellas was there, *kohl*-rimmed eyes locked on her, an arrogant sneer on his lips as he raised his two-handed sword to strike. Issa blocked his attack, even though it opened her up to another blow from the side—she'd be damned if she let the *Dhukari* hit her even once.

A blow to her leg nearly shattered her knee and she sagged, crying out in pain. She tried to block the follow-up strike, only to take a slashing strike across her right forearm. The dull blade opened a deep gash and blood dripped down her elbow to her shoulder.

She fought through the pain, through the knowledge that her comrades were falling behind her. She couldn't tear her eyes from the fight to track

Enyera's movement. All she could do was just hold the enemy off until the trumpet sounded.

Three blows struck at once, to her back, neck, and the top of her skull. Issa toppled forward and crashed to the sand face first. Darkness reached cool, welcoming fingers toward her.

*Where is the trumpet?*

It never came.

## Chapter Nineteen

Evren went rigid, motionless.

"If you're hiding from the Indomitables," said the cold voice, "well that means you've done something wrong, doesn't it? Now, how much coin do you think it'll take to convince me *not* to turn you over?"

Evren tensed as he felt a hand reach into his right trouser pocket, doubtless in search of a pouch. He turned his hips slightly, pulling his pocket away from the searching hand without risking the dagger punching into his spine. When the hand followed his movements, the blade moved a finger's breadth away from his back.

Just enough for Evren to attack.

He spun to the left and whipped his elbow around. The sharp-tipped bone slammed into the side of a face—a very dirty face that belonged to a very dirty young man that looked to be around Evren's age. The blow collided with the youth's jaw and sent him staggering. Evren moved with the spin, seized the boy's flailing wrist, and twisted it behind his back. With his left hand, he seized the scruff of the boy's neck and slammed him into the wall. The boy collapsed, blood leaking from his nose, and Evren leapt atop his back before he could recover. A flick of his wrist dropped his throwing dagger into his palm and he pressed the tip against the base of the youth's skull.

"How much do you think it'll take to convince me not to drive this into your brain here and now?" Evren snarled.

A muffled grunt met his question—it was all the boy could manage with Evren shoving his face hard into the dust.

"If it's all the same to you," came another voice, firmer, with a note of command, "I'd rather we didn't have to kill the both of you here and now."

Without removing the dagger from the boy's head, Evren looked behind him. The speaker was an older man, with strong facial features and sharp eyes. Grey showed at his temples but he had an abundance of black in his short-cropped hair and thick beard. His barrel chest and broad shoulders matched the smith's hammer in his hand.

Evren's eyes dropped to the strange metal contraption on the man's right leg: a brace, articulated at the knee, with thick leather straps that clutched his thigh and calf. The metal *clicked* quietly as the blacksmith took a step forward.

"Let Snarth up and we can talk like civilized people," the blacksmith said.

Ten young boys stood around the man. They looked between the ages of seven and fifteen, though one couldn't be more than four years old. Their clothing ranged from ragged to well-tailored, and they wore headbands of blue, black, red, brown, and white. At a glance, Evren saw a hard wariness in their eyes that could only come from a life on the streets.

Their weapons and posture spoke volumes as well. Two pointed compact handheld crossbows at him, while a third covered Hailen. The rest held daggers, hammers, and assorted metal bars collected from the smithy. Though simple and crude, the weapons would prove deadly effective at this range and with this number.

Yet Evren had stared into the face of death uncowed before. "Given that he threatened to jam a dagger into my spine, I'm not exactly feeling kindly toward your Snarth right now."

The blacksmith's teeth shone white against his beard as he smiled. "To be fair, you were the ones who climbed over my wall. Here in Shalandra, those looking to do legitimate business tend to come through the front door. Those taking the back way tend to get stabbed first, questioned later."

"Fair point." Evren inclined his head but didn't remove the dagger from Snarth's spine. "If I let him up, he's not going to try and stab me again, is he?"

"You have my word he won't." The bearded man fixed Evren with a curious gaze. "Though I will be expecting some sort of explanation as to your presence. I don't know what you did, but you've got the Indomitables spitting blood and fury."

Evren grimaced. "So much fuss over a little punch."

The blacksmith raised an eyebrow. "It all depends on *who* you punched, really."

"Some fat bastard with too little clothing and a golden headband."

Both of the smith's bushy eyebrows shot up toward his hairline. "If you're laying hands on one of the *Dhukari,* you're as foreign to Shalandra as he is." He inclined his head toward Hailen. "How's this? Let Snarth up, and you have my word we won't turn you over to the Indomitables to be sold in Auctioneer's Square."

Evren mulled over the offer. "Kind of hard to say no with those crossbows aimed at us."

"That's the point, isn't it?" A smile tugged at the man's lips as he studied Evren.

Evren stood and stepped back, giving the downed boy a wide berth. Snarth picked himself up off the ground and shot him a venomous glare. Evren tensed in expectation of an attack, hands at the ready.

"Get inside," the blacksmith said. "There's steel that needs working and it's your turn at the bellows."

Snarth looked like he wanted to protest but remained silent at the stern look on the man's face. Instead, he snarled a muttered curse, dusted himself off, and stormed through the now-open back door that led into the forge.

"A few hours spent pounding hot steel should help him forget his clumsy mistake," the man said. Without taking his eyes from Evren and Hailen, he gestured to the youths that held the crossbows. Evren breathed an inward sigh of relief as the sharp-tipped bolts lowered to point at the dusty courtyard.

"Now, I think it's time for that explanation." The man took a few stumping steps toward Evren, his knee brace making that strange *clicking* sound. "Let's start off with names. I'm Killian, master of this blacksmith. Your turn."

Evren hesitated. He'd rehearsed the tale that got him into the city—sick father, dutiful son bringing the grain to market in Shalandra—but had neglected to come up with fake names for him and Hailen. He could always lie, but the wary look in the blacksmith's dark eyes made it clear the man would prove challenging to fool.

He opted for the truth. "Evren."

"I'm Hailen!" Hailen piped up from behind him.

Evren's gut clenched, but he forced himself to relax. The names would mean nothing to this man—bloody hell, they probably meant nothing to anyone except for the Hunter, Kiara, Graeme, the Cambionari, and, in Evren's case, a temple full of vindictive Lecterns two thousand leagues to the north.

"And what, Evren and Hailen, brings you two into my backyard?" Killian cocked his head. "I'd say it was the legendary quality of my wares, but if that were the case, you'd likely be coming in the front. And anyone foolish enough to punch a *Dhukari* is clearly not from Shalandra. So how, pray tell, did two youths from…" He eyed the two of them. "…far to the north end up here?"

Again, Evren pondered his choices. Lie and hope he was convincing enough that this Killian believed him? The blacksmith's dark eyes belied his pleasant demeanor. Evren had known enough hard, cunning men in his time on the streets of Vothmot—and his years with the Hunter—to recognize them at a glance.

"That's a bit of a tough question," Evren said. "On the one hand, if I lie, you'll likely put those little crossbows to the test." He brought both hands up, palms facing the sky. "On the other, the truth's just as liable to get us both killed."

"A quandary, indeed." Killian smiled. "Would it help if I told you that I'm a *very* open-minded individual? You might be surprised to find I'm less fond of the established order than the average Shalandran." His eyes went to the dagger in Evren's hand. "Judging by the blade in your hand and the ones tucked into the back of your belt and the tops of your boots, that's a sentiment you seem to share."

Evren tensed. *How did he know?* Even if Killian had spotted the two *jambiya* blades when he was knocking down Snarth, the daggers in his boots were invisible. The Hunter had special-ordered the boots and weapons from his own personal cobbler and bladesmith.

Killian's smile widened. "I'll take that as a yes." He turned to his boys and gave a dismissive wave. "You all have jobs to be about. Training is done for the day."

"Yes, sir."

"Yes, Killian."

The ten boys trooped out of the yard—*a training yard*, Evren realized, taking in the white chalk square in the center and wooden benches along the wall.

After a moment, Evren slipped the dagger into his wrist sheath. Killian had the sloped shoulders and strong arms of a blacksmith, but Evren reasoned he could defend himself and Hailen should the need arise. If nothing else, the two of them could definitely out*run* the smith.

"Training, eh?" He looked around. "Something tells me this is a secret you'd rather I didn't let out into the world."

"Just as I'm sure you'd rather your assault on a *Dhukari* didn't become public knowledge." Killian inclined his head. "So let's begin this negotiation with the understanding that we both have things we're keeping from the other."

"Negotiation?" Evren scrunched up his face. "What are we negotiating for?"

"Why, for you to come and work for me, of course!" Killian beamed. "In exchange for my assistance in procuring whatever you've come to Shalandra to steal."

Evren's jaw dropped. *Bloody hell!* The man was as brazen as he was insightful. He'd managed to connect dots that Evren hadn't even imagined existed in the first place, and somehow he'd come to the right conclusion.

"Let me speak plainly," Killian said. "Snarth's one of my best Mumblers, but you took him down faster than anyone he's sparred with. That sort of skill would be wasted on the chopping block in Murder Square or lounging in the Pharus' dungeons. I am always on the lookout for resourceful young men to work for me, and you're clearly more than capable of handling yourself."

"What does 'work for you' mean, exactly?" Evren's eyes narrowed as his mind raced through a thousand different scenarios. Young boys living on the streets of Vothmot often had to resort to desperate things to avoid starvation, but he wasn't that boy anymore.

"Gather information to mumble into my ear," Killian said with a wry grin. "Like all the rest of my Mumblers."

Evren frowned. He'd encountered more than a few self-styled thiefmasters, men who offered young boys shelter and protection in exchange for a cut of their profits. Most had been selfish, greedy bastards that cared only for their own enrichment, even at the cost of those that served them.

Yet Killian didn't have that conniving, self-interested look that had marked the others. Wary, certainly, and with a cunning that rivaled Kiara's, but lacking malice. Something about the blacksmith was disarming, friendly even, though it could be simply an act.

"I've shown you my cards, now it's your turn." Killian gestured for Evren to speak. "What have you come to Shalandra to steal?"

Evren didn't hesitate this time. The truth had served him well enough with Killian thus far.

"The Blade of Hallar."

"The Blade—?!" Killian's bushy eyebrows shot up but no trace of outrage showed on his face. He whistled through his teeth. "Damn, you've got a brass set of bollocks on you, indeed."

The man's reaction came as a surprise. He'd just learned that Evren had come to steal one of the city's oldest, holiest relics yet hadn't batted an eyelid. If anything, he seemed impressed.

"I'm sure you've heard just how impossible it is?" Killian asked. "Most secure room in the most secure building in all of Shalandra, that sort of thing?"

Evren nodded. "It's been mentioned."

"Then you know what you're up against." He folded hairy arms over his barrel chest. "Other, more superstitious men might balk at you stealing the Blade. Me, I'm just interested to see if you can pull it off."

Killian's expression grew contemplative and he remained silent for a long moment. Finally, he spoke in a slow voice. "Here's my offer: I'll find a place for you and your…brother—" He raised a questioning eyebrow. "—as a servant in the household of one of the most influential men in the city. The very man who carries the Blade of Hallar out of the Vault of Ancients for the Anointing of the Blades. It's up to you to figure out the vault and how to get out of Shalandra safely."

"And how, exactly, can you pull that off?" Evren shot a pointed glance around. "Unless you're the Pharus' personal blacksmith, I can't imagine you'd—"

Killian cut him off with a chopping motion of his huge hand. "Let's just say I have the right connections in the right places, yes?"

It seemed hard to believe; Evren had never met any blacksmiths with any sort of clout beyond their ability to pound metal into weapons. Then again, if Killian *was* more than a simple smith, he certainly wouldn't flaunt it.

Evren narrowed his eyes. "And *all* you want in return is information." He'd spent enough time around Graeme to know that the right information in the right hands could build empires as well as topple them.

"Correct." Killian nodded. "This certainly isn't me doing you a favor because of any kindness of my heart."

Evren snorted. "Of course not."

"I expect you to produce information that will be of use to me," Killian said. "The *only* reason I am offering you this bargain is because you have the motivation to keep up your end." His eyes went to Hailen, his meaning plain. "You want to keep him safe. I want information. Simple as that."

Evren hesitated. His primary task at the moment was to ensure Hailen was out of harm's way—he needed to have that one worry out of his mind in order to focus on his mission of stealing the Blade of Hallar. Killian's offer certainly came with strings attached, but as long as he knew what those strings were, he could live with that deal.

"What sort of information are you hoping I'll gather?" he asked, more to stall for time to think than out of legitimate interest. Spying was spying, no matter what way he cut it.

"Anything and everything you overhear. Every two days, one of my Mumblers will slip into the Keeper's Tier and meet you someplace to collect the tidbits you've gleaned. You never know what will prove useful to me, so I expect you to leave nothing out. In return, you'll have work—hard work, but preferable to living on the streets. Better still, your brother here won't have to worry about being scooped up by the Indomitables for being out of the Foreign Quarter after dark. No *Alqati* would interfere with a servant of the *Dhukari*, especially one as powerful as the man you'll be serving."

Evren frowned. *The offer seems good, but is it too good?*

Experience had taught him hard lessons, especially when it came to older men that surrounded themselves with young men. He'd fled the Lecterns to escape their abuse. Was Killian the same as the Master's Priests?

"As for you," Killian said with a smile, "you can pass for a Shalandran just fine. You're almost the right color to blend in, and your accent is similar enough to ours that few will pay it much heed. A bit of *kohl* and crushed malachite around your eyes will have you looking like one of us in no time. With the right headband, you'll be free to move around the streets and do whatever you need to do."

Evren hesitated. Throughout the conversation with Killian, Evren had watched the Mumblers moving through the smithy. He knew the signs of young men being exploited and defiled: physical bruises and injuries, quiet and withdrawn natures, indications of fear directed toward their abuser, anxiety, an instinctive submissive nature, and deep, dark shadows in the eyes that spoke of inner torment. The boys showed none of those signs—they appeared like any other children serving in a street gang or thieving crew. Hard-eyed and wary, perhaps even quick to violence like Snarth, yet nothing indicated anything inappropriate about their affiliation with Killian.

Killian might be on the wrong side of the law, but he didn't *appear* to be an evil, ruthless, or self-serving man. That alone made him someone Evren might be able to work with.

He'd come to Shalandra for the purpose of stealing the Blade of Hallar, and now this man was offering him help—a bargain that Killian likely got the better end of, certainly, but nothing in life came free. Evren could play servant for a few days, even weeks, if it got him in a position to steal the *Im'tasi* weapon and get it back to the Hunter.

Better, it gave him somewhere safe to stash Hailen until he figured out what to do with him. He wasn't convinced the Cambionari in Shalandra were the best choice—the Hunter trusted Father Reverentus well enough with Hailen's secret, but Evren didn't know what manner of men called the House of Need in this city home. He wouldn't entrust Hailen to their care until he was certain of them.

*As long as Hailen can play the part convincingly, of course.* He'd have to give the boy a few pointers on being a more convincing liar. But if Hailen could play "mute servant", they had a real shot of making this work.

For now, Killian's offer was his best choice. With a nod, he thrust out his hand. "Deal."

Killian grinned and shook. "From the moment we met five minutes ago, I told myself, 'This is a smart one'. Glad to see you proved me right."

Evren stifled a derisive snort. "Who's this man we'll be serving?" he asked. "The one who'll get me close enough to steal the sword."

Killian smiled. "Arch-Guardian Suroth, high priest of the Secret Keepers."

# Chapter Twenty

Everything ached.

*Ow.* The thought slammed into Issa's mind as a persistent throbbing in her skull dragged her back to consciousness. Even drawing breath hurt—she'd taken a pounding blow to the breastbone that sent spikes of pain radiating through her entire chest.

Yet, as her eyes opened and she caught sight of the stern face hovering above her, she knew she would have no rest.

"On your feet," Tannard growled. "Your duties await."

*Duties?* Issa's brow furrowed in confusion, her sluggish mind trying to make sense of the *Invictus'* words. She hadn't expected anything to take her away from her usual exhausting routine of training and lessons.

She clenched her jaw against the pain as she rolled over onto her stomach. Sand filled her mouth, grinding to grit between her teeth. It was a minor irritation amidst an overwhelming barrage of the pain racing through her back, neck, shoulders, arms, and legs. As she came to her feet, the pounding in her head intensified and the world spun wildly around her. Only sheer effort of will kept her upright.

"Get your armor and weapons and meet me at the Gate of Tombs in five minutes," Tannard rumbled. "If you're late, you'll get no dinner." The *Invictus'* face was as hard as shalanite as he spun on his heel and stalked toward the front gate.

Issa's heart sank. *No way I can limp back to my room, gear up, and get to the front gate in five minutes.* The buckles on her armor alone would take her the better part of ten.

Then she caught sight of Hykos slinking through the halls of the Citadel toward her. The *Archateros* kept an eye on Tannard's retreating back and, when the *Invictus* had disappeared through the arched doorway, he slipped toward her. She wanted to cry out in relief and gratitude as she spotted her armor and flammard in his arms.

"I thought you'd need this." Hykos grinned and held out her gear. He stood in full plate armor, two-handed sword in its sheath on his back. "Figured you could use a hand after that beating."

Issa grimaced. "That bad, huh?" For the first time, she noticed the training field was empty, the Indomitables gone. "How long was I unconscious?"

"Half an hour." Hykos' face tightened.

"And my men?" she asked. "How bad did they get hammered?"

Hykos shook his head. "They won't be walking for a few days. They don't have the Keeper's blessing like we do."

"The Keeper's blessing?" Issa asked as she struggled to pull on her armor. The movements sent pain racing through her battered body.

"One of the marks of his favor," Hykos explained, tapping his forehead, where he bore the circular scar identical to hers. "What could be mortal wounds for most people might not kill us in the end."

Issa's eyebrows shot up. "The Long Keeper makes us immortal?"

Hykos laughed. "Do you feel immortal right now?"

"Not even a little." Issa shook her head.

"Good, because you're not." Hykos' expression sobered. "Too many *prototopoi* have died because they waded into a fight they had no hope of winning. We heal faster than the average person. A wound that might take a week for most to recover from will have us down for five days. A shattered bone will take six weeks to heal compared to eight for any normal person. The Long Keeper will claim us one day, but until then, he expects us to serve him efficiently. Not much you can do to serve from a bed."

Issa's mind raced as she dissected his words. She always *had* considered herself fortunate—not only had she avoided most of the injuries common to youths running around the Cultivator's Tier streets, but on the occasions that she had been injured, she'd recovered far faster than others. Even the bruises sustained from her first beating in the training grounds had only pained her for a day or two.

"Damn!" she breathed. "That's going to come in handy next time Tannard decides I've got to face the entire cohort of Indomitables alone."

"Hey, from what I saw, you did pretty damned good." Hykos clapped her on the shoulder. "Hell, if it wasn't for Kellas and that last line, you might actually have broken through. And that runner of yours came damned close to the pennant. Next time, if Tannard doesn't up the stakes, you've got a good chance of winning."

"So of *course* he's going to make it even harder," Issa growled. "He's determined to make my life impossible!"

Hykos' eyes slid away from hers. "Yeah, I noticed."

"Why?" Issa's voice rose to an angry shout. "What did I ever do to earn his ire?"

"Nothing." Hykos shook his head. "Way I heard it, the *Invictus* didn't even know you were alive until you fought in the Crucible."

"So why in the bloody hell is he getting off tormenting me?" Fury bubbled up from within Issa's chest. "Why does he want me to fail?"

"I don't know," Hykos said. "But I do know that you've got a choice to make."

"A choice?" Issa cocked her head.

Hykos smiled. "Let him win, or fight to prove that you deserve your place here as much as any of us." He winked at her. "And, from what I've learned of you, I'm pretty damned certain which you'll choose."

Issa tried to return his smile—she liked hearing he had confidence in her—but couldn't. Right now, with the weight of her armor and sword adding to the pain throbbing through every fiber of her being, she wanted to give Tannard the satisfaction of seeing her quit. She was too exhausted, hungry, thirsty, and banged up to continue pushing. Tannard wanted to push until she reached the end of her rope—she was getting there fast.

"Let's go." Hykos' words registered through the gloom filling her mind. "We shouldn't keep the *Invictus* waiting."

It took all of Issa's strength to put one foot in front of the other as she followed Hykos from the training yard toward the arched entrance to the western wing of the Citadel of Stone. A long hallway led deeper into the solid stone fortress, in the direction of the towering cliff face that served as the western boundary of Shalandra's uppermost tier.

The Gate of Tombs was an enormous rectangular stone archway, easily thirty feet high and twenty wide. A single wrought-iron gate stood perpetually open on its hinges—it looked as if it would take a dozen strong men to swing it closed.

Issa's mouth went dry as she caught sight of Tannard waiting at the Gate of Tombs. The *Invictus'* face was an unreadable mask of stone and he said nothing as they approached, simply turned and stalked into the Keeper's Crypts.

The Keeper's Crypts served as the final resting places for all the dead of Shalandra. Tombs, graves, and mausoleums had been carved from the very stone of Alshuruq—some estimated there were *millions* by now. Shalandrans were interred on the crypt that corresponded to their castes. Only the wealthiest and most powerful of Shalandra spent their eternal rest on the uppermost tier's crypt. *Intaji* stonemasons spent their lives vying to be chosen by the *Dhukari* and Keeper's Blades to carve the tombs on the Keeper's Tier.

Once, long ago, Issa had visited the crypts on the Cultivator's Tier, and she'd marveled at the ornate scrollwork and images carved onto the simple stone coffins of the wealthier *Earaqi*. The artistry of *Dhukari* tombs stole Issa's breath. The crypt's ceiling rose fifty feet overhead, barely enough room for the pillared mausoleums and sarcophagi covered in gilt and silver leaf. Colorful images frescoed onto the golden sandstone walls and high-relief carvings depicted the heroic deeds of the deceased. Statues with stunningly lifelike features displayed the faces and forms of those long dead. A million precious stones twinkled like the stars in the sky, casting beams of ruby, sapphire, emerald, and brilliant white light on the solemn walls and high-arching domes.

The oil lanterns hanging on the wall bathed the entire crypt in a golden-red light that seemed to make everything glow with a stunning brilliance. Yet there was no mistaking the pall of death that hung over it all. A dusty, dry scent, like corn husks left out too long to wither in the sun. Even the sweet reek of incense, left burning at the *Dhukari* tombs, failed to drown out the smell of desiccated flesh and bone. If anything, it only *added* to the funereal scents that filled the Keeper's Crypts.

Tannard led them a few hundred yards into the mountain before turning his steps north. Issa's muscles ached after her beating, and even the gentle incline sent pain shooting through her body. But as she climbed, she couldn't help noticing the way the tombs began to change. The lavishly-decorated mausoleums of the *Dhukari* gave way to sarcophagi that bore little ornamentation. Yet, instead of golden sandstone, these sarcophagi were made of midnight black shalanite—worth far more than all the wealth of the *Dhukari*. Etched into the lid of every sarcophagus was a two-handed sword with a familiar flame-shaped blade.

*The tombs of the Keeper's Blades,* Issa realized. A reverent hush gripped her; for a moment, it seemed her pain faded as she stared in awe at the final resting places of Shalandra's elite warriors.

"Today, you failed." Tannard broke the eternal silence of the tombs, his voice as hard and cold as the shalanite coffins surrounding them. "Had it been real life and not some staged child's skirmish, you would be lying in one of these." He gestured to the nearest sarcophagus. "Read the inscription."

The stone coffin Tannard indicated looked new, as if someone had just been laid to rest there. She read the words etched into its lid aloud. "Kalune and Lakani, gathered to the Long Keeper's arms." A sad, almost pitiful inscription. She turned a curious expression on the *Invictus*. "Who were they?"

"The *Intaji* youths who claimed the blades in the Crucible with you," Tannard replied. "They passed the trial of steel, but failed the trial of stone."

Issa's sucked in a breath, her blood running cold. *They died?* She'd watched the Necroseti haul away the boys on a stretcher. Their faces had been flushed red and purple, the mark of the bloodstone a burning white on their foreheads. Yet, in everything that had happened this last week, she'd forgotten about them.

"Carry this memory with you always." Tannard fixed her with a piercing glare. "The Long Keeper's wisdom is not for us to understand; when he decides that it is your time, you too will be placed to rest here." His expression darkened to a scowl. "But it is up to you to *earn* that place!"

Issa recoiled from the intensity in his eyes and voice, and it took all her willpower not to retreat a step.

"The blade chose you and the Long Keeper marked you, but you must prove your worthiness to serve him every day." Tannard jabbed a finger into her thick steel breastplate. "Through your deeds, your dedication, your determination. Every time you fail, every time you falter, you insult the Long Keeper and prove yourself unworthy."

He whirled and seized Issa's gorget, pulling her close until their faces were mere inches apart. "Do. Not. Fail." He spoke in a low, harsh voice. "When the day comes that you are laid to rest beside your fallen brethren, what will *your* stone say?"

Fear froze the words in Issa's mouth. Defeat had scrambled her brain, and the ferocity of the *Invictus'* tirade overwhelmed her. It was as if the strong, proud champion from the Crucible had been shattered, leaving only the nervous *Earaqi* girl Issa had been when she started training with Killian. Tannard hadn't just beat down her body—he'd crushed her soul beneath his heel and spat on the splinters.

Tannard released her armor so suddenly Issa stumbled. He rounded on his heel and strode farther up the hill. "Follow me."

A fist of iron squeezed Issa's lungs, and it took a supreme will of effort to stand when she felt a heartbeat from collapsing. Yet Tannard gave her no time to recover. Issa was forced to hurry after him through the sea of black tombs. She didn't try counting—there had to be thousands of them, stacked like neat boxes ready for the market, each bearing the corpse of a Blade fallen in the Long Keeper's service. Each sarcophagus bore the name of its inhabitant, the mark of the two-handed flammard, and a summary of their life and death.

Then came the Tombs of the Pharuses. Each stood nearly a hundred feet tall, with a stone high-relief carving depicting the face of the Pharus, with ornately carved details that set Issa's head swimming. Beloved names like Nofre-kat the Bloody, Anhurmes Thoth III, Thema Amenthes of the Golden Sunrise, and Sen-ma Ramerabai, victor of the Thousand Skull War and hero of Harabai Pass. Despised names like Tachus Snakespine, Pen-Amen Rere, or Odion the Defeated. Every one of the Pharuses since Hallar himself to Mordus Khnemu Nephelcheres, father of the current Pharus.

The sight of such splendor humbled Issa. She felt like a trespasser, a thief stealing among the greatest and most powerful rulers of Shalandra's history. A failure.

Her gut clenched as she realized Tannard's true destination. She had heard the tales of the Tomb of Hallar—everyone in Shalandra had—yet she never dreamed of laying eyes on it. Now, the *Invictus* marched her toward the holiest place in the city.

The Tomb of Hallar was nothing like the rest of the Keeper's Crypts. It lacked the lavish ornamentation, high-relief carvings, and intricate stonework. It had been carved from the single vein of shalanite close to Alshuruq's peak, a solid mass of midnight stone that stood out for its simplicity among the golden sandstone surrounding it. A single slab of shalanite guarded its entrance, its surface marked with thousands of strange-looking symbols.

"This," Tannard said, gesturing toward the black stone wall, "this is the Blades' greatest honor. What you see before you is the Tomb of Hallar."

Hallar, Shalandra's founder and the first Pharus, had defeated the tribes of the four mountains—Alshuruq, Zahiran, Shahkukha, and Dalmisa. Under his rule, which lasted more than six decades, the city of Shalandra had been carved from the mountainside. He had created the system of castes and the five tiers of Shalandra, which had led to peace and prosperity at a time when war gripped Einan. This tomb, his final resting place, hadn't been opened in more than two thousand years. In the center of the slab, at the height of Issa's chest, was a small, perfectly circular hole. Whatever key was intended to be used to open this door had been lost for millennia.

To Issa's knowledge, no one but the Pharus, the Keeper's Council, and the Necroseti ever visited the Tomb of Hallar. Yet the two men who stood solemn and silent before the slab bore the black spiked armor, snarling lion helmets, and two-handed flammards of Keeper's Blades.

"You might have noticed that the Citadel of Stone is set on the west of the Keeper's Tier." Tannard spoke in a quiet voice. "What is an insult to the rest of Shalandra is our highest honor. For thousands of years, since the beginning of our great city, the Keeper's Blades have been set to guard this place. Not only in life, but also in death."

Issa's eyes wandered over the black shalanite sarcophagi that stood arrayed in neat rows—was it her imagination, or did they resemble battle lines?—in front of the Tomb of Hallar. Each bore the same depiction of the two-handed sword, but the inscriptions on the lid were longer, more detailed.

Her eyes roamed over the inscriptions of the tombs nearest her. "*Abethar, Invictus, called Moonspear, fallen at the Battle of Eagle's Crest.*"

Issa sucked in a breath. Abethar was Shalandra's most renowned general during the Hundred Weeks' War, which ravaged the entire south of Einan more than eight hundred years before her time. He'd earned the name Moonspear for his ability to fight in the darkness as well as other men fought in the day. In the Battle of Eagle's Crest, he'd killed more than three hundred enemies before succumbing to his own wounds.

The next name set her heart pounding. *"Kemassis, Ypertatos, called Undying, claimed by the Long Keeper during the Bloody Five."*

Kemassis had earned the name Undying because he'd been wounded more than a hundred times during his years fighting in the Hundred Weeks' War. The Bloody Five had been the final battle in the war, a five-day melee that left more than a hundred thousand dead and thrice that number of wounded.

More and more names met her eyes. Shishak Queenslayer, savior of Shalandra during the Red Queen's Blight. Bicheres the Bold, who sacrificed himself to buy Pharus Ati Bakenrath time to escape the Ravennath hordes. Tosorthros Stilltongued, the mute Blade said to have been twice the height of a man.

So many of the greatest heroes of Shalandra's history had served in the Keeper's Blades. All had been laid to rest here, in front of the Tomb of Hallar. A final honor.

Tannard fixed her with that stern, piercing glare. "We guard this place until Hallar's return, or until the Hallar's Chosen—the Child of Secrets, Child of Gold—arises. But only those that served well in life are selected to guard this place forever." He thrust a finger toward those tombs. "But *those* Keeper's Blades were worthy. Could you say the same of yourself after today?"

Issa's face burned with mingled anger and shame. Shame that she had failed and anger that he'd actually expected her to succeed when he'd arrayed such uneven odds against her. Yet standing here, amid the tombs of the greatest heroes of Shalandra, she couldn't help feeling guilty at her own failure.

She was a Keeper's Blade—as mortal and human as anyone else in Shalandra, yet favored by the Long Keeper. As Tannard had said, by her failures, she insulted the god of death that had chosen her. As if he somehow made a mistake by elevating her above the rest of Shalandra. He needed no words now; the condemnation burning in his eyes buried a dagger in her gut.

The aches and pains of her beating paled in comparison to the torment of her shame.

Tannard turned to the two Blades standing before the Tomb of Hallar and saluted. "Guardians of death, warriors of the fallen, you are relieved of duty. Your brothers stand ready to serve."

The Blades returned the salute, turned to Issa and Hykos, and said in unison, "May the Keeper grant his eternal vigilance over Hallar's final resting place."

Issa repeated the words with Hykos, and she fell in step beside the *Archateros* as he marched toward the black stone wall to take up guard position. Hykos drew his huge black-bladed flammard and grounded the tip between his feet. Issa did likewise, matching his rigid, ceremonial stance.

Tannard's gaze pierced her. "The Long Keeper makes no mistakes. He comes for one and all, from the lowest *Mahjuri* to the Pharus himself, claiming man, woman, and child in equal measure. Death will come for you. When that happens, where will *you* be buried?"

The words rang in Issa's ears as the *Invictus* turned on his heel and marched off behind the two retreating Blades. The weight of her steel armor and flammard suddenly seemed an immense burden—one she had proven herself unworthy to bear.

# Chapter Twenty-One

Kodyn's gut clenched at the anger burning in Arch-Guardian Suroth's eyes, the sharp movements of his fingers. Beside him, Aisha drew in a sharp breath.

*Did Briana betray us?* His eyes went to the petite Shalandran girl standing beside her father. He'd had to tell her his plan to steal the Crown of the Pharus—he'd need her help to get close enough to get his hands on the relic, which only Suroth was allowed to access during the Ceremony of the Seven Faces and the Anointing of the Blades.

"It's not like that, Father!" Briana protested. She turned to Kodyn, eyes pleading and red-faced. "I've been trying to explain it to him."

Arch-Guardian Suroth's fingers fairly flew. *"Explain that they've come here under the guise of stealing one of Shalandra's most holy relics!"* He shifted his stance—a subtle change, from relaxed and confident to wary, alert, one foot slightly back and knees bent, ready for a bare-handed attack. *"Give me one good reason I shouldn't kill you both here and now."*

"Father!" Briana moved to stand between Suroth and Kodyn. "Don't—"

*"We want none of your Night Guild filth here!"* Suroth's eyes blazed.

"You know of the Night Guild?" Kodyn's eyebrows rose.

*"Of course."* The Arch-Guardian's lip curled upward into a half-snarl, half-sneer. *"Every city is home to such human refuse. Even here in Shalandra we have our own version: the Ybrazhe Syndicate. Little more than thieves and thugs, a stain on our city."*

"We're not like that!" Kodyn protested.

"Or at least, *we're* not." Aisha's gesture included the two of them. "We're not here to *steal* the Crown of the Pharus. Or at least not in the way you're thinking."

Suroth's expression darkened. "*Explain,*" he signed.

"No one could ever accuse the Night Guild of being law-abiding citizens," Kodyn said quickly. "But our job is to maintain order in Praamis."

The Arch-Guardian's eyes narrowed and he gave a derisive snort.

"It's the truth." Kodyn squared his shoulders and stood straighter. "My mother is the Master of the Night Guild, and she receives orders from King Ohilmos himself." He heard Aisha's sudden intake of air—he'd have to explain that one to her later. "You know as well as I do that there will always be crime in cities like Praamis and Shalandra. The Night Guild is simply *organized* crime. Our assassins, thieves, poisoners, and brothel-keepers control the crime rate in the city, keeping things balanced and in order. In the last decade, during my mother's reign as Guild Master, Praamis has known a peace and stability not seen for more than two hundred years."

That last bit might have been exaggerated—he doubted that even Darreth, his mother's fussy and all-knowing aide, would have facts that specific. But the grain of truth remained. Since the death of the last Master Gold, the Night Guild had driven the Bloody Hand out of Praamis, eradicated the flesh trade, cut off the supply of Bonedust and other drugs filtering into the city, and maintained order. It didn't matter that they stood on the wrong side of the law; the Night Guild served as another form of justice and peacekeeping that the Praamian Guard could never match.

Suroth didn't look convinced. "*And yet, you are still nothing more than thieves sneaking into Shalandra, using the pretense of bringing my daughter home to me.*" His eyes flashed. "*How are you any better than the ones that took her from me?*"

"Because we don't actually want to *take* the Crown of the Pharus." Kodyn met his gaze without hesitation. "We just need to steal it."

He winced as he realized how stupid that sounded, so he tried again.

"To become full members of the Night Guild, each of us—" He gestured to Aisha and himself. "—have to complete an Undertaking, a task that proves our worthiness. Not only worthy of a place in the Guild, but worthy to serve the Watcher in the Dark, the god of thieves."

*"You claim the Watcher as your patron deity?"* Suroth's eyebrows rose. *"I'm certain Judiciar Tealus might have something to say about that."*

"We're not exactly part of his priesthood." Kodyn grinned. "The Watcher in the Dark is the god of the night, of justice, and of vengeance. What is more just than stealing from those who have more than they deserve? Is there a holier vengeance than seeing murderers, rapists, and arsonists executed?"

Suroth inclined his head. *"A well-chosen god, indeed."*

Kodyn's heart leapt. He could see he was getting through to Suroth, though the Arch-Guardian hadn't relaxed from his combative stance.

"When I found Briana held by the Gatherers," Kodyn pressed on, "I insisted that I would bring her home. Yet I knew that I could not simply abandon my place in the Night Guild, my duties to my House and my mother. So I did the only thing I could: I chose an Undertaking that would bring me to Shalandra. The only thing I could think of was to steal the Crown of the Pharus. But I don't actually need to steal it or take it away from Shalandra. All I need to do is prove that I *can* steal it."

*"That makes no sense."* Suroth looked confused.

Kodyn chuckled. "Let me tell you about my mother's Undertaking. She chose to scale the highest tower in Shalandra—"

*"The Black Spire?"* For a moment, eager excitement sparkled in the Arch-Guardian's eyes. *"I have longed for years to visit that Serenii monument. Is it truly as tall as they say?"*

"Taller." Kodyn grinned. "And it is currently the residence of Duke Elodon Phonnis, Praamis' Chief Justiciar and brother to the king. It was considered an impossible task, yet she determined to do it. All she had to do was scale the Black Spire and place a lit lamp in the uppermost room—simply to prove herself worthy and capable."

*"Ah, I understand."* Suroth nodded, and a fraction of the tension faded from his stance. *"We have similar rituals at the Temple of Whispers."*

Relief surged within Kodyn. *This might actually work!* He had dreaded the inevitable confrontation when Arch-Guardian Suroth found out the truth. He'd hoped the goodwill earned by returning Briana would suffice to smooth over the Secret Keeper's anger and suspicion, maybe even convince the Arch-Guardian to help. His Undertaking demanded that no one *within* the Night Guild offer aid—there were no rules against enlisting the help of others.

"To prove myself worthy, all I need to do is get my hands on the Crown of the Pharus and prove that I am capable of stealing it." He gestured to Aisha. "My trusted companion came not only to help me protect your daughter, but to bear witness that I actually achieved the task."

"See, Papa?" Briana's tone turned scolding. "That's what I was trying to explain!"

"*And once your Undertaking is complete?*" Suroth asked. "*What then?*"

"I have to return to Praamis before my eighteenth nameday," Kodyn said. "But that is almost a year away. There is no reason I cannot stay in Shalandra and help protect Briana. Both of us."

He shot Aisha a glance. Ria had sent Aisha along to watch his back, but something about her behavior since leaving Praamis told him she'd become embroiled in concerns of her own. He wanted to find out what that was and see what he could do to help, but until he did—or until she chose to clue him in—he'd have to focus on his own Undertaking.

Her nod indicated that she agreed. Hell, it had been her plan in the first place, so it was *him* agreeing with her.

"But that's not our *only* reason for coming to Shalandra."

The words poured from his mouth before he realized it. Something about Suroth made him *want* to be honest—if nothing else, he needed to be certain the Arch-Guardian wasn't his enemy.

Skepticism shone in Suroth's eyes. "*There's more? What else have you come to steal?*" A hint of a scowl twisted his lips.

"Nothing." Kodyn straightened and met the Arch-Guardian's gaze without hesitation. "We've come to deal with the Gatherers."

That sparked Suroth's curiosity. He cocked his head, interested.

"The Gatherers murdered Praamians. Men, women, even children." Anger surged within Kodyn. "Their damned rituals nearly killed a friend of mine, and I'll be damned if I let them come back to my city and kill more of my friends. Aisha and I have come to find out as much as we can about them. If we can find a way to stop them, to put an end to their bloodthirsty rituals, I'm going to do it."

He fixed Suroth with a solemn gaze. "You know they're the ones that took Briana, which means *you're* just as invested in dealing with them as we are.

Together, we can find the ones responsible for Briana's kidnapping and take them down."

Suroth's expression changed, his stubborn cynicism wavering in the face of Kodyn's intensity.

"I swear," Kodyn said, "in the eyes of the Watcher in the Dark and upon the life of my loved ones that I intended to return Briana home before I ever found out who her father was. But the fact that you are a member of the Keeper's Council means that you are in a position where you can help me. That influenced my superiors within the Night Guild to accept my quest. That's why I have been permitted to escort her safely home. But while I'm here, I'm going to do everything in my power to deal with the Gatherers."

He fixed Arch-Guardian Suroth with a somber gaze. "From what Briana has told me, you are a good man in a city of vipers wearing the guise of Keeper's priests. I understand if you feel you are unable to help me; indeed, I will not resent it if you decide to have me arrested for attempting to steal the crown. But you have my word that I will do everything in my power to protect your daughter, even if you cannot help me. And if you do help me with my Undertaking, I will do nothing to betray your trust or endanger your position in the city. Together, we can take down the people responsible for harming Briana."

For emphasis, Kodyn drew out a dagger and pressed the edge against his palm.

"*That will not be necessary,*" Suroth's hands flashed. A small smile tugged at his lips. "*When one cannot speak, one learns how to listen. Not just with the ears, but with the eyes as well. I took your measure the moment you walked into my house. What you have just said confirms what I already knew. You are an honorable young man. And woman,*" he added, turning to Aisha. "*I believe that you truly do have my daughter's best interests at heart, and that you will do as you say.*"

The Arch-Guardian's stance relaxed and he thrust out his right hand. "*I will aid you in your Undertaking,*" his left hand signed. "*And, in return, you will help me keep my daughter safe.*"

"Done." Kodyn shook the man's hand. He was surprised to feel the iron in Arch-Guardian Suroth's grip. He'd expected the delicate hands of a scholar and instead found the solid strength of a warrior. "We will do whatever we can to help you find out who is behind Briana's abduction and put an end to the Gatherers."

"*You realize that you are making powerful enemies, do you not?*" Suroth's eyes met his. "*I have some influence in Shalandra, particularly among the Venerated, but the Necroseti wield far more political and financial power than I could ever hope to. It is only my position on the Keeper's Council that has kept them at bay—until Briana's abduction—but if we make moves against them, you may find yourself facing far graver threats than you can imagine.*"

Kodyn grinned. "You really know how to sweet-talk a fellow, don't you?"

Arch-Guardian Suroth's eyebrows rose.

Aisha snorted. "If you'd ever met his mother, you'd understand. That woman hasn't met a challenge she didn't like."

"*So long as you understand what we are up against,*" Suroth said. "*I have already begun marshaling my allies to find out which Necroseti are behind the abduction, and my contacts are scouring the city to find the Gatherers. When the time is right, we will make a move. Until then, our only hope is to pretend as if all is well.*" He pulled Briana into a tight embrace once more. "*Beginning with my joy at my daughter's safe return!*"

"Good." Kodyn turned to Aisha with a pointed look. "Now that we've got that settled, I've somewhere I need to be."

Aisha raised an eyebrow. "Something more important than your new job as the Arch-Guardian's daughter's bodyguard?"

Kodyn nodded. "I need to speak to the Black Widow. Sooner is better, two hours ago is best. This is one woman we do *not* want to keep waiting. Those who do have a nasty habit of winding up dead."

# Chapter Twenty-Two

"He's going to be fine, you know." The quiet words pierced Aisha's contemplation. She looked up and found Briana standing next to her on the garden's balcony.

The girl had changed into Shalandran garb—a tight-fitting *kalasiris* that emphasized her petite figure, lace-up calf-high leather sandals, and a golden headdress decorated with strings of pearls, emeralds, and a single diamond in the center of her forehead—that made her look much more like a *Dhukari's* daughter.

"He has the gold-and-green headband and sigil marking him as my father's servant," Briana said. "The Indomitables won't give him trouble. Anyone else tries, well, you know his skill in a fight better than me."

"Of course." Aisha returned Briana's smile. The Shalandran girl meant well, but she misunderstood the meaning behind Aisha's dour stare.

A part of her couldn't help worrying about Kodyn. *He has his mother's skill and cunning, but also her temper and impetuosity.* Kodyn could fight or talk his way out of a lot of situations, but likely he'd get himself into those situations with his biting wit and stubborn refusal to back down from a confrontation. Ria had sent her along to watch his back, but right now safeguarding Kodyn was the last thing on her mind.

Her eyes strayed once toward the massive cliff wall that marked the western boundary of Shalandra. She'd thought being around the Keeper's Blade was bad. On the road, every time she'd glanced at Ormroth, she couldn't help seeing those translucent, blue-white spirits clinging to that strange black metal sword of his. Yet since her arrival in Shalandra, she had come to understand why it had been named "City of the Dead".

No one but she—or another Spirit Whisperer—would see the spirits, but the presence of the *Kish'aa* in Shalandra was immense. Thousands of ghostly figures fixed their eyes on her, their mouths open in unheard cries and pleas. The *Kish'aa* roamed the streets, drifting about on the wind's currents, floating through crowds that could not hear their desperate cries.

But to the west, near the Keeper's Crypts, Aisha could hardly see the golden sandstone cliff through the mass of *Kish'aa* that clustered around the tombs. The brilliance of their spirits was blinding, a churning, seething mass of energy that gyrated like eddies in a whirlpool. She had not yet learned to hear their words as her father had, but their whispers dug sharp fingers into her mind, pulling at her consciousness. They called to her; it took every ounce of her strength to remain standing still when she wanted to both allow herself to be drawn toward them and flee as far as she could.

A shudder ran down her spine, but she forced herself to keep looking. She would not run from the curse. Eventually, she would have to face the *Kish'aa*. She would have to open her ears to listen to their cries.

*But not now.*

She turned to the Shalandran girl. "Thank you," she said in a quiet voice. "For helping convince your father to help."

"Kodyn did all the convincing," Briana said with a little shrug of her slim shoulders. "And you, with your plan to play bodyguard. You sure you're up for it, especially given my father's plan for tonight?"

Arch-Guardian Suroth had departed to the Palace of Golden Eternity to inform the Pharus and the Keeper's Council of Briana's return. He'd fabricate something to explain her absence, but he had little doubt the Necroseti would know the truth—either they'd been behind it, or they knew of her capture by the Gatherers. And yet, he still intended to parade Briana through high society as if she'd just returned from a long voyage, pretending nothing had happened. All the better to throw off his enemies, he'd said.

Aisha raised an eyebrow. "You doubt our ability to protect you?"

Briana shook her head. "No, it's just…" Her face burned a bright scarlet and her eyes failed to meet Aisha's. A long moment passed before she spoke. "It's pretty obvious how you feel about Kodyn."

Aisha had trained for years to anticipate her enemy's strikes, to spot attacks from the shadows, to be aware of attacks from behind. Yet still Briana's words caught her totally by surprise.

"W-What?" Heat flushed her own cheeks.

Briana gave her a shy smile. "I don't think Kodyn knows. Boys aren't exactly the most perceptive when it comes to understanding feelings."

Aisha gaped. The Briana speaking to her now bore little resemblance to the scared girl they'd rescued from the Gatherers less than a month ago.

"In the short time that I've known Kodyn," Briana continued, "I've come to…appreciate the man he is. Noble, courageous, honest, clever—not what I'd expected of a thief. I'm sure you've seen the same things."

It took Aisha a moment to recover enough to nod.

Briana fixed her with a solemn gaze. "I wouldn't want to do anything to jeopardize your relationship."

Aisha heard the "but" in those words—Briana clearly had feelings of her own for Kodyn. Turning back to the railing, Aisha stared out over the city of Shalandra. The view from the rooftop terrace was breathtaking; the third-story balcony gave her a clear view of the four lower tiers and the farmlands south of the wall. The bright afternoon sunlight washed everything in a golden glow.

The silence stretched on for long seconds before Aisha could speak. "You're right." She turned back to Briana. "About me and what I feel for Kodyn. But I have no claim on him. He's free to do what he wants, to be with whoever he wants. Even if that person is not me."

It felt so strange to say the words. In Ghandia, she and Briana would be fighting rather than speaking. A simpler, more direct approach to such a matter that could prevent it from becoming a problem. But Aisha's time in Praamis had changed her. People did things differently here in the south. She wanted Kodyn to reciprocate her feelings, but couldn't force the issue. Doing so could only drive him away, into Briana's arms.

And, truth be told, she couldn't fault Kodyn. Briana was beautiful, with her golden mahogany skin, well-proportioned features, and arrow-straight nose. The thick lines of *kohl* around her eyes accentuated the smoky-colored crushed malachite applied to her eyelids.

Aisha couldn't help a moment of envy; the tight-fitting Shalandran dress accentuated Briana's slim curves, which contrasted sharply with Aisha's broad shoulders and heavy muscles. Briana had the elegance of a nobleman's daughter and had proven herself an intelligent young woman. Aisha's skill at arms paled in comparison to the wealth Briana could offer.

"I owe you my life," Briana said, "both of you. You rescued me from the Gatherers and brought me safely home. Now, it turns out we'll be spending even *more* time together. I wouldn't want anything as silly as a boy to stop us from being friends." Her face fell. "I don't have a lot of those. It's hard to make friends when you're the daughter of a member of the Keeper's Council. You never know if people are actually your friend for *real* or if they want something from you."

She fixed Aisha with a piercing gaze. "But you're not like that. With you, I know that what I see is what I'm going to get. That's the sort of thing I'd love to have in a friend. I don't want to waste the chance of a true friendship over a man, no matter how handsome or charming he is."

Again, Aisha was struck by how different this new Briana was. There was still the same hint of shyness, but now she saw the truth of the Shalandran girl. Being the secret daughter of a Secret Keeper and one of the city's highest-ranked people made her as much an interloper as Aisha had been in Praamis. Yet unlike Briana, Aisha had had people like Ria, Afia, and the others of House Phoenix—people of her own kind. Briana was an outlier searching desperately for a place to belong, just as Aisha was.

"I'd be honored to call you my friend, Briana of Shalandra." Aisha gave the girl a warm smile and held out a hand. "Our feelings for Kodyn will never get in the way of that, I promise."

Briana dodged the outstretched hand and threw her arms around Aisha's waist. Though the Shalandran girl was small, her slim arms had surprising strength.

Aisha stiffened for a moment, caught off-guard, then allowed herself to relax and wrap her arms around Briana. She, too, was an outsider now, even among her own people. Ria had insisted she accompany Kodyn to Shalandra not only to keep him safe, but so she could find her destiny as a Spirit Whisperer. None of the others in House Phoenix, not even her fellow Ghandians, could understand the burden that rested on her shoulders. Perhaps, with friends like Kodyn and now Briana, she'd have someone to help bear the load.

Briana broke off the hug and fixed Aisha with a bright-eyed grin. "Come, let me show you my favorite part of the garden!" She grabbed Aisha's hand and tugged her deeper into the garden.

Aisha followed, her eyes roaming the garden and instinctively analyzing it for any sign of threat. She might not have Kodyn's skill at finding vulnerabilities in buildings, but she'd spent her life among the bushes, scrub, trees, and grasses of the Ghandian grasslands. She knew how an enemy could hide behind the trunk of that spikethorn tree or use the cover of this maidenhair tree's leaves to slip closer. If Briana truly was in danger, Aisha would keep a wary eye on the rooftop garden.

Yet the Shalandran girl appeared to have lost the fearfulness instilled in her by her captivity. Here, among the nature of her father's home, she finally seemed to be at ease. Her words flowed out in a happy torrent as she flitted between the various plants, shrubs, berry bushes, and trees, describing each in turn. Aisha barely heard the overload of information but she smiled, nodded, and added the appropriate exclamation of wonder.

Then, her eyes fell onto a patch of bright blue flowers, and it felt as if she'd run face-first into a wall.

Aisha stopped, her breath trapped in her lungs, and an icy chill ran down her spine. *It can't be! They shouldn't be here.*

But they were. No mistake, no trick of her imagination.

Her eyes fixed on the little flowers: four petals the color of a cloudless midday sky, with a hint of purple where they joined the delicate stalks. Even from here, she could imagine the smell—sweeter than desert roses, like the scent of belladonna, but with a sharper, spicier edge.

The same smell that had hung around her father every day since the madness claimed him.

Aisha found herself unable to move. The tiled walkway led right past the small patch of the flowers her mother had called "Whispering Lilies". If she kept walking, she'd come close enough to brush the petals that had stolen her father from her.

"What's wrong?" Briana's question seemed to come from a thousand leagues away.

Aisha blinked, found the girl staring at her with worry furrowing her brow. "Those…flowers," was all she managed to get out.

Briana turned to regard the little blue blossoms. "Oh, yes, they can be pretty nasty things. My father calls them Keeper's Spike." Her fingers moved to spell out the word in the hand gestures. "I think in the rest of Einan they're known as Watcher's Bloom."

Watcher's Bloom. To the Night Guild, the Watcher was the god of justice. *Where is the justice in knowing that my father was driven insane by this very plant?*

An *Umoyahlebe* from a neighboring tribe had given him a bundle of dried Whispering Lilies, claiming it could help Spirit Whisperers hear the words of the *Kish'aa* more clearly. It had done precisely that, but too well. For a year or so, he'd actually been more lucid, his mind clear when not using the flower. But slowly, inevitably, the madness of his gift not only returned, the flower had worsened it.

"Be careful with it," Briana said, not seeming to notice the change in Aisha. "Even a single drop of the oil can cause powerful hallucinations."

Aisha knew only too well the effects the plant could have. When her father applied the extract under his eyelids, he'd be lost in the world of the *Kish'aa* for hours, sometimes days.

Once, during his better days, he'd spoken to her of the gift. "The day will come when you, too, must answer the call of the spirits, *bindazi*." *Little gazelle,* his pet name for her. "The Whispering Lily will attune you to the *Kish'aa*. On that day, you must be ready to make the sacrifice. It is the only way to hear what the spirits have to tell you."

She hadn't understood what he'd meant by "sacrifice", but now she did. He'd sacrificed his sanity for the sake of the spirits.

"Come on." Briana plucked at Aisha's hand and pulled her off the walkway, away from the bright blue flowers. "This way."

Aisha allowed herself to be dragged along, her legs as numb as her mind.

Briana led her through a thick screen of dwarf palms and spineberry bushes. She dropped her voice to a conspiratorial whisper. "In here." With a quick glance around to make certain no one was around, she pulled Aisha through a thick hedge.

*No*, Aisha realized, *not a hedge, but a dome.* Leaves and vines climbed upward from the ground to form a natural dome a hand's breadth above Aisha's head. Purple-and-gold flowers filled the interior with dazzling color and a soft scent that brought back memories of running through the patches of aster that grew on the grasslands around her home.

"Isn't it wonderful?" Briana asked, her eyes bright.

Aisha nodded. "Truly, it is."

"It reminds me of her, of my mother." Briana's smile didn't waver, but a shadow passed over her eyes. "I never met her, but Father told me that these dewflowers were her favorite. Sometimes, when I'm here alone, I can imagine that she's here with me."

Aisha's gut tightened. *It's not your imagination,* she tried to say, but no words came out. A single wisp-like form hovered in the dome, a blue-white figure of a woman that seemed to float like a hummingbird between the flowers.

"What was her name?" Aisha finally managed, her eyes fixed on the spirit.

"Radiana," Briana said in a quiet voice. "Father told me it means *bright spirit* in the language of the Secret Keepers."

"Radiana," Aisha echoed. As she'd feared, the ethereal form turned toward her. The spirit's eyes seemed to glow brighter as she caught sight of Briana and her mouth formed words Aisha couldn't hear.

Before her father had lost himself to the *Kish'aa*, he'd told her of the power of names. *"Spirits are connected to us through our memories of them,"* he'd explained. *"Even after the image of their faces, the sound of their voices, the feeling of their warmth fades from our minds, we remember their names. Thus, it is those names that connect us to the Kish'aa."*

A lump rose to Aisha's throat as the spirit's eyes locked with hers. Radiana's lips moved without a sound, but Aisha felt the emotions pouring from the spirit. So much love, all channeled through Aisha, as if the spark of Radiana's life hoped that Aisha could pass that feeling on to Briana.

"If she were here," Aisha forced out, her voice thick, "what would you say to her?"

Radiana's ghostly gaze went to Briana and she floated over to wrap ethereal arms around her daughter's shoulders.

Tears brimmed in Briana's eyes. "I would say I'm sorry." Her words came out barely above a whisper.

"Sorry?" Aisha's brow furrowed.

"She died because of me," Briana said. "I would want her to know how sorry I am for that."

Aisha felt a sudden spike of Radiana's emotions. "I believe your mother would tell you that she is proud of you." Words poured from her mouth beyond her control. "Of the strong, brave young woman you've become. Of how you've cared for your father and brightened his life. And of all you will yet do."

It seemed her feet moved of their own accord, as if drawn not toward Briana, but to the ethereal form floating above the girl. Aisha reached out a hand to rest on Briana's shoulder, and Radiana's spirit placed a ghostly hand atop hers. For that brief instant, the thoughts and feelings of Briana's mother seeped into Aisha's mind.

"And she would tell you that she loves you." Aisha felt Radiana's fingers squeezing Briana's shoulders. "More than anything else, she wants you to know that."

Tears streamed freely down Briana's face, and Aisha couldn't help the emotions roiling through her. She couldn't tell if they were Radiana's or her own—she could only pull Briana into a tight hug as the younger girl wept.

# *Chapter Twenty-Three*

Nervous tension coiled like a snake in Evren's gut as he waited for the grey-haired woman—Nessa, Killian had called her—to finish reading the message from the blacksmith. He had no idea what it said, a fact that heightened his anxiety further, but whatever Killian had penned seemed to have a marked effect on the woman.

"You come highly recommended." Nessa rolled up the scroll and turned a keen-eyed stare on Evren and Hailen. Her voice was crisp and commanding, edged with a hint of disapproval as she studied them. "Yet whether or not you can be trusted remains to be seen."

Evren remained silent; the woman wouldn't care what he said, only what he did. Killian had told them his recommendation—under another name, one he didn't divulge—would get them in the door, but they'd have to earn their way.

"Under normal circumstances," the Steward said, "you would go through a lengthy vetting process, but due to recent events, we will have to make do." She narrowed her eyes and leaned over her broad oak desk, the centerpiece of her well-appointed office, to stare at them. "However, be warned: your every action will be scrutinized."

Killian had warned him of the keen-eyed Steward. *"Nessa will keep a close eye on you,"* the blacksmith had said. *"If you do anything suspicious, she'll pounce on it like a cat on a dead mouse. Be very sure your plan to steal the Blade of Hallar is foolproof before making a move. You've got one chance with Nessa."*

"I do not make threats," the grey-haired woman said, narrowing her eyes, "but you have my word as an *Intaji* that I will not simply dismiss you at the first sign of anything untoward. You wouldn't be the first servants I've had flogged in Murder Square for betraying my master."

"I understand." Evren nodded and held her gaze, though his gut clenched beneath her hawk-like stare. *She might look like a friendly grandmother, but in this case, looks are very deceiving.*

"My brother and I just want to earn our keep in service to the Arch-Guardian," Evren said aloud.

Nessa cocked an eyebrow at Hailen. "Your…brother will serve as the young mistress Briana's personal varlet until I can find a suitable maidservant to fill the role." She fixed him with a critical eye. "As for you, I believe the role of attendant will suit you well."

Evren nodded. "Glad to serve wherever I am needed."

Nessa didn't quite snort—it was more of a snuff of derision. "We shall see about that."

She rang a little bell on her desk, and a moment later a compact man with a red-and-gold headband entered the room.

"Cavad, see that the younger one is sent to Zuima on the upper floor. He is to serve as Mistress Briana's varlet."

"Of course, Steward." The man bowed.

"But first, take the older one to Samall." A grim smile played on Nessa's lips, her eyes on Evren. "And if he proves anything less than efficient, make it clear that I expect Samall to whip him into shape."

Evren's gut clenched as he and Hailen followed the servant Cavad from the Steward's simple yet tastefully furnished office.

The office was located in the rear of the mansion, well away from the lavish ballrooms, grand staircases, and upper-floor wings where the *Dhukari* lived. Back here, in the section of the estate the masters never went, the halls were simple sandstone with bare walls and floors, compact doorways, and doors designed more for soundproofing and privacy than luxury.

The servant, Cavad, led Evren through the narrow corridors toward the southern end of the mansion. "Piece of advice," the man whispered. "Mouth shut and eyes down. Give Samall no cause for complaint and you will be fine."

Evren nodded. "Thank you."

He turned to Hailen. "You got this?" he whispered.

Hailen nodded. "Yes."

"Remember what I told you." Evren fixed him with a stern frown. "Say as little as possible about yourself, and only speak when spoken to. We're servants now, as beneath notice as a chair or rug. Do *nothing* to draw attention to yourself."

"I said I got it." Hailen shot him a frown. "I've been practicing disguises with the Hunter and Kiara."

Try as he might, Evren couldn't get the worry out of his mind. Hailen's innocent, trusting nature made it hard for him to tell a convincing lie. *Let's just hope the lady of the house doesn't bother asking her servants questions.* At that moment, they arrived in the kitchens, and all worries about Hailen faded as Evren found himself face to face with his new superior. Samall was a stout man with a too-neat beard and thinning hair that he wore cropped close and oiled back with a thick layer of grease. He barely reached Evren's shoulders yet affected the stern manner and commanding voice of a harridan. Cavad barely repeated Nessa's words before he grabbed Hailen and fled.

"So you're to be an attendant, eh?" Samall looked Evren up and down. "You've the build for it, so there's that. What do you know about serving the *Dhukari*?"

"I—"

"Nothing, that's what!" Samall cut him off with a chopping motion. "Being one of Arch-Guardian Suroth's staff is an honor that you have to *earn*. Forget everything you learned in whatever piss-hole you came from. I'm going to teach you the right way to serve a member of the Keeper's Council properly." He stepped closer—close enough that Evren could see every neatly-shaven hair on his face and smell the stink coming off three rotting teeth in the back of the man's mouth—and spoke in a low growl. "Maybe, if the Keeper's blessed you with better brains than your looks, there's a chance you won't totally cock this up." His face twisted into a sneer. "But I'm not holding out hope."

*Keeper's teeth.* Evren's heart sank. *What the bloody hell did I get myself into?*

\* \* \*

The afternoon went *far* worse than Evren expected. Over his years as an apprentice in the Master's Temple, he'd picked up skills that would have served him well in any other household, even the noble houses of Voramis. But nothing he did was right to Samall.

When he'd helped shifting furniture in the upstairs sun room, Samall had growled at him for lifting wrong. The curses had turned into a tirade when he set Evren to dusting the bookshelves in the hallway outside Arch-Guardian Suroth's office, then a full-blown dressing-down when Evren failed to place the delicate ceramic dinnerware in precisely the right place on their shelf in the kitchens. Somehow, he even found offense with the way Evren emptied the chamber pots—though that could have something to do with the fact that Evren purposely splashed night waste on his sandaled feet.

Finally, he banished Evren to the shadows of the kitchens and set him to scrubbing pots. That suited Evren just fine; he'd spent hours laboring under the watchful eye of Lectern Ordari as they prepared for the bi-monthly feasts in the Master's Temple. He could scrub a pot with the best of them, but he could turn a ten-minute task into a three-hour job when it suited him. Right now, if it kept him away from Samall, he'd take hours to wash the burned bottoms of the soup tureens.

From within the darkness in the rear of the kitchens, he watched the cooks and servant women moving around. He paid close attention to their chatter. Killian had asked for information, so he needed to gather something that could prove of use to the blacksmith. Servant's gossip often proved very enlightening.

"Did you hear?" muttered one cook to another. "It really *is* the Lady Briana returned!"

"Where d'you think she went?" a maidservant responded. "Do you believe it's true that she was abducted by the Necroseti?"

"Don't know." The cook shrugged. "But I heard it was the Gatherers that took her."

*That could be something of interest.*

Evren had no idea who the Necroseti or Gatherers were, but the fact that one of them had evidently abducted the Arch-Guardian's daughter could prove of interest to Killian. He listened as closely as he could while maintaining the outward appearance of being absorbed in his task.

"Whoever it was, you know that's why Eldesse and Osirath disappeared when they did."

"Disappeared?" asked the second cook. "Or killed like Burum, Attumi, and Engwar?"

"No!" gasped the first. "They found the bodies?"

"Not that I know, but it can't be a coincidence." The second looked triumphant, as if she'd just scored a point in their verbal joust of scuttlebutt. "Either they helped the abductors or they were unlucky enough to get in the way. The fact there are no corpses makes me think it's the first reason."

*That explains why the household is hiring servants, and why the Steward is so suspicious.*

Servants had access to their masters at their most vulnerable, as well as their masters' most valuable treasures. Stewards and majordomos like Nessa had to be careful only to choose those they knew could be trusted. To discover that the Lady Briana's maidservant and her husband were traitors would deal Nessa a severe blow in her master's eyes.

*Killian will definitely want to know about this.*

Evren set the pot down—a little too hard—and the *clank* of metal on stone caught the cook's attention. The rotund, flour-covered woman stared at him through narrowed eyes. Suspicion, or perhaps too much of the wine she was supposed to add to the master's dinner, turned her cheeks a dark red.

"Here now, who are you, then?" she demanded.

Evren gave them a shy smile. "Evren. I'm new."

The cook bristled. "Well, new boy, don't you know it's not polite to eavesdrop?"

"Sorry." Evren made a show of looking apologetic, even wrung his hands in a sham of contrition.

"Sorry's right!" snapped the maidservant. "Best mind yourself, else you'll earn yourself a whipping from Samall."

"Here!" The cook thrust a huge pot filled with filthy water and vegetable peelings at him. "Take this outside and empty it in the horses' trough. Then get yourself to Samall and find a duty that keeps you out of our way."

With a mumbled apology, Evren seized the pot and hauled it out of the kitchens. The pot was heavy and over-full. He grimaced as the filthy water sloshed onto his clothing—he had little doubt Samall would take him to task for staining his new uniform.

The kitchens let out onto a courtyard at the rear of the mansion, bordered by the stables on one side and the sandstone wall on the other. Around a corner from the courtyard stood the tradesman's entrance, which was used to haul in supplies. Evren had just made it to the horses' trough outside the stables when he caught sight of Samall locked in a hushed conversation with another servant in the shadows of the back gate. Something about Samall's dark expression and the way his eyes darted around roused Evren's suspicion. Pot in hand, he ducked out of sight around the corner before the attendant caught sight of him.

Every instinct screamed that he needed to listen in on that conversation and find out what was going on. *They are clearly up to no good.*

After a breathless moment, he peered toward the back gate. He had to creep closer to be able to see and hear them. To his relief, Samall and the manservant were still talking, and they showed no sign of having spotted him.

"…need to go now," Samall was saying in a tense whisper. "Her return cannot bode well for our cause. If we can take her again, this time without bloodshed, our brothers will have the leverage we need over the Arch-Guardian. And if not, her death will convince the father of the folly of ignoring our instructions. Either way, he must be forced to make the right choice when the time comes to act."

"I will get word to our brothers, but surely it would be better to wait until after nightfall," the servant replied. "If the Indomitables catch me, they will—"

Samall cut him off with a slash of his hand. "That is the price of what we do, the price we are all willing to pay for the sake of Shalandra's future."

After a moment, the second man nodded.

"I will cover for your absence," Samall said. "Go, but hurry back. We will be attending the Arch-Guardian in the Pharus' palace tonight. It will be the perfect opportunity to plan tomorrow's strike."

The servant clasped Samall's hand. "Keeper smile on you and guard you from the Final Destruction."

"And you, Brother." With a nod, Samall pulled open the back door for the man to slip out.

Evren ducked back into his hiding place near the stables as Samall turned away. He couldn't risk the man finding out he'd been overheard. Whatever he was planning couldn't be good.

*And they've got something planned for Lady Briana.* According to the kitchen gossip, people had died during the young lady's abduction. Hailen had just been assigned to serve Lady Briana directly. *He could be in danger. Especially given that they're talking about possibly killing her.*

But what was he supposed to do? He had no idea who Samall and his comrade reported to, or what they had planned for the following night. His only goal right now—beyond finding the Blade of Hallar—was to keep Hailen safe.

Strange as it felt, he had only one person he could rely on right now.

*I've got to get to Killian and tell him what's going on.*

But, before he could move, Samall's screeching shout broke the silence of the now-empty courtyard. "Where are you, you incompetent lout?"

Evren contemplated the rear gate for a moment. He could get out before Samall found him, but when he returned, he'd have to explain his absence. It was too early in his employment to do anything that would raise suspicion.

He darted back to his pot, scooped it up, and hauled it toward the horses' trough inside the stable. He'd just finished tipping it up before Samall strode into view in the courtyard.

"What in the Keeper's name is delaying you, boy?" the attendant roared.

Evren, recalling Cavad's advice, kept his eyes on the ground and his mouth shut, but held up the empty pot by way of explanation.

Samall's cuff caught him on the side of the head with enough force to send him stumbling. Yet Evren had taken far harder blows and come back swinging. Instinct and hard years on the streets kicked in, and his fists clenched, his muscles going tense. His right arm actually pulled back into a jab before he caught himself.

*No!* He sucked in a breath and fought to rein in his temper, push back the near-overwhelming urge to fight back. His head rang from the strike, more with anger than pain. He could knock in the attendant's teeth and turn the pudgy bastard into a bleeding, sobbing puddle. But he'd get nowhere assaulting his superior on his first day. Slowly, he let out his breath and forced his fists to unclench.

Samall seemed not to notice the internal war. "Let's go, boy!" He seized Evren's arm and hauled him out of the stables. "There's much to do to prepare for our departure to the Palace of Golden Eternity tonight."

Evren ground his teeth and allowed himself to be manhandled. When the time came, when he uncovered whatever sinister plot Samall was involved in, he'd enjoy returning the man's abuse a hundredfold.

But not yet. Not until he found out what the servant had planned for Lady Briana. He'd listen and watch; his position as footman meant he could keep a close eye on the entrances to the mansion for any hint of threat.

And, at the first opportunity, he'd find a way to send word to Killian. Something told him the blacksmith—clearly more than just a simple artisan—would know what to do.

# Chapter Twenty-Four

"Carry on, then!" The black-armored Indomitable's stern expression didn't waver, but he waved Kodyn through after a few seconds.

"Thank you." Kodyn gave the guard a friendly smile and hurried on his way. Inside, however, his guts churned.

*That's the third time I've been stopped since leaving Suroth's.*

Indomitables patrolled the Keeper's Tier and Defender's Tier, their eyes vigilant as they sought any not wearing the blue or gold-braided headbands that marked them as residents of the uppermost levels. Kodyn's Praamian pale skin made him stand out from the bronzed Shalandrans like a stormcloud in a clear blue sky.

*Good thing I've got this headband.* The strip was made of braided gold and green cloth and a silver disc displaying the Arch-Guardian's sigil on his forehead. Though it set his skin itching, he'd put up with it as long as it got him where he needed to go.

Yet it felt somehow wrong to be strolling around in plain sight. After a life spent in the shadows, he hated the scrutiny. He'd prefer the shadows, sewers, or rooftops any day.

Thankfully, once he reached the Artisan's Tier, the tier of the commerce-minded *Intaji* and intellectual *Zadii*, he should have no problems evading the Indomitables' attention. One more foreigner wouldn't stand out among the marketplaces—Commerce Square and Industry Square, Suroth had called them.

Kodyn had discovered that only one avenue, Death Row, led to the uppermost tiers. With the solid walls, thick gates, and ever-present patrols of Indomitables standing guard, it would be nearly impossible to get back to the

*Dhukari* tier unseen. He'd have to enjoy the anonymity of the crowded Artisan's Tier while he could.

The Indomitables holding the gate that exited the Defender's Tier barely paid him any attention. They focused more about who *entered* rather than those who left. Kodyn was perfectly happy with that. The less people noticed him, the better.

The road descending from the Defender's Tier was mostly empty until it reached the intersection with Artificer's Courseway, the avenue that ran east to west along the Artisan's Tier. The Courseway, however, was near clogged with people, wagons, carts, and draft animals.

Kodyn scanned the crowd warily. He hadn't caught anyone following him, but he wouldn't abandon the cautious habits he'd developed over nearly a decade in the Night Guild. His eyes took in every detail, which his brain quickly categorized as mundane, interesting, or threatening. The mundane was ignored, but he paid attention to everything else.

The graffiti on a nearby wall fell into the "interesting" category. "Child of Spirits" had been painted in crude, crimson letters atop the fresh whitewash of a bakery. Kodyn had seen "Child of Gold" painted on the lower tier, and the near-reverence of the young *Earaqi* men had intrigued him. To see it here on the Artisan's Tier added to his interest.

But he had more important things to focus on than curious street art. As soon as he was out of sight of the Indomitables guarding the Defender's Tier gate, he slipped into the shadows of the nearest side street. His fingers loosened the knots holding his ornate headband in place, and he replaced it with the green band worn by all non-Shalandrans.

On the uppermost tiers, he'd need Suroth's headband to get around. Down here, the gold-and-green with its bright sigil-bearing silver disc would just draw more attention. He'd blend into the crowd far more easily as just one more foreigner roaming through the markets and shops of the Artisan's Tier.

He missed his dull-colored Hawk's clothing, but the *shendyt* and tunic he wore beneath his simple cloak made him look as ordinary as he could manage in a city of dark-skinned Shalandrans. He didn't dare wear the hood of his ornate stole pulled forward—that would only draw more attention—but he tugged his long, dark hair free of its tail and let it hang around his face. That, at least, would obscure his features so he wouldn't be recognized.

He shot a longing glance up toward the rooftops of the Artisan's Tier buildings. *If only this was Praamis, I could run around the Hawk's Highway without worrying about being spotted by the Indomitables.* The maze of rope walkways, wooden bridges, and metal beams that crisscrossed the Praamian rooftops made it easier for the Night Guild to travel around the city undetected.

Here, however, the buildings with their smooth sandstone walls would prove more difficult to scale, and few things would draw unwanted attention faster than a young foreigner crashing through a thatched roof.

With a sigh, he stepped out into the lane. *I guess we're doing this the Fox way.*

Like every other apprentice in House Hawk, he'd spent the better part of a year running with the apprentices of House Fox, the street-level counterparts to House Hawk's third-story thieves. He'd never quite mastered the art of picking pockets to the satisfaction of the older Foxes, but he'd lifted enough to earn his way. But he *had* excelled at moving around the city without drawing attention. Even years later, the old skills came back to him easily.

Sliding through a busy street and thick crowds unseen was an art form. It started with innocuous-looking clothing, which meant he'd had to forsake his Praamian clothing in exchange for more traditional Shalandran dress. Literally, it felt like a dress. He could move well enough, but he missed the pockets and pouches he'd had in his vests and cloak.

He moved in a slight hunch, head tilted down, yet his eyes never stopped moving as they scanned the streets. His movements flowed with the crowds that surged and pushed around him, and he kept close to larger packs of people—servants from *Dhukari* households, pale-skinned foreigners, even heavily-laden wagons. As long as he didn't move too fast or jostle anyone too hard, he could almost blend into the throng of the two marketplaces.

The trinkets of Industry Square and the produce of Commerce Square held little interest to him, but he used the stalls and shops for cover. He doubled back on his trail twice just to be certain no one followed him before finally pushing through Commerce Square and heading west toward his true destination.

He drew in a deep breath as he caught sight of The Gilded Parlour, one of five brothels permitted in Shalandra—one for each tier. It catered primarily to the *Zadii* and *Intaji* that lived on this tier, though some *Earaqi* managed to scrape together enough coin for a night of pleasure with the golden-painted women with their ornate white and brown headbands.

The women of The Gilded Parlour wore the tight-fitting *kalasiris* dresses common to Shalandra, but with the upper hems stopping well below their breasts. Though some used the leather straps for modesty, most used the low-cut design of the dresses to draw attention to the wares they proudly displayed for all passersby. The golden paint that covered every inch of their skin made them seem to glow in the afternoon sunlight like the rest of the city.

But Kodyn hadn't come for the women. He'd come to see the Black Widow.

The interior of The Gilded Parlour was spacious, well-furnished with plush couches and love seats. Everything was gold, from the metal-plated chandelier to the gold thread woven into the bright yellow fabric to the paintings that hung on the wall. It was bright enough to be garish, with the only spot of real color coming from the wooden bar along the north and western edges of the room. Three rough-looking men stood behind the bar serving drinks, watching the men and women scattered around the brothel with keen eyes and hands hovering close to the cudgels on their belts.

Kodyn strode up to the nearest, a slope-shouldered brute with greying hair and dark eyes. He held up two fingers. "Two Spider Legs."

The bartender gave no sign of recognition or interest, simply reached behind the bar and pulled out a glass bottle filled with black liquor. He poured the liquor into two glasses barely larger than a thimble and slid them across the bar to Kodyn. With a nod, Kodyn knocked back the first.

The liquor had a distinctly spicy edge of cinnamon, cloves, and ginger, but just enough sweetness to be enjoyable. Its potency, however, rivaled the strongest Voramian agor, and Kodyn struggled not to cough as the burning alcohol slid a fiery trail down his throat and into his stomach. As the heat settled, he was left with a pleasant spicy-sweet taste in his mouth.

He made no move to empty the second drink. Instead, he plunked a pair of Praamian imperials on the bar, picked up the tiny glass, and strode toward the shadows at the northern edge of the chamber. A small, round booth sized for two people stood empty, and Kodyn slipped into the gold fabric-covered seat.

Kodyn settled back into the couch to wait. Time passed slowly, the liquor burning its way into Kodyn's gut. He'd inherited his mother's taste for sweet wines—Voramian Snowblossom or Nyslian reds—though he'd shared some Praamian rum with Ria at her insistence. But this liquor was far stronger than anything he'd had before.

*Maybe that's why the Black Widow expects her guests to drink it. They'll be too soused to try anything stupid.*

He pretended to relax in his chair, but every muscle in his body was tense as he kept a wary eye on the room. No one paid him much interest—not even the bartenders approached to offer another drink—and he could detect no sign of being followed. If someone was watching him, they were good enough he couldn't spot them.

Half an hour later, the bartender slid out from around the gold-painted wooden bar and strode toward Kodyn. He picked up the tiny glass, emptied it, and gestured for Kodyn to follow.

"This way," he muttered, and disappeared through a small, curtain-covered doorway on the northeastern corner of the room.

Kodyn followed and found himself in a narrow corridor that ran for a few paces, with a single doorway at the end. However, halfway down the hall, the bartender slid aside a panel to reveal a staircase. At the top of the stairs, there was another door, this one built of heavy iron-banded wood, with a steel doorknob to match.

The man produced a key—Kodyn saw it matched an eight-pin tumbler lock—and used it to open the door. He motioned for Kodyn to enter.

Kodyn strode into the room. It was pitch black and, as far as he could see, utterly empty.

"You have five minutes," the bartender said and swung the door closed, plunging Kodyn into darkness.

Kodyn had spent nearly a decade moving around the darkened passages of the Night Guild, the starlit rooftops of the Hawk's Highway, and the pitch black sewer tunnels beneath Praamis, but he'd never felt as nervous as he did now.

He caught a slight hint of shuffling slippers, the creak of wood—*a secret passage?*—and a moment later, a voice drifted from the darkness of the room. "Welcome to Shalandra, Praamian."

It was a woman, of that Kodyn was certain, but her voice had an ageless quality about it. He couldn't tell if she was his age or old enough to be his grandmother. Suddenly, a thread of light streamed through a tiny crack in the heavy shutters barring a window. He caught a glimpse of a slim hand and the outline of her silhouette in the dim illumination. She was neither tall nor short, heavy nor emaciated. With her face concealed by shadow, she looked like a thousand other Shalandran women.

*Which is probably the point,* Kodyn thought. *The less she stands out, the easier it is to protect her true identity.*

The ritual below—ordering the spider-themed drink, waiting to be summoned by the bartender—had likely given the Black Widow's people time to study him.

"What brings you to my city?" she asked.

Kodyn had expected the question—his mother had prepared him for his meeting with the Black Widow, the closest thing to her counterpart in Shalandra. Though she didn't organize crime to the same extent the Night Guild did in Praamis, she had her finger on the pulse of everything that went on in her city. One part spymaster, one part information broker, and four parts deadly when crossed.

Ilanna had emphasized the importance of making contact with the Black Widow immediately upon his arrival in Shalandra. "If she finds out who you are," his mother had said, "you're likely to end up with a dagger in your back unless you have her permission. Better to bring a peace offering than try to talk your way out of a dangerous situation."

Kodyn had spent many hours on his long journey from Praamis mulling over his mother's instructions and trying to decide just how much to tell the Black Widow. Finally, he'd settled on as much truth as she needed to know.

"I've come to steal the Crown of the Pharus," he said without hesitation.

"Have you now?" The Black Widow chuckled, almost a girlish giggle. "And here I thought the Night Guild was far more sensible than that."

"It's my Undertaking." Kodyn reasoned that if she'd already marked him as belonging to the Night Guild, she would know enough about their practices to recognize his purpose for being here. "But I don't intend to take it out of Shalandra."

"Of course not." The Black Widow gave a dismissive wave of her slim hand. "You wouldn't get an hour out of the city before every Keeper's Blade descended upon you. You simply intend to steal it to prove you can, but you have no desire to actually make off with it, is that not so?"

"Yes." Kodyn was impressed. *She knows a lot more about the Night Guild than I expected.*

"And I presume that you intend to use the goodwill earned by returning Lady Briana to convince her father to aid you in this Undertaking?"

"Yes." Again, Kodyn had to marvel. *She really does know as much as Mother warned me.* He'd clearly made the right choice by telling her the truth.

He reached into a pouch and drew out a small pyramid-shaped gemstone. "I offer this as a token of the Night Guild's appreciation for your permission to operate in your city."

The woman reached out a slim hand—the sliver of light revealed a thin iron bracelet encircling her wrist—and took the gemstone. When she held it up to the light, the thin beam of white light from the window was refracted by the diamond and cast six separate beams onto the wall, each a different color of the rainbow.

"A fine gift." She sounded pleased. "Your offering is accepted. For as long as you and your Ghandian companion remain in Shalandra, you have my approval to undertake this quest to steal the Crown of the Pharus."

Kodyn forced himself not to stiffen in surprise. If the Black Widow had known he was escorting Briana, it made sense that she knew of Aisha as well.

"Come to think of it, your mission puts you in a unique position." The Black Widow's tone grew musing. "One that could prove of mutual benefit."

Kodyn raised an eyebrow—an expression lost in the shadows of the room. "I'm listening."

"No one has ever succeeded in stealing the Crown of the Pharus, though not for lack of trying." Amusement tinged her words. "Yet, perhaps, with the right preparation, you will succeed where others have failed. Tell me, does the Night Guild still roam the sewer tunnels beneath Praamis?"

Again, Kodyn struggled to hide his surprise. *She's damned good if she knows that much.*

"Yes," he said when he'd recovered.

"The city of Shalandra, too, is said to be the handiwork of the ancient Serenii," the Black Widow explained. "Much of the city's design—from the structure of the tiers to the palace's heating and ventilation network to the underground channels that supply us with fresh water—were designed by minds far superior to ours. And, like all Serenii cities, there are networks of underground tunnels and passages that run like a honeycomb throughout."

Kodyn frowned, pensive. "Let me guess, you want me to steal the map of this tunnel network."

"Steal?" The Black Widow laughed, a sound that held the sonorous timbre of mature humor. "No, dear boy, there is no need for that. The man responsible for mapping the tunnels owes me far more than just his life. All I have to do is ask."

Kodyn folded his arms. "If so, where do I come in?"

"You will procure the map and use it to aid you in your quest," the Black Widow said. "And, in return, you will answer me one simple question."

"That's it?" Kodyn cocked his head. "Seems a bit of a one-sided bargain, doesn't it?"

"Even a young thief like you has to know that knowledge is power." The Black Widow's voice held a tone of wry humor. "The right secret whispered in the right ear can topple dynasties and build empires."

Kodyn nodded. He'd heard much the same from Journeyman Darreth. "What do you want to know?"

"Who took Lady Briana?"

The Black Widow's question caught Kodyn off-guard. He'd expected something about the Night Guild, his mother, or any number of other things, yet now that he thought about it, he realized the question could carry far more weight than anything he could tell her about Praamis. The Black Widow could use the knowledge of who was behind the abduction in countless ways.

"Have you heard of priests that call themselves the Gatherers?" Kodyn asked.

A deep-throated curse sounded in the darkness, followed by a moment of silence.

Finally, the Black Widow spoke. "The Gatherers took her? You are certain?"

"I saw the priest, Necroset Kytos, die."

"Good." The woman's voice held a tone of grim satisfaction. "Thank you, young Praamian. With this, our bargain is struck."

The woman extended a hand into the thread of daylight. In her open palm lay a round silver coin—larger than Praamian gold imperials, but unlike Shalandran coinage, it didn't bear the Pharus' head on the face side. Instead, it bore the mark of an eight-legged spider. A black widow.

"Show this to Ennolar, a Secret Keeper and member of the Venerated, and he will give you what you desire," the Black Widow told him. "Once you have made use of the map, I would consider it a courtesy if you would deliver it to me."

"Of course." Kodyn nodded.

"But not here." The Black Widow's voice was stern, the commanding tone reminding Kodyn of his mother in her role as Guild Master. "You must never return to The Gilded Parlour. If you wish to speak to me, seek out the children wearing iron bracelets like mine." She held her wrist up to the light. "We communicate through them."

*Of course, children!* No wonder Kodyn hadn't spotted anyone following or watching him. He'd looked for men or women, but never a child. He kicked himself for a fool—he had spent most of his childhood as a thief, so he ought to know to look for the same here. *I won't make that mistake again.*

"I understand," he said and turned to go. "Thank you."

"One last thing, young Praamian." The Black Widow's voice stopped Kodyn in his tracks. "You bring gifts, and now I offer one in return. A warning: the Night Guild may rule the shadows of Praamis, but here in Shalandra, only danger lurks in the darkness. The same Gatherers you faced in your city slither through Shalandra, filling it with their vile words and deeds. The Ybrazhe Syndicate rivals the cruelty and ruthlessness of the Bloody Hand your Guild Master spent years driving out of her city. The Necroseti and the Keeper's Council conceal sharp daggers beneath pleasant words and false smiles. Trust no one but your companion."

Kodyn bowed. "I thank you for your warning."

"Heed my words," the Black Widow said, "and perhaps, with the Keeper's favor, you will survive long enough to tempt fate with your Undertaking."

With those ominous words ringing in his ears, Kodyn left the darkened room and the mysterious Shalandran spymaster.

# Chapter Twenty-Five

The hours seemed to drag on as they stood guard before the Tomb of Hallar. Hykos remained solemn and silent throughout their watch, and Issa didn't dare speak for fear of breaking some unspoken rule. Her mind filled with the gravity of Tannard's words and his warning against her failure. The weight of her armor and the throbbing aches of her body only added to the burden resting on her shoulders.

Finally, the next pair of Keeper's Blades came to replace them on guard. With a silent salute, Hykos and Issa marched off down the path that descended through the tombs.

Issa's eyes roamed over each of the tombs she passed. The stone faces of the ancient Pharuses seemed to mock her, and the black sarcophagi of the Keeper's Blades reminded her that she could never be as strong or unmovable as the mountain. She would *always* fail. It didn't matter that the *Invictus* asked her to do the impossible. Issa had spent the last five years training to be stronger, better, faster, and smarter. Tannard had smacked her over the head with the truth of her own limitations and it rocked her to her core.

Darkness had fully fallen by the time they stepped out of the tunnel and into the Citadel of Stone.

"You okay?" Hykos' words echoed with concern. "You've had a tough day, but—"

"Don't!" Issa growled at him. "I don't need your pity."

"I've none to offer." Hykos held up his hands in a defensive gesture. "Just a friendly word of advice from someone who's been where you are."

Issa bit back on the retort threatening to burst from her lips. "And what's that?"

"You only die when you quit fighting." Hykos shrugged. "Until then, nothing but the Long Keeper himself can stop you."

Issa had no doubt he meant the words to be a kindness, but right now, they just rubbed her failings in her face.

"Thanks," she snarled. Whirling, she stalked away down the hall that led toward her room. Emotions roiled within her as she marched through the empty, bare stone corridors and into her chamber. She hurled her sword and scabbard onto her bed and nearly tore off her armor. The weight and closeness suffocated her, squeezed at her lungs with a fist of iron. Finally free of the burden, she collapsed into her bed, exhausted physically and mentally overwhelmed.

*It's too much!* The thought echoed over and over. The harsh training, the starvation and sleep loss, the endless demands on her body and mind, *Invictus* Tannard's cruelty. All of it was intended to break her, and she had just about reached the point where she felt as if she'd shatter.

She'd felt like this before; Killian had pushed her hard, training her mind and body in anticipation of the hardships inflicted upon her in the Blades. Yet though the blacksmith had been surprisingly kind—when not forcing her to work harder—he wasn't the one that had gotten her through the ordeal.

Issa was suddenly gripped by an overwhelming desire to see her grandparents, to feel their arms around her, to hear their soothing voices and loving words. She didn't know if she was permitted but didn't care. She had to do it before her new life broke her soul.

She fled—armor and sword still on her bed—and hurried back the way she'd come. The Citadel of Stone would be locked at this time of night, but Tannard had shown her another way out.

The entrance to the tombs stood open, and the dust and stink of death welcomed her as she hurried into the cool silence beneath the mountain. Instead of heading up the hill, however, she turned south and began the descent toward the crypts on the lower tiers.

The tombs would be empty at this time of night, she knew. All ceremonial burials took place at sunset and sunrise. Aside from the guard patrols, few of the superstitious Shalandrans traveled the Keeper's Crypts. None would risk tempting the Keeper's wrath by disturbing the dead.

Massive, ornate *Dhukari* tombs soon gave way to smaller, simpler tombs that belonged to the *Alqati*, Shalandra's martial caste. The Indomitables were given homes on the Defender's Tier but earned only a modest wage from the Pharus for their defense of the city. Their tombs lacked the decorative flairs and towering stature of the wealthy *Dhukari*. Instead, they were the same simple sarcophagi of the tombs of the Keeper's Blades, all laid out in neat military order, though made of golden sandstone rather than the treasured shalanite. The hilts of the Indomitables' sickle-shaped khopesh swords protruded from the top of the sarcophagi. Every warrior was buried in full armor, their blades ready to be drawn in defense of Shalandra when Hallar returned.

Issa's stomach did a nervous backflip as she heard the sound of booted feet. The black-armored soldiers had the honor of guarding the crypts on all but the Keeper's Tier, and they took their task seriously. She barely had time to duck into the shadows of a sarcophagus before the troop of Indomitables marched past at a brisk pace.

She waited until the clanking of their half-plate armor faded into the distance before letting out the breath she'd been holding. Heart hammering, she slipped quickly down the path that cut through the *Alqati* tombs. The next patrol would be passing in five minutes, but the *Earaqi* crypts were at least half an hour of downhill travel.

The journey took nearly twice that long, given that she had to keep an eye and ear out for the patrols. Frustration mounted within her as she hid behind a small obelisk dedicated to an Adept, servant of the Swordsman, god of heroism and smithing. The obelisk, and the small forest of identical monoliths surrounding it, matched the Swordsman's Temple on the Artisan's Tier.

She crept through tombs dedicated to the rest of the Venerated, priests serving the twelve lesser gods of Einan, which led to the mausoleums of the intellectual *Zadii* and industrial *Intaji*. The *Intaji* tombs bore the symbols of their crafts: hammer and anvil for blacksmiths, compass and ruler for architects, mallet and chisel for stonemasons, and a hundred more. The crypts, mausoleums, and sarcophagi were decorated with the same lavish artistry that the *Intaji* had demonstrated in life.

The tombs on the *Earaqi* tier were simple: plain stone coffins and sarcophagi, few with a decorative flourish or two. Some had simple engravings on their coffins, but many were bare. Hard-working laborers could scarcely afford to eat well, much less pay an *Intaji* stonemason to carve a lavish tomb for them. Somewhere among this sea of stone, Issa's parents lay to rest under the Keeper's sleepless gaze.

She breathed easier as she stepped out of the Keeper's Crypts and onto the darkened streets of the Cultivator's Tier. The night was cool, with a gentle breeze kicking up dust, but it washed away the smells of the dust and decay behind her.

She tensed as a figure shambled out from a side street onto Commoner's Row a short distance ahead. Her hand dropped to her belt, only for her to remember that she'd left her sword back in the Citadel of Stone.

Yet, to her relief, the man didn't move toward her. He didn't even seem to see or hear her. He looked more skeleton than human, with yellowed and jaundiced skin revealing the blue tracery of veins, bulbous eyes, and a slack expression. Issa didn't know what strong drink or opiate he'd gotten his hands on, but it had left him little more than a husk of a human.

She ducked down a side street to avoid the man—her grandparents had warned her to be wary of anyone who appeared more dead than alive, for they had the least to lose. The back street was neat and clean, yet Issa caught sight of strange words painted onto a fresh-scrubbed brick wall.

*Child of Spirits,* she read. She'd seen similar words—*Child of Gold* and *Child of Secrets,* among others—dotting the three lower tiers of Shalandra, but she'd taken care to avoid the fiery-eyed young men that always seemed to be hanging around the paintings.

A few hundred yards up the road, she returned to Commoner's Row and hurried through the Cultivator's Tier toward her grandparents' home. With every step, the burden on her shoulders grew until she feared it would overwhelm her.

Warmth flooded her as she caught sight of the familiar squat stone building. A sudden wave of homesickness washed over her. Here, she'd been safe, loved, and cared for. Why had she defied her Savta and Saba and fought to join the Blades? The decision, which had seemed so right at first, now heaped mountains of misery on her head.

Issa slipped around to the tiny garden in the back of the house and tapped softly on the rear door. Savta would be up at this time—her grandmother rarely slept more than a few hours a night. A lump rose in her throat as she heard the familiar shuffling of slippered feet, the *thunk* of the deadbolt being pulled cautiously open, and the creaking of the hinges Saba had forgotten to oil for the tenth year in a row. Golden light spilled over Issa, framing the silver-haired figure in the doorway.

"Issa?"

At Savta's voice, the dam of emotions within Issa's chest burst. The fragments of her confidence, held together by nothing more than her iron will, shattered beneath the burden of her shame, misery, and the pain coursing through her body. Her legs seemed to sag and she almost collapsed onto her grandmother. Savta's arms wrapped around her and held her tight, so warm and comforting.

Issa broke down. "I can't," she whispered, tears streaming down her face. "I tried, Savta, but I can't!"

"Peace, *nechda*." Savta's voice soothed her. "You are safe here."

A long minute passed as her grandmother cradled her, until Issa's tears dried up. The weight of her failure and exhaustion dragged at her limbs, and it took all her strength to stay upright as Savta led her to the table. She dropped into a chair—the same chair where she'd shared every meal with her grandparents for the last seventeen years—and buried her face in her hands.

"What is the matter, *nechda*?" Aleema's hand rested atop Issa's shoulder. "Why are you here?"

"It's too much, Savta." Issa's words came out in a hoarse whisper. "I've given all I have and it's not enough."

"Nonsense." Her grandmother's voice was calm, comforting. "You are the strongest person your Saba and I have ever known. There is nothing you cannot do."

"But there is!" Issa lifted her tear-stained face to her grandmother. "The *Invictus*, Tannard, he asks the impossible, then beats me when I fail."

The word elicited a strange reaction from Aleema. Her face tightened, the wrinkles in her aged face freezing in a featureless mask, and something dark glimmered in her eyes. "This *Invictus*, Tannard, he is the one training you?"

Issa nodded. "He is cruel, harsh, and no matter what I do, he always stacks the odds against me so I fail." She realized how petulant she sounded—

like a spoiled child stamping her foot because she didn't get her way—but at that moment, she just needed someone to understand her pain.

"But, *nechda,* you've always known it would be difficult to become a Keeper's Blade." Aleema's eyes fixed her with a gaze at once compassionate and stern. "Was that not what drove you in the first place?"

"Yes, but…" Issa found herself at a loss for words. She *had* known that her chances of becoming a Blade bordered on impossible, but she'd driven on anyway. To her, that impossibility was the most appealing thing about it.

Aleema gave her a soft smile. "When you were young, barely five years old, your Saba and I would take you to an olive grove just outside the city. There was one tree, little more than a stump with a few low branches, that you were determined to climb. Time and again you fell from the tree, sometimes so hard we worried you had hurt yourself. But every time, you bounced up, that stubborn look on your face, and ran at the tree again. We tried to help you, even tried to stop you, but you refused to give up. Do you remember what happened the day after your sixth nameday?"

Issa shook her head. She had little more than a faint memory: bright sunlight dappled through tree branches, the *crunch* of dried leaves underfoot, and the comforting presence of her grandparents.

"You climbed the tree, *nechda.*" Aleema placed a hand on Issa's. "You sat on the highest branch in the tree, looking like the Pharus perched on his throne. You had triumphed finally, after all that effort. Then you did the one thing neither of us expected."

"What?" Issa asked.

"You set about climbing another tree." Aleema's eyes brightened, a broad smile on her beautiful face. "That is how you have always been, Granddaughter. Stubborn as a farmer's mule, yet as unstoppable as a runaway bull." She grasped Issa's hands in hers. "Nothing can stop you, *nechda.* The only one who can stop you is you. You only fail when you stop fighting."

Issa's eyes widened. Hykos had said almost exactly that same thing hours earlier. Yet, hearing them from her grandmother now drove the point home. Issa's burden didn't lighten, but she felt her resolve hardening, her spirit growing stronger to bear the weight. The love in her Savta's eyes and the smile on her face reminded Issa who she was.

"You're right." She straightened, scrubbed her cheeks, and squeezed her grandmother's hand. "I am the way I am because you and Saba taught me to be this way. You would not back down from this, so neither will I."

Aleema chuckled. "Do not blame your hardheadedness on me. That's all your Saba's fault."

As if on cue, a loud snore echoed from the double-sized cot. Issa and Aleema giggled together, and suddenly the weight on Issa's shoulders seemed to dissipate. She had needed to see her grandparents—she'd thought she wanted their commiseration, but that was a childish expectation. In truth, she had simply needed to hear the truth from someone she loved.

"Thank you, Savta!" Issa threw her arms around her grandmother. "Truly, thank you."

Aleema returned the embrace. "Of course, *nechda*. You may become the bravest, strongest Blade in the Keeper's army, but we will always be here to remind you where you come from." She pulled away and fixed Issa with a somber stare. "You are the daughter of greatness, and no matter what happens, know that you are always loved."

Issa felt a tear slip down her cheek—of joy, this time, mingled with gratitude. The Long Keeper had chosen well to give her such wonderful grandparents.

"Now, off with you!" Aleema's tone suddenly grew bossy, insistent—the grandmother Issa remembered. "Get back to the Citadel of Stone before anyone discovers you are missing."

"Yes, Savta." Issa ducked her head, feeling like a ten-year-old child again.

"But first, take one of these." Her grandmother bustled into the kitchens and returned a moment later with a small, sticky ball made of tiger nuts, honey, chopped dates, and seasoned liberally with cinnamon.

"A tiger nut sweet?" Issa's eyes widened.

"Your favorite." Aleema beamed as Issa devoured the treat. "You're looking positively starved. Aren't they feeding you properly up there?"

"Not really," Issa said through a mouthful of sweetness.

"Well, they'd better start!" Aleema's eyes flashed, and she waved a finger at Issa. "Else I might have to come up there and—"

"Oh, look at the time." Issa grinned and stood. "You're right, I do need to get going." She threw her arms around her grandmother and pressed a kiss to the top of the old woman's head. "Thank you, Savta."

"Always, *nechda*." She pulled free and beamed up at Issa. "Go with the Long Keeper's blessing and our love."

A bright smile stretched Issa's lips as she slipped out the back door and into the Shalandran night. She'd come here burdened down and now left light as a feather.

*Savta was right,* she thought. *Impossible's exactly what I specialize in. The harder the better.*

She had no doubt Tannard would throw more challenges at her tomorrow—and every day for the rest of her training. *So be it.* The visit had reawakened her determination. *Let him do his worst. I will not break.*

Her step was lighter, the burden lifted from her shoulder as she hurried through the empty, darkened back streets toward the Keeper's Crypts. She'd rather avoid a run-in with the Indomitable patrols; they'd want to know what business an *Earaqi* girl like her had away from home at this hour.

She had just turned down the side street that led back to Cultivator's Row and the entrance to the Keeper's Crypts when the sound of sandaled feet sliding on stone caught her attention. Heart in her throat, Issa ducked into the shadows of a building and out of sight an instant before dark, cloaked figures appeared around a bend in the broad avenue.

Peering out, Issa caught a glimpse of light from a shuttered lantern held. The thin beam of light didn't illuminate the figures' faces, but it shone on the arm of the man that carried it—and on the strange tattoo inked into the forearm: a crescent moon and star set in the middle of a circle, with two right-angled lines connected.

Issa pressed her back against the sandstone wall as the men reached her hiding place, then passed without a sideways glance at her. The seconds seemed to drag on until the sound of shuffling feet faded into the distance and Issa could finally release the tension in her muscles.

Her brow furrowed in confusion. *Did they just come from the tombs?*

The Keeper's Crypts *should* be empty at this time of night. The Indomitables patrolled the tombs more out of reverence and tradition than any real need; no Shalandran dared profane the sacred resting place of their dead.

The men *could* have come from any of the decrepit, abandoned buildings bordering the western cliff. Only the most desperate *Mahjuri* on the Slave's Tier dared live that close to the Keeper's Crypts. The *Earaqi* refused to live within the shadow of the cliff, so the squat stone homes ought to be empty.

*So did they come from the tombs? If so, what were they doing in there?*

The question followed Issa as she entered the Keeper's Crypts and made her way back up toward the Keeper's Tier. She was so busy mulling it over that she nearly ran into a patrol of black-armored soldiers. Only the Keeper's luck and her training saved her; she ducked out of sight behind a *Zadii* bookkeeper's ledger-shaped headstone barely in time to avoid being spotted.

That snapped her back to her surroundings. If she wanted to reach the Gate of Tombs and get into the Citadel of Stone unnoticed, she'd have to pay more attention.

The climb to the Keeper's Tier took nearly thrice as long as the descent. The incline made for slower going, especially as Issa was forced to wend her way through the tombs, mausoleums, and sarcophagi to evade the patrols. She had no way to mark the passage of time deep in the mountains, but she guessed that sunrise lay less than an hour off by the time she spotted the corridor that led from the *Dhukari* tombs into the Citadel of Stone.

She let out a sigh as she spotted the open gate. It was unguarded, no sign of any Keeper's Blades.

*I made it.*

Her relief died stillborn a moment later as a figure stepped out of the shadows.

Fear drove a dagger of ice into Issa's gut. *Hykos.*

A frown creased the *Archateros'* face and his eyes were dark. "Where in the Keeper's name have you been?"

# Chapter Twenty-Six

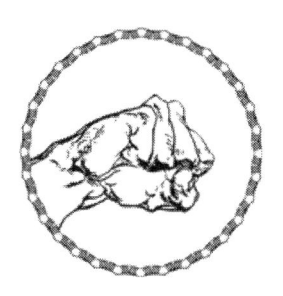

Evren ground his teeth and forced himself not to growl in frustration as he strode along behind Lady Briana's palanquin. *This servant job is taking up time I should be spending hunting down the Blade of Hallar.*

Samall had kept him running all afternoon, preparing the ornate palanquin for the journey to the Palace of Golden Eternity for some celebration or other. Now, he'd been given the unenviable task of hauling a wooden chest—filled with garments in case the *Dhukari* girl wanted a change of clothing—to the palace.

*Now there's no way I'll get away to talk to Killian, at least not tonight.*

He risked a glance to the attendant supporting the other half of the wooden chest—the same one he'd seen talking with Samall earlier this afternoon. Wherever the man had gone on his secretive errand, he'd managed to return in time for the evening departure to the palace.

Evren's one consolation came from the knowledge that Samall's plan—that it was devious, he had no doubt, or else why all the furtiveness?—would take place *tomorrow* night. He had until then to figure out what it was and how to keep Hailen out of harm's way. If he could stop the Arch-Guardian's daughter from being harmed, that would earn him favor with his new master.

*But first I've got to get through tonight.*

The thin leather sandals with their knee-high leather straps that chafed his legs were the worst part of it, though the clothing—a heavy, colorful stole over a thick woolen tunic ornamented with a gold-plated necklace and bracelets to match—came in close second. He'd always hated the long, flowing robes and multiple layers worn in Vothmot, though he couldn't help admitting that the silks popular in Voramis felt wonderful against his skin. Still, Shalandran garb had proven utter torment.

Worse, he'd been forced to relinquish all but one of his daggers. The sleeveless tunic meant he couldn't wear his wrist brace and he had no boots to conceal his blades. He had just one throwing knife tucked into the gold-and-blue sash worn atop his *shendyt*. His twin *jambiya* lay tucked beneath the wool-stuffed mattress he'd been given in the dingiest, dustiest room in the servants' quarters. He'd have to rely on his wits and fists if he found himself in trouble.

Not for the first time, Evren found himself grateful for the years he'd spent bare-handed fighting—first in the Master's Temple, then on the city streets of Vothmot, then training with the Hunter and Kiara. He'd actually managed to land a few good blows during his sparring sessions. Given that the Hunter had the impossible speed, stamina, and strength of his Bucelarii heritage, that was something to be proud of.

Thankfully, the journey to the palace from Arch-Guardian Suroth's mansion proved far shorter than he'd feared. From what he'd learned, there were just two entrances to the palace: from the huge temple to the Long Keeper he'd heard called the Hall of the Beyond, and at the top of Death Row, the avenue that ran along the eastern side of the city. Suroth's mansion stood a few hundred yards from Death Row, so they had less than a mile to travel to reach the palace.

*Damn, that's a big wall!* Evren let out a quiet whistle as their company approached the huge wall of golden sandstone that ringed the sixth and highest tier, dominated entirely by the palace and its grounds. Fifty serious-looking Indomitables bearing the marks of officers—three or four silver bands through the blue ring around the forehead of their flat-topped, spike-rimmed helmets—held guard at the enormous wrought-iron gate. Yet another obstacle Evren would have to get past to reach the Vault of Ancients.

The Palace of Golden Eternity stood on the far side of an enormous open-air plaza, with an ornate balcony where the Pharus could make an appearance before the people gathered in front of the palace. The plaza was covered by white marble tiles that shone brilliantly in the light cast by the lanterns hanging from the front of the palanquin. Black tiles—made of shalanite, Evren guessed—had been interspersed to produce beautiful rosettes in a symmetrical pattern across the square.

The Palace of Golden Eternity was carved from the same golden sandstone as the rest of the city, but its entire surface was decorated with gold, silver, and black shalanite leaves threaded together in ornate mandalas and rosettes. The palace's main building—a structure of solid stone pillars and columns supporting high, crowned arches and a balcony that circumnavigated the outer perimeter of both the second and third floors—spanned fully half of the uppermost tier. Evren caught a glimpse of gardens circling the eastern side of the palace and smaller buildings to the west.

Unlike the Hall of the Beyond, the Palace of Golden Eternity had no spires or lofty towers to draw the eye heavenward. Instead, a face had been carved into the stone above the uppermost dome of the palace. A solemn face, hard and scarred, with a stern expression and eyes that seemed to fix on Evren as he drew closer to the palace. The face of Hallar, Shalandra's founder, watching over his city even in death.

The peak of the mountain Alshuruq ended in a sharp tip a few hundred yards above Hallar's head, but the mountain was sheer, the climb impossible for any but a very experienced climber—*or the Hunter*, Evren thought.

He studied the palace as he followed the palanquin toward the grand front entrance. *No way I'm getting in this way, that's for sure.* Anyone trying to enter through the front would be visible to the Indomitables guarding the gate and patrolling the plaza.

Then there was the matter of the warriors standing guard. They carried two-handed swords nearly as tall as him, with strange flame-shaped blades made of midnight-colored Shalandran steel. Their armor was the same black as the Indomitables', but the spikes protruding from the elbow, shoulder, and knee joints added to the snarling lion helmet to give them an air of deadly menace.

He stopped as the palanquin halted in front of the grand entrance. The six slaves—*indentured* servants, Samall had emphasized the distinction—lowered the palanquin to the ground and stepped aside. Sweat streamed down their faces. They alone of the Shalandrans wore no headbands; the mark of their servitude, he guessed.

Evren struggled to stifle a snorting laugh as Hailen emerged from the palanquin. His pale face had been painted bone-white, with dark lines around his eyes and bright lipstick to emphasize the redness of his lips. He looked absolutely ridiculous in his fancy gold-threaded *shendyt*, long-sleeved tunic, and gold-and-green stole. Even from five yards away, Evren could smell the thick perfumes—a potent mixture of ambergris and musk—that hung in a thick miasma around the younger boy.

*If only the Hunter could see him now!*

Hailen shot him a furious glare, then turned and held out a hand to the young *Dhukari* woman within the palanquin.

Lady Briana was pretty, with skin a deep golden mahogany, oval-shaped face, and arrow-straight nose that reminded him of the young women of Vothmot. Her petite frame brought back memories of the few times he'd roamed the Ward of Bliss, Vothmot's pleasure district. She wasn't too stuck up, either. She'd actually thanked Hailen when he helped her into the palanquin the first time, and nodded to Evren and the other footmen. She was pretty decent compared to most of the nobility of Vothmot and Voramis that he'd had the misfortune to meet.

In the few seconds that he'd been able to catch Hailen alone, Evren had asked about his duties. The young boy had rolled his violet eyes and shook his head. "They've got me fetching things for Lady Briana and her new bodyguards. Not a bad job, but if I wanted to do that, I'd have stayed in the House of Need."

"At least no more of those lessons, eh?" Evren had said with a grin.

Hailen shrugged. "The food's better, too." His expression had grown excited. "But wait until you see what I found in her fath—"

The tinkling of a bell had cut off Hailen's words, and they hadn't had a chance to speak again.

*At least he's been treated well.* That was more than he could say for himself. Samall had come dangerously close to ordering him whipped when he discovered the slop water stains on Evren's clothing. Evren wouldn't have allowed the stocky attendant to strike him, so he'd been relieved when the order came for them to prepare for the journey to the Palace of Golden Eternity. A reprieve from the inevitable confrontation. Samall would take his role as Evren's superior too far, and he'd earn himself shattered teeth for it. Sadly, that would be the end of Evren's short-lived career as a footman—and set back his plans to get close enough to the Blade of Hallar.

*That's already easier said than done,* Evren thought. *Let's just hope there's a side or back way in.*

The last two members of Lady Briana's retinue dismounted from their horses and took up guard positions beside the young woman. One was a fierce, exotic-looking young woman with impressively strong arms and a short spear, the other a young pale-skinned man Evren guessed was roughly the same age as him. Evren couldn't decide if the fellow hailed from Praamis, Malandria, or Voramis—most southerners looked alike to him—but he had a strange, almost familiar confidence about him.

The two were Lady Briana's bodyguards, and they looked capable enough. The young woman, in particular, seemed like the sort of opponent he'd avoid tangling with at all costs. Though, given the familiar ease with which the young southerner carried his sword, Evren guessed he'd be a competent fighter as well.

*Let's just hope they're enough to stop whatever Samall has planned.*

He'd contemplated telling them about what he'd overheard but decided to wait until he had more concrete proof. The fact that Killian had pulled strings to get him and Hailen employment with Arch-Guardian Suroth probably meant that the blacksmith had eyes and ears among the serving staff. He'd want to know about the servants' whispers that the abduction of Lady Briana had been an inside job, and he could offer insight on what Samall and his companion had planned.

If Killian proved a dead end, Evren would go to Nessa or the bodyguards. His evidence might be tenuous at best, but he'd risk it if it meant Hailen was out of harm's way.

Evren made to follow his new mistress into the palace, but Samall stepped in his way with a glower and shake of his head.

"You, stay with Kuhar and watch the palanquin," Samall growled at him. "You're nowhere near ready to serve Lady Briana."

Evren ground his teeth and bit back an angry retort. "Yes, sir." The words came out harsher than he'd intended, but Samall had already turned to accompany Lady Briana and the others inside.

The bare-headed slaves lifted the palanquin and carried it toward an arched gateway on the western side of the palace. There, he found himself amidst a sea of equally luxurious palanquins parked in another massive, albeit less ornate courtyard. It seemed the people of Shalandra preferred the slave-born litters with their plush cushions, silk curtains, lacquered paintwork, and gold-and-bronze finials over the comforts of wagons and carriages. Given his experience riding on Brother Modestus' wagon from Voramis to Shalandra, he couldn't fault them.

To his surprise, when the litter bearers set down their poles, they were ushered into a side entrance. Evren overheard the words "wine and meat" as the bare-headed, broad-shouldered men filed inside. He, however, had to content himself to wait out here with Samall's co-conspirator, far from any sustenance or refreshments.

*Well, isn't that a kick in the bollocks!* He hadn't eaten more than the small flatbread he'd managed to filch from beneath the cook's nose. *I can already tell tonight's going to be a real treat.*

"Stand guard at the front, I'll take the rear, where I can keep an eye on Lady Briana's chest," the man, Kuhar, told him in a curt voice. By the half-sneer he shot Evren, he shared Samall's disdain for the new hire.

Evren nodded. "Got it." He strode around to take up a guard position at the front of the palanquin. He pretended nonchalance, his stance relaxed, but he kept one wary eye on the man.

Back in the mansion, Samall had said that their presence here provided *"the perfect opportunity to plan tomorrow's strike."* If the attendant intended to slip away or try anything duplicitous, Evren would be watching and waiting.

Time seemed to pass at a slow crawl. Evren had developed the patience required to be a successful thief, but even he grew bored after an hour. He occupied his time studying his surroundings. The courtyard was likely the equivalent of the carriage yards common in the homes of Voramian nobles, though thankfully with far fewer horse droppings. The few attendants that had remained in the courtyard were clustered together a short distance away and speaking in voices too low for him to hear.

Solid sandstone walls flanked the western and northern sides of the courtyard, though the eastern side opened onto a cluster of smaller buildings. Doubtless they were the ancillary structures common to palaces: stables for the Pharus' horses, storage rooms for his food, chambers where his laundry was washed, and so on.

Over his years as a thief, Evren had learned that these places tended to be the weak spots in any building's architecture. The Pharus likely preferred his servants to come and go through side and rear entrances, keeping the grand front entrance clear so as to impress his guests. No one would marvel at the stunning architecture if it bore the dust of rugs beaten on the walls, and the black-and-white-tiled courtyard would steal fewer breaths covered in horse droppings.

But those weren't the only vulnerabilities. Evren scanned the second- and third-floor windows and balconies for any way he could get in unseen. Unfortunately, the western side of the Palace of Golden Eternity was as damned-near impenetrable as the front. Black-armored guards patrolled the balconies and kept a close eye on the courtyard. The only place not guarded was a small archway on the northwestern corner.

He shot a glance at the man at the rear of the palanquin. *I doubt he'd let me slip away to do a bit of exploring.*

Just then, Evren's ears perked up at the sound of a low whistle coming from the direction of the palace. He made no move, gave no indication he'd heard it, but his eye snapped toward his fellow servant. The man had straightened and was glancing around the courtyard.

"You awake, new guy?" Kuhar called.

Evren responded with a grunt.

"Gotta relieve myself right quick. You think you can keep an eye on things for a few minutes?"

"You got it." Evren gave a disinterested wave. "Just snag me something from the kitchens on the way back, yeah?"

"Will do," the man replied almost too cheerfully.

Evren pretended to turn away, but tracked the man's movements out of the corner of his eye. The attendant slipped between a pair of silk-curtained palanquins and disappeared from view.

A few seconds later, Evren abandoned his post and slipped in silence after the man. He moved parallel to Kuhar, keeping watch on the attendant from the corner of his eye. As he'd expected, Kuhar was moving in the direction of the whistle, which had come from that archway on the northwestern corner of the courtyard.

His muscles tightened as he caught a glimpse of Samall standing in the archway, framed by the light of the lanterns burning behind him. As Kuhar hurried forward, Samall beckoned for him.

Evren caught Samall's low whisper. "This way."

The two men disappeared through the archway, and Evren followed a few seconds later. *Let's see where you're off to, eh?*

The arch opened onto a short corridor broad enough for two wagons, which gave way onto a smaller courtyard of simple sandstone tiles. The smells wafting from the open doors and windows told Evren that this was the way into the palace's kitchens.

Evren clung to the shadows of the stone corridor, silent as a wraith. The Hunter had honed his skills of fighting, but years spent living on the streets had trained Evren to move without a sound.

Samall led Kuhar away from the kitchen door, and instead to a metal grate set into the ground level. The two men crouched before the grate, studying it, and Samall spoke to Kuhar in a low voice.

Evren pricked up his ears in an effort to overhear the hushed conversation.

"…soon as you can, you must get word to our brothers," Samall was saying to the man. "Harol has found us our way in through the storerooms."

*Thank you, Samall!* Excitement thrummed through Evren's chest. The treacherous attendant had just showed him the perfect way to get in. *I'll still have to find a way through the palace and into the Vault of Ancients to get at the Blade of Hallar, but it's a damned good first step.*

On the other hand, the fact that Samall was planning something in the palace meant he—and whoever his "brethren" were—had something far larger than one simple kidnapping in mind. People only snuck into palaces with the intention of killing monarchs and rulers.

*Killian needs to know about this.* Perhaps the blacksmith could send word to whomever in the palace handled security, have them lay an ambush for Samall and his fellows. Doubtless that would earn Killian a great deal of favor with the right people in the Palace of Golden Eternity—favor that would trickle down to Evren.

But that didn't help Evren keep Hailen out of harm's way. He needed to find out more about whatever Samall and his fellow traitors had planned so he could make his own plans to protect Hailen.

"Get back to your post quickly." Samall's words snapped Evren from his contemplation. "No one can suspect anything. As soon as we return to the Arch-Guardian's house, slip away and get word to our brothers."

Evren's heart stopped as Kuhar nodded and turned to head back toward the carriage. *Shite!*

He scrambled deeper into the shadows of the stone corridor and slunk toward the outer courtyard as fast as he dared. When he reached the concealment of the various palanquins, he broke into a run and dashed back to Lady Briana's litter.

*I can't let him see me!*

He reached his place not a moment too soon. He'd just managed to get his rapid breathing under control when Kuhar appeared from the shadows.

Evren shot the man a glance he hoped looked casual. "Bring me anything?"

The attendant shook his head. "Cooks are watching everything like a mother lion guarding an injured cub."

"Damn," Evren growled. "It's going to be a long, hungry night, then."

Kuhar snorted. "Get used to it. The life of a *Dhukari's* servant is glamorous, indeed."

Evren grunted in response and settled back into a comfortable position leaning against one of the palanquin's arms. Yet though he kept his expression nonchalant, his mind was racing.

When they returned at the end of the night, Kuhar intended to sneak off, to send word to whoever his allies were on the outside. Evren would be ready. He had plenty of experience tailing people through crowded cities.

*I will find out who you're working with, you treacherous bastard.* His fingers tightened around the hilt of the knife tucked into his sash. *And when I do, I'm going to make sure your plans fail.*

# *Chapter Twenty-Seven*

Kodyn exchanged a meaningful glance with Aisha, and she gave him an understanding nod. After he'd relayed to her the Black Widow's ominous warning, they'd both agreed that they needed to stick close to Briana all night long. Kodyn would only slip away long enough to make contact with the Secret Keeper, Ennolar. Once that was done, they'd convince Briana to make excuses to leave early.

*The sooner we're out of here, the better. Who knows what sort of danger lies behind these welcoming facades?*

And people did seem to be welcoming, at least of Briana. A steady parade of *Dhukari* cooed over Briana, offering hollow well-wishes and meaningless words intended to endear themselves to the daughter of a Councilor.

Aisha hovered a step behind Briana, but Kodyn had taken on the task of steering the Shalandran girl through the thick crowds of well-dressed men and women. He ached to scratch his nose—the miasma of musky scents emanating from the throng set his nostrils itching—but feared he'd break his tight-fitting silver-and-gold-threaded tunic if he moved his arms.

Thankfully, Briana hadn't insisted on making him wear the wig-like headdress she'd donned over her wavy locks. She had, however, forced a bright-colored shawl and silk sash on him, using the excuse that "he wanted to blend in among the *Dhukari*". At least he had a few places to conceal daggers. Added to the sword on his hip, he felt confident that he could protect Briana among the perfumed, costumed Shalandran nobility.

*If there's one good thing about this ridiculous style, is that it's nearly impossible for anyone to really conceal weapons.* The women's ankle-length sheath dresses fit too tightly and the men's sleeveless tunics bared hands and arms. He'd have no problem spotting an attack if it came. Still, he kept a hand near the hilt of his sword as he shouldered a path through the crowd.

The presence of stone-faced guards in black armor would likely deter anyone from attacking Briana. The hard warriors with their solemn expressions, heavy plate mail, and enormous swords contrasted sharply with the white marble floors, high-vaulted domed ceilings, colorfully painted walls, and the decorative gold and silver rosettes that seemed to be in favor in the palace's grand hall. The light of a thousand oil lanterns sparkled off the precious metals with dazzling brilliance.

Then there was the music, far too many high-pitched flutes trilling over the gentle strum of an instrument that looked like a lute with too few strings, the thumping beat of a pair of tambors, and the clicking of castanets. To his Praamian ear, it sounded like chaos in a jar.

He kept an eye on his companions as they moved, and he caught the strain in Aisha's face as they passed another pair of black-armored guards. She went out of her way to avoid them, her expression strange. She actually shuddered as they passed one, a towering man with a face that looked cut from stone. He didn't understand her strange behavior—she'd done the same thing with Ormroth on the road to Shalandra—but he hadn't had time to ask her about it.

"Lady Briana!" The call was accompanied a moment later by two familiar faces—Arhin and Feasah, the *Dhukari* they'd met on the road south. Kodyn stopped listening as the men exchanged banal pleasantries with Briana. Instead, he divided his attention between searching the enormous hall for the man he'd come to see and watching for any sign of threat.

He kept a particularly close eye on Briana's new servant—the young boy, who had called himself Hailen, was clearly a foreigner to Shalandra, with the light skin and fair hair common to Malandria. Yet there was something strange about him, something Kodyn couldn't quite put his finger on. He said and did nothing to rouse suspicion, but Kodyn knew that there was far more to the boy than his smiling, innocent demeanor.

When he'd asked Briana about the boy, she'd explained, "It's common among the *Dhukari* to seek body servants not from Shalandra. Somewhat of a game, really, to see who can find the most exotic to serve at their command. Having you as my bodyguard will certainly turn heads."

*That's a bit more of an understatement than I realized,* he thought. He stood half a head taller than most of the people in the room, his skin lighter than even Hailen's. All eyes in the room definitely marked him as they passed through the crowd.

*As long as they're looking at me, they'll be too busy to notice Aisha.*

The Ghandian girl wore an elegant *kalasiris* of colors far more muted than Briana's white-and-gold sheath dress. Her face, however, had been layered with cosmetics to lighten her skin and contour her features. With *kohl*-rimmed eyes, a white-and-gold headband, and four black beauty marks, she could *almost* pass for an *Intaji*. Save for her accent, of course—Aisha's words only revealed a hint of her harsher, clipped Ghandian language, but she couldn't form her words with the same flowing, musical tone of Shalandrans.

Briana had dressed Aisha to look innocuous, unassuming, but Kodyn knew how dangerous Aisha really was. Though she'd left her *assegai* in Suroth's mansion, she could wield the daggers concealed in her elegant sleeves as well as any Serpent. Her face was a mask of calm, but Kodyn knew her well enough to see the wary tension in her eyes, the tightness of her strong shoulders.

He hadn't sparred with her in months, but given what he'd heard from Errik and Ria, he wasn't certain which of them would win. Between the two of them, they ought to more than suffice to keep Briana safe here. The journey to the palace had gone without a hitch, but the return trip had him nervous. If someone intended to make a play to abduct Briana again, that would be the time.

But for now, he simply had to focus on playing the role of Briana's bodyguard while attempting to make contact with the Secret Keeper.

"Point him out when you see him." Kodyn spoke in a voice pitched for Briana and Aisha's ears only, low enough to fade into the hum of the party. "The sooner we can get this done, the sooner we can get you home."

"I know you're eager to be out of here." Briana placed a hand on his arm and guided him deeper into the throng of revelers with a dazzling smile. "But some of us actually *enjoy* this sort of thing. Besides, it's not every day I get to show off my new companion."

Kodyn's brow furrowed at the words. "Wait, I thought I was here as your bodyguard."

"Please, you think *anyone* is going to buy that?" Briana laughed, a high and ringing sound filled with delight. "We've been here five minutes and already I can see people whispering about just what parts of my body you intend to guard."

Kodyn blushed, his face burning.

"Let them whisper." Briana's smile never faded as she spoke from the corner of her mouth. "Anything to keep them away from figuring out the *real* reason you're here, right?"

Kodyn inclined his head. "Fair point." He straightened and extended his arm in the stiff pose he'd seen among the nobles of Praamis. "In that case, allow me to escort you to the banquet table."

He caught the slight shake of Aisha's head as she rolled her eyes at his foppish mannerisms. He brushed it off. *If I'm going to play the part, I might as well do it right.*

The change in Aisha and Briana's demeanor hadn't gone unnoticed. On the road, Aisha had been distant, withdrawn, and polite. He'd returned from his visit to the Black Widow to find the two of them deep in conversation about life in Shalandra and the culture, customs, and etiquette they'd be expected to follow. They'd actually been friendly. Aisha had even become more defensive of Briana, taking her role of bodyguard as seriously as she had her role as a Phoenix guarding the fancy-ticklers and courtesans under the Night Guild's protection.

He welcomed the change—the three of them would be spending a good deal of time together, so it was good the two women could get along.

Briana seemed to be enjoying her grand return to Shalandra, and she flitted from group to group like a hummingbird darting between daylilies. Kodyn paid little attention to the inane conversations—mostly the latest gossip of the *Dhukari*—instead focusing on the people they encountered.

The upper caste of Shalandra bore a strong resemblance to the nobles of Praamis. Their conversations, pleasant on the outside, usually concealed verbal weapons as sharp as any sword. He barely caught a fraction of the hidden meanings and subtle innuendoes, but he heard enough to realize the Black Widow hadn't exaggerated when she'd warned him about the *Dhukari*. *Boom, boom, boom.*

The sound rang out through the grand hall, drowning out the trilling music and the hum of conversation. Immediately, everyone went dead silent as the two gold-embossed double doors at the northern side of the vast chamber swung open.

*Boom, boom, boom.*

Again, this time followed by a loud voice announcing, "Amhoset Nephelcheres, first of his name, Pharus of Shalandra, Guardian of Dawnbreaker, Chosen of Hallar, Word of Justice and Death, and Revered Servant of the Long Keeper."

All in the room turned toward the opening doors and bowed. Kodyn and Briana did likewise, and as he straightened, he caught sight of the Pharus.

Pharus Amhoset Nephelcheres was a tall man with broad shoulders, features both handsome and strong, and a high forehead, upon which sat the conical crown and golden headdress of his office. Beneath his gold fabric shawl, his golden-skinned chest was well-sculpted, his abdomen surprisingly muscled for a monarch. He stood straight, his posture upright, and carried himself with confidence as he strode through the doors. Two women wearing low-cut sheath dresses clung to his arms, their ample hips swaying as they glided alongside him.

People gave way in front of the Pharus, and a path opened before him. To Kodyn's surprise, he found the Pharus' eyes fixed on him—no, on the beautiful young woman on his arm—and the monarch moved straight through the crowd toward them.

"My Pharus." Briana bowed low again as the Pharus approached.

The man stopped before Briana, close enough that Kodyn could see the thick layers of cosmetics that accented his high cheekbones and deep-set eye sockets, the lines of *kohl* and malachite ringing his eyes, and the eight black beauty marks painted on his cheeks and chin.

"Young Briana." Amhoset Nephelcheres inclined his head in greeting. "It does our heart good to see you safely returned to us. Your adoptive father has not been the same these last weeks." A shadow flashed in his eyes, never touching his face, so quick Kodyn might have missed it had he not been a step away. "You have our welcome on your joyous return."

"My Pharus does me honor." Briana bowed a third time.

The Pharus turned to Kodyn. "And is this the brave young man who escorted you?"

Kodyn met the Pharus' gaze and found himself staring into eyes that glinted with the same sharp intelligence that marked his mother. The Pharus might hold a figurehead's title, but cunning and ambition burned bright within him.

"We would know your name," the Pharus said.

"Kodyn…" He didn't know how to address the ruler of Shalandra—"my Pharus" didn't feel right—so he settled on "…sire."

"A strong name." The Pharus pursed his lips, a perfectly sculpted eyebrow arching upward, though in displeasure, curiosity, or amusement, Kodyn couldn't tell. "We bid you welcome to our city. You have done us a great service by returning the daughter of our honored Arch-Guardian. The time may come when we will be in a position to repay your bravery."

*How about you give me the Crown?* Kodyn thought, struggling to hide a grin. Instead, he bowed and said, "You honor me, sire."

"Indeed." Pharus Amhoset gave a little nod to Briana and turned away, his concubines on his arm. As he moved, the crowd swirled around him, until Kodyn, Aisha, and Briana stood in their own little island amidst the people jockeying for the Pharus' favor.

"Wow!" breathed Briana. "The Pharus himself welcoming you. What an honor!"

Kodyn nodded, but he didn't feel particularly honored. In addition to his mother's skill, determination, and wit, he'd inherited her distrust of nobility and royalty. He'd caught a glimpse of the true Pharus: a man as calculating, cunning, and relentless as any Guild Master.

"Young Lady Briana." A new voice cut through the crowd. "The Keeper truly smiles on you to bring you safely home after what must have been such a trying ordeal."

The voice, as unctuous and oily as a merchant peddling forgeries, immediately set Kodyn's teeth on edge. One glimpse of the man to whom it belonged confirmed his instant dislike.

"Councilor Madani." Briana smiled, but her tone was as warm as the Frozen Sea. "I'm certain the Long Keeper heeded your prayers for my return."

Councilor Madani looked to be in his late forties, with a hint of grey around his temples and wrinkles lining his prim lips. His hooked nose and insincere smile gave him the appearance of a vulture circling a dying man, and Kodyn imagined his long, thin fingers were claws ready to sink into Briana's flesh. He wore all black—from his ornate stole to his black-dyed silk tunic and *shendyt* to his high-strapped sandals—accented with enough gold to purchase a small kingdom. His belly drooped so low it engulfed the sash that hung around his thick thighs.

Behind him stood four more equally obese men wearing equally rich robes. One looked to be nearly a hundred, though age hadn't bent his back or stooped his shoulders. The other three were fairly unremarkable, save for the opulence of their clothing and the haughty disdain on their faces. They were the Keeper's Council, the most powerful men in Shalandra.

A flock of servants and attendants huddled behind them, all clad in the black robes of the Necroseti. They hung on the Councilors' words and waited patiently to do their bidding.

One man, however, caught Kodyn's eye. He stood near the rear of the retinue, far from the prestigious positions near the Councilors. His robes were simpler, though still the same gold-trimmed black. But it was his appearance that made him stand out. Short, with a hunched back, bald head, and face twisted by some malady, he stood tilted at an awkward angle, as if his crooked spine threw off his balance. He never lifted his eyes to Kodyn's, simply kept his gaze fixed on his masters.

"I can only give thanks to our god and his wisdom." Madani's devout expression and pious tone grated on Kodyn's nerves far more than the trilling flute music. "With all the rumors of unrest among the lower castes, I was concerned that you had been taken by someone intending to use you to gain leverage over your adoptive father."

The man was as brazen as he was smug. Arch-Guardian Suroth had suspected the Necroseti from the onset, and Madani's words danced along the line of an admission of guilt.

"It is only by the Keeper's grace that I am safely returned," Briana said, her face a mask of civility. She gestured to Kodyn. "My father has taken steps to ensure my protection."

"Ah, yes, the young foreigner." The Councilor turned dark, *kohl*-rimmed eyes on Kodyn. "Guard her well, young man. Even a city as beautiful as Shalandra may conceal dangers one so youthful will be unprepared for."

"I'll remember that," Kodyn let a dangerous edge into his words. "I've already found a few threats that I fully intend to deal with when the time comes."

Madani raised an eyebrow and pursed his lips.

Briana interjected before the man spoke. "If you will excuse me, Councilman, I see my adoptive father beckoning me." She gripped Kodyn's arm tight and steered him away from the priest.

"Heed my words," Madani called after them. "I would *so* hate to hear that something untoward happened to our dear Secret Keeper's daughter."

Kodyn allowed himself to be dragged away. He had to wrestle down a near-overwhelming desire to drive his fist into the Councilor's face—or a sword in his gut.

"Kodyn, that's Ennolar." Briana's voice whispered in his ear. "There, by the banquet table."

The words shoved the smug Necroseti from Kodyn's mind. His eyes sought out the man Briana had indicated.

The man was short, shorter even than Briana, and nearly as round, with a perfectly oval-shaped head and hooked nose above a thick-lipped mouth. Beneath his ornamental white headdress, a single lock of braided hair hung down his back and his scalp had been shaven bald and waxed to a bright sheen. He moved with purpose along the table of delicacies laid out along the eastern wall of the grand hall. His brown robes marked him as a Secret Keeper, priest of the Mistress—the man the one the Black Widow had instructed him to seek out.

Kodyn nodded and turned to Aisha with a questioning look.

"Go," Aisha told him. "I'll keep an eye on her."

"Allow me to bring you something to eat, my lady," Kodyn said in a loud voice.

"Thank you." Briana gave him a little curtsy, her dazzling smile returning.

Kodyn squeezed Briana's hand before slipping his arm free of her grip. He strode toward the far end of the banquet table, scooped up a golden platter, and began heaping it high with treats and delicacies—the sort of thing a young girl should enjoy. He continued until he stood beside the Secret Keeper.

"The Black Widow sends her greetings," he said in a low voice. At the same time, he turned up his hand and uncurled his fingers to reveal the silver spider-faced coin he'd palmed from his pocket.

To Ennolar's credit, he managed not to stiffen or twitch, but simply turned a silent, questioning glance toward Kodyn.

"*She has sent me to collect a map of the...*" He didn't remember the hand signs for Serenii. "*...tunnels beneath the city.*"

Now surprise cracked Ennolar's stoic expression. "*You know our language?*" he signed.

"*I am the one who saved Briana.*" He met the man's gaze. "*She taught me.*"

Ennolar gave a little nod of understanding. "*Dare I ask why the Black Widow wants the map?*"

Kodyn shrugged. "*You can ask her. I'm just the messenger.*" He had to spell out the last word—yet another sign he hadn't yet learned.

After a long, silent moment, Ennolar's fingers flashed again. "*So be it. The Temple of Whispers at noon tomorrow. But not you. Your pale skin makes you stand out. Send someone in your place, someone you trust. Give them that.*" He thrust his chin at Kodyn's right hand, which held the coin. "*And tell the Black Widow that this cancels our debt.*"

Kodyn nodded. "*Noon, then.*"

Their exchange ended, Kodyn moved around the Secret Keeper and continued filling Briana's plate. Finally, once he'd heaped the sweetmeats high enough, he turned away from the table.

Excitement thrummed within him as he strode back toward his comrades. *One step closer to getting my hands on the Crown of the Pharus and completing my Undertaking!* With the map, he'd know how to get into the palace using the underground Serenii tunnels. There were still a lot of details left to figure out—chief among them, how the hell to get into the Vault of Ancients. Hopefully he could convince Suroth to fill in those gaps.

When the time came—and it seemed to be coming sooner than he'd anticipated—he'd be ready to make his move and prove his worthiness to be a Journeyman of the Night Guild.

# Chapter Twenty-Eight

As Aisha steered Briana through the crowd toward her father, she felt the tremor running through the young Shalandran. She squeezed Briana's arm, a gesture intended to help calm the girl. But when Briana turned toward her, Aisha caught the spark of anger burning bright in the girl's eye. The interaction with Councilor Madani hadn't scared her; it left her enraged.

"The smug bastard!" Outrage tinged Briana's harsh whisper. "You heard him. He all but confessed!"

Aisha nodded. "It proves your father's theory right. The Necroseti really *did* plan to take you. Maybe they actually managed it, but somehow the Gatherers got their hands on you. That just means we need to be doubly cautious about keeping you safe. Maybe we should—"

"If you're about to recommend that we leave, you'd better rethink that." Briana rounded on her, eyes flashing. "Madani did that to rattle me, to send me running scared and send a clear message to my father. I may not be a warrior like you and Kodyn, but I'm not some little girl to hide at the first sign of danger."

Aisha couldn't help admiring Briana's spark of defiance, her resilience. She'd known too many others that had crumbled during their enslavement by the Bloody Hand. Only a handful of girls—those that had stayed in Praamis to join House Phoenix—had walked away from the horrors of their captivity stronger in body, mind, and will. Briana hadn't endured the same things she had, but she recognized a kindred spirit.

Briana's face was a mask of polite courtesy, but she fairly stomped through the throng toward her father. Arch-Guardian Suroth looked up from his conversation with a *Dhukari* and a furrow rippled his brow at the sight of his daughter.

"*What is the matter?*" his hands flashed.

Briana's fingers moved so quickly Aisha could barely keep up. The angry gestures made the emotions behind the message clear.

The concern in Arch-Guardian Suroth's eyes turned to white-hot rage. For a moment, as he scanned the crowd, Aisha thought the Secret Keeper would storm off and hunt down his fellow Councilor. Aisha had seen his fighting stance when he first discovered their true purpose for being in Shalandra. He was a dangerous man even with nothing but a crystal goblet in his hand and the fire of fury burning in his chest.

"*I will not let his actions go unanswered,*" Suroth signed, his face a mask of anger.

"*Nor should you,*" Briana responded. "*But we need to move carefully. You know better than I just how much power the Necroseti wield.*"

Suroth scowled. "*Accursed priests!*"

Briana's eyes widened. "*Father, beware you do not blaspheme yourself. They are the Keeper's chosen!*"

"*They are no more chosen than the stone beneath our feet or the wine in our glasses.*" His grip tightened around the goblet until Aisha feared the delicate crystal would shatter. "*They are but men, regardless of their title.*"

"*Powerful men,*" Briana retorted. "*With more power and influence among the Dhukari and Alqati than you.*"

"*But with the Pharus?*" Aisha asked.

Both pairs of eyes—so similar in their almond shape, their dark color, and the bright, burning anger—turned toward her.

"*The Pharus himself sought you out to welcome you back,*" Aisha continued. "From what you've told me, that doesn't seem like the sort of thing he'd do needlessly, even to keep up appearances."

Arch-Guardian Suroth's eyes widened a fraction. "*You speak truth, Ghandian.*" He turned to Briana. "*The Council knows that the Pharus favors me—perhaps simply because I am* not *Necroseti and have no desire to control him. That could be one of the reasons they moved against me by capturing you. They know that I will turn the Pharus against something they intend to do.*"

*"So speak to the Pharus, then,"* Briana insisted. *"Tell him your suspicions."*

*"It will achieve nothing unless I can prove the truth."* Suroth's expression soured, then grew pensive. *"Perhaps I may have a way of doing precisely that."*

He rounded on Aisha. *"As soon as your companion returns from convincing Ennolar to give him the map of the Serenii tunnels, get Briana back home."*

The words stunned Aisha. It took her a long moment before she could remember the hand signs to ask, *"How did you know?"*

Suroth's expression went flat. *"I am Arch-Guardian of all the Secret Keepers in Shalandra. I know what each one specializes in, where their interests lie. The moment I saw Kodyn heading toward Ennolar, it was a simple matter to decipher his intentions."* He nodded. *"A plan I intended to suggest to you on the morrow. It is good to see that your companion is as clever as you are strong. When I move against whichever of the Councilors were behind the plot to abduct Briana, I will have need of wits as well as brawn."*

Aisha nodded. *"We will stand with you, Arch-Guardian."*

To her surprise, gratitude filled the man's eyes. *"Thank you, truly."* It remained a moment, barely a glimpse, before hardening once more. *"Now, I've got to make contact with my sources in the Necroseti. I will return to the mansion late. I trust you with my daughter's life."*

Aisha squared her shoulders. *"A trust I do not take lightly."*

*"Good."* Suroth squeezed Briana's hand quickly and bustled off into the crowd. Within moments, his brown Secret Keeper robes disappeared among the mass of swirling gold, silver, blue, and white.

Aisha searched the crowd until she found the cluster of black amid all the dazzling color. The *Kish'aa* hovered around the Keeper's Priests, clinging to them like shadows. A shudder ran down Aisha's spine—she could only imagine what the Necroseti had done to these poor souls to tether them so close in death.

Her attention returned to her surroundings as Kodyn came over to them, a look of triumph in his eyes. "Tomorrow at noon."

"Good." Aisha swallowed the acid swirling in her throat and turned to Briana. "Now I think it's time we do as your father says and get out of here."

"I won't run scared just because of a threat," Briana protested. "Even from a member of the Keeper's Council."

"I'm not asking." Aisha gave Briana a stern look. "We're here to guard you, and right now, I'm telling you that it's time to leave. There will still be enough traffic moving around the Keeper's Tier that we can travel safely. And the fact that no one's expecting you to leave so early means we'll be out of here before anyone realizes we're gone."

Briana's face fell and she opened her mouth to protest, but Kodyn spoke first.

"Aisha's right." He shot Aisha a nod. "Our job's to keep you safe. Let us do that. Once we're back safe in your mansion, we'll be able to figure out our next step."

"Remember," Aisha whispered, "you just found out that the most powerful people in your city have it out for you and your father. That's not a threat anyone should take lightly."

Briana looked ready to protest, but common sense prevailed. "Fine, but at least allow me to say farewell to—"

"No!" Aisha shook her head. "We leave *before* anyone knows we're out of here."

The look on Briana's face made her displeasure clear. At that moment, the Shalandran girl's pleasure was the last thing on Aisha's mind.

\* \* \*

The night air in Arch-Guardian Suroth's rooftop garden was cool and comforting. The gentle breeze set the leaves rustling and carried the delicate aromas of a hundred exotic flowers to her. Aisha basked in the darkness and silence—peace after what had been an intense day.

The return journey to Suroth's mansion had passed without event, though Briana had bordered on sulky as Aisha and Kodyn fairly dragged her out of her own celebration. She'd barely spoken two words to Aisha as they hustled her inside and deposited her and Hailen, the strange pale-skinned servant boy, in the care of Nessa.

At Aisha's insistence, Kodyn had given the exterior of Arch-Guardian Suroth's mansion a thorough examination. His years as an apprentice Hawk had taught him to spot hidden ways in and out of buildings even as fortified as this.

If there was a way assassins or kidnappers could get at Briana—from the ground or the rooftops—he'd find it.

She'd stood silent guard outside Briana's room until Kodyn relieved her.

"Go, get some sleep," he'd told her. "I'll hold the door until morning."

He meant it as a kindness, but Aisha couldn't even begin to even consider sleep. She'd come straight to the garden, the only place in the massive house where she could be certain of solitude.

She lifted her right hand and held it in front of her face. The darkness highlighted the tiny spark of energy that danced around her hand. Crackling, surging, a little rush like lightning that leapt from finger to finger like a firebug.

But this was no bug. Growing up on the plains of Ghandia, Aisha had spent many summer nights chasing the lightning bugs with her baby sister. The bugs glowed a soft golden yellow, but this light shone a pure white.

*The power of the Kish'aa.*

She'd never understood it when her father spoke of the energy a Spirit Whisperer could control. To her, the gift conveyed the ability to see the spirits of the dead, even speak with them and call upon their aid. Now she knew what it meant to wield the power of the *Kish'aa*.

Her eyes wandered toward the flower-covered vine dome in the heart of the garden, but she knew she wouldn't see the ethereal, translucent blue form of Radiana floating there. Briana's mother had gone, her spirit dissipated on the wind, the spark of her life absorbed into Aisha. She felt it in the core of her being, like the last glowing ember as the fire died. But when she focused, she could see it glimmering within her veins and darting between her fingers.

Her father had tried to explain it to her once. *"When a fire dies, its heat is not lost forever. Instead, it simply reunites with the air around it, dispersed until it can no longer be felt. But, when the fire is rekindled, the heat returns to its source. Thus it is with the Kish'aa. A Spirit Whisperer can gather the heat unto himself until he becomes the fire."*

The words, so confusing at the time, had begun to make terrible sense. More than once, she'd thought she caught a glimpse at that same energy within her father. Always from the corner of her eye, and always gone when she turned fully toward him. What she'd written off as her childish imagination now revealed the truth to her.

*My father wielded the Kish'aa like fire, and it consumed him.*

She glanced to the west, toward the Keeper's Crypts where the dead clustered like a storm cloud. Those spirits held a terrible power—if she dared to approach them and claim their sparks for herself. Yet the memories of her father's descent into madness haunted her. The laughing, quick-tongued man had transformed into an emaciated husk, nothing remaining but two empty eyes that stared into a world she could not see.

With effort, she tore her eyes away from the tombs, but found her gaze now resting on the bright blue petals of the Watcher's Bloom. The plant that had enhanced her father's ability and stole his mind.

"Can't sleep either?"

Aisha spun to find Briana coming up behind her. The Shalandran girl wore a loose linen dress and a shawl pulled tight around her petite shoulders. Bare-footed, she'd moved with such silence that Aisha, distracted by her worries, hadn't heard her coming.

"Don't worry." Briana smiled at her. "Kodyn understood when I said I needed to take a walk in the garden, to clear my head. And when he saw you here..." She trailed off and glanced over her shoulder. "He's waiting at the gazebo. Giving us space to talk. Sometimes, only another woman can understand what you're going through."

Aisha forced a smile but could find no words to explain the tempest brewing within her. How could anyone understand the truth? The Einari worshipped the Thirteen Gods of Einan, while the Shalandrans held the Long Keeper in reverence. They could never understand the power of the *Kish'aa*. Worse, they could think her mad.

Yet the burden had grown heavy, almost too much for her to bear alone. If she didn't tell someone soon, she feared she'd crack beneath its weight.

"This plant," Aisha began hesitantly, pointing to the flowers Briana had called Keeper's Spike, "you say it causes hallucinations, yes?"

"Correct." Briana shot a curious glance at her. "Don't take this the wrong way, but I never expected you to be a Deadener."

Aisha's brow furrowed. "Deadener? I'm not familiar with this word."

"Someone who deadens their pain through drugs or drink," Briana explained. "Here in Shalandra, the people who take Night Petal are called Deadeners. As the plant drowns out their pain, it slowly deadens them to the world until they are nothing but empty husks, the walking dead." She fixed Aisha with a piercing stare. "I know you've endured a lot in your life, but—"

"No." Aisha shook her head. "It's not that."

"Oh." Briana's face relaxed, relief visible.

Silence hung between them for a long moment. Aisha couldn't bring herself to share all the details, but Briana seemed at a loss for words.

Aisha spoke first. "You know what happened to me and the others of House Phoenix?"

"Kodyn told me," Briana said in a quiet voice. She almost looked embarrassed. "I asked him about it back in Praamis, after I saw that look in your eyes, the one that speaks of deep-rooted pain and loss. I see it in my father's eyes every time he speaks of my mother."

Aisha felt a jolt in her chest, as if Radiana's spirit reacted to the words. Perhaps the woman's life force hadn't truly gone, simply absorbed into Aisha's soul, where it lived on.

"The ones who held me prisoner, the Bloody Hand," Aisha went on slowly, "they gave me a narcotic, Bonedust."

Briana winced. "My father has told me about it. Truly horrible." She placed a hand on Aisha's. "For what it's worth, I'm sorry that you had to endure that."

Aisha nodded. "Yet, without that, I would not be here right now. Right where I need to be."

Her gaze went once more to the Watcher's Bloom. "That plant, back in Ghandia we called it Whispering Lily."

"What a pretty name!" Briana's eyes lit up. "I like it a lot better than either Watcher's Bloom or Keeper's Spike."

"Some of those who took it said they could..." She didn't want to say "speak to the dead" for fear she'd sound crazy. "...see things. Even hear things."

"That makes sense," Briana said. "Hallucinations, both visual and auditory, are one of the flower's side effects."

"But it did more than that." Aisha hesitated. "It affected their minds. Made them...empty, like one of your Deadeners."

"Oh." Briana's expression registered her understanding. "Someone close to you?"

Aisha drew in a deep breath. "My father."

Briana squeezed her hand, her slim fingers surprisingly strong and comforting on Aisha's. "I'm sorry. That's difficult for anyone to see."

"Yes." A lump rose to Aisha's throat at the memories of her father's vacant stare. She swallowed for fear tears would overwhelm her. "But, I thought, maybe with your father's expertise, he might know of something to counteract the effects of the plant."

Briana's brow furrowed. "You mean, like the hallucinations without the plant dulling your senses?"

Aisha nodded. *"The day will come when you, too, must answer the call of the spirits, bindazi,"* her father had said. *"The Whispering Lily will attune you to the Kish'aa. On that day, you must be ready to make the sacrifice. It is the only way to hear what the spirits have to tell you."*

But what if she could somehow use the Whispering Lily without sacrificing her sanity? Her father had told her that she would find her destiny in the City of the Dead. What if her destiny was to save the Spirit Whisperers of Ghandia from madness by bringing them a cure? She'd watched the Whispering Lily drive her father mad. She knew the high cost that came with the gift of the *Kish'aa*. Perhaps she'd been sent to Shalandra to find a way to spare future generations of *Umoyahlebe* from that suffering.

"I'd have to ask my father," Briana said, "but I think you might be on to something."

Excitement surged icy hot within Aisha's chest. "Really?"

"Well, the psychotropic properties in the Keeper's Spike…er, sorry, the *Whispering Lily* act on specific parts of our brains." Briana's brow furrowed in concentration. "But, if we could somehow come up with something to neutralize or diminish those cognitive effects, we might actually have a real solution."

Aisha didn't understand half of what Briana was saying—the Secret Keepers delved into every complex discipline of science, something she, a simple warrior, didn't have a hope of understanding. But the light in Briana's eyes made Aisha think there really was a chance.

She threw her arms around Briana's slim shoulders. "Thank you!" The words burst from her chest.

For the first time since she'd discovered her gift, Aisha had a sliver of hope.

# Chapter Twenty-Nine

As Issa met Hykos' angry glare, a thousand excuses ran through Issa's head. She could lie, could invent a story of where she'd been. But that didn't sit right with her. Hykos had been kind to her, even helped her in defiance of *Invictus* Tannard, his superior officer. Lying to him felt paramount to spitting in his face.

"I went to visit my grandparents," she said. He'd earned her honesty.

For a moment, Issa feared he would snap, shout, or threaten. She hadn't been explicitly ordered to remain within the Citadel of Stone, but she'd sworn to the Elders of the Blades that she would sever all ties to her past. Her choice to sneak out had been made knowing full well that there could be consequences for her actions. What those were, remained to be seen.

To her surprise, Hykos just nodded. "Good. Everyone needs someone to cling to in the tough times." He fixed her with a small smile. "I was fortunate enough that my older brother was chosen to join the Indomitables. He was my rock through my training until I was able to stand on my own. Without him, I don't know if I would have made it through to become a sworn Blade. And my training wasn't half as challenging as what Tannard is putting you through."

Issa's jaw dropped. "You're not…angry?"

Hykos shrugged. "The *Invictus* told you a Blade needed to be clever and stealthy. The fact that you chose this avenue of escape and that I alone saw you leave proves that you will one day be both." His expression grew wry. "Let us say you simply interpreted Tannard's instructions a tad more obliquely than he intended."

For a moment, Issa could do nothing, stunned by Hykos' response. Then she threw her arms around his neck.

"Thank you!" she whispered.

Hykos stiffened, equally surprised. Issa remembered herself and pulled away before he recovered.

"Er...right." The normally calm, composed *Archateros* seemed flustered. "Unfortunately for you, dawn is almost upon us. You've just enough time to arm yourself before Tannard summons you for your morning run."

Issa groaned. "Keeper's teeth!"

"That's the spirit." Hykos grinned. "Now hurry before someone else sees you out and about."

Issa raced through the corridors that led toward her rooms in the Citadel's western wing. She fairly flew, taking the stairs two and three at a time. Her heart was light, her mind at ease. Now, she just had to survive another day of Tannard's brand of brutality, then another. As her grandmother had told her, she specialized in impossible.

She pulled on her armor as quickly as she could, fumbling with the buckles, straps, and cinches. After more than a week of wearing it, she'd grown accustomed to the many fastenings required to hold the heavy, segmented plate mail in place. Her eyelids drooped but she forced herself to blink away the sleep. She'd be ready to face Tannard when he came for her.

By the time she strapped the last of her armor in place and slung her baldric and sword sheath over her back, the first rays of morning light had begun to appear in the eastern sky. Her stomach tightened in expectation of the harsh banging on her door that would announce Tannard's presence and the beginning of her day's torments.

Yet it never came.

She splashed water on her face and hurried out of her room, anxiety lending wings to her feet. *He's going to be waiting in the courtyard and give me some fresh punishment for showing up late for my morning run.*

The courtyard stood silent and empty, save for Hykos.

"Tannard?" she asked.

"Not here yet." Hykos seemed as surprised and confused as she.

"We'd better get on with our run, then," she told the *Archateros*. "That way, he won't have any excuse to torment me when he finally shows up."

"Agreed." Hykos grinned. "I'll be joining you this morning."

Issa shot him a sly smile. "If you think you can keep up."

"Careful, *Prototopoi*." Coming from him, the word held far less insult than when Tannard growled it. "You wouldn't be the first recruit to get a big head."

"Can't hear you back there!" Issa called as she sprinted off across the field. "Too busy winning!"

The clanking of her armor and the pounding of her boots drowned out Hykos' retort.

A laugh burst from Issa's throat as she ran. Without Tannard here to torment her, she could actually look forward to the day's training. For the first time since she'd met the *Invictus*, she once again felt proud and excited to be a Keeper's Blade.

* * *

"Don't get overconfident." Hykos knocked aside her blow with contemptuous ease and brought his two-handed sword whistling around toward her head. "Cocky gets you killed."

Issa responded by ducking his blow and lunged forward with a quick thrust. Hykos actually had to leap to the side to avoid the tip. Her dulled practice blade glanced off his armored side with a clang.

"Hah!" Issa recovered and transitioned to a Silver Sword defensive guard before he could counterattack.

Hykos looked unimpressed. "You know I'm taking it easy on you, right?"

"Is that so?" Issa grinned. "Maybe it's time you actually give me your best."

Hykos shook his head. "You're good, *Prototopoi,* but not that good."

Issa cocked an eyebrow. "Sounds like you're scared I might actually win."

Hykos said nothing, simply shrugged.

"Come on," Issa said, curling her finger in a beckoning gesture. "Show me what you've got, *Archateros*."

The young man stared at her for a long moment. Finally, he lifted his empty hand palm skyward. "You asked for it." He stepped back into a low guard position.

Issa tensed, flammard held at the ready, eyes locked onto Hykos. His stance was confusing, half-Darting Arrow and half-Windy Mountain. She couldn't tell where he'd attack from but didn't waste her time trying to guess. Instead, she locked her gaze on his torso and midsection. Those muscles in his spine, chest, and abdomen would tense before he raised his arms or moved his feet. They would signal his movement even as he made it.

His attack came so fast she barely registered it. His sword swept up toward her chin, and it was all she could do to jerk her head backward. Before she could recover her balance, he whipped his two-handed blade around and drove it point-first into her chest.

The armor stopped the dulled tip but did little to lessen the impact. Pain flared through Issa's breasts and the force of the blow knocked her backward hard enough to send her to the dirt. She fell as Killian had trained her—chin tucked to her chest, hands outstretched to slap the ground—but she'd barely hit the dirt before she found the point of Hykos' sword at her throat.

Hykos' face was an expressionless mask, but humor glinted in his almond-colored eyes. "How's that, *Prototopoi?*"

Issa gaped up at him. His attack had caught her totally by surprise and knocked her on her back. Yet one look at his face told her he hadn't done it to humiliate her the way Tannard had. Instead, it was simply a sign of respect—he'd given her what she asked for.

"Damn!" Her breath caught in her lungs; the blow had stolen her wind and she fought to draw in a full breath. "You really were holding back."

For answer, Hykos grounded his tip in the dirt between his feet and held out a hand to help her up.

"No way you should have been able to move that fast," Issa said as she pulled herself to her feet. "That was…inhuman!"

"The Keeper's blessing." Hykos met her gaze levelly. "Like our healing abilities, our god's gift confers upon us speed, strength, and stamina beyond that of normal men."

Issa's eyes widened. "You mean *I'll* be that fast one day, too?"

"Maybe." Hykos shrugged. "It's different for each of us. Take Chirak, there." He gestured to a tall, strong-featured woman training with Etai. "She's no faster than you are, but *never* face her in an arm wrestling match." He winced and rubbed his wrist as if at a painful memory. "Or Byrach. He's strong enough, but there are few of us that can match his stamina. Once, he ran a full day straight without stopping. In full armor!"

Issa glanced over to where Byrach was hammering away at Kellas' guard. She'd noticed that the hulking man rarely grew tired, even when swinging around his flammard, which was easily a foot or two longer than the other Blades'.

"The Keeper blesses each of us in his own way," Hykos told her. "We first see his gifts manifest during our Anointing, but it's only as we continue to serve him that we truly understand the full scope of what he's given us."

Issa's mind raced as she tried to picture what abilities she'd discover during the confirmation ceremony. She'd take Hykos' speed any day, though enhanced strength and stamina sounded damned awesome just the same. Either way, she would be gifted with something that few in Shalandra—or all of Einan, for that matter—ever received.

"Go," Hykos told her. "Get a drink and we'll get back to it."

For the first time, she noticed that the sun had risen close to its zenith, its golden radiance turning the air around her sweltering. She felt as if she'd sweat a barrelful into her tunic and padding. Some water, even water gone tepid from sitting in a wooden barrel all morning long, would be welcome.

Issa had just turned toward a nearby water barrel when a sound like thunder reached her ears. No, not thunder. The rhythmic *stomp, stomp, stomp* of booted feet marching in order.

Acid roiled in her stomach. *Again?*

To her dismay, a familiar figure appeared through the front gate of the Citadel of Stone. Tannard wore full armor, his heavy flammard carried in a comfortable rest on his shoulder. Behind him marched a full sixty-man company of Indomitable trainees, clad in their black half-plate mail and carrying dull-edged blades.

At the rear of the line came eight of the ten trainees that had fought with her the previous day. Bruised, bloodied, and battered to a man, they had survived the battle with the fewest injuries. The other two had sustained broken bones, one a concussion severe enough the Ministrants of the Bright Lady, goddess of healing, weren't certain he'd recover fully.

Tannard led the Indomitable trainees onto the practice yard in neat formation, and they ground to a halt in precise unison. The *Invictus'* eyes locked on to her. Cold, hard, no sign of mercy.

"Yesterday, you proved yourself a failure," he growled. "Today, redeem yourself in the eyes of the Long Keeper. If you do not, you are unworthy to call yourself a Keeper's Blade."

Ice ran through Issa's veins. *He's going to kick me out if I lose again?*

"The greater the failure, the greater the victory is required." Tannard's voice was emotionless, yet Issa thought she caught a hint of disdain cracking his mask. "To prove yourself truly worthy of the Keeper's blessing, you must face a true challenge." He lifted his huge sword off his shoulder and grounded the point in the training yard's sand. "Me."

Issa sucked in a breath, and Etai's gasp echoed from behind her. Even Kellas' face had gone pale.

"Kellas," Tannard said without taking his eyes from Issa, "you hold the same place as last time."

"Yes, *Invictus*." Kellas' voice sounded somehow smaller, weaker than usual, all trace of arrogance sucked away by relief.

"The Keeper gives us the strength to bear every challenge he sends our way." Tannard's smile was as cold as the first snow on Zahiran's southern slopes. "You will not stand alone."

Relief washed over Issa. If he let Hykos fight with her, she actually had a—

"Etai!" Tannard's words shattered Issa's momentary hope. "You will fight with Issa."

"Yes, *Invictus*." Etai sounded terrified; she'd stood watching yesterday's skirmish, had seen Issa's small company utterly demolished.

"May the Long Keeper guide your aim and strengthen your arm," Tannard growled. "In his service, failure is not an option."

# Chapter Thirty

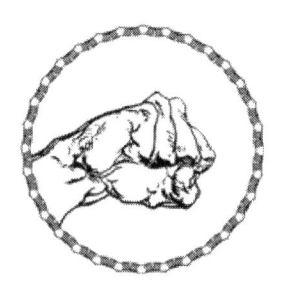

*It's about bloody time!*

Evren stifled a frustrated growl as he slipped out of Arch-Guardian Suroth's mansion an hour before dawn, hot on Kuhar's heels. Everything about the attendant—from his dark cloak and hood to his furtive glances to his surreptitious movements—reeked of villainy. If only the man hadn't taken so damned long to make his move.

The moment they'd returned from the Palace of Golden Eternity with Lady Briana's palanquin, Evren had ducked out of Samall's sight, hurried to his room, and retrieved his weapons and thief's clothing. Then he'd lain in the stables waiting for the footman to sneak out. His vantage point from the shadows of the stone building gave him a clear view of the mansion's rear gate. No way Kuhar would be stupid enough to sneak past Arch-Guardian Suroth's private guards at the front gate.

Evren had had to bide his time for nearly two full hours before Kuhar appeared. He'd slunk toward the back door like a rat creeping through a muddy alley and, after glancing around to be certain no one followed, slipped out of the back gate. The door had barely closed behind Kuhar before Evren slithered through the darkness after him. He was free from duties until noon, so he'd make good use of his time to track the treacherous attendant.

The weight of his boot daggers, wrist knives, and twin *jambiya* tucked into the back of his belt comforted him. He had no idea what he'd find when Kuhar reached his ultimate destination. If it came to a fight with Kuhar and Samall's "brethren", he'd be ready.

At this time of night, the Path of Gold was mostly empty, but a good deal of traffic flowed out of the palace down Death Row toward the lower tiers. Kuhar took full advantage of the palanquins and litters to slip through the gate unseen. For the next hour, he tailed Kuhar down Death Row, keeping close enough to remain within eyesight yet not alert the man that he was being followed.

Finally, just as the sun began to rise and light brightened the eastern horizon, Kuhar slipped through the gate that let out onto the Artisan's Tier. The Indomitables paid him and the others leaving the Defender's Tier little heed; their job was to keep out the riffraff from the lower tiers. As Evren reached them, he straightened and lifted his head so his gold-and-red headband was visible to the guards. They waved him through without a second glance.

He caught sight of Kuhar descending toward the Artificer's Courseway. Evren sped up to close the distance to the man. But halfway down the hill, he found himself caught in a small cluster of people. It took him less than two seconds to extricate himself, but in the moments that he took his eyes off Kuhar, the attendant disappeared.

Evren raced down toward the Artificer's Courseway and scanned the streets. Even though dawn traffic was light at this time of the morning, Evren could see no sign of the attendant. Kuhar's dark cloak could conceal him in any of the myriad of shadows on the Artisan's Tier. The sun would be fully risen in less than half an hour, but by then, Kuhar would be long gone.

Evren swore under his breath. *Now what the bloody hell am I going to do?*

Without knowing who Kuhar was sneaking messages to, he had nothing to help him convince Nessa or Briana's bodyguards of anything amiss. He could voice suspicion, but that might only earn him scorn—and a beating if Samall found out.

He couldn't go back to the mansion empty-handed, with no idea what dangers awaited him that evening. The clock was ticking and Hailen would be in harm's way as long as he remained beside Lady Briana. But Evren couldn't simply abandon his post in Arch-Guardian Suroth's house—he needed more time to figure out how to get his hands on the Blade of Hallar.

One option remained to him: *I need to talk to Killian.*

The blacksmith and thiefmaster had proven himself far well-informed. If he didn't already know of Samall and Kuhar's plot, he'd certainly have information that could help Evren put the pieces together.

A question nagged at the back of his mind. *Could Killian be in on it?*

Killian wouldn't be the first to deal in murder and kidnapping as well as secrets. Yet, from what Evren had learned in his short interaction, the blacksmith hadn't struck him as that sort. He might steal, lie, and manipulate with the best of them, but Evren's intuition—honed over years of surviving in the Master's Temple and on the streets of Vothmot—told him that the blacksmith had lines he wouldn't cross.

*Besides, if Killian was planning something like that, he'd have filled me on in it, wouldn't he?* That thought led to another. *Maybe he even* expected *something to be going on, which is why he put me in Suroth's household in the first place. It can't be a coincidence that there's a plot to abduct the Arch-Guardian's daughter the very day after he gets me that job, can it?*

Evren didn't know, but he certainly had a way of finding out. Killian had said he expected reports—Evren had a lot of information the blacksmith would want to hear.

He turned his steps westward on the Artificer's Courseway. Smith's Alley was a quarter-league away from Death Row, so if he hurried, he could reach it in just under half an hour. The sun would be fully up by then, but with his gold-and-red headband, he had no reason to fear the Indomitable patrols. He'd be just one more servant on an errand for his *Dhukari* master.

His heart leapt when, twenty minutes later, the sound of clanging hammers echoed from a street ahead of him. He'd drawn within a hundred yards of Smith's Alley when he caught sight of a familiar face—a face still bearing the bruise left by Evren's fist. The youth didn't seem to see Evren. Indeed, he was looking back over his shoulder, as if searching for something behind rather than ahead of him.

Evren slid up beside Snarth. "Lovely morning, isn't it?"

Snarth half-jumped, half-spun, hand dropping toward his belt.

"Nice to see you, too." Evren hid a mocking smile. "Going somewhere?"

"Yes," Snarth snapped. "To find you. Killian's expecting a report."

Anger purpled the youth's face, yet Evren caught a hint of something else in his eyes. Guilt. *No way he'd look like that if he was actually doing something for Killian. So what the hell is he up to?*

"Oh, perfect!" Evren gave him a too-cheerful smile. "I was just on my way to see Killian myself. Why don't we walk together?"

The offer caught Snarth off-guard. Just for a moment and he recovered quickly enough, but Evren caught it. *Yes, there's no way he's on an errand for Killian.*

"N-No," Snarth said, the tiniest hint of hesitation in his voice. "Killian's…busy at the moment, training the other Mumblers. I can pass your message on to him. It's protocol. We don't want anyone connecting you to Killian."

"Hmm." Evren made a show of contemplating the boy's words, furrowing his brow and giving a theatrical frown. "You're right. That's good thinking."

He let the silence drag on for a long moment, content to watch Snarth squirm. The boy's eyes darted up the Artificer's Courseway, back the way Evren had come, a hint of urgency written in his expression.

"So," Snarth finally said, "your message for Killian?"

"Oh, right, of course!" Evren smacked his forehead. "Let me see…" He trailed off as if deep in thought, which only served to amplify Snarth's irritation and impatience.

*He's definitely up to something.* The boy would never be so antsy if he truly was on Killian's business as he said.

Snarth's face twitched, agitation etched into the tight line of his lips. "The message!"

"Yes, the message." Evren delayed just long enough to annoy the boy, then quickly spoke. "I thought he should know that Arch-Guardian Suroth has hired two foreigners to guard his adoptive daughter. A man and a woman, and they look like they mean business."

"That's it?" Snarth cocked an eyebrow, a sneer on his face. "You risk drawing suspicion to yourself and Killian for that?"

"Hey, Killian told me he wanted to know anything and everything," Evren insisted, continuing his charade of naiveté. "This seems important." He dropped his voice to a conspiratorial whisper. "Maybe the Arch-Guardian has enemies in the city, so he's hiring outside help because he doesn't know who in Shalandra to trust."

He made it sound like the most important discovery of an age—on par with finding the Lost City of Enarium or the sunken continent of Aegeos. Yet, that was something anyone with even a half-functioning eye and mostly-deaf ear could figure out. Where there was power and wealth, intrigue and betrayal followed close on its heels.

Snarth nodded. "You're right, that *is* information Killian should hear." His tone made it clear he found nothing of value in Evren's words, yet he had to continue his own pretense to avoid Evren's suspicion. "I'll get it to him at once."

"I thought you said he was busy training the Mumblers?" Evren asked, all innocent curiosity.

"H-He is," Snarth said quickly, "but he'll see me for certain. I am, after all, one of his most trusted."

Evren stifled a snort. *Not if he knew you were up to something seriously questionable.*

Outwardly, his expression showed only gratitude. "Thank you. I want to make sure Killian knows that I'm holding up my end of the bargain."

"Very well." Snarth nodded. "If that's all…?"

"Right, of course," Evren said. "I'd best get back to the mansion before anyone discovers I've left."

"Can't have anyone suspecting you work for Killian," Snarth confirmed.

With a nod, Evren turned and hurried back the way he'd come. He didn't glance back—he had no doubt the Mumbler was watching him closely. He moved up the street until the early-morning stalls along the avenue blocked him from Snarth's view, and then ducked out of sight into a side street filled with goldsmith's shops. His heart hammered as he waited in breathless silence.

Tailing an unsuspecting mark was as easy as stealing coins from a passed-out drunk, but it grew harder when the one being followed suspected pursuit. He'd made a show of pretending to return to Suroth's for Snarth's sake. As long as the Mumbler didn't think anyone knew he was away from whatever task Killian had given him, he wouldn't expect a tail.

But to sell the ruse to Snarth, he'd had to gamble that the Mumbler wouldn't actually return to Killian's with his message. The urgency in Snarth's eyes had told Evren that the youth had somewhere important to be. He'd taken the chance that Snarth would wait a minute or so to be certain Evren truly *had* gone before continuing on his original path.

His gamble paid off. Less than two minutes later, Snarth appeared from up the road. Evren ducked deeper into cover and waited until Snarth passed. The Mumbler cast wary glances around him, but he never saw Evren sliding out into the street behind him.

*Let's see where you're off to,* Evren thought with a grim smile.

He tailed Snarth toward Death Row and, to his surprise, down toward the gate that led to the Cultivator's Tier. The boy cast furtive glances over his shoulder, but Evren kept out of Snarth's direct line of sight. He hung back, keeping a wide enough gap between them that the flow of traffic obscured him from Snarth's questing gaze but allowed him to keep a close eye on the Mumbler. After losing Kuhar, he wouldn't take any chances with Snarth.

Finally, Snarth seemed to decide that he wasn't being followed, for he picked up his pace, his steps more determined. Evren actually had to jog along to stay within safe tailing distance as Snarth descended to the Cultivator's Tier, then farther downhill to the Slave's Tier.

The Mumbler turned west on the Way of Chains, past Auctioneer's Square. Evren's gut clenched; the square was packed at this time of the morning, the sale of men and women—not just bronzed Shalandrans, but people from all over Einan, including pale-skinned Voramians, thin-eyed Hrandari, and the swarthy desert dwellers from the Twelve Kingdoms—in full swing.

Evren had to push his way through the thick crowds, but thankfully it seemed Snarth was having the same difficulty. By the time he burst free of the throng fifteen minutes later, the Mumbler had gained a few yards on him. Evren hurried just enough to close the gap then once more settled into a pace suitable for tailing the boy.

His curiosity grew with every step. Snarth *could* truly be on a mission for Killian, but his reaction to his earlier encounter with Evren made that seem unlikely. The question nagged at Evren: *what business does a Mumbler have in the Slave's Tier.*

His answer came half an hour later as Snarth ducked into a side street that intersected with the Way of Chains. Evren paused at the corner, glancing sidelong down the street in time to catch a glimpse of Snarth turning onto a smaller back road running parallel to the main avenue. Again, Evren peered around the corner rather than stride out into the alleyway.

His caution proved well-founded. The alley stood empty save for three tough-looking men sitting in front of a doorway. Though the house looked as decrepit and ordinary as every other stone buildings around it, the way the thug-looking men straightened at Snarth's approach made it plain that they were guarding it. The question was: what was important enough down here to require guards? And who in the Slave's Tier, the poorest level of Shalandra, could even *afford* guards?

Evren couldn't hear Snarth's hushed conversation with the thugs, but whatever the Mumbler said seemed to work. One stood and pushed the door open. Evren ducked out of sight as Snarth glanced around. When he peered around the corner again, Snarth had disappeared and the door stood closed.

*Well, that complicates things.*

Evren hesitated, uncertain what to do. He couldn't walk in the front door, so he'd have to find another way in.

His eyes traveled to the golden sandstone wall that served as the northern border of the Slave's Tier. A contented smile broadened his face. His training with the Hunter and Kiara hadn't been limited to learning weapons. The Hunter, in particular, had placed special emphasis on the ability to climb: cliffs, walls, the sides of buildings, anywhere he could find handholds and footholds.

Evren had watched in breathless awe as the Hunter scaled the Palace of Justice, Voramis' tallest building. The Hunter had insisted Evren take a turn climbing Dead Man's Cliff, the sheer rock face a half-day's ride outside of Voramis. He'd even set up a climbing wall of sorts in the warehouse that had become their center of operations over the last year.

*That'll do nicely.* The house Snarth had disappeared into was built right up against the rock face. If Evren could slip into the nearby alley without alerting the guards, he'd have no problem scaling the rock wall. Surely he'd find a balcony, window, or rooftop to give him an unseen way into the house.

A passing trio of *Kabili* women gave him the perfect opportunity. The guards' catcalls filled the air, and one of the women shouted in reply. This led to a loud exchange of Shalandran insults—very creative, and riddled with slander about the guards' ancestry—that distracted the men long enough for Evren to slip into the alleyway.

Evren grinned as he studied the cliff face. Sandstone was easily eroded and fairly fragile, but offered excellent friction and plenty of handholds and footholds for climbing. It took him less than a minute to scale high enough up the jagged wall to peer over the lip of the second-story window.

The window looked into a small room, more like a low attic set beneath the thatched roof. A crude table stood in the middle of the chamber, with five rough-looking men seated in the rickety chairs that surrounded it. Their rough, scarred hands and grim faces immediately brought back memories of the time Evren had lived on the streets.

*These are definitely the sort of men that make a living through vice and crime.*

At that moment, the door opened and Snarth entered the room.

# *Chapter Thirty-One*

Though Aisha still had the better part of four hours until her noon appointment at the Temple of Whispers, a sense of urgency drove her to depart Arch-Guardian Suroth's mansion just after the morning breakfast. She'd picked at her meal, her stomach a mess of knots. Though her conversation with Briana had given her a shred of hope, her gloom had returned with the overcast morning.

The Whispering Lily would give her the ability to not only see the spirits, but actually speak with them—to answer their call, as her father had told her. Yet, until she could find a way to counteract the effects, she feared what would happen if she took it.

For the tenth time since leaving Suroth's house, she touched the small pouch hidden beneath her simple servant's garb. The pouch contained a few Whispering Lily petals she'd plucked. She hadn't dared to use it yet—she didn't know when she would summon the courage to take the risk. But she carried it for the same reason she'd ridden *toward* the graveyard at Rosecliff. Her mother had taught her not to flee her fears, but to confront them. Few things terrified her more than the thought that she would turn into that same dead husk of a human that her father had. Keeping the flower close was her way of defying that dread.

Thankfully, she didn't have to worry about the flower or its effects, at least not right now. For the next few hours, her mission to the Temple of Whispers would consume her full attention. The challenge of moving through the streets unobserved by anyone watching would prove a welcome distraction from her troubles.

Her outfit provided ample cover for her mission. She wore a servant's *kalasiris* free of insignia with a headband—strips of *Dhukari* gold and *Earaqi* red braided together—to mark her as a low-caste servant in a high-caste household. Nessa, the Steward, had insisted that no one would interfere with or question her as long as she wore the headband. A loose, flowing cloak completed her ensemble.

She felt naked without her *assegai,* but she hadn't hesitated to leave it with the rest of her weapons back at Suroth's mansion. Shalandran servants didn't carry weapons, at least not in plain view. Years spent training with Ria, Errik, and the rest of House Serpent had accustomed her to fighting with a wide range of weapons both bladed and bludgeoning, as well as bare-handed.

*Besides, what are the chances that someone's going to attack a Dhukari's servant?*

If it came down to it, Kodyn had lent her a pair of flat throwing daggers, which she'd tucked beneath the wide red-and-gold silk sash around her waist.

Her greatest concern at the moment lay in being spotted. She had no idea who'd watch her—she and Kodyn had been in Shalandra for all of a day and night—but that didn't stop her from taking her usual precautions. Her short time in the city had proven that Arch-Guardian Suroth had enemies that wouldn't shy away from killing servants or kidnapping the Councilman's daughter.

As always, Aisha took the most circuitous route possible. Only one road led from the Keeper's Tier to the Artisan's Tier, but three broad avenues connected the Artisan's Tier to the lower two levels of Shalandra. Aisha descended Death Row toward the Slave's Tier and cut westward through Auctioneer's Square.

Acid rose to her throat as she spotted the familiar *choclat*-colored skin and broad features of her people. Not just Ghandians, but Issai and Tanirians as well. All people like her, ripped from their homes and dragged thousands of leagues away to live as slaves.

But hers weren't the only ones to be enslaved. Men, women, even children with skin of every shade—from pale white to rich bronze to the midnight black of the Dynari tribe far to the east of Ghandia—stood on the auctioneer's platform and watched in mute, defeated silence as their lives were sold to the highest bidder.

The *Kish'aa* hung thick around the stone columns and wooden stockades behind the platforms. Countless people had died here: thousands, perhaps even tens of thousands over the centuries of Shalandra's existence. The spirits of the dead fixed lifeless eyes on her, their mouths gaping in wordless cries, little more than whispers too low for her mind to comprehend.

*What are they saying?* The thought of what she'd hear if she took the Whispering Lily sent a shudder of fear down her spine. Her father had never had a moment's peace; the cries of the dead had haunted him and stolen his mind.

It took all her willpower not to clap her hands over her ears, to break into a run to flee the dead. They tugged at her, the energy within their blue-white glowing forms pulling at her. They wanted her to come closer, to make contact with them. She was their only connection to the living. Without her, they would fade into obscurity, even their names forgotten by time, left to drift on the winds invisible to all but her.

She sucked in deep, gasping breaths and picked up her pace to get through Auctioneer's Square at a fast shuffle. Anyone following would have to speed up, making them more visible to her as well.

Once free of Auctioneer's Square, Aisha ducked into the shadows of a side street and waited, eyes fixed on the Way of Chains. For nearly fifteen minutes, she remained motionless and silent, until her heart slowed its hammering. When she caught no sign of pursuers, she resumed her trek through Shalandra.

Her steps led due west, toward Traders' Row. Just beyond the broad avenue stood another square, similar to Auctioneer's Square but with far more dried, crusted blood staining the platforms. Murder Square, Briana had called it. Here, the Indomitables carried out the harsh sentences imposed upon the people ground beneath their heels. Thousands of *Kish'aa* hovered around Murder Square, the combined sparks of their lives so bright she could barely look at them.

Shalandra truly was the City of the Dead, and she alone could see and hear them.

Thankfully, her path turned to the north, and she sighed in relief as she climbed toward the Cultivator's Tier. The guards took one look at her headband and let her through without a second glance. The tier, home to the *Earaqi* laborers that made up the largest percentage of Shalandra's population, was neat and clean, the streets laid out in a precise order that the haphazard buildings of the Slave's Tier had lacked. Fewer of the dead hovered in the air, their numbers diminished enough that she could ignore their pleading looks and silent cries.

After a quick search for any sign of pursuit, she turned westward, toward the Foreign Quarter. From there, it would be a quick climb to the temples that stood in the shadows of the cliff that served as Shalandra's western border.

Her fists tightened as the ghostly figures grew thicker. Every step led her closer to the Keeper's Crypts, toward the mass of *Kish'aa* clustered there. Their whispers rose to a dull hum at her approach, like a fly hovering inside her ear. An almost tangible energy crackled in the air. The spark of Radiana's life flowing within Aisha burned like a match touched to kindling.

Aisha clenched her jaw and forced herself to keep moving despite the strange sensations coursing through her. The writhing, seething mass of blue-white light called to her, tugged at the core of her being. The souls of the dead pulled her toward them, their lifeless, empty eyes fixed on her. The hum in her head grew to a pulsing, thrumming that rattled against the inside of her skull until she had to grit her teeth against the pain.

By the time she climbed the Path of Sepulture to the Artisan's Tier, she had all but forgotten to search for any sign of pursuit. She cast a glance backward but her eyes refused to focus. The wordless cries of the *Kish'aa* pushed into her thoughts and tore at her mind.

Relief washed over Aisha when she finally turned eastward, away from the Keeper's Crypts tombs. The tugging sensation diminished with every step away, yet she could not truly escape it. The dead remained behind her, and they would not let her go so easily.

She tried to push the humming to the back of her mind as she entered the Temple District on Shalandra's Artisan's Tier. The temples here were massive buildings; none near the size of the Hall of the Beyond on the Keeper's Tier yet still unique marvels of construction.

All had been carved from the stone of the mountain, but each had been built in their own style. The Master's Temple was the grandest, nearly half again as large as the other temples, with a huge marble statue of Kiro dominating the courtyard in the center of the horseshoe-shaped building. An army of Shalandran heroes stood silent vigil in front of the squat, sturdy Temple of

Derelana, each statue carved in lifelike size and bearing the features of the greatest warriors in the city's history.

The Temple of Prosperity, home to the Illusionist Cleric, bore the same bizarre façade that seemed to play tricks with Aisha's eyes if she looked too closely. For a moment, the swirling lines carved into the golden sandstone shifted to form ghostly figures of the dead. When Aisha blinked, the images seemed to change to form the gently rising hills and swaying grasses of her homeland.

The Swordsman's obelisk rose thirty paces into the sky, a white marble dagger that reflected the sunlight with dazzling brilliance. Aisha had to shield her eyes as she hurried past.

Aisha's destination, the vault-like Temple of Whispers, was just beyond the obelisk. Built from the same golden sandstone as the rest of the temples, somehow the stone seemed to have lost its brilliance, turned a dull ochre as if to match the muted brown robes of the priests that served there. The only opening Aisha could see in the entire temple was the enormous concave steel door at the front.

Two Secret Keepers stood silent vigil before the door. As she approached, they stepped forward to bar her entry to the temple, fixing her with a questioning gaze.

Her fingers flashed in the hand signing Briana had taught her. "*Ennolar is expecting me.*"

The Secret Keepers' eyebrows rose to disappear beneath their white headbands. When they made no move to get out of her way, Aisha repeated her silent statement.

After a moment, one of the Secret Keepers nodded. "*Wait here,*" his fingers said. He strained to open the steel vault door enough to slip through, but his companion didn't lend a hand.

Less than a minute later, the same Secret Keeper stepped out. "*Come.*" A single gesture, universally understood in any language. He made no move to enter, but stepped aside to make way for her.

Aisha had to twist sideways to enter the barely-opened vault door. Surprise raced through her as she caught a glimpse of the temple's interior. She didn't know what she'd been expecting, but she'd been expecting *something*. Instead, she stood inside a perfectly cubical room of blank stone walls, ceiling, and floor. The single object in the room was an oval-shaped glass globe embedded in the ceiling. The liquid within the globe filled the room with a dim glow, similar to the beamer lamps she'd used in the Night Guild. Aside from that, the room was utterly devoid of details.

Even inside their temple, it seemed, the servants of the Mistress guarded their secrets from the world outside.

Aisha nearly jumped as a section of stone wall in front of her slid aside in utter silence. Ennolar—she recognized the short, bald-headed man from the previous night's party—appeared in the opening and strode toward her. *"What do you want?"* his hands asked.

For answer, Aisha reached into her pocket and pulled out the silver coin Kodyn had given her—the Black Widow's coin bearing the depiction of an eight-legged spider.

The Secret Keeper studied her through narrowed eyes. After a long moment of silence, he nodded. *"The light-skinned one did well in sending you. You pass for a Shalandran far better than he, Ghandian."*

The fact that he knew where she was from came as only a small surprise to Aisha—Ria had told her the story of Ilanna's visit to the Temple of Whispers in Voramis and the many wonders she'd encountered there. No one outside the Mistress' priesthood knew the full breadth and depth of the knowledge stored in these halls.

He pressed a finger to his lips. *"No words. The walls have ears, but within this room, we are unobserved."*

With a furtive glance around, he reached into his dull brown robes and produced a leather scroll tube. *"Here."* He held it out to her. *"As promised."*

*"Thank you."* Aisha took the scroll tube and tucked it into the large pocket in her flowing cloak. The large, heavy tube sat awkwardly, but she could make it work.

*"What you have there is more than three decades of my life's work."* Ennolar fixed her with a stern gaze. *"The Arch-Guardian has given his permission to share this information with you, but I will warn you, should it fall into any other hands, the consequences will be severe."* He finished his words with a hand gesture she didn't understand, but which mimicked a very painful form of execution.

*"Understood."* Aisha nodded.

With a bow, the Secret Keeper turned and strode toward the wall. To her surprise, he made no move to touch the stone, yet the wall slid aside for him as he approached. When he stepped through, it slid silently back into place behind him, leaving Aisha alone in the temple.

She hurried toward the vault-like door, once again forced to squeeze sideways through the narrow opening. The two Secret Keepers stared at her curiously but asked no questions as she ducked into the flow of traffic moving through the Temple District. At this time of the morning, just after the noon hour, the streets around the temples were busy. She welcomed the press of people—it provided ample cover for her to lose anyone following her.

Aisha's heart stopped as her eyes fell on the stone pillars and marble-tiled stairs of the Sanctuary. Her feet hesitated, horror thrumming within her. The *Kish'aa* hovered by the thousands, a thick wall of blue-white light that swirled like a whirlpool around the building. She sucked in a breath as the spirits of the dead turned toward her, their empty eyes locking onto her face. With a force beyond her control, she began striding toward them as if in a trace. She could not escape the dead, not so close.

The Ministrants, healers of the Bright Lady, were too busy treating the ill to pay her attention. The white-robed women wore thick cloth bandages wrapped around their hands and arms as they ministered to emaciated men and women covered with crusted blue blisters that oozed pus.

A sudden swell of nausea crashed into Aisha, and she sucked in a breath as the energy crackled through her skin. The single spark of life within her danced between her fingers and set her nerves tingling. All around her, the sparks of the thousands that had died here surged toward her like moths drawn to a flame. The humming in her head grew to a deafening ringing that set her head pounding and drowned out her surroundings.

Aisha heard herself cry out, a muted, wordless whimper of panic and fear. Her legs moved of their own accord, as if the power of the *Kish'aa* controlled her body like a puppeteer's marionette made to dance on its strings. She wanted to shut her eyes and stop up her ears, yet she could not. All she could do was watch in helpless horror as the dead swirled around her.

Someone bumped into her and she faintly heard a voice asking, "You hurt, girl?" But it came as if from a great distance. She was in the world of the *Kish'aa* now.

Energy tingled across her skin and thrummed to her marrow. She could see the sparks dancing around her fingers, running across her hands, rippling through her veins. Yet it felt…wrong. She'd absorbed Radiana's spark, yet these spirits would not join her. Without their names, she could not control them, could not stop them from setting every nerve in her body ablaze. She could see and feel the dead, but she lacked her father's ability to hear them, to summon them to do her will.

The *Kish'aa* held her rooted in place, imprisoning her within a swirling vortex of crackling blue-white light. Their ghostly lips moved but she could not hear their words. She felt as if her head would explode with the force of their cries.

Her father's words flashed through her mind. *"The day will come when you, too, must answer the call of the spirits, bindazi."*

Tears streamed down Aisha's face. They were brought on partly by the pain that threatened to rip her apart from the inside out. For the first time in years, since the day she had regained consciousness in the Night Guild's tunnels, Aisha knew real fear.

Fear of the power around her, of the whirling energy that set her nerves and muscles on fire. Fear of the madness that would claim her if she yielded to the power of the *Kish'aa* and chose to use her gift. Fear of losing herself to the power of the Whispering Lily, of deadening herself until only a husk remained.

A part of her wanted to curl up in a ball, to close her eyes and block out the world around her. She was terrified of this gift, this curse. She had no one to call on, no one to offer advice or lend support. Kodyn and Briana could try, but what did they know about being a Spirit Whisperer? This was a burden that she alone could bear. A burden too heavy for her shoulders.

Yet another part of her, the part she'd fought so hard to strengthen for the last four years, screamed at her to fight. Not to fight the power of the spirits, but to fight the fear that held her paralyzed.

Aisha curled her fingers into fists. Even the tiny movement sent pain flaring through her arms, but she bit down on a cry.

She had chosen to come to Shalandra. Even knowing what lay ahead, she'd made the decision because she *had* to. She had come to find her destiny, to embrace the gift of the Spirit Whisperers.

*So be it.* Resolve hardened like a block of stone in her gut. *I will embrace it as my father instructed.*

Reaching into her pouch, she pulled out the petals of the Whispering Lily. So small, so delicate, such a lovely shade of blue, yet their beauty belied their danger. She hesitated, wrestling back her fear. There was no going back from this.

Aisha drew in a deep breath and closed her fist around the petals, crushing them in her strong fingers. *I will answer the call of the dead. I will make the sacrifice.*

Her hand came up to her mouth and, without pause, she swallowed the crushed petals. A sweet fragrance filled her nostrils and a single drop of oil coated her tongue. Sweet at first, then bitter and biting, then sweet once more.

The buzzing stilled, so suddenly it staggered her. The pounding in her head stopped, and it seemed the world had fallen silent. Yet Aisha could still hear the muted hum of traffic, the muttered conversations around her, the moans of the sick lying before the Sanctuary. But it all faded into the background, as if someone had stuffed cotton into her ears.

A new sound reached her then: whispers, quiet at first but growing steadily louder. Words from a thousand lips, washing over her like a thundering cascade, a torrent of pleas and cries that she could not understand.

The swirling mass of energy coalesced into individual shapes. Men, women, children, old and young. Their figures were sharp, as clear to her eyes as the people moving through the streets around her. She reached out a hand toward one, a girl that looked around her age. The moment her fingers touched the ghostly form, a spark crackled through her skin. But it no longer brought her pain. Instead, the power set her muscles alight with energy, vitality.

She met the spirit's lifeless gaze. "What do you want?"

The ethereal form seemed to solidify, the details of her face, form, and clothing almost becoming tangible. "*Justice.*" A single word, drifting like a leaf on the wind, yet it echoed in Aisha's mind with the force of a hurricane. It was perfectly clear, as if someone had just said it aloud.

"Justice for what?" She shook her head.

"*Justice.*" The spirit of the young girl fixed pleading eyes on Aisha. As her figure came into focus, Aisha's eyes flew wide. The girl's body was covered in crusted, pus-oozing sores. The same sores that covered the men and women being tended by the white-robed Ministrants.

Confusion twisted Aisha's face into a frown. "I don't understand."

The ghostly figure's eyes seemed to flash, a spark of lightning in her empty gaze. "*Justice.*" The cry was louder, piercing. More and more ghostly throats echoed the word, until it rippled through the spirits swirling around her.

Aisha felt helpless. She had answered the call of the spirits, but she could not understand what they wanted. She could do nothing for them. There could be no justice for disease—it claimed all alike, rich and poor, powerful and enslaved.

Yet she could listen. She could hear their cries. It was the gift she'd been given—the gift of the Spirit Whisperer—and though it came at a heavy price, she would bear the burden.

# Chapter Thirty-Three

Anxiety set Kodyn's gut churning as he paced the garden balcony that overlooked the front of the mansion. He scanned the Path of Gold again and glanced at the sun's position high in the cloudless sky.

Noon had come and gone more than two hours earlier. *She should be back by now.*

He knew he shouldn't worry about Aisha—she could take care of herself. Yet, with everything he'd learned about the enemies they faced, he couldn't help his nervousness. They were up against the most powerful people in Shalandra, outnumbered, with no allies he could call on. Arch-Guardian Suroth's lips had remained sealed on what he intended to do to move against the Necroseti and the Gatherers.

"You're going to wear a rut in the tiles," Briana called from where she sat on a high-backed stone bench in the shade of a strange-looking tree with silver bark, leaves, and fruit to match. "And you know how costly Praamian ceramic can be."

"Sorry." Kodyn shot a last glance back at the Path of Gold then turned toward the Shalandran girl. "Even with all the precautions she'd take to avoid anyone following her, she should have returned by now."

"And worrying isn't going to get you anywhere." Briana gave him a little smile. "Better you join me and actually get some food in your stomach. Keeper knows you hardly ate at breakfast."

Kodyn had to admit the food on the tray beside Briana looked appetizing. Sweet rolls, candied nuts, dried fruits, crushed date paste, goat cheese, salted butter, and strange prickly fruits harvested from one of Suroth's trees. He plucked a few dried fruits from the tray.

"There, happy?"

Briana gave him a broad smile. "Very."

Kodyn glanced around but saw no sign of the Malandrian boy, Hailen. Briana had dismissed the servant, wanting some time alone in the garden. The brow furrowing the girl's forehead told Kodyn that she was deep in thought.

*Likely mulling over her encounter with Councilor Madani and what to do about the bastard.*

The sound of boots *clacking* on the ceramic tiles tore his attention away from the food. His hand dropped to his sword as he stepped in front of Briana, but he relaxed as he caught sight of Arch-Guardian Suroth striding toward them.

*"Good to see you take your job seriously, young Praamian."* The Secret Keeper smiled. *"I take it by your worried expression that your companion has not yet returned?"*

Kodyn shook his head. "She's probably just being extra careful," he said aloud, more for his own benefit.

Suroth nodded his approval. *"Wise."* He turned to Briana. *"With your permission, Daughter, I'd speak to the young man alone."*

Briana cocked an eyebrow. "What's so secretive you can't say it in front of me?"

*"Nothing."* The Arch-Guardian brushed an affectionate hand across his daughter's cheek. *"I simply doubted you'd be interested in the Vault of Ancients Kodyn intends to access to steal the Crown of the Pharus."*

"You doubted that?" Briana's eyes flashed, and her fingers moved through the hand signs in sharp, short gestures. *"I have always shared your fascination for anything Serenii-made. If there is something you want him to know, I'm damned well going to hear it, too."*

Suroth turned a helpless smile on Kodyn. *"My daughter could out-stubborn her mother any day."*

Kodyn chuckled. "Trust me, that's something I'm very familiar with." His mother could challenge a stone statue to a staring contest and walk away victorious.

*"If you insist, Daughter."* Suroth addressed the both of them now. *"As the highest-ranking Secret Keeper in Shalandra, nothing goes on in the Temple of Whispers without my knowledge. Ennolar informed me of your request for the map, though he believes it is going to the Black Widow."*

Kodyn raised an eyebrow. "You know about the Black Widow?"

Suroth snorted. *"Of course I do! I've availed myself of her services on a number of occasions. Indeed, she was one of the first people I contacted in my search for Briana. That is how I knew my daughter was* not *in Shalandra. I swear that woman has every grain of sand counted. Makes her a truly effective ally in our efforts to punish the Necroseti responsible for Briana's abduction."*

The Arch-Guardian squeezed his daughter's shoulder, and Briana leaned her cheek against his hand for a moment.

*"But the map is just the first step in your quest to steal the Crown of the Pharus,"* Suroth continued. *"The Serenii tunnels will get you inside the palace, but they do not lead directly to the vault where the crown is stored with the rest of Shalandra's relics. You will need to enter the Tomb of Hallar on the western side of the Palace of Golden Eternity."*

Kodyn's gut clenched. *If it was easy, it wouldn't be a worthy Undertaking.*

*"The Vault of Ancients sits beside the holiest place in all of Shalandra: the Tomb of Hallar."*

Briana drew in a sharp breath. "Truly?"

Kodyn's brow furrowed. "Someone important, I take it?"

Both sets of eyebrows rose, and Briana's eyes widened. "Did I never tell you about Hallar, Shalandra's first Pharus?"

Kodyn shook his head.

"Hallar's origins are shrouded in mystery," Briana explained, "though it is agreed that he belonged to one of the tribes of the four mountains. He was a champion—of which tribe, no one knows—a peerless warrior that defeated every challenger sent against him. He was the one to unite the tribes into one, and under his rule, the city of Shalandra was built."

"Carved from the mountain, you mean."

Briana nodded. "Of course. He founded the Keeper's Blades and the Indomitables, and, we believe, created the caste system, which has maintained order and prosperity in Shalandra since his days. His death is as much a mystery as his birth, but everyone in Shalandra knows that his body lies at rest in the

Tomb of Hallar, at the highest point of the city, above even the level of the palace."

"In that stern-looking face?" Kodyn had seen the stony features of Hallar glaring down at him as he entered the Palace of Golden Eternity. "That's his tomb?"

"Yes, or..." Briana hesitated. "At least that's what we believe."

*"The Tomb of Hallar has been sealed for two thousand years,"* Suroth put in, *"and the key lost to time. Few written records exist from that long ago. All we have are the stories and legends passed down to us by our ancestors, and those carved into the tombs in the Keeper's Crypts. My Secret Keepers and I have dedicated ourselves to uncovering as much of Shalandra's history as we can."*

"But the Vault of Ancients *can* be accessed, right?" Kodyn cocked his head. "It's not locked up tight like the tomb?"

*"Of course."* Suroth nodded. *"But, and this is a secret that no one beyond myself and a few of my most trusted priests know, the vault does not open on our command."*

Kodyn's brow furrowed. Briana had told him that Suroth was the one who brought out the relics from the Vault of Ancients for ceremonies. Yet the look on her face revealed confusion on par with his.

Suroth glanced around, *"The Serenii designed the vault door to only open four times a year. The Vault opens of its own accord—I alone know how to move through the vault safely without setting off the traps left by the ancient people. Only I can safely enter to retrieve the relics stored there."*

Kodyn's gut tightened. *Serenii traps? That's going to make things damned difficult.* He'd heard his mother's story of her escape from the Black Spire in Praamis. Only her skill combined with a healthy dose of the Mistress' luck had gotten her out alive.

"If this is such a big secret, why are you telling me?" Kodyn asked.

*"Because I need your trust if I am to trust you to keep my daughter safe."* Suroth fixed him with a pointed expression. *"The vault will open in three weeks, on the day of the Anointing of the Blades. But if, for some reason, we fail to find a way to help you succeed in your efforts to claim the Crown of the Pharus, you will know that I am speaking the truth when I say that we can only try again in three months."*

"Ah, of course." Kodyn smiled, understanding dawning. "Trust is built on truth, after all."

"*Precisely.*" Suroth returned the smile. "*With everything that we face—the Necroseti, chief among them, but I doubt the threat of the Gatherers is truly passed—I need to know that I can count on you to keep my Briana safe. I would give anything to ensure her protection.*"

Kodyn held out a hand. "You have my word that I will do everything in my power to protect her. And, as long as you need us, we are here to help."

"*Thank you.*" Suroth shook his hand, and once again Kodyn was surprised by the strength of the Secret Keeper's grip. "*I am father first, priest second, and Councilman third.*" He shot a glance up at the sun and his brow furrowed. "*Speaking of the Council, I am late for our weekly meeting.*"

Briana's face fell. "Must you go, Father? Those Necroseti wear masks of courtesy but they want nothing more than to see you gone."

Suroth shrugged. "*I do what I must. My duty is to serve this city as best I can. And, after the Council meeting, I will find a way to speak to the Pharus and share my suspicions. He has no love for the Necroseti and the rest of the Council, either.*"

Briana sighed. "All the same, I'll still worry about you until you return. Maybe Kodyn can—"

"*Kodyn's place is by your side.*" Suroth cut off his daughter with a firm shake of his head. "*I am more than capable of protecting myself, Daughter.*" He pressed a kiss to Briana's forehead, and she threw her arms around his neck.

Kodyn looked away—after the last few weeks, they deserved a private moment of tenderness. Suroth had made an effort to spend a few hours with Briana the previous afternoon, but his duties as Arch-Guardian of the Secret Keepers and a member of the Keeper's Council had kept him busy.

"I love you, Papa." Briana's words, spoken aloud, held a depth of emotion that brought a lump to Kodyn's throat. He'd never had a father just as Briana had never had a mother. They'd both had to make do with one parent—one parent that cared for them with every shred of love they could muster. He'd been truly fortunate to have Ria there as well.

A strong hand rested on Kodyn's shoulder. He turned to find Arch-Guardian Suroth standing behind him.

"*Take this to the Black Widow.*" The Secret Keeper held out a small pouch. "*She will understand the meaning of the message.*"

Kodyn cocked an eyebrow, curiosity burning as he took the pouch. The object within felt round, smooth, and hard, small enough to nestle in the palm of his hand.

"*To face the Necroseti, we need help.*" Suroth gave him an enigmatic smile. "*The Black Widow makes a powerful ally—for the right price.*" His expression grew stern. "*But deliver it only to her and no one else. In the wrong hands, this can be used for truly terrible things.*"

Kodyn nodded understanding. "I will get it to her as soon as Aisha returns." The ominous look in Suroth's eyes inflamed Kodyn's innate curiosity. He ached to find out what could be so important to the Secret Keeper, yet respect for the man stopped him from opening the pouch.

"*Good,*" Suroth's fingers said. "*Time is of the essence.*" He gripped Kodyn's forearm. "*She is my sun, moon, and stars. I could not bear to lose her again. Keep her safe, Kodyn.*"

"With my life." Kodyn met his gaze.

With a nod, Arch-Guardian Suroth released his grip on Kodyn's arm, turned, and hurried away across the walkway that led through the rooftop garden.

Kodyn glanced at Briana. Worry sparkled in the Shalandran girl's eyes.

"He'll be fine," he told her. "I may have only known him for a day, but I've met few people as capable as him." Errik, Ria, his mother, and the Hunter numbered among the few he'd wager on against the Secret Keeper.

"I know," Briana said, "but that doesn't stop me from fearing for him. Especially now that we know Councilor Madani and the rest of the Necroseti are against us."

"We'll figure it out." Kodyn placed a hand on her shoulder. "The four of us."

Briana squeezed her eyes closed and leaned on his hand, a smile on her face. "I feel much safer, just having you here. Both of you. I don't know what I'd do without you and Aisha."

"You won't have to find out, I promise." Kodyn crouched in front of her and scooped up her hands in his. He spoke in an earnest voice. "We're not going anywhere until we're sure you're safe."

Briana smiled, and suddenly Kodyn was aware of how close she was. Her hands were warm in his, her skin soft and fragrant with the smell of tiger lilies. The lines of *kohl* accented the dark color and almond shape of her eyes, and she'd painted her lips with a deep purple color that seemed to glisten in the sunlight. The fabric of her simple dress shimmered, the thin straps over her shoulder revealing an abundance of the golden mahogany skin of her slim shoulders, neck, and upper chest.

Heat raced through him as his eyes locked with Briana. He saw that same glimmer of fire in her eyes, the flush in her cheeks. Her hands in his had grown suddenly hot. Her lips parted, her breathing speeding up to match his. For a moment, he almost thought she was leaning forward, closing the distance to—

A sound from behind him shattered the moment. He stood and turned in time to see Aisha striding through the garden toward them. A momentary surge of disappointment, even anger, flashed through him. Yet one look at Aisha's face wiped it all away.

"What's wrong?" he asked. A shadow hung in Aisha's eyes, her shoulders tense, as if beneath a great weight. "Was there a problem with the Secret Keeper?"

Aisha shook her head and, without a word, produced the scroll tube. Kodyn took the leather tube but his eyes never left hers. She was still the same young woman he'd known for years, but there was something else, something new that he couldn't quite put his finger on. Something within her had changed.

"I'm fine," Aisha said. "Just tired. Didn't sleep much."

A lie, but Kodyn let it pass. She'd been carrying a burden since the day they'd left Praamis, one she hadn't chosen to share with him. Either she would do so in her own time, or he'd press her a bit when they had a moment of peace. Right now, if she wanted him to treat her as if nothing was wrong, he'd go along with it.

He pried the lid from the scroll tube and pulled out the scroll—made from a pithy plant Briana had called papyrus. Eager anticipation coursed through him as he unrolled the thick paper.

Excitement turned to confusion, and his brow furrowed as he stared down at the scroll.

"What is it?" Aisha asked.

Kodyn turned it over and held it up. "There's nothing!"

The map was blank.

# Chapter Thirty-Three

Issa swallowed the acid surging into her throat. She, Etai, and eight Indomitable trainees faced sixty enemies bolstered by Kellas and the heavily-armored, stone-faced *Invictus* Tannard.

*There's no damned way we can pull this off.* Not against six times their number. Again, they wore padded jerkins and wielded wooden batons against sword-wielding Indomitables in solid half-plate mail.

Yet her grandmother's words from the previous night echoed in her mind. *"That is how you have always been, Granddaughter. Stubborn as a farmer's mule, yet as unstoppable as a runaway bull. Nothing can stop you, nechda. The only one who can stop you is you. You only fail when you stop fighting."*

She gritted her teeth. *I will never stop fighting.* Anger burned in her gut as she fixed her eyes on Tannard at the rear of the line. *I refuse to let you force me out of the Blades, you bastard!*

Tannard's stony expression never changed. He simply stood ready, huge two-handed sword carried on his shoulder. An immovable obstacle she'd somehow have to surmount in order to succeed.

*So be it.* Resolve hardened like shalanite in her stomach. *Somehow, I'm getting past you.*

She turned to her small company—bloodied and beaten, but defiance shining in their eyes. Last time, she had nearly carried them to victory against impossible odds. Even Etai, the slim *Mahjuri* girl she'd helped in the Crucible, looked at her with mingled hope and trust. They wanted her to triumph. No, more than that. They *expected* her to.

The realization bolstered her courage and determination. She was their commanding officer, and they counted on her to keep them alive in this mock battle. Issa wouldn't let them down.

"I'm dreading the words about to come out of your mouth." Nysin's tone dripped sarcasm. Clearly, he refused to let a few bruised ribs and a split lip dull his cutting edge. "Hopefully it'll be a better plan than last time."

Issa smiled. "The same plan, actually." Her grin widened as Nysin's jaw dropped. "Almost."

"You got us all killed last time." Nysin shook his head. "If it's all the same to you, I'd just as soon skip the pummeling on my second day in a row."

"You should be used to that by now." Viddan, another *Mahjuri* trainee, snorted. "You've taken a beating in just about every training session with Rilith."

Issa shot a glance at the tall, slender *Earaqi* girl. "You're good with your blades?"

Rilith shrugged.

"Yes," Enyera put in. "I may be lightest on my feet, but none of us can match the speed of her hands."

"Good." Issa nodded. "Then you're with Etai and me at the tip of the spear." She glanced at Viddan and Nysin. "The two of you behind them, and the rest of you filling out the formation. And you," she told Enyera, "I want you at the back again, ready to run."

Nysin rolled his eyes. "Because that worked so well last time!"

"Put yourself in their place," Issa said with a sly grin. "Would you expect us to try the same maneuver twice?"

Nysin shook his head. "Given its spectacular failure last time, only an idiot would do that!"

"Which is *exactly* why we're going to do it." Issa laughed at Nysin's incredulous expression. "They'll realize we're trying to outthink them by doing the last thing they expected us to do, so they'll have to adjust their battle lines. As soon as they see Enyera taking her place at the rear of our group like she did last time, they'll expect her to run around them again."

"So they'll have to expand their lines in preparation." Etai's eyes went wide as realization dawned. "And when their lines are spread out, we'll have an easier time driving through them."

"Never mind that the lines are now fifteen men strong instead of twelve," Nysin interjected.

"They could be a hundred strong." Issa nodded her chin toward their enemy's ranks. "They're still only two deep, and they've still got the same distance between the four lines." Had she been the one in command on the opposite side, she'd have used the additional twelve to form a fifth line—making it truly impossible for her to break through.

Confusion clouded Enyera's face. "But *am* I going to run for the pennant?"

Issa shot her a smile. "That's what we want them to think. But I've got something else in mind. Something that none of them will expect."

She relayed her plan—utterly desperate, and impossible in full armor, but their only hope of winning this challenge—and Enyera's eyes widened.

"Damn!" The *Earaqi* girl shook her head. "You're either insane or the cleverest person here."

"We'll find out which soon enough," Issa said with a grin.

Her eyes traveled over the bruised, battered faces of her company. "We face an impossible challenge. No one could hope to succeed here, and everyone in that battle line across from us knows it." A brazen grin split her face. "Let's prove them wrong!"

Nine pairs of eyes filled with grim determination, defiant. The Indomitable trainees gripped their wooden batons tighter, adjusted their padded jerkins one last time.

"We do this," Etai told Issa in a low voice, "you'll only make things worse with Tannard. You'll be defeating *him* personally."

Issa met the *Mahjuri* girl's eyes. "I know." The words came out in a low growl. "But it's bloody well worth it!"

Etai grinned. "May the Long Keeper strengthen your arm—"

"—and guide your aim," Issa finished. She saluted, right fist to left shoulder, and Etai returned it.

Issa strode toward their battle line and took her place at the tip of the spear. She tightened her grip on her twin batons and drew in a deep breath.

*This is for you, Savta.*

She charged.

Batons held low, jaw set, eyes fixed on her first opponent, Issa pounded toward the enemy's lines. Behind her, nine pairs of boots *thumped* in the sand. The Indomitable trainees facing her crouched behind their wooden shields, braced for impact.

Issa slammed into the front rank with bone-jarring force. Instead of striking out with her truncheons, she lowered her shoulder and drove straight into the trainees before her. The force of her charge backed by the power of her muscles bulled through the first rank, then the second, and she burst free of the battle line with a cry of rage.

Her momentum carried her forward, and she poured fury and determination into her muscles. She hit the second line seconds after plowing through the first. She, the tip of the spear formation, punched into the enemy like a dagger through parchment. Her batons crunched into outstretched arms and exposed heads.

This time, she aimed for her enemy's hands and arms. She couldn't face Kellas or Tannard with wooden clubs. She needed a sword, even a shorter Indomitable blade. As one trainee struck at her, she dropped the club and reached out her right hand to close fingers around his wrist. She squeezed, her forge-hardened grip painfully tight. The trainee's grip on his blade loosened long enough for Issa to tear it from his grasp.

Her momentum had slowed in that instant, but Etai and Rilith on her flanks drove through the second line. With a gasp, she raced on toward the third line.

Kellas held the center of the line, eyes fixed on her, two-handed flammard held at the ready. She could see desire written in every contour of his arrogant *Dhukari* face: he wanted to be the one to take her down this time.

*Let's see what you've got, you pompous prick!*

"Now!" she shouted.

Kellas' face hardened, a smile curling his lip upward into a half-sneer, and he echoed her words. "Now!"

Even as Issa and her company raced toward Kellas' line, the fifteen-man company suddenly split into three. Kellas and four trainees held the center, but the ten trainees on the right and left flanks spread outward in expectation of Enyera's desperate race toward the flag.

*Got you!*

She'd known that Kellas would think himself clever for anticipating her maneuver. He'd have come to the same realization she had: only a fool would try the same maneuver twice, so she'd try to outthink him by doing that. He'd simply outthought himself—and, in doing so, given her a fighting chance at succeeding.

Kellas' triumph turned to horror as the ten-man company raced toward him. Enyera made no move to sprint either right or left. Issa saw the moment he realized that he'd split his forces in an attempt to trap her, and now left his position vulnerable.

To his credit, he managed to block her right-handed sword strike. His flammard was far heavier than the Indomitable blade she'd scooped up, so he'd have a chance of defeating her in a duel. But this was no duel. This was battle, quick, brutal, and efficient. Her shorter sword and the truncheon in her left hand gave her all the advantage she needed.

Even as Kellas batted aside her right-handed strike, Issa brought her club up and slammed it into the side of his head. Kellas staggered, swinging wildly, but Issa deflected the blow with her sword. She barreled into him with enough force to send him staggering. He crashed to the sands, taking two more trainees down in tangled heap of limbs.

Issa almost paused—she wanted nothing more than to whale on Kellas, unleash her frustrations on the arrogant *Dhukari*. Yet if she did, their line would slow and the attack would fail. They had gotten through and their only hope of victory would be to capitalize on their momentum, even if that meant leaving Kellas unpunished.

Issa's heart leapt as she drove on. The third line gave way before the force of their charge, and now they had only one line left.

Tannard's line.

Hope turned sour in Issa's mouth as Tannard brought his sword up to a ready position. She'd never seen that stance; his blow could come from high or low, right or left. He wielded his own blade, honed to a razor sharp edge, backed by the power and skill of an *Invictus*.

And he prepared to meet her head on, his face as hard as stone, a cruel glint in the gaze he fixed on her.

*Please let this work!* A single thought, edged with desperation, was all she had time for.

With a wordless cry, she brought her stolen Indomitable blade whipping around. In the same instant, Tannard stepped forward into a thrust—the one attack Issa hadn't expected. Her blood turned to ice as she realized the tip of his five-foot blade would punch through her padded armor, skin, organs, and spine. She had no time to block or dodge; she could only twist her body and hope she survived.

Pain skewered through her abdomen as the length of Tannard's blade laid open her torso. She half-expected to fall, blood splashing out of her severed intestines onto the sand. Yet even as she staggered backward, hand clapped to her bleeding belly, a dim part of her realized that Tannard hadn't aimed to kill. He'd turned the tip of his sword aside at the last moment to wound her, deep enough to drive home his disdain but not enough to kill.

But that searing pain was worth it.

Enyera soared over her head, propelled by the strong arms of the two trainees she'd used to anchor the rear of their formation. The light *Mahjuri* girl, clad only in light trousers and a padded jerkin, seemed to hang suspended in the air for a long second.

Issa's heart stopped as she watched Enyera stretch out her arm, the girl's slim fingers closing around the pennant.

The clarion call of the trumpet was the sweetest sound Issa had ever heard.

The clash of weapons and the cries of the trainees seemed to go suddenly silent. Issa heard nothing but that high, ringing note and the blood pounding in her ears. The world faded around her until only she and Tannard remained.

The *Invictus'* face revealed nothing—no disappointment, anger, pride, or his usual contempt. He simply nodded and said, "The battle is yours."

Issa wanted to weep, shout, laugh, but she forced herself to stand still and meet Tannard's gaze. "Thank you."

That was it. Every curse she'd wanted to hurl, every bit of rage she'd wanted to unload on him, all faded away in that moment of triumph. He'd tried to break her and failed. That realization was all she needed.

"Get yourself cleaned up," he said, his voice brusque as ever. "For your reward, you have the honor of standing guard in the Palace of Golden Eternity tonight."

Without another word, he turned on his heel and strode away.

Silence reigned for a long moment, shattered by the cries and cheers rising from nine throats. Enyera rose to her feet, pennant clutched in her hand, and held it aloft.

Issa's company pressed in around her, hands clapping her back, their pain wiped away by exultation.

In that moment, Issa felt as if she would shatter. Not from exhaustion, anguish, or defeat, but from the joy swelling like a thundercloud within her. She threw back her head and laughed, and her company laughed with her.

Against all odds, despite facing an impossible task, they had won. More than that. In her personal battle against Tannard, she had finally triumphed.

And victory tasted sweet.

# Chapter Thirty-Four

Evren's brow furrowed. *What the bloody hell is Snarth doing here? More importantly, who are these men?*

He climbed higher until he reached a more comfortable perch. Though he couldn't see from his new position, he could listen in on the conversation within the room.

"We had a deal!" Snarth's voice held a high-pitched, plaintive whine. "I gave you what you asked for. You agreed I'd get a place in the Syndicate, but not as a low-level street ruffler, but a proper Crewman."

"We *did* have a deal." The voice that answered held a gruff note, deep with gravel and disdain. "But what you've brought me isn't enough. If you want in, you need to do better."

"What more do you want from me, Annat?" Snarth sounded ready to cry. "I just know how he runs all of us in the streets. He doesn't let any of us see where his fortune is stored or what he writes in that book of his. But you can just *ask* him about it when you take him down. Torture it out of him if you have to."

"Sounds like you're expecting to be rewarded for making *us* do all the hard work," replied the man, Annat. "If you want what you ask for, you'll have to do better."

Evren's mind raced. *He's talking about Killian.* He was fairly certain Snarth was working for this Syndicate, either as a plant in Killian's Mumblers or a defector. Either way, he planned to betray Killian to these people.

Anger surged within Evren. He had no true love for Killian—the man had helped him get his current position within Suroth's household likely out of self-interest—and he owed the blacksmith nothing. Yet Evren had suffered too many betrayals in his life, both in the temple and on the streets. The thought of such treachery set his blood boiling.

"Tell you what," Annat continued, his words softening to a haggling tone, "you want in as a Crewman, you get your hands on Killian's book. Or, at the very least, find out where he keeps it."

"He's too careful," Snarth whined. "He never lets anyone—"

"The Syndicate don't give two shites of a horse's arse for your excuses." Annat's voice rose to a snarl. "Your place in our ranks must be earned. We are poised to take power over this city. The Pharus will soon lie dead, and in the chaos that ensues, we will claim the Artisan's Tier for our own. But we cannot have that accursed blacksmith and his Mumblers roaming the streets. That book of secrets holds the key to Killian's power in this city. Until you get it and deliver it to us, you are not worthy to call yourself one of us."

"But—"

Evren didn't hear the rest of Snarth's protest. His stomach lurched as the stone beneath his right hand crumbled free of the sandstone cliff. Acting on instinct, he released his grip on the falling rocks and reached for another handhold. Even as he regained his balance, his eyes flew wide as the stones clattered atop the rubble and debris littering the alleyway. Right atop the discarded remains of a cracked metal pot. To Evren's ears, the noise was deafening.

"What was that?" Annat's voice came from within the room, filled with suspicion.

Without hesitation, Evren began climbing down the cliff face as fast as he could. He'd just reached the ground when he heard Annat's angry shout from overhead.

"Spy! Get him!"

Adrenaline surged in Evren's veins as he sprinted toward the mouth of the alley. His only hope of escape lay in reaching the street before—

Two thugs appeared around the corner and raced into the alleyway, their eyes fixed on him. Evren caught the glint of steel as they began drawing their belt daggers.

He had a single heartbeat to decide his course of action—draw his *jambiya* or try to bull-rush them. If he got bogged down in a knife fight, he might not get out before Annat and anyone else within the building arrived to reinforce the guards.

Evren leapt up onto an overturned wooden crate and shoved off with all the strength in his legs, hurtling through the air toward the man. His right fist drew back for a flying punch aimed at the thug to his left. Not the smartest blow in a brawl, but the best choice for taking down an enemy quick and dirty.

His fist crashed into the man's jaw with teeth-shattering force. Evren's knuckles, hardened by years of bare-handed fighting, protested at the collision with the jawbone but didn't break. The thug's head snapped around and he stumbled backward, sagging into unconsciousness.

The second guard had managed to draw his dagger and swiped at Evren, but Evren's momentum carried him past faster than the thug had anticipated. He tensed in expectation of pain yet none came. Instead, he heard a quiet *rip* as the strike tore cloth.

Then he was past the guard and racing east on the Way of Chains, toward Auctioneer's Square. He had to get up to the higher tiers, hopefully high enough that the thugs wouldn't be able to follow him.

Angry shouts echoed behind him but he didn't dare look back. The thugs in the alley, caught up in the rush of battle, wouldn't remember his face. Annat, Snarth, and any others pursuing him would only see his retreating back. His dull street clothing blended into the shouting throng in front of the auctioneer's blocks and would make it easy to hide among the crowds on the Cultivator's and Artisan's Tiers. His headband gave him easy access to the uppermost tiers, and he could be back in the uniform of Suroth's servants as soon as he returned to the Arch-Guardian's mansion. Once he lost his pursuers, their chances of actually hunting him down bordered on slim to none.

Yet escape wouldn't prove as easy as he'd hoped. The shouts and cries from the men behind him matched his pace. He was fast, but they knew the city better than he. Worse, he couldn't skirt the crowds—he'd stand out far too much—so he'd be forced to slither through the crush of people in Auctioneer's Square. He'd have to move slower, be more cautious who he shoved aside for fear of drawing attention.

*I have to find another way!* The back streets of the Slave's Tier tended to be fairly empty at this time of day. He could use those to evade the crowds.

He ducked out of sight into an alleyway and glanced over his shoulder for any sign of pursuit. Ice ran down his spine as he caught sight of Annat striding down the Way of Chains, flanked by a dozen bull-necked thugs.

"Spread out," Annat snarled. "I want him found and brought to me now!"

Heart pounding, Evren glanced around for any avenue of escape. He had no choice but to flee deeper into the back alleyways as Annat's thugs surged down the side streets. His gut tightened as he caught sight of more men cutting off the way ahead and behind him. He'd be in serious trouble if he allowed himself to be boxed in.

He shot a glance at the towering sandstone cliff. *The only way out is up.*

The cliff face rose eighty feet—fifty to the level of the Cultivator's Tier and another thirty for the height of the tier's wall—but the stone buildings of the Slave's Tier stood just fifteen or twenty feet tall. If he could just get up the cliff and onto the rooftops, he could hide out until his pursuers passed or gave up the search. He might even be able to find a way of escape that way. The Hunter had used the rooftops of Voramis as his own personal highway—Evren might be able to do the same.

He glanced at the street and, finding his pursuers momentarily distracted searching nearby homes, raced toward the cliff face. Hand over hand, he climbed as quickly as he could. The rough stone gave him plenty of holds but tended to crumble beneath his weight. He had to pick a careful path else risk getting stuck with no way up, down, or to the side. It took him a full two minutes to make the climb.

His heart clenched as his fingers closed around the stone lip of the roof and he pulled himself up. The thatching creaked and rustled beneath his feet, sagging precariously, but to his relief it held. He tested with his feet until he found a section that seemed sturdier, supported by the roof beams, and raced up the gentle stope toward the ridge. He hauled himself over and down the other side just as a pair of thugs turned into the alleyway he'd just vacated.

Climbing down the roof proved easy work, and the stone wall provided him with solid footing to make the leap to the next roof over. Yet as he scrambled over the second house, he found himself confronted by an alleyway.

The gap was less than six feet wide, a jump he could make any day. Yet two of Annat's thugs stood below, kicking through debris and muttering curses. Evren waiting, heart hammering, until they left and counted to thirty before making the leap.

Two more roofs, then another alley, this one wider than the first. He barely made the eight-foot jump and had to throw himself flat onto the thatching to avoid falling backward. His mouth was dry, his palms sweaty as he continued his rooftop trek.

The next alleyway was narrow, but the roof on the far side had crumbled away, revealing the sways and spars that held up the thatching.

*Keeper's teeth!* Jaw clenched in frustration, Evren paused to consider his course of action. He could see the roof beams, warped by sun and rain yet solid enough to hold his weight. If he didn't get his leap just right, he would crash through roof.

The caution saved his life.

Just as he prepared to make the leap, two figures appeared at the mouth of the alley and set about searching it. Evren threw himself flat on the rooftop, heart hammering. *Bloody hell, that was too close.* If he'd attempted the jump, they would have spotted him for sure.

The thatch was hot and bristly against his face, yet it had the sweet smell of grass and hay. He glanced up at the bright sun. It had to be the first or second hour after noon—the trek to the Artisan's Tier had taken the better part of two hours, and he'd followed Snarth down here to the Slave's Tier for more than an hour. If he didn't lose his pursuers soon, he wouldn't have time to get to Killian's before racing back to Suroth's mansion.

Whatever Samall and Kuhar had planned for Lady Briana was happening tonight, and Evren *had* to return as soon as possible to at least try to warn the bodyguards. But he felt Killian deserved a warning as well. More as a professional courtesy than any genuine concern, truth be told. If he got to Killian in time, the blacksmith would owe him.

He had enough time, barely. *If only these damned thugs would hurry up and get out of here!* They seemed far more interested in kicking through the litter covering the alley than looking up at the rooftops. *I need to get out of here now, else I won't have time to warn Killian and get back to Suroth's mansion.*

Time dragged on for what felt like an eternity, but was likely no more than three or four minutes, before the thugs concluded their search. Evren breathed a silent sigh of relief as they hurried away. He waited another minute to be certain they'd gone before standing from his hiding place. Without hesitation, he made the leap.

He landed hard on the beam, but to his horror he found the nails holding it in place had rusted away. The beam swayed and creaked beneath his weight. Evren had to throw himself to another section of roof just before the wood crumbled beneath him. His gut clenched as he watched the patch of grass and reed thatch sag inward and collapse into the house. Thankfully, the attic stood empty. Heart in his throat, he listened for any indication that he'd been overheard. When no cries or shouts echoed from the streets below, he continued his trek across the rooftops of the Slave's Tier.

He made far slower progress than he'd like. Though Auctioneer's Square stood just a few hundred yards from Death Row, he had to pause to check the streets for his pursuers before leaping over the alleys. By the time he decided he'd covered enough ground to evade the thugs, he'd lost at least an hour.

Clambering down the wall, he slipped down the alleyway toward the side streets. Relief flooded him. No sign of the thugs. He raced down the street and ducked into the press of people on the Way of Chains. The throng would give him ample cover. He'd spent years slipping through thick crowds unseen. This time, instead of picking pockets and lifting purses, he only had to concentrate on escaping his pursuers.

He had just broken free of the crowd and headed toward Death Row when he felt a sense of danger prickling at the back of his neck. His heart sank as he caught sight of four hard-faced, thick-necked men guarding the road up to the Cultivator's Tier and freedom.

# Chapter Thirty-Five

Kodyn couldn't believe it. He'd been prepared for a secret code, like the Illusionist's script used to encode the map of Lord Auslan's vaults his mother had stolen from Duke Phonnis.

But not empty paper. He turned the scroll over in his hands, held it up to the light. Nothing. The same rolled-up papyrus utterly devoid of even a single line or character.

*Keeper's teeth!* Anger surged within him.

Aisha frowned, confusion on her face. "You think Ennolar made a mistake?"

"Maybe." Kodyn scowled down at the map. "Either that or he deceived us."

His mind raced. *If he's afraid of the Black Widow, he could have given Aisha this fake to buy time enough for him to get out of Shalandra.*

That didn't fit. The Secret Keeper had had all night to flee if that had been his plan all along. He wouldn't have waited in Shalandra just to hand over a fake to Aisha.

He stared down at the blank scroll in his hands. *So what the hell is this thing?*

Try as he might, he couldn't figure out the Secret Keeper's actions or the meaning of the blank map.

*The Black Widow might know,* he decided. *At the very least, she will know what to do with Ennolar. If he did betray us or her by giving us this fake, she'll have a plan on how to get the information I need—even if it means hunting down a fleeing Secret Keeper.*

Kodyn controlled his anger long enough to roll the scroll up and slide it back into its tube, but he shoved the lid on so hard he nearly broke it. He drew in a deep breath in an effort to tamp down his anger.

"I need to visit the Black Widow," he told Aisha and Briana. "Not only about this map." He showed them the purse Suroth had given him. "The Arch-Guardian said that this would convince the Black Widow to help us in our efforts to bring down the Necroseti responsible for Briana's abduction."

Both young women studied the purse, curiosity written in every line of their faces. Kodyn couldn't help sharing their interest. He hadn't opened the strings to look inside, and he only felt that impossibly round, smooth object within. The thought that something so small could hold such value only added to his desire to know what Suroth was sending to the Black Widow.

"Go," Aisha told him. "I'll stay with Briana. We'll be safe here."

Kodyn studied the Ghandian. Aisha's face was paler than usual, a sharp contrast to the shadows in her eyes and the tightness around her mouth. Yet if she wanted him to think nothing was wrong, he trusted her enough to honor her wishes.

"I'll be back as soon as I can." He'd wait until he spoke with the Black Widow before deciding what his next step would be. He had three weeks to figure out how to get into the Serenii vault, but he had to balance the need to complete his Undertaking with his desire to keep Briana safe.

*One thing at a time.*

He left Aisha and Briana in the rooftop garden and descended to the second-floor room he'd been given beside Briana's private quarters. The room's luxuries far surpassed the few comforts he'd had in House Hawk. There, he'd had a simple wooden bed with a straw-filled mattress suspended by ropes, a chest to hold his valuables, a desk and chair, and armoire for his Hawk clothing and equipment. Here, the double-sized bed was covered in plush pillows, a velvet-covered comforter, and a mattress stuffed with soft goose feathers. The table, chair, and furniture were made of oak, teak, and ebony, the hardware gold-plated metal, with ornate etchings of gold and platinum. There was even a soft, deep shag rug to cover the white Praamian ceramic tiles.

He strode to the armoire and pulled the heavy doors open. Pulling out simple servant's clothing left for him at Briana's orders, he stripped off his armor and unbuckled his long sword. He dressed quickly and, donning the green-and-gold headband that marked him as a *Dhukari's* servant, he strode out of the front gate with the determined stride of a man on a mission. His clothing hid enough of his favorite daggers for him to feel safe, but he carried a wooden basket as cover for whatever errand he was pretending to be on. No one would question him—a servant headed to the Artisan's Tier to shop for his master.

As he strode toward Death Row, his eyes scanned the crowds until he found what he sought. A boy, no more than ten or eleven, clad in simple servant's clothing, wearing a braided gold and white headband, but with a black iron bracelet on his right wrist.

Kodyn sidled up to the boy. "Tell the Black Widow the Praamian wishes to speak with her. I'll be waiting by the blacksmiths' road in the Artisan's Tier in an hour and a half."

The boy didn't so much as glance at him. Kodyn continued on his way but watched the lad out of the corner of his eyes. He'd gone nearly fifty paces before the boy stirred from his position and scampered away. He lost sight of the small boy instantly, but continued on down Death Row, confident that his message would reach the Black Widow soon enough.

The guards at the gate to the Defender's Tier waved him through without a second glance. The Indomitables patrolling the *Alqati* level seemed uninterested in a *Dhukari's* servant, even a foreigner, and the soldiers guarding the entrance to the Artisan's Tier paid him little heed.

*Good to see I chose the right disguise for this mission.*

A glance at the sun told him he'd used up an hour of the time he'd allotted to reach the blacksmiths' road on the Artisan's Tier. He quickened his pace—he'd have to hurry if he wanted to reach the meeting place in time to—

"You there!"

Kodyn's blood turned to ice and it took all of his self-control not to freeze or reach for a dagger. He continued on his way, refusing to look over his shoulder. A backward glance was the surefire mark of a guilty thief.

"Get up!" The gruff voice roared behind him again.

Relief bathed Kodyn as he realized the shout wasn't aimed at him. Now he allowed himself to turn and seek the source of the voice.

A four-man Indomitable patrol stood on the eastern edge of Death Row, glowering down at a pathetic figure huddled on the ground. The man was wasted by age, hunger, and the strange blue blisters that dotted his hands, face, and sunburned skin. Emaciated ribs and gaunt, bony shoulders showed beneath the tatters of the man's robes. A thin strip of filthy, dust-stained black rope encircled his head, marking him as one of Shalandra's wretched caste.

"Up!" One of the Indomitables, who had a line of silver etched into the blue stripe across the forehead of his spike-rimmed helm, kicked at the old man. "Up!"

The old man cried out and attempted to crawl out of the way. His arms and legs quivered with the effort of trying to stand, and he fell with a little groan.

"On your feet, now!" The Indomitable bent over the man, a scowl on his face. "You *Mahjuri* know better than to dirty up the Artisan's Tier with your filth. Get out of here before we're forced to arrest you!"

Again, the withered man tried and failed to stand.

"So be it!" The Indomitable snapped his fingers at his men. "Take him."

"Why?" The angry shout came from nearby. Kodyn scanned the passersby that had stopped to watch and found the speaker was a young man wearing the red headband and simple clothing of an *Earaqi* laborer. "There's no call for that. He's just—"

"You dare?" The black-armored officer stepped up to the young man and loomed over him, his face a mask of outrage. "You've one chance to step back before you get hauled in as well."

"For speaking up against such mistreatment?" This time, the voice belonged to a woman with threads of grey running through her black hair and a simple brown strip of leather around her forehead. "There's no reason to…"

Kodyn hurried away from the scene before he got caught up in anything nasty. The mood of the crowd was dark, anger blazing in the eyes of the *Mahjuri*, *Earaqi*, and even a few *Intaji* and *Zadii* on Death Row.

Reaching the Artificer's Courseway, he hurried west, in the direction of the row of blacksmith shops. He reached it five minutes before he'd told the Black Widow's courier he'd be there, just enough time to find a comfortable place to wait and watch from across the street. He preferred to see the Black Widow's courier before they spotted him—his mother had taught him the value of *always* having the upper hand in any sort of clandestine activities.

A hint of anxiety roiled through him at the thought of meeting with the Black Widow. Their last encounter had gone as well as he could have hoped, but life in the Night Guild had taught him *never* to take such things for granted when dealing with powerful people—especially powerful people in the criminal underworld. Allies could turn to enemies with the wrong word or the right coin.

At this time of the afternoon, the crowd of people was thick, men and women hurrying to conclude their business before the sun set and the day ended. Kodyn had always loved to watch the crowds in Old Town Market or the Path of Penitence in Praamis. From his perch on the rooftops of the Hawk's Highway, it felt like following the shifting tides of the ocean. He could see the way people flowed out of the path of heavily-laden carts, shuffled around the thugs guarding the goldsmiths' and jewelers' shops, or swirled between people headed in the opposite direction. Like a dance with an entire city's population taking to an open-air dance floor.

Something in the street caught his attention. Four men—clad in laborer's clothing and black *Mahjuri* headbands—moved through the crowd in a strange way. Instead of flowing with the surging traffic, they seemed to cut at a strange angle. Kodyn had spent enough time as a thief on the streets of Praamis to instantly recognize sneaking, suspicious behavior. Everything from their wary gazes to the way they always looked over their shoulders to their pulled-up hoods set his instincts immediately on alert.

He kept his head down and his posture relaxed, but his eyes tracked their movement through the swirling crowds. The more he watched them, the more convinced he became that they were up to no good. He'd learned to move that way from Errik, Master of the assassins of House Serpent, and every Fox and Grubber he'd run with during his years on the streets.

An *Earaqi* hauling a huge bale of hay bumped into one of the men, nearly knocking him from his feet. Had the man been about honest business, he likely would have snarled or hurled an insult. Instead, he simply recovered and hurried after his comrades.

But as he'd flailed to regain his balance, his sleeves had slipped up to his elbows—high enough for Kodyn to catch a glimpse of the tattoo on his right forearm.

Ice seeped down Kodyn's spine. *The mark of the Gatherers!* The woven basket fell from his fingers and clattered to the street.

The Gatherers in Praamis had carved that same symbol—an almost-complete circle connected to two lines that bent outward in a perfect right angle, with something that resembled a sun and moon in close alignment in the center of the circle—into the chests of their victims and painted it on the wall of their secret underground lair in blood. The symbol was a combination of two Serenii glyphs: "death and rebirth" and "life beyond". It had tied the string of murders to the death-worshipping cult that originated here in Shalandra. The threat of their return had been enough to convince his mother to grant permission for him to accompany Briana home.

*And now I've found them here!*

Nervous excitement set his heart thumping against his ribs. He had no doubt they'd try to kill him if they caught him following them, but it was worth the risk. If he found their secret lair, he had little doubt Arch-Guardian Suroth could call on the Keeper's Blades, Indomitables, or even his own Secret Keepers to raid the Gatherers. Suroth wanted vengeance on the ones that had kidnapped his daughter more than Kodyn did.

Yet, the weight of the pouch in his pocket stopped him. Suroth's words flashed through his mind. *"In the wrong hands, this can be used for truly terrible things."* Whatever lay within that pouch had to be an object of supreme importance. But *more* important than finding the Gatherers?

*No*, he decided. *The Black Widow can wait. The Gatherers are the more important threat!*

Grim determination hardened in his gut as he slipped from his perch and dove into the crowd, abandoning his basket. Even though he hunched to diminish his height, he couldn't cover up his pale skin. He had to keep far back enough that he could watch the Gatherers without being spotted.

Thankfully, traffic in Industry Square and Commerce Square reached a peak at this hour of the day—men and women hurried to finish up their late-hour shopping. Kodyn could see over the head of most Shalandrans, so had no problem keeping an eye on his quarry.

Savage triumph twisted in his stomach as the Gatherers turn down a street that intersected with the Artificer's Courseway a short distance west of Commerce Square. He followed them toward the golden sandstone cliff that served as the northern boundary of the Artisan's Tier, then down the smallest back alley within the shadow of the wall. Peering around a corner, he saw them duck into a one-story structure built against the cliff's face. He hung back for a minute, waiting to be certain they wouldn't spot him as he slipped toward the house.

His mother had hammered home the importance of learning the architecture of every city, neighborhood, and street. During the ten-day journey from Praamis, he'd discussed Shalandran architecture with Briana—and eventually Ormroth, after the Keeper's Blade joined them. Ormroth, a former *Zadii* and son of an architect, had proven surprisingly well-versed in the city's design. The Blade had revealed a truly important gem: houses on Shalandra's, originally carved from the stone of Alshuruq, lacked basements. Even the most decrepit one-room shanty on the Slave's Tier had at least an attic.

Thatching had to be secured to sloping wooden beams that supported the sways and spars, which meant there would be unused space between the top of the stone walls and the ridge of the roofs. That space would be converted either into storage or an additional room—just the sort of place where a clandestine meeting would be held.

He smiled as he scanned the rough-hewn walls and the rocky cliff face. *It's like they're begging me to climb it!*

The climb took less than a minute—he'd honed his skills on the Perch in House Hawk and the Hawk's Highway. He didn't clamber onto the rooftop for fear the rustle of thatching would give him away. And, one glance at the dips and sags in the center of the roof told him that the support beams were either rotten or warped. One of the first lessons every Hawk learned was how to read the surfaces of rooftop for stability and reliability. No way he'd risk plummeting through the thatched roof, not when he could simply hang onto the wall and listen from beneath the eaves.

A low sound reached his ears: voices, muffled by the thatching and stone wall. The opening between the roof and the top of the wall was small, but wide enough that he could hear the conversation within.

"…time is now, Brothers!" a man's voice said. "We've received word from our brother in the Councilor's mansion. The father will be at a Council meeting tonight, which leaves the daughter guarded only by two foreign youths."

Kodyn's gut clenched. *They're talking about Briana.*

"I'd prefer taking her alive, but her death will send a clear enough message to the father that he must fall in line. For the sake of a smooth transition, it must be so. Are we clear?"

A round of muffled "Ayes" echoed in the room below.

Kodyn had heard enough. He didn't understand what "transition" they were talking about or what they expected Suroth to do, but he knew one thing for certain: the Gatherers were making a move on Briana. Tonight.

He glanced up at the sun and found it had already sunk dangerously low over the western horizon. Darkness would fall within an hour.

Heart pounding, he scrambled back off the wall under the eaves and slithered down the side of the house as silently as he could manage. The moment his boots touched the alley, he was racing south toward the Artificer's Courseway, then west toward the road upward.

*Damn, damn, damn!* He *had* to get back to Briana. Arch-Guardian Suroth had his private guards posted at the front gate and patrolling the grounds, but they would be treating it like business as usual. Boredom could dull even the sharpest guard's attention. Kodyn needed to warn the guards and get to Aisha. *We're Briana's last line of defense, and I need to be there to protect her.*

The slapping of his sandals echoed loud off the stone streets, but he didn't care. The time for caution and stealth had passed. He'd have to hurry to get back to the Keeper's Tier and Suroth's mansion in time to prepare for whatever the Gatherers intended tonight.

*Come on!* He pushed himself to run faster. *Please let me be in time!*

Yet, as he turned to race up Death Row, the sight ahead stopped him cold, sent ice flooding his veins.

The incident with the Indomitables had riled the crowd into an ugly mood. More than a hundred low-caste Shalandrans faced a line of black-armored guards that stretched east to west across the highway. Angry shouts and yells echoed from the crowd, and Kodyn could feel the fury simmering just beneath the surface. One wrong word, one misstep from someone in the crowd, and this could turn violent. If he tried to squeeze through, he could be the one to incite uproar.

Horror flooded Kodyn. *No!* He couldn't afford even a moment's delay, not with the looming threat of the attack. He scanned the crowd, trying to find a clear way through, but people were packed too tightly together. *Keeper take it!*

A wave of hopelessness washed over him. He couldn't delude himself into believing the Gatherers would be stymied by this crowd. The fact that they'd evaded the Indomitables and Suroth's searchers for so long meant they had to know secret ways around the city. Ways like the Serenii tunnels that were supposed to be marked on the map Ennolar had given him.

*Did Ennolar betray us to the Gatherers?* He had given *them* the map instead, fully expecting the Gatherers to kill Kodyn and Aisha during their attack on Briana's mansion. With them dead, no one could tell the Black Widow that he'd given them a fake.

Right now, it didn't matter. Kodyn dove into the crowd, slipping through where he could and shoving where the people packed tightest.

A single thought rang over and over in his mind. *I have to get to Briana and Aisha before the Gatherers make their move.*

But the reality of his situation filled him with a nagging fear. Could he get through the crowd in time?

*I have to!* If he didn't, his friends could end up dead.

# Chapter Thirty-Six

Issa struggled to keep her eyes open, her head up. She hadn't slept in nearly forty-eight hours and after two days of hard training, she felt one breath away from collapse.

But that was precisely why Tannard had done this.

"A Blade's greatest weapon is not his sword, but his mind," the *Invictus* had growled with his usual expressionless severity. "You must be able to fight through your fatigue, to remain clear-headed despite exhaustion. Hunger, pain, weariness—all are weaknesses a Keeper's servant cannot afford."

Hunger and weariness, she'd grown accustomed to. Her triumph in the training yard dulled her pain far better than any physicker's healing draught.

That, and the fact that Kellas had been forced to join her and Etai on guard duty. The bruises and cuts she and Etai had sustained—even the long gash on her belly, courtesy of Tannard's sharp sword—paled in comparison to the battering he'd taken.

The *Dhukari* youth's helmet sat slightly askew atop the bandage wrapped around his head, and he winced every time he drew in a deep breath. Issa had hit him hard enough to make him feel it for a day or two, even with his accelerated healing. The bruises on his face, left by the stamping boots of the charging trainees, had turned an ugly purple. He'd escaped broken bones...barely.

Yes, the sight of Kellas looking so bedraggled certainly made Issa feel better.

*He looked like a wet cat in a golden bathtub. Or, in this case, a golden palace.*

The Palace of Golden Eternity lived up to its name. From the floor tiles to the pillars to the high-arched ceilings, every inch of the palace's interior was either plated with or made of gold. Threads of silver and black shalanite ran throughout, adding a color contrast and another layer of extravagance. Any room in the Palace of Golden Eternity held more wealth than the entire Slave's Tier saw in a lifetime.

That thought set anger burning within her. *Such wastefulness! All this for show, when it could be used to feed the people of the lower tiers for the rest of their lives.*

Since her tenth nameday, she'd realized the difference between the castes. The *Mahjuri* were despised, left to starve or succumb to thirst. Only those *Kabili* actually in service to the Pharus and the Keeper's Council received anything approaching decent rations, and their access to fresh water on the Slave's Tier was severely limited. As long as the *Earaqi* tilled the fields and served the *Dhukari*, they were fed, but never in abundance. Some *Zadii* and *Intaji* could afford the exorbitant prices levied on food supplies by the Keeper's Council, but most simply survived on their monthly rations.

The *Alqati*, however, were fed well—Shalandra needed them strong to maintain law and order. Yet their training and service to the city kept them lean. Only the *Dhukari* could actually afford to be fat. The plumper a *Dhukari*, the wealthier they were. She'd seen men, women, even children too obese to walk hauled around on litters borne by sixteen slaves. They flaunted their riches in the face of the starving lower castes.

There were a few exceptions. Some of the *Dhukari*—Kellas, for example—actually *chose* to remain thin. Mostly those who sought to join the Blades. They remained in good physical condition as their service to the Long Keeper required. The Pharus was another example of a man that hadn't allowed his wealth and power to go to his belly. It was whispered around the Citadel of Stone that he trained daily with a hand-picked Blade or Indomitable.

"This is an insult," Kellas' grumbling drew Issa's attention back to their duty. "We are Keeper's Blades and as such should be above such mundane tasks worthy only of an Indomitable."

"You're not a Blade yet." The words were spoken under Etai's breath—her victory in the training yard had helped her recover from her defeat at Kellas' hands their first day in the Blades, but the deference of the *Dhukari* ingrained in every low-caste Shalandran had proven harder to shake.

Issa winked at Etai and shot Kellas a smug grin. "And, to be fair, you were just trounced by a group of Indomitables."

"You got lucky, *Earaqi.*" Kellas scowled at her.

Issa shrugged. "If that's what you have to tell yourself." She glowed with the knowledge that she'd not only outsmarted the arrogant *Dhukari* youth, but she'd gotten one up on Tannard, a twenty-year veteran of the Keeper's Blades. Kellas couldn't write that off only as luck.

They fell silent as the Keeper's Council appeared at the far end of the corridor they'd been set to guard. She and Kellas stood rigid as statues, flammard tips grounded on the gold-tiled floor between their feet, while Etai pulled one of the double doors open for the Councilors. The fat Necroseti in their black robes gave no sign of even acknowledging the Blades' existence—to them, Issa and the others were as much fixtures in the palace as the golden statues, ornate pillars, or servants in their gold-and-silver clothing.

The brown-robed Secret Keeper—Arch-Guardian Suroth, the man that had administered Issa's trial of stone—nodded at her.

Issa didn't move but a small smile tugged at her lips. *Yes, today is definitely a good day!*

Etai closed the double door and returned to her position between Kellas and Issa.

Issa settled in for a long night of standing guard—Tannard had warned them that their relief wouldn't arrive until daybreak. She tried to ward off her fatigue by occupying her mind taking in the details of the opulence around her.

They stood in a long corridor that connected the grand hall to the private Council Chambers in the heart of the Palace of Golden Eternity. However, more corridors running east and west intersected with the main hall, providing access to the various wings of the palace. One, the first corridor to Issa's right, led toward a side door on the eastern side of the Council Chambers. It was used only by the servants delivering refreshments to the Council while they were in session. Two more Blades would remain on guard there until the Councilors had finished their late-night session and left the palace.

Forty-two Blades stood guard in the palace at any given time. Most held the entrances to the Pharus' private wing, the wing belonging to his concubines, and the row of rooms reserved for Lady Callista Vinaus and the other Elders of the Blades. By tradition, the highest-ranking Blades were kept close at hand to provide council to the Pharus in time of war.

The rest of the entrances, exits, and chambers were guarded by Indomitables. It was seen as an honor for the military caste to be chosen to guard the Palace of the Golden Eternity.

To Issa, the "honor" felt more like a burden, but she wouldn't echo Kellas' sentiments aloud. Hell, she'd *request* the duty if it meant Kellas suffered. The *Dhukari* had earned her enmity. Though, she had to admit humiliating him on the training yard made her feel a lot less hostile toward him. Perhaps, one day, he'd pull the spear out of his arse long enough to remember that they were *all* chosen by the Long Keeper. That made them equals.

Issa stifled a yawn and shuffled her weight to her other foot. The warmth in the palace added to her fatigue to make her feel drowsy.

That was one of the first things she'd noticed when taking up her guard position. The night air had a hint of chill, not quite an icy bite but cool enough that most people would wear a shawl or cloak. But the air within the palace bordered on hot and stuffy.

Etai's remark on the temperature earned a lengthy explanation from Kellas on the Serenii-built machines that harnessed the heat from geysers deep within the mountain's core. Issa had wanted to know more, but the *Dhukari's* tone was so infuriating she'd been happy when he finally shut his mouth.

Right now, Issa wanted to shut her eyes and let sleep claim her. The warmth and her exhaustion from the day dragged her toward slumber with an unrelenting determination. Issa shifted from foot to foot, blinked her eyes hard, and even slapped herself to stay awake. Despite her best efforts, she found her head lolling on her chest, her eyelids drooping shut.

A hand on her arm snapped her awake. She turned to find Etai staring at her, concern written in her expression.

"Go, do a sweep of the corridors," the *Mahjuri* girl told her. "Kellas and I will hold the door."

"Yes, desert your post, lowborn," Kellas sneered.

Issa resisted the urge to punch him. "Not deserting, doing a patrol."

Tannard hadn't explicitly stated that she couldn't leave, especially if she intended to search the corridors for anything amiss. Yet she had little doubt the *Invictus* would punish her if he found out.

*If* he found out. She could trust Etai, just as she could trust Kellas to get her in trouble at any opportunity.

*So what's worse? Falling asleep at my post or patrolling the corridors for a few minutes?*

Finally, she decided to go with Etai's suggestion.

"Thank you." She nodded to Etai. "I'll be back in a few minutes."

Her boots clacked on the gold-tiled floor as she strode down the corridor. The weight of her armor and the sword resting on her shoulder tugged at her sore, tired muscles, but she forced herself into a steady march to push back her fatigue.

She scanned the corridors as she went, her eyes roaming over the colorful paintings of Shalandran history splashed across the walls, the ornate details etched into the columns and pillars, and the images frescoed onto the domed ceilings. She had never seen so much wealth in one place—it wouldn't hurt to enjoy it for a few minutes while she patrolled.

A part of her wished she could head outside to the Terrestra, the gardens that spanned the eastern side of the palace's tier. The Terrestra was one of the marvels of Shalandra, reserved exclusively for those *Dhukari* and *Alqati* fortunate enough to receive a private invitation from the Pharus, the Keeper's Council, or the highest-ranking Blades.

*One day,* she told herself. *One day I'll be able to visit them anytime I want.*

She turned down one of the side corridors, which connected the kitchens to the main entrance of the Council Chambers. A cluster of servants pushing wheeled trolleys laden high with pastries, fresh and dried fruits, nuts, and other delicacies hurried past. Like all servants, they moved with eyes downcast, shoulders stooped. Issa took little notice of them as she patrolled, but just as she was about to turn the corner, something glinted in the moonlight. For a moment, she thought she'd been imagining it. Yet, as she turned back to scrutinized the figures, she realized how un-servant-like they appeared.

*Too broad in the shoulders, and those boots.* The Pharus' servants wore high-strapped sandals so as not to scuff the soft golden tiles. Only Blades and Indomitables were permitted to wear boots in the palace.

*That's not right.*

"Hold!" Issa called after them. "Stop where you are."

The servants seemed not to hear her, which only confirmed her suspicions. No one could miss her voice echoing through the high-ceilinged corridors.

"Stop!" she shouted. Every trace of fatigue faded as adrenaline coursed through her body.

The rearmost figure glanced back over his shoulder, and Issa's heart stopped as she caught sight of the tattoo inked into his bare forearm—the same strange crescent moon and star figure she'd spotted on the Cultivator's Tier near the Keeper's Crypts.

Without hesitation, Issa raised her sword and charged. "Assassins!" she shouted. "Assassins in the palace!"

With a growled curse, the man threw back his cloak, revealing metal-studded leather armor, and drew a long sword from within the cart—the source of the metallic glint. He tore his sword free and turned to face her charge. His companions, more than a dozen, drew their own weapons.

Issa raced forward, heedless of the fact that the assassins outnumbered her. She'd been charged to guard the Pharus and the Keeper's Council—not even a horde of demons would stop her from fulfilling that oath.

# Chapter Thirty-Seven

Evren's mind raced. He couldn't go back; it would cost him too much time backtracking to Trader's Way. The only way he'd get to Killian's and return to Suroth's mansion was forward.

His lessons with the Hunter flashed through his thoughts. In addition to the art of combat, the assassin had taught him the tricks of disguise. The Hunter's skills enabled him to walk straight into his enemies' strongholds or distract them as he studied their defenses. He'd always preferred to rely on cunning and false-facing rather than brute force.

Evren had relished those lessons far more than the bare-handed and armed combat sessions. During his years on the streets, he'd picked up a few tricks that helped him stay unnoticed among dense crowds. Yet his training with the Hunter had taught him a whole new parcel of skills.

"The key to a successful disguise is belief," the Hunter had emphasized. "Believe that you *are* who you say you are and your target will as well."

The Hunter's facades typically included a false face—once, he'd required alchemical masks, until he'd discovered his strange shape-shifting abilities. Evren had neither Bucelarii skills nor the alchemical flesh required. He could, however, do a few things to change his appearance.

Crouching, Evren scooped up a handful of dirt and rubbed it onto his face. He just needed enough to slightly alter the shape of his cheekbones, nose, and chin. A bit of dirt rubbed around his mouth saw to that—similar to the way the women of Voramis contoured their faces using a plethora of cosmetics.

Next, he removed his red and gold headband on the off-chance someone had spotted it as he fled. Bare-headed, he went from a highly-placed servant to one of the *Kabili* slaves. He changed his posture as well, letting his shoulders droop and adopting the weary walk of a laborer. Face downcast, clothes askew, he moved in a tired shuffle toward the thugs.

His gut clenched, but he forced himself to keep moving at a steady pace, never lifting his head to glance at them. None of the four thugs had seen him back in the alley, so their orders were likely to be on the lookout for someone matching his description. Doubtless they'd be looking for a furtive-looking mark rather than just one more bare-headed *Kabili* youth. As long as he didn't show fear at their presence or appear like the spy they sought, he wouldn't arouse their attention.

His heart leapt as the sound of booted feet echoed from behind him. A glance down Death Row revealed a patrol of black-armored Indomitables marching at a quick-step up from the East Gate. The thugs reluctantly cleared out of the guards' path and took up position on the far side of the road.

Evren seized the opportunity and quickened his step. Not enough to appear hurried, but just enough that he slipped past the thugs under cover of the Indomitable patrol. The moment he passed through the gate to the Cultivator's Tier, he ducked out of sight of the watching thugs and set off at a run up Death Row.

The guards at the gate to the Artisan's Tier fixed him with stern glares, but they were distracted by the arrival of a *Dhukari's* litter descending to the Cultivator's Tier. Evren used that moment of inattention to slip past.

He raced toward the Artificer's Courseway and turned west, heading toward the side street where he'd find Killian's smithy in the shadows of the cliff that bordered the Artisan's Tier's northern edge. When he reached Smith's Alley, he paused long enough to glance up and down the street to be certain no one followed him, then ducked into the cacophony of hammers ringing off metal.

Three boys, two around his own age and one a couple of years younger than Hailen, worked the bellows and anvils in the smithy, but Evren saw no sign of the blacksmith.

"Where's Killian?" Evren demanded of the nearest Mumbler.

The boy shrugged. "Dunno," was his only reply before he turned back to pumping air over the glowing coals.

Evren ground his teeth. "Listen, I have something important that Killian needs to know *now*."

The boy looked up at him, his expression blank. After a long moment, he called out, "Serias, you know where Killian's at?"

"No," called the youngest boy. He wore a red *Earaqi* headband and looked as if he hadn't seen a decent meal in his life. "Heard him say he was headed out but didn't say where or when he'd be back."

"There's your answer," the first boy said. "I can pass the message on, if you want. Or you can wait."

Evren fixed the boy with a hard stare. He had the same hard-eyed, wary appearance of every Mumbler, but looks meant little on the streets. Some of the kindest, friendliest faces he'd seen hid all manner of vices and villainy. He had no idea if Snarth was working with the Syndicate alone, or if he had others within Killian's Mumblers also double-dealing. He wouldn't risk it.

"I'll wait." He settled onto a nearby stool.

The minutes seemed to drag on as Evren sat, impatient for Killian's return. His stomach twisted in knots when he shot a glance at the sky. His detour to follow Snarth had cost him close to two hours, and it had taken him nearly twice as long to evade Annat's thugs and return to the smithy. It could be close to the second or third hour after noon by now. He'd have to leave soon if he wanted to return to Suroth's mansion in time to warn Lady Briana's bodyguards of Samall's treachery.

Finally, after half an hour, Evren could wait no more. "I've got to go, but the moment Killian returns, tell him I've urgent news." Right now, Hailen was his priority. He'd still have time to get back to Suroth's mansion and speak with the bodyguards before nightfall. "I'll be back as soon as I can."

The boy nodded. "Will do."

Evren hurried from the smithy and rushed east, back toward Death Row. It took him the better part of a half-hour to reach the broad avenue that led up to the higher tiers, and every moment spent dodging a wagon or slipping around a gaggle of basket-carrying shoppers only added to his worry.

Anxiety thrummed within him as he spotted a dense cluster of people crowding the road ahead of him. His instincts, honed over years on the streets, warned that this wasn't a typical crowd gawking at some spectacle or listening to a religious tirade. Instead, this was a dangerous beast: an angry throng.

Crowds could be volatile and unpredictable, changing from mild-mannered and placid one moment to seething, hate-filled, even violent the next. The most passive gathering could become aggressive and hostile with a single word or action. It took just one inciting incident to turn a group of law-abiding citizens into a bloodthirsty mob.

Evren recognized the temperament of the crowd at once. They were angry, shouting, pressing toward whatever held their attention or attracted their ire. Any second, things could turn far uglier and break out into savagery. With a crowd of this size, easily five or six hundred men and women wearing the red and black headbands of the city's lowest castes, it could become a riot in the space of minutes.

He had to get through the crowd *now* before it turned violent. If it ignited into a brawl, he'd never get past in time to reach the Keeper's Tier before dark.

Gritting his teeth, he slithered through the crowd as fast as he could without jostling or elbowing too many people out of his way. Even one wrong shove could be the spark that lit the fuse of the throng's fury. Most of the people he passed were too focused on shouting at the line of black-armored soldiers guarding Death Row that they barely paid attention to him, though a few hurled angry curses at his retreating back. Evren ignored them and kept pushing, struggling, slipping through any gaps he could find.

*Come on, come on!* Fingers of panic crept into his brain. He could feel each second passing by too quickly. He'd never make it to the mansion in time, not at this pace. Yet he couldn't move any faster through the densely packed throng. It felt like swimming upstream against a current determined to sweep him away, suck him under.

An iron fist gripped his heart and squeezed the air from his lungs. The emotions seething within the mob thickened the air until Evren was gasping, clawing for each breath. It took all his willpower to keep moving, keep searching for the holes in the crowd. He had to get through!

As he approached the front of the crowd, he found his progress slower, the people packed tighter together. The sound of their rhythmic chanting grew deafening.

*"Child of Secrets, Child of Gold,*
*Child of Spirits, bring the judgement foretold!"*

Evren's brow furrowed. *They're shouting those words written on the walls.* He had no idea what the words meant or why the crowd would chant them, but he could worry about that later. Right now, he had to focus on getting out of this throng in one piece.

It seemed an eternity before he burst free of the crowd. Sucking in a great breath, he stumbled toward the Indomitables. The line of men stood steady, their man-high, seven-sided shields planted firmly on the stone street. Their faces were grim, yet a hint of nervousness flashed in their eyes as they studied the angry throng.

"I need to get through!" Evren shouted at the nearest soldier, though the angry chants drowned out his words.

"Back in line, *Kabili*!" roared an Indomitable. "I won't tell you twice!"

Evren's brow furrowed, but before he had time to react, someone shoved him from behind. Thrown off balance, he lurched forward, right at the line of Indomitables. He didn't have time to see the vicious strike, much less dodge it. Pain exploded in the side of his skull. One moment he was on his feet, the next he lay on the ground, his head ringing and the world spinning dizzily around him.

Gasping, Evren blinked away the stars whirling in his vision and pushed himself up onto one knee. *He hit me!*

Anger pushed away some of the vertigo as he pressed a hand to the wound on his forehead. Blood trickled from a cut right beneath his scalp. Yet, a part of him realized that something was off. His mind struggled to understand what it was. The skin was severed but his skull hadn't been crushed. He prodded the bare flesh of his forehead.

*Bare flesh!* Suddenly, he realized why the Indomitable had called him slave and struck him. He'd taken off his red-and-gold headband to evade the thugs' notice and forgotten to replace it. Only the *Kabili* slaves went around Shalandra bare-headed.

His fingers were clumsy, his movements jerky as he pulled out the headband and knotted it around his forehead.

All around him, the shouts of the crowd turned ugly, threatening. Fruits, vegetables, even a few metal and clay trinkets rained down around Evren, some landing dangerously close to him and the Indomitables. Even in his disoriented state, Evren recognized that it would only take one hit on a guard's shield or helmet to turn things ugly.

Headband in place, he staggered upright and stumbled left, away from the Indomitable that had struck him. A few paces down the line, he tried again.

"Please!" he shouted, and motioned to his headband. "My master will be expecting me."

The Indomitables before him exchanged glances. "Hurry!" called one and beckoned for Evren to pass.

Gasping, Evren stumbled through the gap and away from the raging crowd. Relief flooded him, followed a moment later by a surge of acid to the back of his throat. He recognized the symptoms of a minor concussion—he'd taken more than his fair share of blows to the head during his days bare-handed fighting in the Master's Temple. Yet he swallowed the rising vomit and forced himself to stagger onward up the hill.

A dull throbbing engulfed the entire right side of his face. He winced and wiped blood away from his forehead, but the touch set the world spinning once more. A wave of dizziness seized him and he was forced to find a seat at the edge of Death Row for fear of collapsing. He breathed heavily, sweat streaming down his face, and clenched his jaw against the nausea.

Hailen's face spun through the dizzying images before his eyes. Smiling, bright, friendly, those strange violet eyes of his sparkling with mischief. Evren couldn't let anything happen to Hailen. The Hunter and Kiara would never forgive him; Evren would never forgive himself.

He didn't know how long he spent seated, slumped against the golden sandstone wall—it might have been five seconds or five hours—but finally the dizziness and sickness passed enough that he could lever himself to his feet. The analytical part of his mind took stock of the injury; as long as he didn't lose consciousness, he should be fine.

*I've got to keep going,* he told himself over and over. *I've got to get to Hailen in time.*

Twice more—that he could remember—he had to pause in his ascent of Death Row to let the nausea and vertigo pass. Each time, the effects grew noticeably less, his brain recovering from the jolt. Even the headache began to dim until he could move faster without fear of emptying his stomach

The journey to the Keeper's Tier, which had taken him just over an hour before, now seemed to take an eternity. Evren risked another bout of dizziness to glance at the sun and found it had dropped dangerously close to the horizon. Night would fall within half an hour. He had to hurry to reach Suroth's mansion before Samall and his conspirators went for Lady Briana.

His heart leapt as the gate of the Keeper's Tier came into sight. The guards took one look at his headband and let him through, though not without close scrutiny. He knew he looked a sight—bloodied forehead, staggering like a drunk—but he didn't care.

He half-ran, half-shambled east along the Path of Gold. *I made it!*

His relief died a moment later when he spotted a group of dark-robed figures slipping down the alley that led to the rear entrance of Suroth's mansion. The tradesman's gate swung open and Samall appeared in the archway, a small lantern in his hand. At his low hiss, Kuhar and more than twenty other figures in dark robes slipped from the shadows and raced toward the back way in.

Evren had arrived too late.

# Chapter Thirty-Eight

Issa's two-handed sword carved a deadly arc through the air. The Shalandran steel blade hacked off one assassin's arm at the shoulder and plowed through his ribcage before biting deep into his spine. The man screamed and collapsed, sliding off Issa's sword as she stepped back into a Silver Sword guard stance. The next assassin that came at her died with her sword tip through his stomach—the same thrust Tannard had used on her in the mock battle earlier that day.

"Assassins!" she shouted again. Not out of fear for her own safety, but to alert Kellas, Etai, and the other guards protecting the palace. If there were other assassins, she needed to sound the alarm at once.

Six robed figures charged in a rush. Issa knew what they intended—close the distance and get inside the reach of her flammard, where their long swords and daggers could give them the edge—but that knowledge did little to help her. Though she took one down with a quick cut that opened a gash in his throat, the other five closed the distance before she could recover. Their long swords and knives flashed at her chest, arms, throat, face, and legs.

Her Shalandran steel armor saved her life. Blades rang on her gauntlets, breastplate, and helmet, hard enough to knock Issa back a step. She allowed herself to be driven backward—she had to keep her face, the only vulnerable body part, away from their blades. And she needed to clear space to swing her sword.

Her quick upward cut caught one of the assassins in the stomach. Issa heard a *clang* of steel on steel followed by a cry of pain as the Shalandran steel hacked through whatever armor the man wore beneath his robes. Issa whipped the pommel of her sword into the face of another opponent. Teeth shattered, cartilage crunched, and blood gushed from his nose and split lips.

Issa hissed as one dagger carved a slash across the bridge of her nose, and responded by driving her shoulder into the assassin's chest. The spikes in her armor punched through his armor and slammed against bone. In the second it took the man to recover, Issa straightened, released her grip on her sword's hilt, and seized it by the blade. The heavy steel pommel, hilt, and crossguard clubbed the man into unconsciousness.

She whirled to face the remaining two assassins, flammard held in the half-swording grip popular at the Academy of the Windy Mountain. The heavy sword could do enough blunt force damage to shatter an enemy's skull, and the shortened grip on the blade made it as versatile as a club or mace.

She drove the pommel into one man's gut, whipped the crossguard into the other man's face, and dragged the razor sharp edge across the first's throat. Even as the assassin collapsed, hands clasped to his gushing neck, Issa reversed her grip on the sword and brought the blade spinning across in a blindingly fast horizontal strike. The steel blade separated the man's head from his shoulders like a hot knife through tallow.

Issa found herself alone, surrounded by eight dead or dying men, and her heart sank as she saw the remaining seven assassins racing down the corridor. Without hesitation, she leapt over her dead enemies and gave chase.

Determination spurred her on—she had to get back to Etai and Kellas before they were overwhelmed by the attackers. Her marvelous segmented plate mail made barely a sound as she ran, the weight almost negligible after long days spent running and training fully-armored. By the time she reached the main corridor, she had closed within ten yards of the assassins.

Her stomach clenched as the clash of steel echoed from her post, followed by a cry of pain. *Etai!*

Issa charged around the corner in time to see the remaining seven assassins join the five already attacking Kellas and Etai. Six more corpses lay at the Blades' feet, but Etai was stumbling back, a hand pressed to a bleeding wound in her cheek. Her one-handed grip on her sword sufficed to block the next attack, but Issa could see that the two assassins would break through her guard at any second.

Three dark-cloaked assassins kept Kellas tied up, though the *Dhukari* youth seemed to be holding his own. However, with their backs against the Council Chamber's double doors, they couldn't retreat.

Issa couldn't get to them in time, not with the seven assassins in her way. All she could do was buy them a split second.

"For the Long Keeper!" The cry burst from her lips with every ounce of strength she possessed.

It worked. The seven assassins nearest her whirled, blades sliding free of their sheaths. But the five locked with Kellas and Etai made the mistake of glancing over their shoulders at the new threat. Kellas seized advantage of the momentary distraction to hack down one of his enemies and finish off one of Etai's.

Issa's sword, backed by all her strength and the force of her charge, sheared through an upraised arm, laid open the assassin's chest, and carved a deep gash into the thigh of the assassin on her left. The two men fell with cries of pain. Issa strode through the widening puddle of blood to attack the assassins behind the dying men. Two more assassins fell to her twin hacking strokes, and her armor turned aside one lucky blow aimed at her chest.

Kellas' sword punched through the stomach of the rearmost assassin. Issa's heart leapt as she saw Etai cut down another.

Three enemies remained, and as one, they reached within their cloaks. Issa caught a flash of glass as the nearest assassin drew out his hand—she severed his arm with a backhand stroke before he could throw it at her. Etai dodged the glass object thrown at her, and it shattered on the gold-enameled door behind her with a loud *crash*. A moment later, the *Mahjuri* girl drove the tip of her flammard into the man's chest.

Issa's blood turned to ice as the third assassin drew out the glass object and prepared to hurl it at Kellas. The *Dhukari* youth had gotten his feet tangled in the arms of a fallen assassin, and his eyes had left his enemies for that single second.

Issa never hesitated. Her desperate one-handed blow shattered the assassin's forearm. The limb bent at a terrible angle, and the glass object fell from useless fingers. Issa removed his head as the glass shattered on the ground.

The moment the falling body struck the pool of liquid seeping from the glass vial, a loud *hissing* filled the air. Issa felt her meager lunch coming up at the stink of charred flesh—not burned by fire, but eaten by something as corrosive as the sulfuric acids used by Killian to pickle his steel and remove impurities.

She leapt backward. "Watch out!" she called to Kellas and Etai. "That stuff in their glass bottles was acid!"

Etai gave the body a wide berth, but Kellas stared down, wide-eyed and pale-faced, at the bubbling, smoking mass of flesh that had once been an assassin. After a moment, he lifted his eyes to her.

"Y-You...saved me?" Confusion knitted his brows.

"Why in the bloody hell would you do that?" Vitriol dripped from Etai's words. She fixed Issa with a disgusted look. "After all he's done?"

Issa shrugged. "He's a Blade." Sure, an arrogant, hot-headed prick. But the Long Keeper had chosen him just as he'd chosen her and Etai. As Tannard had told them, the Long Keeper did not make mistakes.

The sound of clashing steel from down the eastern corridor snapped her into motion. "Stay here!" she shouted as she turned and sprinted away. "Hold the door and make sure the Keeper's Council is safe!"

Even as she turned into the intersecting corridor, Issa knew she'd find assassins sneaking around to the Council Chamber's side entrance. The Pharus, the Lady of Blades, and the Keeper's Council would all be within. All targets for assassination gathered in a single room. Her only hope was that the two Blades guarding that side entrance would hold long enough for her to reach them.

But when she sprinted around the corner, Issa found only one figure locked in combat with the six assassins assaulting the door. A woman, bare-headed, long hair hanging loose around her shoulders, yet clad in the black plate-mail of a Keeper's Blade and wielding her two-handed flammard. Five corpses lay on the ground around the broad-shouldered, well-muscled form of Callista Vinaus, Lady of Blades.

Issa couldn't help marveling at the lethal grace of the *Proxenos*. Lady Callista finished off two of the assassins before Issa took a single step, and another fell a heartbeat later. But the sight of two assassins reaching into their robes spurred Issa to greater speed. She brought her flammard's tip slicing across the backs of the two rearmost enemies' necks. The Shalandran steel hacked through flesh, blood vessels, and bone. The assassins flopped forward, spines severed.

And then there was only Lady Callista, alone in a pool of blood, the bodies of fifteen assassins at her feet. Sorrow clutched at Issa's heart as she spotted the acid-twisted corpses wearing black plate mail among them. Those unfortunate Blades hadn't received warning in time.

Lady Callista seized Issa's arm. "Protect the Pharus!" she commanded. "Leave the assassins to me."

"Yes, *Proxenos!*" Issa saluted, but Lady Callista had already stalked off bare-footed through the puddles of blood.

Issa sprinted into the Council Chamber and found a scene that would be laughable if not for the corpses littering the floor. The six Necroseti of the Keeper's Council huddled in a corner, pudgy faces twisted in fear as their eyes fixed on the ten dead bodies near the door. Judging by the positons of the bodies, the assassins had managed to get through the Blades and within five paces of the massive marble table dominating the room before they'd been taken down. Nine assassins and one figure in dull brown had died here.

Pharus Amhoset Nephelcheres stood in a wary crouch, bloody dagger gripped in his hand. A fierce light shone in his eyes as he saw Issa enter the room.

"What's happening out there?" the Pharus demanded. "How many have fallen?"

"I know of just two casualties, My Pharus." Issa held her sword in a firm grip. "But don't worry, Bright One. They're not getting through me!"

The Pharus actually straightened and gave her a calm smile, a strange expression given the blood staining his face. "I can see that."

With grim determination, Issa turned toward the door, ready to cut down any assailants who entered. Her commander had given her an order; she'd die before she failed now.

321

# *Chapter Thirty-Nine*

Aisha glanced nervously at the sky. The sunset shades of purple, gold, and orange had given way to dull grey-blue as the daylight faded. *Where is he?*

Kodyn had been gone far too long. The meeting with the Black Widow should have taken him no more than two or three hours—including time to reach the Artisan's Tier and make the return journey. The fact that he hadn't yet returned worried her. He was more than capable of taking care of himself, yet he was alone, weaponless save for a few daggers, and in an unfamiliar city.

Her stomach clenched as an image flashed through her mind: a ghostly, ethereal Kodyn stared at her with empty eyes, his mouth open in a scream.

*No.* She forced the image away. *He'll be back soon. He probably just got delayed or found something interesting.* The thought rang hollow in her mind. Try as she might, the nagging worry refused to leave her alone.

To distract herself, she toyed with the smooth wooden shaft of her *assegai* and replayed over her encounter with the *Kish'aa* in the Temple District. Truth be told, it wasn't a distraction—it was *all* she'd been able to think about since Kodyn left. Those pleading cries of *"Justice"* repeated by a thousand spectral lips, rising in a crescendo until she had no choice but to run.

The Whispering Lily had opened her ears to the call of the spirits, but she could not understand what they wanted. Perhaps *that* was what had driven her father mad. Endless pleas for help, help he could not give. Suddenly, she understood the quiet hopelessness that had glimmered in her father's eyes. He'd heard the *Kish'aa* and found himself drowning in turmoil that even death could not ease.

The effects of the Whispering Lily hadn't fully worn off. Like a hangover after too much rum, Aisha felt a quiet throbbing in the back of her mind, and Radiana's presence within her felt far more noticeable than it had before. She almost imagined she could hear Briana's mother whispering in her mind.

She didn't know if it was real or her imagination—so far from the Spirit Whisperers of Ghandia, she had no one to ask. She'd have to muddle through it on her own.

A sharp prickling suddenly coursed down her spine. Like an itch, but painful and persistent. Issa ground her teeth and tried to ignore it, but it came again, more forceful this time.

"Ow!" A spark crackled between her fingertips, scorching her skin.

Her brow furrowed as she stared down at her hand. The blue-white light of Radiana's spirit danced beneath the flesh of her palm, bright enough to light up the evening shadows.

*What is it?* It almost felt like Radiana wanted to tell her something.

Suddenly, Aisha's hand darted forward, as if the spark had triggered an instinctive reaction in her muscles. Aisha's eyes went wide—not only at the strange, jerky motion, but at the sight she saw *beyond* her outstretched hand.

Close to thirty figures in dark cloaks moved through the settling gloom. None looked up toward her, concealed beneath the shadows of an overhanging mangrove tree, but she could see them clearly limned in the light of the torches burning in the courtyard.

For a heartbeat, she hesitated. Those figures could just be servants going about their tasks. Yet a moment later, when a loud clatter echoed from somewhere in the distance, the figures froze as if fearful of being discovered. In that instant, Aisha's senses screamed that they were interlopers. No servant would act so suspicious.

Radiana's spirit sent a jolt of energy down Aisha's spine. Instantly, her senses went on full alert and she spun to race across the garden to the gazebo where Briana sat with the pale-skinned servant, Hailen.

"Something's going on," Aisha said as she pounded into the circle of light cast by the twin oil lanterns hanging from hooks on the gazebo's pillars. "There are cloaked men inside the mansion."

Briana paled, her eyes going wide, and her hand flew to her mouth. "Th-The Gatherers?" She gave a little shudder. "T-They've come for me again!"

Aisha shook her head. "I don't know, but—"

"No!" The terrified cry burst from Briana's lips and her arms wrapped protectively around her waist. "Y-You can't let them take me. Not again. I-I can't..." She trailed off as tears brimmed in her fear-filled eyes.

Aisha crossed the distance to Briana in two long steps. "Listen to me," she said in a firm voice and gripped Briana's arm hard. "I'm not going to let anything happen to you. We're going to get through this."

Aisha shot a glance at the servant. "Do you know how to sound the alarm?" she demanded.

Hailen nodded. "Yes." To her surprise, he produced a knife from his belt. The blade was utilitarian, well-honed, and worn by use—not the sort of weapon she'd expect from a servant. "I can fight, too."

"No! Go sound the alarm." Aisha commanded. "We need to alert the guards that there are intruders in the mansion." Twenty would be too many for her to defeat alone.

With a nod, Hailen dashed from the garden.

Aisha shook the girl, trying to snap her out of her panic. "We need to get inside, now! There's no way to defend this garden. We can lock ourselves in your room and hold them off."

Briana was a barely coherent mess of tears. Finally, Aisha simply lifted the girl to her feet and half-dragged, half-carried her down the stairs. She wouldn't let Briana's panic get them both killed.

The *Dhukari* girl's rooms were two adjoining suites—one a bedroom, the other a sitting area with plush couches and ottomans. Depositing Briana on the bed, Aisha raced toward the door that led out into the hall, slammed it shut, and threw the deadbolt. She cast about for anything that could be used to block the entrance. Her gaze settled on a heavy four-drawer oak dresser.

She turned to Briana. "Help me barricade the door."

To her dismay, she found the Shalandran girl frozen in terror. Briana's face had gone deathly pale and she quivered like a leaf in a hurricane.

"Briana!" Aisha shouted. "I'm trying to protect you, but I need your help."

Briana turned fear-numbed eyes on her and began moving slowly, as if in a fever dream.

"Hurry!" Aisha's voice was hard, edged with urgency. "I can hear them coming up the stairs."

The lie spurred Briana to action. The Shalandran girl darted forward and, with a frenzied flurry of activity, set about shoving at the dresser. Together, they pushed until the oak furniture blocked the entrance.

"Good." Aisha nodded. "Now we need to barricade the other way in."

Aisha raced into the sitting room, a hand around Briana's wrist. She had to keep the girl close. If Briana panicked and went into shock, she could end up putting both of them at risk. She and Briana had just set about hauling a heavy stuffed wool couch toward the door when it burst open.

Time slowed to a crawl as the first of the assailants rushed into the room. They wore dark cloaks over boiled leather armor and carried simple, straight-bladed long swords and daggers. As one lifted his weapon to strike, Aisha caught a glimpse of that same strange Gatherer tattoo she'd seen in Praamis.

Aisha's blood turned to ice, but her hands were already moving, reaching toward her *assegai*. The short-hafted spear glinted in the candlelight as she drew it and thrust out at the first man to reach her. The leaf-shaped spear blade punched through the man's armor and drove deep into his chest. When Aisha tore the weapon free and danced backward, the assassin cried out and slumped in the doorway, blocking his comrades.

Drawing in a deep breath, Aisha unleashed a Ghandian war cry with all the force of the battle thrill rushing through her. The shout slowed the foremost assassin for a single moment, long enough for Aisha to leap forward and bring him down with a quick thrust of her *assegai*.

She crouched, spear and dagger ready for the next attack. "Stay behind me!" she called to Briana. "I'll hold them off."

She never heard Briana's reply. Instead, she heard one of the assailants call, "Go around!"

Her gut clenched—even if she managed to keep them busy here, the assassins would get through the locked door and barricade if they were persistent enough. She pricked up her ears for any sign of the alarm bell, but only the shouts of the assassins and the moans of the bleeding, dying man met her ears.

The next assassin leapt over his comrade, and Aisha drove her spear into his throat before his feet touched the floor. Blood sprayed as she tore her spear head free and used it to block a strike of another assassin's long sword. Her dagger opened a long gash up the length of his forearm and her kick to his chest sent him stumbling backward, once more to block the doorway.

She had to keep them out of the room. If she held the door, forced them to come at her one at a time, she had a chance. *I just need to hold them long enough for the servant to sound the alarm and for Kodyn to return.*

But, in the end, she couldn't count on anyone else to protect Briana or save her. She alone stood in this room, facing more enemies than she could hope to defeat. Her mother had trained her to be a warrior in body, mind, and spirit. Years in the Night Guild had hardened her, prepared her to fight with cunning and trickery as well as honor and skill. Facing these assassins intent on slaying her and making off with Briana, that was precisely who she needed to be.

Aisha's hands moved in a blur, spear thrusting and slicing, dagger stabbing and cutting. Her lithe body, honed by years of training, spun and leapt in the familiar rhythm of the *Kim'ware* war dance taught to her by her mother, the greatest warrior of the *Ukuza* tribe. Even the Serpents of the Night Guild had learned to respect the strange, dance-like movements of the Ghandians. Only Ria, Master of House Phoenix, had surpassed Aisha in combat.

The assassins, unaccustomed to the fighting style, fell back before her. Three died in the space of two heartbeats, Aisha's sharp spear blade and dagger's edge taking their toll in blood. She managed to push them back beyond the doorway and out into the hall.

But only for a moment. One assassin clutched the spear embedded in his chest, slowing her down with his last breath. Aisha managed to tear the weapon free of his lifeless grasp, but by then, two more assassins had leapt over the fallen body and charged her, swords raised.

Aisha had no choice but to give ground, which opened the way for more assassins to flood into the room. As she retreated, she risked a single glance behind her to find Briana. The Shalandran girl had gone rigid, eyes fixed on the killers, and she blocked Aisha's retreat through the doorway into the bedroom beyond.

With a growl, Aisha dropped into a low crouch and spun, foot swinging out and spear coming up to protect her head. Her heavy boot crunched into one knee with bone-shattering force as an assassin's blade clanged against her dagger. As she finished the spin, her leg muscles propelled her upright and into a high leaping kick that drove the toe of her boot into the underside of an assassin's chin. The man's head snapped back with an audible *snap* and he sagged, silent and boneless.

The sudden ferocity of her assault gave her a single moment to breathe, and she used it to turn, grab Briana, and shove the girl hard into the bedroom. Her gut clenched as she heard the rhythmic *thumps* echoing from door. The assassins were serious about breaking through her barricade. When that happened, she'd have to face an assault from both sides.

One problem at a time. She'd taken down eight of the dark-cloaked figures but five more remained. Even as she retreated through the doorway, the assassins followed, long swords swinging at her head, arms, chest, and legs. Only the doorway saved her from being hacked to pieces; long swords *clanged* as they struck solid sandstone. But two lucky strikes got through her guard, slicing a cut across her thigh and into the side of her face.

Aisha fought down the instinctive wave of fear. There were too many for her to deal with, not if she wanted to keep Briana safe. She fought alone, with no one coming to help.

The sound of the alarm bell echoing through the mansion sent hope surging through Aisha. She wanted to shout, laugh, to cry out in glee. Hailen had sounded the alarm. Help was on the way!

Two of the assassins were distracted by the sudden ringing, and Aisha used their inattention to bring them down with twin thrusts of her dagger and *assegai*. The attack nearly cost her—she barely managed to throw herself to the side to evade a hacking slash aimed at her neck. A line of fire opened along her shoulder and down her bicep as the sword's tip dug a furrow into her skin.

Yet against three, she had a chance. She'd faced as many as four Serpent apprentices in Master Serpent's sparring bouts and emerged victorious. These assassins lacked the speed, skill, and cunning of the Night Guild's assassins. Indeed, they fought artlessly, their attacks backed by brute strength yet lacking any real skill.

Aisha ducked beneath a high strike and slashed her dagger across one assassin's thigh, just above the kneecap. As the man sagged, she brought her knee up and plowed it into his face. She leapt back to avoid a rapid thrust, twisted out of the path of a vicious chop, and brought her spear whipping around to slam into the man's head. The tip of the spear, weighted with a metal ball the width of two fingers, crushed bone. The assassin collapsed in a boneless heap. A moment later, the final assassin died at the end of Aisha's dagger.

The sound of splintering wood set Aisha's heart lurching into her throat. The assassins, wielding a heavy stone bust, had broken through the door and five now leapt over her barricade.

She turned to meet them but slipped in the blood puddling around the corpses at her feet. She fell, hard, her head striking the ground before she could catch herself. In that moment, the world spinning dizzily in her vision, she heard Briana's terrified scream.

Aisha lifted her head in time to see an assassin seizing Briana in rough hands, while a second stuffed a dark sack over her head.

*They're going to take her!*

The words echoed in Aisha's mind clear as if someone had spoken in her ear. She recognized the emotion that drove the voice—Radiana, Briana's mother. The spark of life within Aisha flared to a sizzling energy that begged to be unleashed. Almost of its own accord, Aisha's hand snapped forward. The tiny flickering blue-white spark surged from her fingers and flew toward the man holding Briana's arms. The moment it struck him, the man's muscles seized up, his face going rigid, and he toppled to the side.

The second assassin, the one holding the sack, shot a stunned glance toward his companion. Aisha watched, equally surprised, as the spark of Radiana's life leapt from the downed man toward the other like a shooting star cutting the night sky. The blue-white glow slammed into the assassin hard enough to throw him backward. He crashed into the wall and fell, his neck twisted at a terrible angle.

Aisha froze, her jaw agape. For an instant, the figure of Radiana appeared before her, the blue-white light coalescing into the form of a beautiful woman.

Ghostly eyes fixed on Aisha and a contented smile broadened Radiana's face. "*Thank you.*" Barely more than a whisper that caressed the back of Aisha's mind, yet unmistakable. Slowly, like a trail of smoke carried away on the wind, Radiana faded from view.

More figures appeared in the hall and began clambering over the dresser. Aisha staggered upright, her mind struggling to comprehend what had just happened. *That was the work of the Kish'aa?* Such a tiny little bit of energy, yet it had enough force to bring down two men. Her father had been right; a Spirit Whisperer could truly wield terrible power.

Suddenly, she understood what it meant to be *Umoyahlebe*. The *Kish'aa* needed someone to hear them, to help them find peace. More than anything in the world, Radiana had wanted to protect her daughter, and she'd done so even in death.

The spirits would tell her what they needed, and it would be her task to help them. The burden weighed heavy, yet after what she'd just witnessed, she could no longer consider herself cursed.

Her father truly had passed on a gift to her.

*I am a Spirit Whisperer,* Aisha told herself as she prepared to meet the next wave of assassins. *I answer the call of the spirits!*

# Chapter Forty

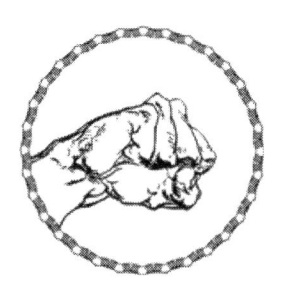

*What in the bloody hell do I do now?* The thought set the acid in Evren's stomach churning.

He knew what the Hunter would do in this situation: charge in, swords flashing, and kill everyone that stood between him and Hailen. But Evren wasn't the Hunter. He didn't have the Hunter's speed, skill, or healing ability. He'd seen what happened to the apprentices that had tried to fight with a head wound like his—some took one blow and died or, worse, suffered permanent impairment of their mental and physical functions.

Then there was the fact that there were at least twenty men—far too many for him to handle alone. He didn't have time to try to race around to the front; Samall would have the intruders up inside the house long before Evren ever convinced the guards at the front gate to let him through. His only hope lay in sounding the alarm.

Nessa had insisted on showing him the various mechanisms around the house that would trigger the alarm bell—installed after Lady Briana's kidnapping. The nearest was in the entrance, just around the corner from the grand staircase. He'd need to cut through the kitchens, but from there it would be a short sprint to his final destination. All he had to do was ring the alarm to alert the guards and Lady Briana's bodyguards; they could deal with the kidnappers, leaving him free to focus on finding Hailen.

He waited until the last of the dark-cloaked figures disappeared into the mansion, counted ten seconds, and raced down the alley toward the gate. In his hurry to get his accomplices inside, Samall had forgotten to lock the rear door.

Or he'd simply neglected to lock it—they might be planning to use that as their escape route once they'd abducted or killed Lady Briana.

Heart thundering, Evren scanned the darkened courtyard. He caught a glimpse of dark cloaks slipping through the shadows of the pathway that ringed the western edge of the mansion. Relief flooded Evren. Samall was leading the kidnappers *away* from the kitchens, toward the servant's hallway that led directly from the stables toward the grand staircase. Yet that meant Evren would have to move faster to reach the alarm before they climbed the stairs to Lady Briana's room on the second floor.

The wound in his forehead still sent jolts of pain radiating through the right side of his face, but he forced himself to move quickly. Not quietly, though. As he sped through the kitchens, he seized the largest of the cook's wooden spoons and struck every pot he passed. The clatter was deafening, at least to anyone in the servants' section of the house. He just hoped it would suffice to get people suspicious and looking for anything out of the ordinary, thereby raising the chance that someone would see the kidnappers.

Once through the kitchens, he raced down the narrow corridor that led toward the grand staircase. *Please let me be in time!* He didn't know who he prayed to—the Hunter had told him the truth of the thirteen "gods" of Einan—but right now, all that mattered was that he got to Hailen before the kidnappers attacked.

Hope surged in his chest as a piercing alarm bell rang out around the mansion. Someone had seen the intruders and sounded the alarm. Arch-Guardian Suroth's guards would come running to help Lady Briana's bodyguards. If Hailen was with them, he'd be safe, too.

But Evren couldn't take the chance. Hailen might be in the small servant's room across the hall from Lady Briana's chambers. If the kidnappers entered the wrong door, they might kill Hailen to stop him from crying out.

Fear lent wings to Evren's feet and drowned out the hammering in his head. He'd just reached the main staircase when a familiar commanding voice echoed from a nearby hallway.

"Evren!" Nessa strode from the hall that led to her Steward's office at the southeastern corner of the mansion. Her hair was a mess, her white *Zadii* headband crooked, but anger blazed in her eyes. "What is the meaning of this? Where have you been all d—?"

"Kidnappers!" Evren shouted. "They've come for Lady Briana. Samall and Kuhar are with them!"

Nessa's eyes widened and she recoiled. "Blessed Keeper!"

"I've got to find Hailen," Evren said.

"He was with Lady Bria—"

Evren didn't hear the rest of Nessa's sentence. He was already halfway up the stairs, racing toward the second floor and Lady Briana's room. A sudden wave of dizziness gripped him and forced him to stop for a breath. It passed in a moment, and he was just about to keep climbing when a piercing scream sounded from above him, accompanied by the clash of steel. Evren's gut clenched as he reached for his *jambiya*. He'd fight his way through all of the kidnappers to get to Hailen.

Movement on the second floor caught his attention. He recognized Hailen's white-painted face and servants' robes. The youth was running back in the direction of Lady Briana's room—right toward the assassins! Hailen was gone before Evren could call out. Heart thundering, Evren sprinted up the stairs and onto the second floor.

There, he came face to face with Samall, Kuhar, and two men wearing the black robes of the kidnappers.

Samall's eyes went to the daggers in Evren's hands and his lip curled into a sneer. "Kill him," he commanded.

Evren felt calm descend over him, the way it always did when he fought in the Master's Temple. Time seemed to slow around him, and he watched, almost detached, as the two kidnappers and Kuhar charged him. Their long swords hung in the air, moving slowly toward his head. He took in the nervous fear and grim determination in their eyes, the sweat trickling down their faces, even their heavy, ragged breathing.

Instinct and years of training took over. Evren ducked the first blow, deflected the second with the blade in his right hand, and slashed his left-handed *jambiya* across Kuhar's forearm. The attendant cried out and fell back, dropping his sword to clutch at the wound. Evren spun, right hand whipping around in a quick right hook. His fist crashed into an assassin's jaw, backed by the force of his anger and the weight of his dagger. The man fell like a pole-axed drunk.

The Hunter's training had emphasized Evren's strengths—speed, precision, and his excellent coordination at landing punches—and paired them with the lethal efficiency of his daggers. Just as Evren had taken down apprentices in the Master's Temple far larger and stronger than him, he brought down these kidnappers with short, sharp blows.

Before the first man hit the ground, Evren was ducking beneath a long sword strike and bringing his left hand around for an uppercut. But instead of striking with his bare knuckles, the curved edge of his dagger opened the underside of the man's chin. The blow missed the jugular vein, barely, but it laid open flesh to the bone. As the kidnapper cried out and fell back, Evren snapped a kick into his knee. Bone shattered with a loud *crack* and the man crumpled. A boot to the face rendered him unconscious.

Evren stalked toward Kuhar, who was clinging to the wall and desperately trying to stanch the flow of blood gushing from his arm. The strike had severed the artery—the attendant's legs, weakened from blood loss, gave out as Evren broke into a run. Kuhar might live, *might*, if he got to a physicker in time.

Samall had frozen in horror at the sight of Evren taking down his comrades, his eyes wide. Now, he turned to flee from the young man charging at him. Anger burned hot and bright in Evren's gut as he chased the cowardly traitor through the mansion. Something warned him that Samall would try to use the servant's staircase to descend to the ground floor, where he could flee out through the tradesman's gate. The attendant was far better-acquainted with the layout of Arch-Guardian Suroth's mansion, but Evren pursued him with the same grim determination that had won him freedom from the Master's Temple.

He raced down the stairs in time to hear a curse and loud clattering as Samall stumbled over the pots Evren had knocked from their shelves. Evren leapt over the pots and burst out of the rear door. Racing across the courtyard, he caught up to Samall just as the man reached the stables. Evren kicked the back of the man's knees, sending Samall stumbling into the pile of horse manure he'd had Evren shovel the previous day. He landed face-first with a loud *splat*. When he managed to extricate himself from the muck and turned to Evren, his expression had gone from disdain to desperate supplication.

"Please!" Samall begged. "I had no choice. The Gatherers, they made me do it! They threatened my family if I didn't help them."

Evren didn't bother listening. His fist drove into the man's face hard enough to shatter teeth. Samall's head snapped back and he sagged, once more face-first into the droppings.

For a moment, Evren stared down at the daggers in his hand. The treacherous Samall deserved punishment, preferably something painful and permanent. He had betrayed his employer and, in doing so, put Hailen's life in danger.

The moment passed and Evren sheathed his *jambiya*. Seizing Samall's pants, he set about dragging the unconscious attendant through the courtyard and down the pathway that led to the front of the house.

Evren was a fighter; he'd *had* to be in order to survive in the Master's Temple and on the streets of Vothmot. Yet he was no killer, not if he had a choice.

He had the skills. The Hunter and Kiara had both trained him to kill, with blades and fists. He wouldn't hesitate to take a life in the defense of someone weaker and smaller—someone like Hailen, or like his friend Daver from Vothmot—or if someone threatened to kill him. Yet given a choice, he would prefer to avoid taking a life. The Lecterns' cruelty and years of hard living on the streets hadn't completely eroded his humanity. There would always be a part of him that would fight to make the right choice.

The stout Samall proved a heavy burden to drag, but Evren didn't release his grip on the man's pants. He lugged the attendant around to the front of the building, where Nessa stood with Rothin, the head of Suroth's guard. The two of them were snapping orders and shouting commands to the twenty-odd guards in golden breastplates.

The Steward's eyes widened at the sight of Evren dragging the unconscious Samall. Evren stopped in front of her and dropped Samall's leg. It hit the ground with a loud *thump* and the man himself gave a quiet groan.

"He's alive, eh?" Nessa cocked an eyebrow.

Evren nodded. "Kuhar's inside on the stairs. He's wounded bad. If he gets to a physicker in time, he might live long enough to talk."

"He's not worth the bother." Nessa's face hardened as she stared down at Samall. "He'll be made to speak, and when he's done, his head will decorate a spike in Murder Square like the traitorous dog he is."

"What about his family?" Evren asked. "Will they—"

"Family?" Nessa's brow furrowed. "What family?"

Evren thrust a finger at the now-stirring Samall. "He said the Gatherers threatened his family if he didn't help them."

Nessa snorted. "He has no family." Her lip curled into a sneer. "Traitors will do anything to save themselves. But no lies will save him now."

She snapped her fingers. "Get him out of my sight!"

Two of the guards hurried to gather up Samall. The attendant awoke then, his eyes opening. Fear creased his blocky face and his face turned white as marble. A loud wail burst from his lips as the guards dragged him away.

Nessa turned to Evren. "I will deal with him. As for you, I will make certain the Arch-Guardian hears of your actions here."

Evren bowed. "Thank you, Steward." The Councilor's favor could go a long way toward getting him closer to the Blade of Hallar. He might be able to leverage it into a better servant's position, one that brought him inside the palace.

Thoughts of the *Im'tasi* blade sent his mind flashing back to Hailen.

"Hailen!" The words burst from his lips. "Have any of you seen him?"

"He the pale-skinned bodyservant?" asked one of the guards.

"Yes!" Evren nodded. "Is he alive? Is he safe?"

"He was the one that triggered the alarm," the guard continued. "Where he is now, I don't know."

Evren turned and sprinted off, in the direction he'd seen Hailen running. He raced through the front door and up the stairs toward the second floor, cursing himself for giving Hailen that dagger. The boy would follow the example set for him by the Hunter and Evren; he'd throw himself in harm's way to protect Lady Briana.

"Hailen!" he shouted and reached for his twin daggers. "Hailen!"

Fear clenched in his belly. He had to find the young boy, make sure he was safe.

"Hailen!" Desperation tinged his voice as he reached the second floor.

"He's in here." The words echoed from down the side corridor that led toward the rear staircase—the same way Evren had pursued Samall not ten minutes earlier.

Evren raced down the corridor, toward the small coat room where he'd heard the voice. Confusion furrowed his brow. *That voice! It can't be!*

There, in the coat room, stood Snarth with a dagger pressed to the side of Hailen's neck.

# Chapter Forty-One

Kodyn's heart hammered a frantic beat as the crowd surged around him, slamming into him and shoving him backward. He had no way to break through the ranks of angry, shouting people or the solid line of black-armored Indomitables.

Gasping, he burst free of the back of the crowd, staggered by the rage that hung thick in the air. The throng surged up Death Row, their enraged cries ringing off the golden sandstone wall that barred the way to the Defender's Tier.

*The wall!*

An idea born of desperation slammed into his mind and he acted without hesitation. Instead of trying to barrel through the crowd, he turned and raced back down Death Row, toward the Artificer's Courseway. He sprinted down the decline until he reached the main avenue, turned west, and rushed toward the nearest intersection. The side street stood barely fifty paces from the edge of Death Row and cut northward, toward the border of the Artisan's Tier.

Kodyn kept one eye on the chaos on Death Row as he ran. The road rose toward the tier above it, but the two- and three-story houses had been built along the leveled surface. He could see the ranks of Indomitables and the swirling, shouting crowd above the level of the rooftops—and the small gap of cleared space between the soldiers and the gate to the Defender's Tier.

*If I can get there, I can get through the gate in time!*

He ran until he reached the cliff face on the northern edge of the Artisan's Tier before turning down the alley that ran east. The back lane dead-ended at the stone wall, and Kodyn skidded to a halt, studying the coarse stone surface in the fading daylight. The climb would be precarious—sandstone tended to crumble if he wasn't careful, and the incline of Death Row rose fully ten paces above his head. Yet he never hesitated. Aisha and Briana's lives were on the line.

Seizing the first handhold, he hauled himself up the cliff face. Sandstone crumbled to dust in his fingers but he was already on to the next step, his left hand gripping a narrow fissure and his right foot digging into a slight indentation. One hand and foot at a time, he scrambled up the wall like a spider. Skill, strength, and instincts honed over his years as a Hawk, a third-story thief, kept him moving upward at a steady speed.

Yet no matter how fast he climbed, he couldn't outpace the setting sun.

The shadows deepened around him as he scrabbled for purchase on the hard stone. As night fell, it grew more and more difficult to find his next handhold and foothold. Soon, he was forced to feel his way up the cliff.

Every delay, every moment of hesitation, added to his mounting frustration and fear. Not for himself or his wellbeing—though he knew a fall from this height would shatter bones at best or kill him at worst—but for Aisha and Briana. The Gatherers were coming for Briana, and Kodyn knew Aisha would fight to the death to protect the *Dhukari* girl. If there were too many cultists…

*No!* He pushed the image of Aisha's bloodied corpse from his mind. *I won't let that happen. I'll get to them in time, no matter what!*

Slowly, one step at a time, the stony ground grew more distant below him and the upper lip of the cliff drew nearer. Five paces became four, three, two, then one. Kodyn hesitated only an instant—shooting a glance at the rear of the Indomitable ranks holding off the crowd—before pulling himself up onto the slope of Death Row.

He was on his feet in an instant, hands held wide. A trio of black-armored soldiers rushed toward him, sickle-shaped swords at the ready.

"I'm a *Dhukari* servant!" he shouted. The roar of the crowd behind him drowned out his words. To his relief, the sight of his pale skin and the gold-and-green headband encircling his forehead caused the guards to slow.

"I need to get to the Keeper's Tier!" Kodyn moved toward them. "It's a matter of life and death."

"Go!" With a nod, the nearest Indomitable—an officer, judging by the vertical stripe of silver on the blue band of his helmet—beckoned for the guards to let him pass.

Kodyn sprinted through the gate and onto the Defender's Tier, heart racing in time with his flying feet. His pulse hammered in his ears. *Run, run, run, run,* it seemed to say, filling him with a renewed sense of urgency.

For the last nine years as a Hawk apprentice, he'd been subjected to Bryden's vindictiveness—Master Hawk hated Kodyn's mother with every fiber of his petty being. Kodyn had been forced to weather the storm of Bryden's enmity on his own. His mother couldn't protect him; he had to stand on his own feet.

That, perhaps, had caused him to be so protective of others. First the younger Hawk apprentices, like Sid, the boy that had nearly died at the Gatherers' hand in Praamis. Now Briana, the girl he'd found, freed, and sworn to return home. He hadn't had a shield to protect him from the cruelties of the world, but he had vowed to be that for others.

And now he was about to break that vow. He'd barely saved Sid in time; the boy had been strapped to the Gatherers' table, their cruel poison killing him slowly. He couldn't fail Briana, too.

*Please!* he begged silently in his mind. *Please don't let it be too late.*

The run to the Keeper's Tier couldn't have taken more than twenty minutes, but to Kodyn, it felt as if a lifetime passed before he finally saw the gate. He slowed only long enough to point out his headband, which elicited the same response as with the Indomitables below.

*I made it!* Hope surged in his chest. The sun hadn't set more than half an hour earlier—he still had time to get to Briana and Aisha, to warn Suroth's guards before the Gatherers attacked.

He raced down the side street that led to Suroth's mansion. "Open the gate!" he yelled as he approached. Rothin had ordered the gates closed at sundown, as usual. "Open the Keeper-damned gate!"

The wicket gate opened and a puzzled-looking Rothin appeared. "What the—?"

Kodyn barreled past the man, nearly knocking him over in his haste. "The Gatherers!" he shouted as he raced up the walkway toward the front door. "They're going to attack."

He didn't pause to find out if or how Rothin and the other guards responded. He never slowed, but maintained his desperate dash through the front doors and down the hall toward the staircase. His mission was to reach Aisha and Briana before—

Icy feet danced down his spine as he caught sight of the figures moving up the stairs. Five of them, clad in dark hooded cloaks, carrying short swords. From the second floor came the sound of something heavy *crashing* against a wooden door.

Horror brought acid surging to Kodyn's throat. He was too late. The Gatherers had arrived before him. Even now, they could be standing over Aisha's corpse and hauling Briana away.

A war cry, bellowed in Ghandian, sent a sudden rush of energy coursing through him. Aisha was still alive! He'd arrived in time.

He answered Aisha's war cry with one of his own. "Die, you bastards!" Daggers in hand, he charged up the stairs to attack the rearmost Gatherers.

Five faces turned toward him, but too late for the cultist in the rear. Kodyn's right-handed dagger took the assassin in the spine, just below the base of his skull. The man sagged when Kodyn ripped it free, his body flopping limply onto the assassin on the stair above, tangling the two of them in a mess of flailing limbs. Kodyn scooped up the fallen man's short sword and hacked down another cloaked figure, blocked a wild swing from the man on the floor, and drove his dagger into the first man's face. The stolen short sword put an end to the prone assassin before he could disentangle himself from his dying comrade.

A wordless roar of rage ripped from his throat as he fell on the remaining assassins. He'd left his long sword on his bed before leaving, but his training with Master Serpent made him deadly even with just his daggers. Now he had a short sword in one hand and a knife in the other—the assassins would know the wrath of the Night Guild.

Two men died in quick succession, throats slashed and bellies opened by a quick thrust of his short sword. Their patchwork leather armor could turn away a slicing attack, but Master Serpent had taught him to use quick, hard thrusts that could punch through anything short of studded leather, chain mail, or solid plate. The assassins wore little more than hardened leather jerkins, no match for the ferocity of his attacks.

The remaining Gatherer proved skilled, turning aside Kodyn's thrusts with deft strokes of his short sword. Kodyn's charge slowed and stalled as the cultist battled him to a halt. The man fought with surprising skill, his sword darting and flashing at Kodyn so fast that it took all his concentration to deflect, block, and dodge.

Kodyn gasped as the Gatherer's blade carved a line of fire along the back of his knife hand. The man grinned as the dagger fell from Kodyn's grip. Triumph blazed in his eyes as he raised his sword to renew his onslaught.

In that moment, a terrified scream echoed through the house—high, shrill, reeking of panic. Kodyn's blood turned to ice. He'd recognize that voice anywhere. *Briana!*

Grim determination hardened within Kodyn. He'd sworn to protect Briana, and now was his chance to prove it. There was no retreat, no escape, no clever plan to outmaneuver his enemies. He had to fight—for her, and for Aisha, who doubtless was already locked in a desperate battle of her own.

With a roar, he brought his short sword around in a wild swing at the Gatherer's head. The man knocked aside the blow with a contemptuous snort. His backhand drove at Kodyn's face, the sword slicing straight at his throat.

But Kodyn wasn't where the Gatherer expected. The moment he'd felt the sharp *clang* of his blow being blocked, he threw himself into a dive at the man's legs. Jarl, his mother's giant of a friend, had taught him the art of the low tackle. Wrapping his arms around the man's knees would give him leverage to bring him down. Kodyn didn't want to bring him down. He wanted to end the man here and now.

His right shoulder drove into the Gatherer's kneecap with the force of his charge. Bone *crunched* and the cultist's leg bent backward at a terrible angle. The man screamed, his sword swinging high above Kodyn's head. He fell with a piercing cry of pain—a cry silenced a moment later as Kodyn drove his short sword into the man's side.

*I'm coming!*

He leapt over the dying Gatherer and sprinted the remaining distance to Briana's room.

Five men had charged in, but two more remained in the hall. They turned to engage him, but he was an unstoppable force of rage-backed steel and muscle. His block knocked one's wild swing into the other's arm, eliciting a wail as the sword bit deep into muscle, all the way to the bone. His dagger punched through the unwounded assassin's leather armor and slid between ribs. Even as the man sagged, Kodyn brought his short sword down in a powerful chopping blow that cut deep into the side of the assassin's neck. The dark-cloaked figure fell with a gurgling, gasping cry.

Kodyn spared a single glance to make sure everyone in the hall was dead or incapacitated, then hurtled the dresser barricade in a powerful leap. He had to get to Aisha and Briana before—

Aisha's final opponent sagged as she ripped the head of her *assegai* free of his chest. Kodyn's heart stopped at the sight of the blood covering her face, arms, and clothing.

He crossed the three steps toward her in an instant. "Are you hurt?"

"Not badly." Aisha winced and pressed a hand to a cut on her thigh. Blood flowed from a small cut in the side of her cheek.

"Let me take a look," Kodyn insisted.

Reluctantly, Aisha allowed him to examine her leg. A quick glance told him the cut, while painful, hadn't severed any arteries or damaged the bone. He tore off his servant's shawl and used it to bind the wound.

Kodyn met Aisha's eyes. "That one will leave a scar."

Aisha shrugged. "I'd take that over being dead any day."

Relief washed like a cool balm over Kodyn and, before he realized what he was doing, he threw his arms around Aisha's neck. "I was worried I wouldn't make it in time." He felt as if he could finally breathe. They were safe.

Aisha stiffened, then relaxed and wrapped her arms around him. "Glad to see you did." Her voice echoed the emotion surging within Kodyn.

After a moment, Aisha broke off the embrace and turned to where Briana crouched between her massive canopy bed and the stone wall. "Are you hurt?" Genuine concern echoed in her voice.

"N-No." Briana shook her head. She accepted Aisha's help to stand. "Thanks to you." Her eyes went to Kodyn and the bloodstained weapons in his hands. "Both of you."

As Aisha helped the Shalandran girl to the bed, she shot a glance over her shoulder at Kodyn. "What happened to you? You were supposed to be back from your meeting with the Black Widow hours ago."

"I never made it to the meeting." Kodyn crouched beside one of the fallen assassins and used his dagger to slice the man's sleeve. "I ran into a few of our old friends instead."

Aisha grimaced as her eyes fell on the Gatherer's tattoo.

Briana cried out and clutched at the Ghandian girls' arm. "Gatherers!"

Brow furrowed, Aisha fixed Kodyn with a worried look. "How did you know they were coming?"

Kodyn related everything that had happened from the moment he spotted the Gatherers to his eavesdropping on their secret meeting to his hurry to return to the Keeper's Tier with the warning.

"I don't know what happened, but something caused that crowd to turn ugly fast," Kodyn said. "I barely made it out of the press of people in time to avoid the impending stampede."

Aisha shot him a questioning glance. "But if you couldn't get up here, how did *they*?" She thrust a finger at the fallen assassins.

"The same way they've managed to avoid the Necroseti, Indomitables, and everyone else hunting them." It was a guess, but years spent slinking around secret ways above and beneath Praamis were enough to confirm his suspicions. "The Secret Keepers might not be the only ones that know of the Serenii tunnels around the city. The Gatherers could be using them to move around the city's levels unseen."

Aisha swore in her native Ghandian—the salty language would have made any Praamian laborer's ears burn, but thankfully only Kodyn understood the words.

He smiled. *Good to see she's still the same Aisha.* He'd noticed the shift in her since leaving Praamis, but now something *more* had changed. The shadow had left her eyes, the burden gone from her shoulders. She stood straighter, head held higher, and she seemed almost…happier. He didn't understand but he determined that he'd ask her about it the first chance he got. Whatever she'd been through, she'd endured enough alone—he was here to help her as much as she'd come to help him.

Aisha once more spoke in Einari. "If they *are* using the tunnels, the Secret Keepers need to know about it." She turned to Briana. "As soon as your father returns from the Palace of Golden Eternity, we'll show him the blank map Ennolar gave us."

Briana stared blankly at Aisha. Kodyn noted the vacant expression, the fearful tremor in Briana's hands, and the way her eyes darted around as if seeing enemies in every shadow. She'd recovered from her captivity at the Gatherers' hands, only to find herself attacked once more in her home. That could leave scars on even the strongest person.

To her credit, the Shalandran girl finally managed to speak. "Yes," she said in a quiet voice. "My father."

Aisha went over to sit beside the girl, provide the reassurance of her presence. Kodyn knew of what Aisha had endured at the hands of the Bloody Hand—she'd be best-suited to help Briana get through the traumatic experience.

Uncertain of what to do, Kodyn set about examining the corpses scattered across the floor. Each of their right forearms bore the mark of the Gatherers. However, none wore headbands, *kohl*, or beauty marks to identify their caste. He hadn't been in Shalandra long enough to distinguish the upper and lower castes. Yet, the fact that they were hard, lean men told him that they couldn't be the heavy-set *Dhukari*. Perhaps *Alqati*, but he guessed it was more likely they were *Kabili*, *Mahjuri*, or *Earaqi*.

Not that that information helped much right now. But at least the discovery confirmed the suspicions that had led him to accompany Briana here to Shalandra. The Gatherers in Praamis had been a fraction of their true number, which meant killing them hadn't put an end to the threat to Briana. Had he and Aisha—*Aisha, mostly*—not been here, the girl would have been captured again. Or, worse, killed in the attempt.

He tensed as the sound of pounding feet echoed in the corridor and spun toward the door, dagger and sword held ready. He'd fight to his last breath—the Gatherers would die before he let them take Briana.

The tightness faded from his shoulders as men wearing the gold breastplates of Suroth's household guard charged into the room. They, however, didn't relax. Instead, they seemed to perceive him as a threat—despite the fact that the bodies of the assassins clearly lay littered around him and Lady Briana was safe—and raised their swords to attack.

"Hold!" The shout came from Rothin, the head of Suroth's guards. "They're Lady Briana's bodyguards."

Kodyn only lowered his weapons *after* the guards sheathed theirs. He wouldn't take any chances, not after hearing that one of the guards and Briana's own maidservant had played a role in her abduction.

Rothin's eyes widened as he stared at the bodies littering the floor. "The two of you did this?"

Kodyn inclined his head toward Aisha. "Mostly her. I arrived in time for the clean-up."

Rothin shot an incredulous glance at the Ghandian girl on the bed beside Briana, then back at Kodyn. "The Arch-Guardian clearly made the right choice in bringing you on." He held out a hand. "Without you, we would have had only bad news to deliver to our master upon his return from the palace."

Kodyn gripped the man's hand. His eyes mirrored the sincerity that echoed in his voice.

"We got lucky," Aisha said. "Lady Briana and I were on the garden terrace and saw them coming."

Rothin winced. "Some of our own were working with these men and opened the tradesman's entrance. We managed to take one alive. Nessa will have the truth out of them by daybreak." He crouched and stared down at the tattoo inked into one of the assassin's forearms.

"Gatherers," Kodyn said. "They were responsible for taking Lady Briana out of Shalandra last time."

"Accursed cultist!" Rothin growled down at the body. "Twisting our reverence of the Long Keeper as an excuse for their bloodshed and murder." He stood and fixed Kodyn and Aisha with a solemn gaze. "The guard will be doubled, and I will *only* put men I trust on duty. By the Sleepless One, I swear this will never happen again."

"Thank you, Rothin." Briana had recovered enough to speak in a quiet voice. "My father always trusted you, even after everything that happened with Osirath and Eldesse."

"My lady honors me." Rothin bowed. "And I will do everything in my power to live up to the Arch-Guardian's trust."

He turned to his men. "Search the rest of the mansion. If there are any more of these damned death worshippers hiding, I want them found at once."

With a nod to the three of them, Rothin stalked out of the room, his guards on his heels. Kodyn had little doubt the man would be as good as his word. Rothin seemed to be a good man put in the unfortunate position of finding himself surrounded by traitors.

At that moment, Nessa appeared at the door.

"Oh, Nessa!" Briana stood and ran toward the Steward. "I'm so glad you're…" She trailed off, her brow furrowing. "What's wrong?"

Nessa's face had gone the same ashen grey as her hair. Sorrow glimmered in her dark eyes and tears streamed down her age-lined face.

"Word has come from the Palace of Golden Eternity," she said in a quiet voice. "The Gatherers made an attempt on the Keeper's Council."

Briana sucked in a sharp breath. A dagger of ice drove into Kodyn's belly. From the look on Nessa's face, he knew *exactly* what she was about to say.

"The Pharus and the Necroseti survived." Nessa wiped her tears and reached for Briana. "But your father…"

"No!" Briana gasped, hand flying to her mouth. Kodyn leapt forward to catch her as her legs gave way.

"Forgive me, Lady Briana." Nessa bowed her head. "Your father was slain in the attack."

# Chapter Forty-Two

Anxiety thrummed within Issa's chest as she marched through the Palace of Golden Eternity. Bodies lay strewn everywhere, the golden tiles and walls splashed with the blood of traitors. Servants, Blades, Indomitables, even a member of the Keeper's Council had died in the attack on the Pharus.

What started out as a good day had ended in anguish. At least Etai had survived the attack—she'd bear a scar on her cheek, but she'd gotten lucky to escape with such a minor wound. Kellas' armor and skill had saved him.

A six-man squad of Keeper's Blades—all *Ypertatos* assigned to the Pharus' personal guard—had relieved her two hours earlier. The adrenaline rush brought on by the attack had refused to let her rest despite her fatigue. She'd volunteered to aid in the clean-up efforts.

Then the summons had come in the form of a stone-faced Tannard.

"The Pharus demands your presence," was all the *Invictus* had said.

Now, striding along behind Tannard, Issa could only swallow down her nervous anxiety. *Did Kellas tell the Invictus I abandoned my post? Is the Pharus going to personally expel me from the Blades for deserting my comrades?*

She tried to tell herself that worrying wouldn't solve anything, that she'd find out what the Pharus wanted with her soon enough. It didn't help. Her stomach was a mess of knots as she followed Tannard through the massive gold and silver leaf-decorated double doors that led into the Pharus' private chambers.

Pharus Amhoset Nephelcheres sat on an enormous golden throne, with massive eagle's wings at the crest, velvet-cushioned armrests, and a plush seat. Above and behind him, high-relief carvings in the sandstone depicted the stern faces of men—likely the Pharuses before him—frowning down at the back of his head. A reminder, perhaps, that his ancestors knew every decision he made.

To Issa's surprise, the Lady of Blades stood guard beside the throne. General of the Shalandran military, the highest-ranked officer in the Keeper's Blade, yet she was given the duty of guarding the Pharus that all in Shalandra knew she hated. She hadn't bothered to wash the blood off her armor, face, and hands.

Tannard stopped at the silver line that marked the respectful distance from the throne and Issa did likewise.

"Issa of the *Earaqi*," the *Invictus* said.

The Pharus stared at her in silence for a long moment. His eyes, dark and almond-shaped like all Shalandrans, bored into her with a piercing scrutiny that discomfited her far more than Tannard's cold disdain. His lips twisted into a pensive frown, his strong brow furrowed.

Issa forced down her anxiety and stood straight, head held high. No matter what happened here, even if the Pharus decided to punish her for deserting her post, at least she had the knowledge that she'd saved the Lady of Blades and helped to foil the attack.

"I find myself in a curious position," the Pharus said, his tone musing. "It is not often that I am indebted to one of my subjects."

Issa held her breath. *Indebted?* That, and the fact that he addressed her with the informal "I" and "me" rather than the regal "we" and "us", set her curiosity burning. Whatever he had summoned her for, it bore greater importance than she currently understood.

"I am told that you are the one that gave warning of the attack." The Pharus raised an eyebrow. "Is that so?"

After a moment, Issa nodded. "Yes, Bright One. But my comrades—"

"Yes, I know of the actions of your fellow Blades-in-training, Etai and Kellas." Pharus Amhoset Nephelcheres gave a dismissive wave. "I have heard all about it from your commander." He shot a glance at Lady Callista, the sneer on his lips a match for the venom in his words. "Despite our…differences, I can admit that the Lady of Blades may have something wise to offer from time to time."

Callista Vinaus' face could have been cut from shalanite for all the emotion her face revealed. Despite her well-known disdain for the Pharus, she was on duty and would comport herself with the respect due her monarch.

The Pharus snapped his fingers and a servant hurried forward. The Pharus lifted a small glass vial from the tray in the servant's hands. "Do you recognize this?" he asked Issa.

Issa stared at the vial a long second. "Yes," she said finally. "The assassins carried them." The acid had very nearly killed her, Etai, and Kellas.

He pursed his lips. "It seems these assassins not only plotted my death, but they intended to make me suffer. A truly cruel, agonizing end." His eyes fixed on her and he leaned forward. "An end I was only spared by *your* actions."

"It is no more than my duty," Issa said. "I swore myself to serve the Long Keeper and his servant on Einan. You, My Pharus."

"A good answer." A smile tugged at the Pharus' lips as he leaned back in his throne. Long seconds passed as his strong fingers toyed with the little glass vial filled with acid.

"Tell me, Issa of the *Earaqi*," he finally said, "if I offered you anything in Shalandra, what would you ask for?" His almond-colored eyes once again pierced her, as if reading her soul.

Issa hesitated. He clearly expected an answer, but what? Her next words could have a direct effect on the rest of her life.

She chose the honest answer. "Nothing, my Pharus."

"Nothing?" The Pharus arched a dark eyebrow. "Is there nothing your heart desires?"

Issa drew in a deep breath. "I have already been honored with everything I desire. I am chosen by the Long Keeper to serve him, you, and the city of Shalandra. When I am Anointed, my grandparents will be elevated to the *Dhukari* and given the better life they deserve. I serve the Lady of Blades and my Pharus. What more could I want?"

The Pharus' face revealed nothing, but the intensity of his gaze set Issa's insides quailing. Had she said the wrong thing? Had she offended him by not requesting a reward?

To Issa's surprise, the Lady of Blades broke the silence. "See, my Pharus?" Her stiff guard posture relaxed for a moment as she turned toward the ruler. "She is as I told you."

"Indeed." A broad smile wreathed Amhoset's handsome face and he leaned back in his golden throne. "For once, you do not disappoint me, Lady Callista."

Callista Vinaus' face hardened and her spine went rigid as she returned to her guard stance.

"Many in your position would have asked for wealth, power, even a place in my court." He steepled his fingers beneath his chin and stared at her with that same curious smile. "Yet the fact that you do not shows an innate nobility that not even the thugs in the Keeper's Blades could hammer out of you. A person like that is a person that can be trusted to serve me."

Issa bowed. "I am honored to serve in whatever capacity my Pharus requires."

The Pharus snapped his fingers. "Clear the room."

The two servants that stood at attention behind the throne scurried out of a side door. Issa struggled to conceal her surprise as not only Tannard turned and marched out of the room, but Lady Callista as well. The door closed behind the black-armored Lady of Blades, leaving her alone with the Pharus.

"What I am about to say, few outside this room know." Pharus Amhoset Nephelcheres spoke in a grave voice, his face a solemn mask. "With your deeds and words, you prove yourself one I can trust as I seek to root out the *true* threat behind tonight's attack."

Issa remained silent, but nervous anxiety hummed within her.

"The Lady of Blades has questioned every one of the Blades and Indomitables on duty tonight and found them innocent of treachery." The Pharus' brows pressed together into a frown. "Which means someone else, someone within my own household, played a role in tonight's attack."

He leaned forward and spoke in a low voice. "The assassins belong to an offshoot of the Necroseti, a cult that calls themselves 'the Gatherers'. As of yet, we have not ascertained if they serve the Necroseti directly or operate on their own. For now, we are operating on the assumption that they answer to Councilor Madani and the others of the Keeper's Priests."

Issa sucked in a breath. *What?*

The Pharus nodded. "The Gatherers did not enter the palace through any of the side or rear gates, and the guards all swear that no one got past them. Which means the assassins had help from the inside. The Palace of Golden Eternity has many hidden ways, vulnerabilities that not even Lady Callista and I know the full extent of. Right now, there are only three people in the world I do not suspect. You, myself, of course, and Arch-Guardian Suroth."

Issa's gut tightened at the memory of the silent, brown-robed form lying among the assassins. Arch-Guardian Suroth had been kind to her during the trial of stone.

"Suroth was one of the few people in the city I fully trusted," the Pharus explained. "He sacrificed himself fighting off the Gatherers to give me and the rest of the Keeper's Council time to flee to safety. He killed nearly a dozen before the accursed Gatherers brought him down." Sorrow filled his eyes. "His death is truly a great loss to all of Shalandra."

The sight of the Pharus' sorrow struck Issa as terribly odd. The Pharus was revered by all in Shalandra as the Long Keeper's servant on Einan, yet the man before her seemed so...human.

The Pharus bowed his head. "He died protecting me," he said in a quiet voice. A long moment of silence passed before he looked up. "It is only fitting that we honor his sacrifice by protecting the thing he cared about most in the world: his daughter. A job I entrust to you."

Issa barely managed to stifle her protest. *Dhukari* were bred to arrogance—Kellas served as a prime example of their haughty disdain for the lower castes. *And he wants me to babysit one?* That was the last thing she wanted. Issa ached to continue her training and help hunt down the Gatherers, not take care of an entitled girl.

Yet she managed to school her expression and conceal her true thoughts. "It will be an honor, my Pharus."

The Pharus' lips quirked in to a wry smile. "I'm certain." Evidently, she hadn't done as good of a job of concealing her thoughts as she'd believed.

"I have received word that Lady Briana was also the target of an attack by the Gatherers tonight," Pharus Amhoset Nephelcheres told her. "And, I have it on good authority that the Gatherers were the ones behind the young lady's mysterious disappearance in the first place."

Issa frowned. The only reason she could think of for abducting the Arch-Guardian's daughter would be to use her as leverage against him. His position on the Keeper's Council and guardian of the Vault of Ancients made him a prime target, especially if the Necroseti *was* the hand behind the Gatherers.

"The Arch-Guardian may be dead," the Pharus told her, "but until I am certain his daughter is safe, I must have someone I can trust watching out for her."

"Of course, my Pharus." This time, Issa meant it.

"When the time comes, you *will* be summoned once more," the Pharus told her. "When I am ready to move against those who sought my death, I would have you leading the charge."

"My Pharus honors me," Issa said with a bow.

The Pharus nodded and sat back in his chair. "Go, young Blade. Carry out this duty with the eternal gratitude of your Pharus." With a wave, he dismissed her. "As a Blade I once knew used to say, 'Strike first, strike true'."

Issa froze halfway into her ceremonial bow. The words sent a chill down Issa's spine. *A...Blade?*

She recovered quickly, turned, and marched out of the room. Yet her mind raced as she strode through the double doors. The words had been the last thing her grandfather said to her as she departed.

Suddenly, the way Saba had reacted when she told him she'd been accepted into the Blades took on a new meaning. *Was my father or mother a Blade? Both of them?* Her grandfather had always refused to tell her about them.

The thought set her head whirling, adding to the chaos in her mind. She'd walked into the Pharus' Chambers expecting punishment, only to find herself drawn into something far larger than anything she'd imagined as an *Earaqi* girl training to fight in the Crucible. And possibly someone who knew her parents—the Pharus himself!

*What the fiery hell have I gotten myself into?*

The huge double doors *boomed* shut behind her, driving home Issa's confusion. She stared in numb silence at the two Blades that stood waiting for her.

Lady Callista fixed her with a gaze as piercingly sharp as the Pharus'. Yet there was something strange written in her eyes. She was searching Issa's face for…what? Issa couldn't decipher the meaning of the tight expression on Lady Callista's face. She could only hold her head high and try to conceal the turmoil raging within her.

"We will speak again soon, *Prototopoi*. Count on it." The words, so sudden, spoken in a sharp voice, were the last thing Lady Callista said before turning on her heel and marching into the Pharus' Chambers.

This only added to the knots forming in Issa's stomach. The words held a depth of meaning, one Issa failed to understand. Too many things were flying at her from all sides. The revelation of the Gatherers. The Pharus' gratitude. Her grandfather's words from the Pharus' lips. And now something strange from Lady Callista.

*What the hell is going on?*

"The Pharus honors you." Tannard spoke in a hard voice, edged with a sneer that made the word "*honor*" sound like he was spitting in her face.

At least *this* was one thing that hadn't changed. She knew how to face up to Tannard's contempt.

She turned toward him, her jaw clenched. "I swore to serve him, just as you did."

Tannard loomed over her, his face the same icy mask as always. "Do not for *one second* think that this new duty absolves you of your duty to the Keeper's Blades."

Issa's gut clenched. "I would never—"

"You will continue your training as befits a *prototopoi*," Tannard snarled. For an instant, anger cracked his expressionless façade. "I will see to it that you make time for your lessons and practice, no matter what."

He jabbed a finger in her chest. "This reward does not give you a way to escape me. We're not done, not by a long shot, little *Earaqi*." He spat the word like a curse and lowered his voice to a growl. "We're just getting started!"

# Chapter Forty-Three

Ice slithered down Evren's spine and he sucked in a sharp breath. *Hailen!*

Snarth pressed the edge of his dagger harder against the boy's throat. "Do anything stupid and he'll have to breathe through a hole in his neck." His eyes darted to the twin *jambiyas* in Evren's hands. "Drop those, now."

Evren's gaze locked with Hailen's. He saw no fear written in Hailen's violet eyes, only the sort of wary hesitance one experienced with a blade a heartbeat from severing their throat. Hailen's eyes indicated his hand, his lips pressed into a resolute line.

"So be it." Evren didn't drop the daggers, but crouched and placed them on the floor.

"Kick them over to me," Snarth ordered.

Evren shook his head. "I don't think so."

Snarth's eyes widened a fraction, and he seemed taken aback. "I'm the one holding the knife to your brother's throat, here. You do what I tell you."

"You *are* the one with the knife," Evren said, "but think about what that means." He gestured at their surroundings. "Right now, you're threatening the personal servant of Lady Briana, daughter of one of the highest-ranking men in Shalandra. One word from me brings the guards running. What do you think they'll do when they find you here?"

Snarth scowled. "It'll be too late for your brother! He'll be bleeding out onto the floor and beyond a physicker's help."

"Yes, he will." Evren snarled, his face hardening. "But right now he's the only thing that's stopping me from pounding the shite out of you." He bared his teeth in a growl. "And if you harm him, I won't just stop at a bruised jaw. I'll break every traitorous bone in your Keeper-damned body, then I'll drag you through the streets to Killian's—"

"Shut up!" Snarth growled, but a hint of desperate fear cracked his anger. "Killian can never know that you saw me meeting with the Ybrazhe. I'd rather die here than let him find out I'm working with the Syndicate." His lip twisted into a snarl. "But, by the Keeper, I'll be damned if I die alone!"

Evren's gut clenched as Snarth's dagger arm tensed. "Or," he said before the Mumbler could drag the blade along Hailen's throat, "you could take the third option."

"Third option?" Snarth sneered. "What's that?"

"You run." Evren shrugged. "You leave Shalandra before Killian finds out you've betrayed him to the Syndicate." He didn't know who the Syndicate was, but Snarth's fear of discovery made it clear they were at odds with Killian. "Go to Praamis, Voramis, hell, even go across the Frozen Sea. Run and never look back."

The doubt that flickered in Snarth's eyes brought a surge of hope to Evren's chest.

"If you leave right now," he pressed, "I swear on my brother's life that I won't say anything to Killian. You can start a new life somewhere far from here." He dropped his voice to a low growl. "But *only* if you run now."

For a moment, Snarth almost gave in. Evren could see it in his eyes; he wanted to flee, wanted to escape his life as a Shalandran street rat.

Then the moment passed and Snarth's sneer returned. "Think you can trick me with your clever words?" He pressed the dagger harder against Hailen's neck. "It won't work on me!"

Evren's eyes followed the crimson droplet that slid down Hailen's pale skin. He'd heard the Hunter's stories of what the boy's blood could do—his heritage as a *Melechha,* descendant of the Serenii, gave him extraordinary abilities when his blood came in contact with Serenii artifacts.

But none of that mattered. He cared nothing for the blood or the power it promised. All that mattered was Hailen, the boy that had become his younger brother. Snarth was threatening Hailen's life and Evren wouldn't let that stand.

His eyes darted around the coat room in search of anything he could use to distract the Mumbler. Snarth had fast reflexes, but Evren was faster. He just needed to get that dagger away from Hailen's throat!

"It's no trick," he told Snarth. "I'm offering you a chance to get out of here before Suroth's guards find you. That's a better offer than you'll get from Killian when he finds out that you're working for the Syndicate."

"Which is why you're not going to tell him!" Snarth shouted.

"Think about that for a moment." Evren cocked an eyebrow. "Play this out. You cut Hailen's throat, I beat you senseless then either call Suroth's guards or haul you to Killian myself. You try to drag Hailen out of here, someone sees you and the end result is the same. Even if you somehow get out of the mansion the same way you came in—" Evren guessed Snarth had used the distraction of the kidnapping attempt to slip through the open back gate. "—you're not going to get far threatening a *Dhukari's* servant. One look at your headbands and the Indomitables are going to be all over you."

Snarth's face fell and dismay twisted his expression as he came to the same conclusion.

"The only way out of here is without bloodshed." Evren took a step toward Snarth, then another. "Leave now and no one gets hurt."

"Back!" Snarth shouted. "Stay back, or I'll—"

The Mumbler made the mistake of removing the blade from Hailen's throat and pointing it at Evren. With surprising speed, Hailen spun in Snarth's grip, his right hand driving straight at the older boy's torso. The dagger he'd concealed in the folds of his robe punched into Snarth's stomach.

Snarth fell back with a cry, and Hailen leapt backward and ducked to avoid the desperate swipe of the Mumbler's dagger. At the same moment, Evren snatched Hailen's collar and dragged him farther backwards, well out of Snarth's dagger range.

Snarth stumbled against a rack of coats, a hand clasped to the wound in his gut. Blood trickled down the front of his tunic and stained his trousers. Pain pinched his face and turned his skin pale. He stared wide-eyed at the crimson-stained dagger in Hailen's hand.

"Go!" Evren shouted and thrust a finger toward the narrow door. "Get out of here, Snarth, and pray to the Long Keeper that you get to a physicker in time."

With a half-groan, half-cry of terror, Snarth stumbled out of the little room and into the mansion's main corridor.

Evren didn't need to pursue—if Snarth lived long enough to get out of the mansion and to a physicker, he'd be confined to a bed for days, maybe weeks, as the torn muscles in his gut healed. By then, Killian would know of his treachery.

Instead, he turned, tore a linen dress from a metal hanger, and pressed it against Hailen's neck.

"Evren!" Hailen tried to shove his hands away. "It's just a scratch!"

Evren's heart hammered in his ribs as he removed the linen and studied the wound. To his relief, it really *was* just a scratch.

He pulled Hailen into a tight hug. "Keeper's teeth! You know the Hunter and Kiara would *never* forgive me if I let anything happen to you."

"I'm not a child anymore," Hailen protested and squirmed out of Evren's embrace. "I don't need everyone always looking out for me. I'm here to *help* you find the Blade of Hallar. If I wanted to be babied, I would have stayed in the House of Need in Voramis."

Evren wanted to argue, but he couldn't deny that Hailen *had* grown a lot since they first met. The naïve child he'd met on the road to Enarium had grown. As he'd proven today, he could take care of himself. He was more than just Evren's burden—he was his brother and, like it or not, they were on this mission together.

"You're right," Evren said with a nod. "You're not a child. But that doesn't mean I'm not going to worry. I've got to have your back, just like you've got mine. Like the Hunter and Kiara, we've got to watch out for each other."

"Always." Hailen grinned. "But don't think for a minute that you're getting your dagger back!" He used the bloody linen to wipe his blade clean.

"No, I think it's better that you have it."

Hailen's eyes went wide. "Really? You mean it?"

Evren nodded. "You need to be able to protect yourself."

"So I can have a sword, too?" Hailen's violet eyes sparkled. "Like the Hunter has?"

Evren expression went flat. "Let's just start with a dagger." He had *no* intention of letting Hailen anywhere near a proper weapon if he could help it. The boy had proven far more adept at letters than swordplay.

Evren's mind raced as he tried to figure out his next move. He hadn't gotten anywhere near close enough to the Blade of Hallar, but over the last couple of days he'd made progress on his mission. He knew of the secret way into the Palace of Golden Eternity, the way Samall and his traitors had gotten in. By aiding in the defense of the mansion, he'd earned the Arch-Guardian's goodwill—perhaps enough that he could use it to get inside the palace to start scoping it out for a safe route to the Vault of Ancients.

But first, he had to get to Killian with news of Snarth and the Syndicate—the Mumbler had called them the *Ybrazhe,* whatever that meant. That, and the information on the people that had attacked Suroth's mansion, would more than satisfy the blacksmith that Evren was holding up his side of the bargain. And, if Evren was lucky, he might be able to talk Killian into giving him more information to aid him in his mission to get into the vault.

"Hailen, I need you to get to Lady Briana and stay as close to her as possible," Evren said. "Right now, the mansion's going to be on high alert, so the safest place to be is by her side."

"What about you?" Hailen asked.

"I need to get to Killian and tell him everything." Evren placed a hand on Hailen's shoulder. "But I'll be back before—"

"Wait!" Excitement sparkled in Hailen's eyes. "Before you go, I need to show you something."

Evren's brow furrowed. "Can it wait?" He'd had a long couple of days and nights—he could use a few minutes of rest before the sun rose.

"No!" Hailen seized his hand and hauled on his arm. "You need to see this."

With an internal sigh, Evren allowed the boy to drag him through the corridors.

The guards in gold breastplates fixed the two of them with a hard look, but they'd all seen Evren dragging the unconscious Samall. Right now, he guessed the guards would mostly leave him alone—at least until it came time for someone to serve Lady Briana's breakfast. He was, after all, a servant.

Hailen led him to the door at the far end of the hall. Evren recognized it—it was the one room in the mansion that he *hadn't* been permitted to clean.

"Hailen!" Evren hissed. "This is the Arch-Guardian's private study. We're not supposed to be here."

"Just trust me," Hailen whispered. "This is important." He slid open the door and slipped inside.

Evren's brow furrowed as he followed. *What's important?*

Suroth's office was surprisingly neat, for a Secret Keeper. Evren had expected chaos on par with the hurricane of clutter that adorned every surface in Graeme's secret back rooms. Here, parchments lay strewn across the vast desk that occupied the center of the room, but the shelves stood empty save for a handful of strange-shaped stone ornaments. He could make out no discernible use for the objects, but his eyes flew wide as he recognized the strange Serenii symbols etched into their smooth black surfaces.

Hailen strode over to the shelf and reached for one, a long cylindrical stone roughly the width of Evren's middle finger and half the length of his forearm.

"Remember when I told you that Father Reverentus and the Cambionari were teaching me magic words?" Hailen asked, hefting the object. "Serenii words of power?"

Evren narrowed his eyes. "Yes, but what does that—"

"Watch."

Excitement sparkling in his eyes, Hailen touched a finger to the wound in his neck. The bleeding had slowed but crimson still glistened on his skin. He pressed his crimson-stained finger to the flat end of the cylinder.

Hailen began to chant in a strange language Evren had never heard. Though the words held no meaning to him, there was no mistaking the power they held. A shiver ran down Evren's spine and the room seemed to fill with a subtle crackle of energy. Evren could almost feel his hairs standing on end as Hailen's voice grew louder, the power filling the room.

His eyes flew wide as the cylindrical stone in Hailen's hands started to glow, brighter and brighter, pushing back the gloom of Suroth's office with an azure brilliance.

Evren stepped back as the blue glow emanating from the stone in the boy's hand grew blinding. He shielded his eyes, but it seemed the light passed through his palms to pierce his eyelids. The energy grew so thick Evren felt he could cut it with a knife. Something pressed on his eardrums and thrummed deep within his stomach, all the way to the core of his being.

With a loud *fwash,* the stone gave off one final brilliant flash of light and dimmed to a low radiance, as if the room was lit by torches and oil lamps rather than the midday sun.

Yet the light came from no lantern or torch. Instead, a soft glow emanated from the stone in Hailen's hand, which shone with an internal light.

At that moment, the door to the adjoining room burst open.

# Chapter Forty-Four

Kodyn had never felt as helpless as he did at that moment. He sat on Arch-Guardian Suroth's bed and held Briana as she wept, but he could find no words of comfort to offer.

She wouldn't care that her father had slain nearly a dozen of his assailants and saved the Pharus' life. All that mattered was that her one parent, the only one she'd had since birth, had been taken in the Long Keeper's arms. She was alone in the world now.

A twinge of guilt ran through him. *If I'd delivered Suroth's purse to the Black Widow, would it have changed anything?* He still felt the smooth, round object sitting in the purse in his pocket, a burden far heavier than its true weight. The question had no answer—if he hadn't followed the Gatherers, he wouldn't have been back in time to help fight off the last of the assassins. The Gatherers hadn't spoken of killing Suroth, so Kodyn had made the choice to come for Briana first.

He didn't regret the decision, yet he couldn't shut off the part of his mind that felt he deserved the blame. Just as he'd blamed himself when Sid got kidnapped in Praamis. He'd promised to protect them—look how that had turned out both times.

Aisha stood nearby, a solid presence that filled him with a sense of comfort. She hadn't let Briana down. Aisha had defeated more than a dozen assassins alone. Her strength and determination throughout the entire ordeal—including whatever internal struggle she'd been fighting—humbled him.

Aisha tensed as the door opened, but relaxed as she caught sight of Nessa. The grey-haired Steward nodded at the Ghandian girl and padded quietly across the plush carpets surrounding Suroth's massive bed.

"Briana," Nessa said in a calm, soothing voice, "I know this is the last thing on your mind, but you need to eat." She glanced around. "At the very least, let me get you out of those clothes and into something clean."

Briana hadn't washed the crimson from her hands and face or changed out of her blood-splattered dress. She shrugged off Nessa's hands. "No," she sobbed. "Just let me be here a little longer."

Upon learning of her father's death, she'd fled to the safety of his bedroom. Her tears stained the velvet pillowcases, but she was beyond caring.

Nessa tried again. "Please, *taltha*. A little broth or some fruit? You need to keep up your strength."

For answer, Briana only shook her head.

Nessa's expression looked as helpless as Kodyn felt. With a little sigh, the grey-haired Steward stood.

"When she finishes grieving, I'll have a servant standing by with food and fresh clothing," Nessa told Aisha in a quiet voice.

Aisha nodded, sorrow sparkling in her dark eyes.

As Kodyn watched Nessa slip out of the Arch-Guardian's room, his eyes fell on the strangely smooth black stone trinket on Suroth's bedside table. No, not a trinket. An object of indeterminate purpose, yet upon closer inspection, he saw the familiar strange, intricate markings of the Serenii etched into the stone.

*With Suroth's death, where does that leave my Undertaking?* The thought came to his mind unbidden, and he shoved it away, cursing himself for his selfishness. He worried about something as inane as stealing the Crown of the Pharus when Briana had just lost her father.

The Arch-Guardian's death made it all the more important for him to stay in Shalandra. Not only because it was a huge setback to his plans to get into the Serenii vaults, but because he felt obligated to protect Briana. He'd brought her home knowing the danger she faced—had he unknowingly caused her father's death?

*Blaming myself isn't going to get vengeance for Briana's father.* He clenched his jaw. *I'm going to make sure the Gatherers are stopped, once and for all. Even if I have to kill them all myself.*

That would be stupid. He couldn't take them all on alone. He'd need help—from the Black Widow, certainly, perhaps from Ennolar and the Secret Keepers. They'd want vengeance for their Arch-Guardian's death as much as Briana.

But he couldn't do that if he had to worry about her wellbeing.

"Briana," he spoke in a quiet voice, "how would you feel about returning to Praamis? My mother would—"

Briana sat bolt upright, eyes flashing. "You're thinking of running?"

"Never!" Kodyn shook his head. "I'm staying in Shalandra so I can hunt down every damned one of the Gatherers. I will avenge your father's death, I swear on my life." He let out a slow breath. "But I'd feel better knowing *you* were somewhere safe, far out of the Gatherers' reach. In the Night Guild—"

"No!" Briana's response, a defiant shout, surprised him. "I will not flee!"

Defiance shone through the tears filling her eyes. Her face, puffy from crying, twisted into a mask of determination.

"The Gatherers tried to use me to cow my father into submission," Briana said, her voice a half-snarl. "They attacked my home and killed my father. I'll be damned if I let them get away with that."

"But here, you're in danger," Kodyn protested. "At least in Praamis I'll know you're out of harm's way."

"I will not let them win!" Briana straightened, a hand dashing the tears from her cheeks. "They seek to use fear as their weapons, but they will find I am not afraid of them."

The fear in Briana's eyes belied the firmness in her voice, but Kodyn had to admire her strength of spirit. Despite everything she'd lost, she still stood strong. Or, at least, tried to. It would take her time to grieve her father and come to grips with his death, but just hearing her words brought a sense of peace. She would get through this. And he'd be here beside her to help any way he could. He owed her that much, at least.

Briana stared down at her hands, still covered in blood, and suddenly she gave a little gasp. "Oh!"

Kodyn was instantly alert. "What is it?" His hand dropped to his sword. "What's wrong?"

"The map!"

To Kodyn's surprise, Briana leapt up and darted out of the room. He raced after her, Aisha on his heels, as she rushed into her bedroom. She grimaced at the disaster of her bedroom—the guards had dragged out the bodies, but blood still stained the floor.

She scooped up the leather scroll tube and turned back to the door. Kodyn's eyes flew wide as she stooped and dipped a finger into a puddle of crimson.

"Here." She thrust the scroll tube into his hands. "Open it and spread out the map on my father's table." Tears still rimmed her eyes, but a strange excitement seemed to have pushed back her sorrow.

Stunned, Kodyn followed the girl back into Suroth's bedroom, fumbled open the scroll tube cap, and, with Aisha's help, unrolled Ennolar's map. He spread the blank scroll out on the table and fixed her with a curious gaze. "What now?"

Triumph shone in Briana's eyes as she held up her bloody finger. "The blood is the key!" She pressed the finger against one corner of the paper.

Kodyn sucked in a breath as the material seemed to absorb the blood from her skin. Instantly, thin lines of crimson began to appear on the papyrus, spreading outward like a spider web. But these lines were neat, crisp, drawn by a confident hand. Beside them were neat annotations written in a language he didn't understand, but recognized as Secret Keeper script—the same script that filled the book Journeyman Donneh of House Scorpion had stolen from the Temple of Whispers in Voramis.

"My father called it invisible ink," Briana told them. "It only works on a particular type of papyrus, made using a recipe known only to the Secret Keepers. The more mundane inks work with the heat of a candle's flame or acids, but for something this important, only blood can activate it."

Kodyn's mind raced. "So Ennolar *did* give us the real map!"

Briana nodded. "He assumed my father would tell us how to use it." Sorrow flooded her eyes and her face fell.

Kodyn placed a hand on her shoulder, and Aisha gripped her arm. Briana brushed a tear from her cheek and gave them a sad smile. "I-I'm fine."

"You don't have to be," Kodyn said. "I know I wouldn't be if I were you."

"Here in Shalandra, we view death differently than the rest of Einan." Briana gave a little shrug of her shoulders. "Each of us is called to the Long Keeper's arms when it is our time. If my father is gone, it was meant to be." She looked like she was trying to convince herself of the words. "He would want us to continue fighting. And he would want me to honor the bargain he made with you."

The words, spoken with such strength and determination, caught Kodyn by surprise.

Briana fixed him with a firm gaze. "I might not be the Arch-Guardian of the Secret Keepers, but I will do what I can to help. Starting with this map." She bent over the parchment and studied the thin crimson lines and markings. "I can read a few of these symbols, but I'll need time to fully understand what they're saying. And I'll need my father's private journals."

She strode around the bed and set about rummaging through the drawers in her father's bedside table.

"My father used two types of ciphers to write," she explained. "One was the secret language used in the Temple of Whispers, but the other was a special cipher he devised just for the two of us to understand. That way, he could translate everything he wanted to share with me into that code, but the information would still be protected. No one would be able to steal it and the Secret Keepers would never know what secrets he was teaching me. Aha!"

Briana held up a thick, leather-bound volume in triumph. "This holds the key to translating the Secret Keepers' language into our shared code." She plopped the book onto the bed with a loud *thump,* opened it, and flipped through the stiff pages. The markings within made no sense to Kodyn, but Briana seemed to recognize their meaning.

"Huh?" She stopped on one page, which bore six lines of neatly printed symbols. "That's odd."

"What is it?" Kodyn asked.

"I've never seen this before." Briana ran a thumb along the symbols and read aloud:

*When sword and scepter unite*
*The blood of ancients revived*
*Child of Secrets, Child of Spirits, Child of Gold*
*Half-master seeks the relic of old*
*Then Hallar's blood shall rise*
*And sew the final destruction from midnight eyes*

She looked up, confused. "What does that mean?"

Kodyn's blood ran cold. He knew *exactly* what it meant.

"The Gatherer, Necroset Kytos, he rambled on about some Final Destruction before my mother ended him," Kodyn said. "He warned of 'Hallar's prophesied destruction', said the world would be washed away in a torrent of blood and scoured by fire." He frowned. "It sounded like the ramblings of a madman, but—"

"But if my father wrote it here, it has to mean something!" Briana stared down at the symbols, her lips moving as she read.

"When we were coming into the city, did anyone else notice the words 'Child of Gold' painted onto the walls?" Aisha asked.

"Yes!" Kodyn sucked in a breath. "And I saw 'Child of Spirits' painted on the Artisan's Tier." His mind raced. "That can't be a coincidence."

His brow furrowed. "The way Kytos talked about it, he was terrified of this Final Destruction. And it seems your father placed some importance on it as well."

"But what does it mean?" Briana's expression grew puzzled. "Hallar's blood shall rise? Blood of ancients revived? Sew the final destruction from midnight eyes? That makes no sense!"

"I don't know." Kodyn shrugged. "But if your father put it in his private journal, it has to be important enough for us to find out, right?"

After a moment, Briana nodded. "He only included things related to the Serenii in here." She tapped the journal with a delicate finger. "Somehow, that strange poem is connected to the Serenii that built the city thousands of years ago."

Eager excitement burned within Kodyn. He'd always loved stories of the ancient race of immortal beings that had disappeared from Einan, leaving only their strange buildings behind. But as Kodyn looked around the bedroom, he realized that the Serenii hadn't just left *buildings*.

"These things," he gestured to the black stone objects sitting on Suroth's bedside table, "they *are* Serenii artifacts, aren't they?"

Briana nodded. "Yes, my father was studying them."

Kodyn couldn't help gasping. Serenii artifacts were beyond rare, considered some of the most valuable objects on Einan. Few in the Night Guild could ever boast of seeing any, much less stealing one. Yet here, hundreds of leagues from home, he stood in a room littered with them. He couldn't help marveling—*how much power does this room hold?*

Something strange reached his ears, and every muscle in his body tensed. It was a sound, yet like nothing he'd ever heard before. A deep humming that set his heart racing, piercing to the core of his being. It seemed to come from everywhere around him at once, yet his eyes caught a glimmer of light through the closed doors that led to Suroth's office.

Aisha seemed to see it, too, for she drew her *assegai* just as he pulled a dagger from his belt.

"Get down!" Kodyn hissed to Briana. The Shalandran girl ducked behind the desk as Kodyn and Aisha slipped toward the closed doors.

The light in the room beyond grew painfully bright, almost shining through the dense wood of the doors. Kodyn exchanged a nervous glance with Aisha and, together, they reached for the door handles.

A loud humming echoed in the room, setting Kodyn's ears buzzing. Two figures stood in the room beyond. One was a youth roughly Kodyn's age, with the dark skin of a Shalandran and a red-and-gold headband that marked him as a servant. His jaw hung agape. "Hailen, what in the bloody hell did you do?"

The other figure, the light-skinned Hailen, Briana's servant, stood a few paces away. Kodyn's eyes flew wide at the sight of the glowing stone sitting in the boy's hand.

"I don't know," said Hailen, "but I think I can wield Serenii magic!"

# *Our young heroes' journey continues in Crucible of Fortune (Heirs of Destiny Book 2)*

# Chapter One

The songs of the dead echoed loud in the hall of the Long Keeper, god of death. A mournful tune, as heavy and cloying as the incense that hung thick in the temple, underscored by a shrill chorus of flutes that grated on Kodyn's nerves. Yet he forced himself to stand still, to remain a firm bulwark for Briana to lean to as she mourned her father's death.

Arch-Guardian Suroth, high priest of the Secret Keepers, servant of the Mistress, and member of the Keeper's Council, lay silent and still atop the golden sandstone that dominated the center of the sanctuary. Death slackened his features and turned his umber skin to a brown as dull as the simple Secret Keeper's robes he now wore. His strong hands rested atop his chest, a peaceful pose that belied the violent nature of his passing.

He'd fallen in defense of Pharus Amhoset Nephelcheres and the rest of the Keeper's Council. Nine Gatherers, members of the death-worshipping cult, had died at his hands before he succumbed to his wounds. Yet one look at Briana told Kodyn that her father's courage or the heroism of his sacrifice meant next to nothing in this moment. She'd never known her mother, who had died giving birth to her. Now she had lost the most important person in her life.

And Kodyn had no idea how to comfort her.

He'd sat by her bedside as she wept, held her hand through her tears, feeling useless all the while. He couldn't wipe the sorrow from her heart or the pain of loss from her eyes. Behind her pale features and vacant stare she fixed on the body atop the altar, she had to be wrestling against a seething ocean of emotions that he could only begin to understand. He had never felt as helpless as he did now, watching her suffer in silence.

Aisha, his companion and fellow Night Guild apprentice, stood on Briana's other side. She held Briana's hand, lending her strength as well. Sorrow glistened in her almond brown eyes—she hadn't known Suroth long, but she'd become close friends with Briana over the last few days.

Now, the two of them were the closest thing Briana had to friends and family in the world.

The music fell silent as High Divinity Tinush, the oldest member of the Keeper's Council, stepped up toward the altar. Above his head, the stone-carved face of the Long Keeper stared down at Suroth's body. The god of death had already claimed Suroth's soul—all that remained was to commend his flesh to the Crypts.

"Mercy, change, justice, vengeance, sorrow, joy, and eternity." Despite his age, his voice rang out loud and strong, echoing off the sandstone walls, ceiling, and floor of the sanctuary atop the Hall of the Beyond. "These are the seven faces of the Long Keeper. Mercy, for death is just the first step toward eternal bliss in the Sleepless Lands. Change, the one inevitable constant. Justice for the deserving and vengeance against the wicked."

Tinush bowed his head. "Sorrow, for in passing we leave behind those dearest to our heart, yet with it comes joy in finding peace and rest in the eternity of the Long Keeper's arms."

The hand he rested on Suroth's pale forehead was spotted with age and tattooed with seven black dots. "Go into infinity, Suroth, secure in the knowledge that the world was a better place for your presence. May you find the peace you deserve." With that, he bent and placed the ceremonial kiss on the dead man's lips.

The trilling of flutes and forlorn strumming of harps filled the sanctuary chamber once more, and singers took up a funereal chant. Kodyn felt a burden of sorrow settle onto his shoulders at the doleful lyrics. He glanced toward the double doors, which stood open to reveal the lines of people crowding onto the golden sandstone steps that descended the broad stairway carved into the southern edge of the Hall of the Beyond. The golden morning sunlight failed to drive back the pall that hung over the gathered mourners.

Hundreds of Dhukari, Alqati, Zadii, and Intaji had come to see the Arch-Guardian off. For one so well-respected and revered, the funeral rituals would last hours until the early afternoon, when the Necroseti, priests of the Long Keeper, began the final journey to Suroth's resting place. According to Nessa, Arch-Guardian Suroth's household Steward, burial rites always took place at sunrise and sunset. The sun had already fully risen by the time the commotion in the palace after the assassination attempt had died down, so Suroth would be interred beneath the fading twilight.

That seemed an eternity away. He and Aisha had accompanied Briana just after dawn to the Hall of the Beyond, the temple to the Long Keeper, for the embalming and final blessing rites carried out by the Necroseti. She had sat beside the lifeless, pale-faced corpse that had once been the strong Secret Keeper, holding her father's limp hand as the priests prepared him for an eternity in the Long Keeper's arms.

Kodyn and Aisha hadn't been allowed entrance into the private room where the body was prepared—only the family of the deceased could enter—but they'd taken up guard in front of the door. Aisha, in particular, had scrutinized every priest that entered the room. After last night's attempt to kidnap or murder Briana—he couldn't know *which* the Gatherers had intended—she took her role as the Shalandran girl's bodyguard with the utmost severity. More than a few of the lower-ranked priests in attendance had wilted beneath her furious glare.

At the tenth hour of the morning, they'd undertaken the solemn procession up the stairs to the rooftop sanctuary, the more sacred chamber in the Hall of the Beyond. They had passed beneath the gold sandstone statue of the Long Keeper and laid Suroth's body atop the ceremonial altar in preparation for the ceremony.

Pharus Amhoset Nephelcheres had met them at the bottom of the stairs. "I owe your father my life." Genuine sorrow had sparkled in his kohl-rimmed eyes. He'd even worn simple clothing, for a Pharus—a plain gold-threaded tunic over an ankle-length shendyt, with a narrow black mourning shawl draped about his shoulders and a finger-thick headband of solid gold, a far cry from his typically ornate headdress and conical crown. "He saved us all. I will not forget the debt I now owe him."

They hadn't needed to hire dancers and mourners for Suroth's ritual journey to his final resting place in the Keeper's Crypts—hundreds of men, women, even children from the Artisan's Tier, Defender's Tier, and Keeper's Tier had turned out to accompany him. Suroth might never have spoken a word, yet it seemed they had loved him nonetheless. Well-wishers had pressed condolences and kind sentiments on Briana. She could barely bring herself to nod.

Now, as the people of Shalandra trooped into the sanctuary to bid farewell to Suroth, her red-rimmed eyes had a vacant stare, her brows hooded.

The highest-ranked men and women in Shalandra stood silent vigil around the altar. Secret Keepers in dull brown, Warrior Priests in full suits of splinted mail, even Lecterns in long green-and-silver robes. The Venerated, the council formed of a representative from each of the twelve temples, watched over their fallen brother. Keeper's Blades armed in spiked black plate mail and carrying huge flame-bladed swords took up position at the four sides of the altar. Callista Vinaus, the Lady of Blades and commander of Shalandra's military herself, guarded Suroth's head.

Kodyn's gut twisted at the black-robed priests that flanked the west side of the temple chamber. Six heavy-set men with double chins and sagging paunches occupied the front of their ranks. These Necroseti served on the Keeper's Council. These were the men Suroth had died to protect.

And Kodyn was all but certain *they* had a role to play in the Arch-Guardian's death.

Sorrow tightened Kodyn's chest as a little girl, no more than three or four, slipped shyly up to the altar. She wore the simple brown headband of an Intaji, Shalandra's artisan caste, and held a small stone figurine in her pudgy fingers. With a hesitant glance at Briana, she darted toward Suroth and set the statuette—the figure of the Mistress, goddess of secret trysts and whispered truths—on altar the next to him. One more treasure to accompany him on his journey into the Keeper's arms.

Briana turned away, a strangled sob escaping her throat. Aisha wrapped an arm around her shoulder for support and comfort.

"I-I'm fine," Briana said, barely above a whisper. "I just can't…" She scrubbed the tears from her cheeks. "I can't see him like this anymore."

"Of course." Aisha nodded. "Let's get you home." They didn't need to be here any longer—the Necroseti and the crowd of mourners would see Suroth to his final resting place in the Keeper's Crypt.

Briana allowed Aisha to escort her through the crowds, which parted to make way.

One of the black-robed priests stepped toward her as if intending to have words, but Kodyn stepped in the way. "Whatever you have to say to Lady Briana," he growled, "it can wait."

Councilor Madani's kohl-rimmed eyes darkened. "Beware your tone, pup." His thin mouth pressed into a tight line, which only made his hooked nose look even more like a vulture. "Your mistress has enough burden with the death of her father; I would hate to see her grieve an insolent bodyguard as well."

Kodyn straightened to his full height, looming over the priest. "You know where to find me, *priest*." He almost spat the words. "But remember that it was *your* Gatherers that did this, and the Pharus knows the truth."

Madani's upper lip curled into a sneer. "We were in the Council Chamber when they attacked, beside the Pharus and the Arch-Guardian. The actions of those rabid dogs cannot be blamed on us. Perhaps, in a few years, your young mind will come to understand such intricacies."

Anger burned within Kodyn, but he pressed back on it, hardened it into a tight, bright core. Not at the insult—he could return the priest's scorn a hundred-fold—but at the priest himself. The vulture-faced bastard had been behind the attempt to kidnap Briana the first time. Despite Madani's protest of innocence, Kodyn wasn't ready to believe that the priest had no hand in the attempt.

Yet now wasn't the time for accusations. Soon, Kodyn would be free to unleash his anger at these pompous priests, the ones truly responsible for so much of Briana's anguish and loss. When that time came, woe to Madani and his cronies.

"This will not go unanswered." Kodyn fixed the Necroseti priest with a hard stare. "There will be vengeance. May the Long Keeper have mercy on the guilty, whoever they may be." His tone of voice made it abundantly clear who he blamed.

Madani bristled and opened his mouth to speak, but Kodyn turned on his heel and stalked down the broad stairs after Aisha and Briana.

The view from atop the Hall of the Beyond was breathtaking, offering an unbroken view of the entire city. The four lower tiers looked like colossal stepping stones cut into the golden sandstone of Alshuruq, the mountain upon which Shalandra sat. Green and yellow farmlands spread out from the southern edge of the city.

Yet the beauty faded beneath the pallor of his mood. At that moment, Kodyn had no eyes for gorgeous vistas or masterpieces of architecture. His mind was consumed by concern for Briana and anger at the Necroseti.

The descent took them the better part of half an hour, each step downward accompanied by words of condolences from the people lining the staircase. Kodyn and Aisha supported the pale, tired-looking Briana until they reached the palanquin waiting for them on the Path of Gold.

Aisha helped Briana climb into the litter, then glanced at Kodyn.

"Go," Kodyn told her with a nod. "She needs someone with her right now."

Aisha hesitated, as if wanting to say something. She seemed to think better of it and climbed into the palanquin.

Kodyn climbed into the saddle of his horse and shot a nod to Rothin. "Let's get her home."

The captain of Arch-Guardian Suroth's private household guard called an order to the eight men he'd brought as the honor guard. They formed a protective square of gilded breastplates and stern faces around Briana's litter, with Kodyn riding at the front, and began the long, slow march across the Keeper's Tier back to the Arch-Guardian's mansion.

Kodyn's eyes never stopped moving as he scanned the Path of Gold for any sign of danger. The Gatherers, a death-worshipping cult offshoot of the Necroseti, had been behind Briana's kidnapping the first time—they'd hauled her north to Praamis, where he had met and subsequently rescued her. Now, they'd tried to kidnap her again, though it seemed they would settle for murdering her as well?

Both times, the attempts had been made on the Keeper's Tier, the uppermost of the five levels of Shalandra. The Tier, home to the wealthiest Dhukari, was supposed to be well-guarded, with guards patrolling the broad avenues and taking up station at the single gate that gave access from the lower levels. Yet somehow the Gatherers had gotten past—or around—the black-armored Indomitables at the gate. Kodyn suspected the cultists used the secret Serenii tunnels built into the mountain. The same tunnels he'd intended to use to steal into the Palace of Golden Eternity to get his hands on the Crown of the Pharus.

Right now, all concerns for his Undertaking took second place to Briana's safety. He knew he'd have to figure out another way to get into the Vault of Ancients—without Suroth's help, it would be near impossible. Worse, he had less than three weeks until the Serenii-designed locks opened the Vault, then it would be re-sealed for another three months.

*But that's a problem for after I figure out what our next steps with Briana are.* He had to make sure she was safe. *And that starts with getting her home.*

Worry tied his stomach in knots as he rode, and his hand never strayed from the hilt of the sword strapped to his waist. His Night Guild armor—quality leather treated with one of House Scorpion's special alchemical potions—could turn aside most attacks, but Briana wore only a gold-and-white kalasiris with straps of white leather. Vigilance would prove her best defense at the moment; his sword would turn aside the attacks her ornate cloth gown could not.

Relief flooded him when he caught sight of the high walls of Arch-Guardian Suroth's mansion a quarter of an hour later, yet he didn't truly breathe easy until the steel-banded wooden gate shut behind him and the bare-headed *Kabili* slaves set the litter down.

Aisha leapt out before he'd fully dismounted, and one look at the tightness of her shoulders told Kodyn she'd felt the same nervous tension he had. Yes, she was taking her role of guardian very seriously.

The Briana that emerged from the litter bore little resemblance to the young woman that had laughed and danced among the Dhukari in the Palace of Golden Eternity just a few nights earlier. She looked more like the Briana he'd rescued from the Gatherers: almond eyes red-rimmed from crying, her kohl streaked by tears, her hair rumpled. Yet sorrow hadn't diminished her beauty; if anything, the evidence of her emotions only deepened her maturity and grace.

Nessa, the grey-haired Steward, bustled out of the mansion's front door. "Come, my lady," she said in a soothing voice. "Let's get you in a bath then bed. You've had enough to deal with for one—"

"No." A hint of iron had returned to Briana's voice. She brushed away her tears, a spark of defiance shining in her eyes. "I will not lie in bed, not while my father's murderers are free."

"I am told that the Keeper's Blades slew all of the Gatherers in the Palace," Nessa said.

"But not all of the Gatherers in Shalandra." Briana's face hardened. "Not the ones who ordered the attack, or the ones responsible for the Gatherers in the first place."

Nessa's brow furrowed, and her eyes darted around. "Beware, my lady. The Keeper's Council has eyes and ears everywhere."

"Good!" Briana straightened, her face creased with anger. "Let them hear me! Let them know that I'm going to make them pay for what they did to me, and to my father."

Nessa's expression grew tight. "Anger is a part of the mourning process, Lady Briana, so we will say that this is simply your grief talking. No one, not even your father, was foolish enough to move against the Necroseti. They are more than just the most powerful men in Shalandra—they are the Keeper's voice and will on Einan."

"Then the Long Keeper is served by cowards and fools!" With a snarl, Briana stalked into the house.

Surprise rooted Kodyn to the spot for an instant. He had seen Briana's strength before—she had recovered from the traumatic ordeal of captivity by the Gatherers—yet this new display astounded him. The fearful girl he'd met in Praamis had disappeared, replaced by a defiant young woman. Her resilience of spirit spoke of deep reserves of inner strength, but his job of keeping her safe would be much more difficult if she took on the Necroseti.

He hurried into the mansion a step behind Aisha, and the two of them moved quickly to match Briana's stride. The Shalandran girl fairly stomped up the stairs toward the second floor.

"Nessa wasn't wrong," Kodyn said. "The Necroseti are too powerful to go after directly. Your father knew that, which is why he didn't attack them head-on."

Briana whirled on him with a glare. "Don't tell me *you're* about to try and convince me not to go after them or the Gatherers that did this?" She gestured around her at the blood that stained the pristine white carpets covering the staircase.

"No." Kodyn shook his head. "I came to Shalandra to make sure the Gatherers never came back to Praamis, and this makes it perfectly clear that they need to be dealt with once and for all. But if your father couldn't find them, even with all the resources at his disposal, I'm not so arrogant to think I'll miraculously succeed. And I'm not stupid enough to charge at the Necroseti like a mad warrior jousting a windmill. I'm just saying that we need to be smart about what we do. We need to find a way that *doesn't* get us all killed."

Briana scowled, but Aisha spoke first. "He's right. We're exhausted, and it's going to be nearly impossible to think straight. We need to plan, but first we need food and rest."

"You want to sleep now?" Briana's eyebrows shot up.

"If we want any hope of making a plan that works, yes." Aisha's jaw took on a stubborn set. "And you know I'm right."

Briana looked ready to shout, to rage, to attack Aisha, but Kodyn was fairly certain it was more due to the overwhelming flood of emotions. And it was to be expected, given what had just happened.

"If we're going to have any chance of taking on the Necroseti," he told her, "we're going to need all the help we can get. That means the Secret Keepers, and the Pharus, if we can get in to speak to him. But there's another place we can look for help."

Briana's brow furrowed, and even Aisha seemed curious.

Kodyn met their eyes with a firm gaze. "We can use the power of the Serenii."

# Chapter Two

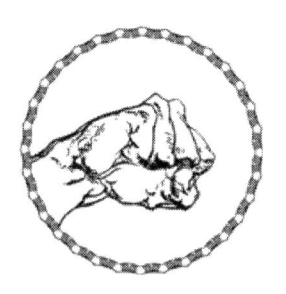

Evren's gut tightened as the deadbolt *thunked* open. He leapt to his feet and positioned himself between Hailen and the door. "Remember," he growled, "let me do the talking."

Blinding light flooded in as the door swung open. Evren tried to blink away the pain, but his eyes had grown accustomed to the pitch blackness within the storeroom where he and Hailen had been locked away for hours—how many, he didn't know, but enough that he'd been able to catch a nap—in the darkness.

The minor concussion didn't help. He'd been struck on the head while trying to slip past the Indomitables guarding the Defender's Tier. The dizziness and nausea had diminished, though the ache remained.

*The Hunter always said I had a hard head.*

He reached for his daggers, only to remember that Lady Briana's bodyguard—*that tall, pale-skinned Praamian*—had taken them. Yet that didn't stop him from clenching his fists and squaring his shoulders. He'd won enough battles bare-handed not to go down fighting.

The moment a hand grabbed his right arm he swung with his left, a quick hook aimed at his opponent's jaw. Pain flared through his hand as his knuckles slammed into a hard skull. The grip on his arm fell away and the man staggered back with a grunt, but before Evren could lash out at the next blurry figure, two more men seized him.

"Cease your struggling before you end up dead."

Evren recognized the voice—it belonged to Rothin, the captain of Arch-Guardian Suroth's household guard. The man that had imprisoned him here on Lady Briana's orders.

His eyes had adjusted to the light enough to make out the blurry forms of four guards in their bright gold breastplates. Two clung to his arms while a third leaned against the door frame with a hand pressed to the side of his head. Rothin's broad shoulders and strong-featured face loomed in his vision, and Evren didn't need his eyes to feel the cold steel resting against his throat.

"What do you want?" Evren snarled.

"Lady Briana commands your presence," Rothin said. "Both of you." His voice held no anger or malice, only a tone of stern authority. He'd been present when Evren warned of the Gatherers' attack.

*Let's just hope that means he doesn't think I'm a traitor or spy.*

To be fair, he'd likely have come to that same conclusion himself, given how they'd been discovered in Arch-Guardian Suroth's private office, with one of his most valuable possessions clutched in Hailen's hand. *I'd probably have arrested me, too.*

He relaxed and dropped his hands. "Then let's go." No sense fighting, not where Hailen could get hurt. The boy had very nearly been killed the night before by Snarth, one of the Mumblers working for Killian the blacksmith.

The guards half-led, half-hauled him and Hailen out of the storeroom, down the servant's corridor, and into the main room of the mansion. The eyes of Suroth's servants followed their journey up the stairs, and Evren could hear their whispered gossip. Doubtless they were trying to figure out what Evren and Hailen had done to earn the ire of Nessa, Briana, or Suroth himself.

Evren's curiosity blazed bright as the guards marched him not into Lady Briana's private chambers, but into the very same study where he and Hailen had been discovered the previous night, just after the assassination attempt.

Lady Briana sat behind her father's vast wooden desk, in the straight-backed leather armchair. Her eyes were red-rimmed, her kohl smeared and faded from crying—Evren had heard of her father's murder in the Palace—but her expression was an unreadable mask of calm composure.

Her two bodyguards—the pale-skinned Praamian and the fierce woman with skin darker than Evren's own—hovered behind her like mother hawks guarding a hatchling. Given what had happened, Evren didn't begrudge them their caution.

"Thank you, Rothin." Briana inclined her head to the captain of the guard. "You may leave him with us."

"Of course, Lady Briana." Hesitance echoed in his voice, yet he simply bowed and turned to leave. The guards released Evren and Hailen, then followed their captain.

Silence hung thick in the study for long seconds after the door *clicked* shut behind the departing guards. Three pairs of eyes bored into him, but Evren stood tall, defiant. He hadn't let fear of anything—not the Lecterns in the Master's Temple where he'd served as apprentice, not the monsters roaming the Empty Mountains, not even the Hunter of Voramis, the legendary assassin that had become his trainer and mentor—shake him for years. He'd be damned if he showed a Dhukari girl or her bodyguards even a hint of worry.

"What is your name?"

Lady Briana's question caught him off-guard. He'd been expecting threats and accusations, yet she spoke in a tone bordering on civil.

"She asked for your name," growled the pale-skinned bodyguard, a scowl on his face as he took a step toward Evren.

Evren sized up the man before him. Long, dark hair pulled back into a tight tail, high cheekbones, and deep blue eyes. Yet he was surprised to find they were roughly the same age, though the bodyguard stood a hand or two taller, with broad shoulders and the easy confidence of a warrior trained to use the sword hanging on his belt and the five or six daggers Evren spotted concealed around his armor and clothing. He'd spent enough time around the Hunter to recognize the lethal grace of a killer, yet something about the Praamian reminded Evren of the slimmer, quicker thieves he'd known on the streets of Vothmot.

*An interesting mix of the two, certainly.*

The other one, the woman with braided hair and a fierce scowl on her full lips, was a bit more of a mystery. The breadth of her shoulders almost matched Kodyn's and thick muscle corded her forearms and biceps. She stood in a slight crouch, expression wary, hand hovering near the short-handled spear on her back. A warrior, for certain, yet up close, something about her seemed different than he'd expected. There was a strange glimmer in her eyes that he didn't quite understand.

He didn't know what to make of these two, but if they were threatening Hailen, they'd find him more than just a simple servant.

"Why?" He poured all his defiance into the word. "What does it matter?"

"It matters," Lady Briana spoke before the tall Praamian could, "because I have to know what sort of person I'm dealing with."

Evren's eyes narrowed. *Dealing with? That sounds less like a threat and more like a conversation.*

Understanding dawned when Lady Briana placed a palm-length stone as thick as Evren's middle finger atop the table. "What he did should be impossible," she said. "Had I not seen it with my own eyes, I would never have believed it. So I want to know exactly how it happened."

Evren's gut tightened. He'd been dreading this since the moment they'd been caught in Suroth's study hours earlier.

"This stone is the handiwork of the Serenii." Lady Briana's eyes slid past Evren to Hailen. "My father is..."

Sorrow twisted her face and she swallowed hard, her eyes dropping. The fierce-looking woman placed a hand on her shoulder.

A long moment passed before the girl continued in a quiet, tight voice. "My father *was* studying it and all the other Serenii artifacts in this room in the hopes of unlocking its secrets. He had begun to decipher the runes etched into its surface. However, he never hinted that it would do anything like it did last night." She narrowed her eyes at Hailen and leaned forward. "So tell me, how did you make it hum and glow like that?"

Evren heard Hailen draw in a breath but spoke quickly first. "Before I tell you, I will have your word that my brother will not be punished. It was my idea to sneak into your father's study. The blame lies with me, and the punishment should as well."

"Evren—" Hailen began.

Evren whirled and shot a stern glare at the younger boy. Hailen's face grew stubborn but he held his tongue.

"Your brother?" The tall Praamian youth cocked an eyebrow. "Intriguing."

Evren met the bodyguard's gaze without hesitation. Curiosity burned there, and a wary suspicion, but that seemed more innate, the result of hard years of living, rather than personal. It simply served to reinforce Evren's suspicion that the youth was *not* the traditional sort of bodyguard. Then again, a Praamian in such a trusted position in a Dhukari household didn't scream tradition, either.

"My *brother*," Evren emphasized the word, "is special." He didn't know how to explain that Hailen was *Melechha*, a descendant of the ancient Serenii, not without sounding crazy. "Serenii things have a tendency to come to life when he's around."

"Is that so?" Lady Briana inclined her head and turned to Hailen. "What is your name?"

"Hailen," Hailen responded before Evren could stop him.

The young woman beckoned. "Come here, Hailen."

Evren made to stop Hailen, but both of the bodyguards tensed, hands dropping to their weapons. Clearly, last night's attempt on Lady Briana had them on edge. Evren decided *against* doing anything to raise their suspicion any further.

"Here." Lady Briana held out the cylindrical stone. "Take it."

Hailen hesitated a moment before reaching for the object. Evren's gut tightened as the boy's fingers closed around the cylindrical black stone etched with those strange Serenii runes. The blood on Hailen's fingers had dried hours ago—the stone required fresh blood to activate.

Lady Briana and her bodyguards drew in sharp breaths and leaned back as Hailen took the stone. But, when nothing happened, suspicion flashed across their faces. The young Dhukari woman looked confused.

"Last night, how did you make that work?" she asked Hailen.

Evren shot Hailen a meaningful look and a slight shake of his head. *Don't do it, Hailen!* He couldn't straight out shout at the boy to hold his tongue, but he had to hope Hailen had the common sense to—

"It's my blood." Hailen said after only a moment of hesitation. "It's what activated the stone."

Evren stifled a curse. *Damn it!* The boy had an innately trusting nature—a remnant of the *Irrsinnon*, the madness inherited from the Serenii that had nearly claimed his mind years earlier—which had gotten him in trouble on more than one occasion. Now, he'd just revealed the secret of his *Melechha* blood to these three perfect strangers.

"Your blood?" Lady Briana's brow furrowed. "What do you mean?"

"What he means," Evren interjected, "is that his blood can interact with Serenii artifacts." Hailen had revealed enough for now; better Briana *not* know that he was the last surviving *Melechha* on Einan. That knowledge would give her far too much power over Hailen—and, by extension, Evren. Already, they were at the mercy of the Dhukari noblewoman. She had only to order her guards to execute them and Evren be forced to fight his way to freedom.

"Interact with the artifacts, how exactly?" For a moment, curiosity pushed back the dark sorrow lingering in Lady Briana's eyes. "Like what happened last night, with that bright light and loud noise?"

"Yes." Evren met the young woman's gaze. "Or, at least, that's what that one artifact did. I don't know about the others, but I know that they will work when they come in contact with Hailen's blood."

"Fascinating!" Excitement sparkled on Lady Briana's face. "My father dedicated his life to studying these artifacts, and you two unlock more secrets in three minutes than he did in three decades." Suddenly, questions bubbled from her lips in a torrent almost too fast for Evren to follow. "Is there anything else your blood can do? Can you use *all* Serenii artifacts or just this one? Do you read the Serenii language? How much do you know about what these things can do? Can you truly wield the power of the Serenii like you said?"

"Uhh…yes?" Confusion echoed in Hailen's voice. "I mean…"

Lady Briana suddenly stood, a look of grim determination in her eyes. "Listen to me, both of you. Last night's attempt to kidnap or kill me was the work of the Gatherers, a cult of death-worshippers that either work for the Necroseti or rebelled against them. Either way, the Keeper's Priests and the members of the Keeper's Council wanted to eliminate my father. They have their wish, so I shouldn't have to worry about them coming for me."

"You're certain?" the tall Praamian asked. "Your father had a great deal of influence among the Secret Keepers—"

The Dhukari girl shook her head. "But the only reason he posed a threat to them was because of his influence with the Pharus and his position on the Keeper's Council. With him gone, the Necroseti won't bother with me. Or, at least, they have no reason to. Same for the Gatherers. They wanted me to use as leverage against my father. Now that they don't need leverage, I should be safe. Safe enough that no one will see it coming when I take down the Gatherers and the Keeper's Council."

Evren raised an eyebrow. *An ambitious plan, though one likely to get her killed.* He wasn't certain the two bodyguards could keep her safe from the secret cult or the most powerful priests in Shalandra.

"But I can't do it alone, even with all of my father's connections," Lady Briana continued. "They are too powerful for just the three of us to take on. Which is where you two come in."

"Or *him*," Evren said, inclining his head at Hailen. "You want to use the power of the Serenii in your private war for revenge."

"Yes." A simple reply, with no hint of deceit. Lady Briana met his eyes. "In return for his help, I will give you anything that is within my power as the daughter of Arch-Guardian Suroth."

Evren's eyebrows rose. "Anything?" Quite the tempting offer, certainly, though he couldn't be sure what she would have to give him. He'd come to her father's household intending to use his position to get into the Palace of Golden Eternity to steal the Blade of Hallar, an ancient relic he believed was one of the Bucelarii *Im'tasi* weapons—weapons the Hunter needed in his mission to sustain Kharna and protect Einan from the threat of the Devourer of Worlds.

*She might not be her father, but she may still be able to help me get what I need.* She could get him into the Palace, maybe even close enough to the Vault of Ancients that he could get his hands on the Blade of Hallar. From there, it would be a simple matter of collecting Hailen and fleeing Shalandra before anyone realized what he'd done.

Lady Briana shrugged. "Ask, and I will see what I can do."

Evren pondered his request, but before he settled on anything, a knock sounded at the door.

The two bodyguards tensed, eyes fixed on the door.

"Come in," Lady Briana called.

At the *creak* of door hinges, Evren glanced over his shoulder to find the grey-haired Nessa entering the room. Though the Steward shot a curious look his way, she addressed Briana.

"Forgive me, my lady, but there is someone here to see you."

"Who is it?" Lady Briana asked.

Nessa's face went a shade paler and her eyes went wide. "By the looks of her, one of the Keeper's Blades, sent by the Pharus himself!"

# *Crucible of Fortune*
# *(Heirs of Destiny Book 2)*

**Five young warriors, one mission. Will they stand together or die alone?**

**Kodyn** and **Aisha** are losing the battle to save the City of the Dead.

Stripped of rank and wealth, they must use all their wits, skill, and courage to survive the cruel streets of Shalandra and bring justice for their murdered protector.

Kodyn's cunning and Aisha's growing power over the dead are all that stands between them and an untimely end. New allies emerge to join the fight: a thief, an elite warrior-in-training, and a boy with ancient magical abilities

In a world of greed and cruelty, only the strongest bonds of unity can triumph against death cultists, bloodthirsty criminal gangs, and the most powerful politicians in the kingdom.

*If you love action, adventure, plot twists, and intrigue, you'll love every heart-pounding second of Heirs of Destiny! For fans of Jeff Wheeler, Robin Hobb, and A.C. Cobble, take a journey through Andy Peloquin's dark epic fantasy world...*

# In the Heirs of Destiny series:

Trial of Stone (Book 1) – Jan 22, 2019

Crucible of Fortune (Book 2) –Feb 5, 2019

Storm of Chaos (Book 3) – Feb 19, 2019

Secrets of Blood (Book 4) – Mar 19, 2019

Ascension of Death (Book 5) – Apr 16, 2019

AND BONUS:

The Renegade Apprentice (Book 0) May 12, 2019 <--- Evren Novella

# Try the Prequel Novella for FREE

**A desperate breakout. A perilous life on the streets. A fight to the death.**

Evren's life as an apprentice priest is an endless torment, until he seizes the chance to escape his slavery. But his freedom, and his life, may be cut very short because the dark alleys of Vothmot hold their own dangers…some deadlier than others!

Sign up for my VIP Reader List at
https://andypeloquin.com/join-the-club-hod/
and read the prequel novella for FREE

# *More Books by Andy Peloquin*

**Queen of Thieves**
Book 1: Child of the Night Guild
Book 2: Thief of the Night Guild
Book 3: Queen of the Night Guild

Traitors' Fate (**Queen of Thieves/Hero of Darkness Crossover**)

**Hero of Darkness**
Book 1: Darkblade Assassin
Book 2: Darkblade Outcast
Book 3: Darkblade Protector
Book 4: Darkblade Seeker
Book 5: Darkblade Slayer
Book 6: Darkblade Savior
Book 7: Darkblade Justice

Different, Not Damaged: A Short Story Collection

# *About the Author*

I am, first and foremost, a storyteller and an artist--words are my palette. Fantasy is my genre of choice, and I love to explore the darker side of human nature through the filter of fantasy heroes, villains, and everything in between. I'm also a freelance writer, a book lover, and a guy who just loves to meet new people and spend hours talking about my fascination for the worlds I encounter in the pages of fantasy novels.

Fantasy provides us with an escape, a way to forget about our mundane problems and step into worlds where anything is possible. It transcends age, gender, religion, race, or lifestyle--it is our way of believing what cannot be, delving into the unknowable, and discovering hidden truths about ourselves and our world in a brand new way. Fiction at its very best!

### [Join my Facebook Reader Group](#)
for updates, LIVE readings, exclusive content, and all-around fantasy fun.
### Let's Get Social!
Be My Friend: https://www.facebook.com/andrew.peloquin.1
Facebook Author Page: https://www.facebook.com/andyqpeloquin
Twitter: https://twitter.com/AndyPeloquin

Printed in Great
Britain
by Amazon